SHE DIDN'

Charlie took in... ...m-
bered what had ... ...he
first place. Nightmares, longings, loneliness. And now
this man's touch brought forth a deep desire within
her, a desire almost forgotten. No matter what her
good sense told her, she didn't resist him.

Instead she turned slightly and let Mitch hold her
close. The hammering of his heart challenged the
thrumming of her own.

Naked beneath the thin fabric of her gown, she could
feel the roughness of his jeans, the cut of his belt,
every button of his shirt pressing against her warm
flesh.

He put a finger under her chin and raised her face,
his mouth so close it was a blur. His warm breath
whispered over her cheeks and lips as his hands
spanned the curves of her body. Out here on the prairie in the quiet of the night, his desire for her was
explosive. He wanted her so much he could taste her
sweetness. . . .

Brightspun Destiny

~

Elizabeth Gregg

A TOPAZ BOOK

TOPAZ
Published by the Penguin Group
Penguin Books USA Inc., 375 Hudson Street,
New York, New York 10014, U.S.A.
Penguin Books Ltd, 27 Wrights Lane,
London W8 5TZ, England
Penguin Books Australia Ltd, Ringwood,
Victoria, Australia
Penguin Books Canada Ltd, 10 Alcorn Avenue,
Toronto, Ontario, Canada M4V 3B2
Penguin Books (N.Z.) Ltd, 182–190 Wairau Road,
Auckland 10, New Zealand

Penguin Books Ltd, Registered Offices:
Harmondsworth, Middlesex, England

First published by Topaz, an imprint of Dutton Signet,
a division of Penguin Books USA Inc.

First Printing, September, 1996
10 9 8 7 6 5 4 3 2 1

 REGISTERED TRADEMARK—MARCA REGISTRADA

Printed in the United States of America

To Charle and Judy
who led the way
I'll always be grateful

Chapter One

A cross the sprawling valley patches of new grass shared space with winter-dried bare earth to form a crazy quilt. Purple mountains cut into a brilliant columbine sky; along the ground clouds of dust moved in the wind like ghost herds pursuing the cattle drive. Mitch squinted into the bright spring sunlight. He was late. Spring roundup had begun.

Between his legs the powerful stallion shifted restlessly, nostrils flaring in a puff of wind. He held the animal yet another moment to absorb the intangible emotions that poured through him, hot, raw, and bittersweet. He'd never expected to return to Montana Territory. Yet the past that had kept him away had ultimately chased him back like an angry, wounded animal bent on revenge.

With an impatient grunt, he settled the black Stetson firmly on his head, tilting it so that the brim shadowed a scar that slashed through his left eyebrow. The vivid mark never let him forget what he had lost.

He shook off the memories. He'd come here to use his gun, and it was time he got to it, long past time that someone paid for what had happened. Besides, the man who had hired him was waiting. No need to look back any longer. If he did he might catch sight of the beast that pursued him with such fury.

He loosened the reins. The black stallion neighed into the wind, tightened his haunches, and tore down the incline.

Most of that day Mitch rode across Circle D land until at last he reached the colonel's house, a rambling, low structure squatted on high ground at the horseshoe bend of Little Porcupine Creek. Before dismounting, he rested a moment to study the enormous ranch house, its extravagant glass windows, the wide veranda skirted by freshly dug flower beds. At last he dropped wearily from the horse and pulled a leather gunbelt and holster from his saddlebag. Without removing the black cowhide gloves he strapped on the Colt .44 and settled it low so the gleaming butt rested a trifle below his right hip.

Charlie rode easy in the saddle and let the roan work the milling longhorns. The tough little mare deftly turned the cows and calves and headed them back in the direction of the branding camp. Other cowboys rode in, all herding cattle from their assigned sections.

The rowdy exuberance of spring roundup chased away Charlie's winter doldrums. She grinned broadly. Grains of dust gritted between her teeth and she uncapped a canteen to rinse her mouth and take a long swig. The bawling and bellowing, the cracking of the cattle's horns as they clashed, the pounding of hoofs, were as sweet as first light after a cold night on the trail.

For the first time since her father died, she felt good! The long boring winter of grief and utter, complete isolation behind her, Charlie actually looked forward to life in this new country. She would have to be tough as nails to make it without her father, for Matthew Houston had truly been the strength of the Double H Ranch.

"We'll call it the Double H," he'd said, "for the two Houstons." And then he'd grinned at her and rumpled her hair, the closest he ever came to showing affection.

Could she hold on and fulfill his dream here in this wild and vast country? Its merciless conditions tested the endurance of even the hardiest man. Even so, she enjoyed the turmoil of roundup, the feel of the roan shifting and dancing between her knees, the sweat trickling down her backbone as the sun climbed the sky. The dirt, the smell, the aching muscles. All glorious. And she wouldn't think of Matt's tragic death today. Fury always came on the heels of such thoughts, and she was weary of being angry. Winter had been the time for mourning; spring was for celebration of this new life.

She leaned forward and urged Belle closer to the bunching cattle, laughing aloud at the antics of a calf lumbering awkwardly in a halfhearted gallop after its mother, tongue hanging from the side of its mouth dribbling with foam.

A Rocking R puncher whooped and charged his pony in a wide circle to corral an escaped steer, and Charlie could contain her pleasure no longer. With an answering shout she swept off her worn Stetson. The wind twisted through her cropped hair, cut short like a man's so that the black curls just touched her shoulders.

The herd circled and milled, and she reined up to let the expert cutters begin their exhausting work of roping the calves and dragging them to the flankers for branding.

"Dammit, Matt, we made it," she cried aloud. "We got through the winter. How do you like that, by God, just how the hell do you like that?" She squeezed her eyes shut, willed away moisture that gathered there, and swallowed the thick lump in her throat.

She pulled herself away from the brink of grief. She mustn't let go. Not now, not ever.

After a filling meal from the chuck wagon, Charlie rested on her haunches and listened to the tally from the branding fire.

Neighboring rancher Cal Malone settled in beside her, picking up a stick to doodle in the dust between his scuffed boot toes.

"We made 'er, Charlie, we surely did," he said, and traced a gigantic X in the dirt for emphasis.

She glanced at her friend and nodded. Lingering smudges under his eyes told of his own grief last winter. Maybe that's why they had gravitated toward each other like they had.

"Glad to see spring, Cal, I surely am."

He gazed out across the sprawling countryside and breathed deeply. "Wish Becky could ... well, you know she loved the springtime. But then, who could blame her? Winters in Montana ain't no picnic." Cal sniffed and rubbed at his nose. "Aw, hell. Anyway, how you think you did?"

Charlie knew the question didn't call for a specific answer, it was just trail talk. Until the tally was done they'd neither one have any idea how their herds had fared over the winter. "Well, Cal, they say it was a mild winter. Being from Texas I wouldn't know, but I'll tell you one thing. If thirty below for two weeks at a time is mild, I'm dreading the tough ones."

Cal laughed, "Well, hell, gal. Two weeks ain't nothing. I've seen it forty below for a month or more, forty inches of ice and snow and a wind straight off the pole."

"Yeah, yeah, Cal. I've heard the stories."

The two chuckled comfortably. Of all the ranchers, Cal treated Charlie the most fairly. It was like he knew she was a woman and allowed for that, but yet figured her to do just about anything she set her mind to without qualification.

They had another bond too, one that no one else knew about. Cal wrote poetry and Charlie made up music for the words. Of all things, they'd discovered their similar inclinations at the gathering after Rebecca's funeral the previous October.

Neither of them ever discussed it much, the poetry and music nonsense, like maybe they were a bit embarrassed by it even though they couldn't seem to stop the creating. Every once in a while Cal would hand Charlie a wrinkled piece of brown paper with a poem scribbled on it, words crossed out and rewritten, some nearly illegible, and the next time they met she'd sing him the words, and neither of them able to read a note of music.

"Gawd, don't that smell like money?" Cal said, and pointed with the stick toward the buzz of activity around the branding fire.

As the brander shouted out the mark a calf's mother carried, the iron tender would fetch that particular branding iron from those lined in the fire. Too hot meant a bad blister on the calf's hide, not hot enough meant the brand would likely hair over and become indistinct. Few mistakes were made, for these men were all experts at what they did.

"They're calling twenty Circle Ds to every Double H or Rocking R, though." She inhaled the stench of burned hair, grimaced at the fearsome bawling of the calves when the cherry-red iron sizzled their hides.

"That's okay. The colonel, he's got a spread the size of one of them eastern states. Bound to have more cattle than us."

Before it was finished the joint roundup would cover several hundred square miles and encompass the grazing land of more than half a dozen ranches. And it was true the Circle D belonging to Colonel Hulbert

P. Dunkirk was immense, much of it gained by devious means. Still, they'd all work together, it was the only way in this majestic and demanding territory where one mishap could mean death.

Contemplating death made her think of Matthew, even though she tried not to. What a dreadful memory, watching powerless and grief-stricken as they lowered her father's canvas-wrapped body into a muddy grave alongside the trail near Ogallala last fall. Nebraska Territory was a far piece and those heartrending days long behind her. It made her angry that she couldn't bury the worst of the memories and keep only the best.

She tried by joshing with her friend. "Well, hell, Cal, there's another Double H calf."

Cal grinned.

She was happy to see that. He'd taken his wife Becky's death real hard, especially since their baby had not lived either. He was mighty alone, and she hoped someday he'd find himself another woman. Good women, though, were as scarce in this territory as were the conveniences that attracted them.

She rose and stretched, standing still to enjoy the sun's warmth through her shirt as she raised both shoulders and rolled her head backward to loosen some of the kinks.

"Double H," the brander shouted again.

Smiling, she screwed the bedraggled hat back onto her head, then turned sharply at the rattle of horses' hooves approaching from the southwest.

"Who in thunder is that?" Cal asked, coming to his feet.

Together they shaded their eyes and squinted into the bright white glare.

"Looks like that bastard of a colonel," she said. "Wonder what brings him out here?"

"Got an army with him. What you reckon he's up to?"

She figured whatever the colonel had in mind boded no good. Colonel Dunkirk, a man of reasonable girth, rode in a fancy carriage drawn by a white horse, and he reined in near the rope corral where the extra horses were tied. He wore what appeared to be a military uniform. She knew it wasn't. He ordered his wardrobe in Miles City and the style signified nothing but his ego. Flanking him on either side were more than half a dozen gunhands, men hired not to herd cattle or do any ranch work, but to ride roughshod over smaller ranchers so that sooner or later Colonel Dunkirk would own all they had.

Because Circle D was the biggest spread, Dunkirk's ramrod, a fellow by the name of Bodwell, was running the wagon for this roundup. He bossed the riders, his own and the smaller ranchers', with a harsh fist. Charlie had tried not to dislike the bully of a man, but it wasn't easy. He treated her as if she didn't exist, assigning duties without so much as a glance at her. She was left to pick her own jobs, which she did without comment. He deserved a good punch in the mouth, and she figured she might give it to him if he didn't watch out.

"Well, he sure as hell never rides out to roundup," Cal said. "Not since I've been here. Let's go see what's up."

The colonel acknowledged Cal, another rancher by the name of Duffy McGrew who owned a spread up on the Missouri, and the Double H ramrod Yancey Barton. His eyes wandered to Charlie and he touched the brim of his hat with two fingertips.

She sucked in a frustrated breath. "Surprised to see you out here, Colonel." Red anger flashed through her good humor.

He didn't meet her gaze, but stared out across the

prairie. "Why wouldn't I be? My interest in this roundup is a hundredfold more than any of yours." He waved a doeskin-gloved hand to include the other ranchers.

"Depends entirely on how you look at it," Cal Malone said.

Charlie nodded curtly in her rancher friend's direction, and as she swung her attention away the agitated movement of a long-legged black stallion caught her attention. Eyes rolling wildly, nostrils flaring, the magnificent animal pranced into view from behind the colonel. On the stallion's back sat a man every bit as untamed in appearance as his mount. This was no cowhand, nor was he an ordinary gunhand. Back ramrod-straight, long legs taut in the stirrups, he gave the impression of a predator stalking prey. The way he sat his horse reminded her of the vaqueros in the paintings in her grandparents' home in south Texas. Men who were cowboys long before this country knew the meaning of the word. Proud, stalwart, mysterious. There the resemblance ended. His eyes, as green as the deep summer woods on a stormy day, were fathomless and frosted like crystals. They registered nothing, even though his glance flicked over each of the ranchers in turn. He wore a pistol slung low on his right hip and carried a rifle in his scabbard. The black stallion never stopped its restless motion, and the man's body moved lithely to compensate.

After a moment he noticed her studying him and tipped his hat back away from his face to get a better look. A jagged pale scar cut upward from his left eyebrow into a streak of white in the black hair. His expression remained as stoic as a finely hewn statue. Her skin prickled like it did when a sudden thunderstorm approached.

Dunkirk cleared his throat loud enough to get everyone's attention. "Just wanted to introduce all of you to my new man, in case you run across him on the range. This here's Mitchell Fallon, he's my rep, come to help me keep a tally. He'll make sure none of you small ranchers overstep your bounds and burn a few brands where they don't belong."

Charlie's loosely reined temper flared. She tightened her lips and kept her eyes hard on the colonel. "If anyone is likely to do that, sir, it's you and your collection of ratty gunfighters."

Mitch gave the brash cowpoke a second look. On first glance, he had thought her a young man, but now saw that she was a rough and hardened female who looked like a good scrubbing wouldn't hurt her any. Damn shame, considering the shortage of good-looking women, that this one chose to go as a man. But what the hell? It made him no difference. If he came up against her, he'd treat her just like all the rest and do what he'd been hired to do.

He rode for a brand, he honored it. Suited him fine that Colonel Dunkirk had a dark craving to rule this land. To the strongest and meanest go the spoils. Mitch didn't much care, one way or the other, who came out on top. This was a job that suited his temperament; it gave him plenty of excuse to get back at men who deserved to pay for what had happened to him.

The colonel ignored Charlie's comment.

Of course, that only made her angrier and mouthier. "As for your hired *hand,* keep him and his kind off my ranch. I may be new up here and I may be a woman, but don't make any mistakes you'll regret. I don't intend to lose my land to thieves and killers."

Despite her anger Charlie couldn't take her eyes off the man in black who gazed right past her as if she didn't exist. Though he appeared to be paying no attention to his immediate surroundings, he held his right arm slightly bent, hand almost touching the pistol. Dunkirk had been heard to vow more than once that he would own all of Montana's grazing land one day. And this man was here to help him do just that. He was a gunslinger, pure and simple. The way Dunkirk accumulated land was nothing short of stealing. Even if he did give it a fancy name like possessory rights, it was still illegal.

Yancey Barton slid to her side, said under his breath, "We don't need the likes of him, but if I was you I wouldn't rile him."

"You don't have to rile a man like that. He comes riled. Besides, it looks to me like we don't have a choice," Charlie whispered back to her ramrod.

The man in black startled her by belatedly acknowledging Dunkirk's introduction in a voice hard-edged and emotionless. "I'll be around."

Abruptly he met her gaze with a calculating expression that gave her the shudders right down to the depths of her soul. She had never feared any man or beast in her life, but this man's lifeless tone and granite stare were terrifying in a way she couldn't explain. Her mouth dried and her heart paused in its beating. Whatever she might have been about to say to Yancey or Cal, or for that matter the colonel, evaporated. She turned on her heel and almost ran from the confrontation. As she untied Belle she noticed her fingers were trembling. A familiar, unwanted sensation settled in the pit of her stomach, like some long-lost desire no longer recognized. Her reaction to the man terrified her even more than he himself had.

Yancey sat beside Charlie that evening while they were eating. He didn't say much until both had finished off their plates of beans and biscuits, but she knew he had something on his mind.

"The man's gonna take all the land, Charlie, and I don't see a way in hell we can stop him. It's just a matter of time."

She sipped at her coffee and stared off across the campfire at the lone figure of Mitchell Fallon. He had backed up under a tree and lit a thin black cheroot. In the dark he might have been staring at her, she couldn't tell.

Swiftly she turned her attention to Yancey. "What would Matt do?"

"Fight, I reckon. He always did."

"But he had Richard King to back him up. The most powerful rancher in Texas. When you have friends like that you don't have to do too much fighting."

"Did to get where he was though, same as King. You don't think someone handed him that spread in Santa Gertrudis on a platter, do you?" Yancey tossed the dregs of his coffee to the ground.

"You telling me to fight, Yancey? Is that what you're telling me? And if so, will you and the men back me?"

The ramrod studied her for a long moment, squinting his blue eyes so that the sun-wrinkled skin folded in around them. "Ain't no place for a woman, fighting for a spread."

"Don't you dare tell me that, Yancey Barton. Every woman who takes up with a rancher fights for the life as much as her man does. She wears herself out fighting." Hot tears stung her eyes and she turned quickly away, not wanting him to see. Dammit, she had to be tougher than this.

"Now, sweetheart, don't go getting touchy on me. You know blamed well what I meant. Nobody knows better than me how hard you've worked, or any rancher's wife, for that matter.

"It's just you don't have no business going up against men like that'un"—he gestured toward Fallon—"with a six-shooter in your hand. He'll win 'cause he's meaner, not 'cause you're a woman, and that's a fact."

Charlie sighed and drank the last of her coffee. "Then what do I do? Hire someone like him?"

"Well, there's that, and ..." Yancey hove to his feet and looked down at her. "... then, of course, we could band together, you and the others Dunkirk wants to force out. Go to the law about his thieving ways."

She snorted. "Nobody cares that he rookered a bunch of war widows out of their land-bonus privileges, or that every man in his outfit has filed a claim and signed it over to him. Sheriff Newton turned a blind eye to the vigilantes who strung up those homesteaders a while back. Dunkirk found them squatting on his land and that was all that mattered. And what about poor Ruell Denver? Just happened to be unlucky enough to ride up on some bad doin's and ended up getting blamed for rustling and strung up. What makes you think a man of Sheriff Newton's caliber, lawman or not, would help us?"

"Well, gal, then I reckon you have to go higher than the sheriff. Contact the territorial governor or the marshal."

Charlie stood and stretched. The idea didn't appeal to her. Ride all over hell and creation chasing some politician who would have no inkling what was really going on out here even after she explained it. No, sir, she was a rancher not a crusader, but maybe Yancey did have something in suggesting that the small ranchers band together. Once the roundup was over she would speak to Cal and Duffy about it, see what they thought. There was that Englishman Hawthorne east of the colonel's and Les Burris whose place laid alongside of Duffy's, and a couple more whose names she hadn't learned yet even though their cows had turned up at the branding fire.

That night, asleep in her bedroll until time for her watch, Charlie dreamed of the man in black with the snowy streak in his hair. Sensual perceptions brought her awake with that all too familiar deprived ache deep inside, and it was a long time before she went back to sleep. She had dreamed of him satisfying those needs in a most unthinkable way, and it disturbed her deeply.

The man in black was certainly not to be desired, even if she harbored such thoughts, which she didn't. She had played the role of her father's son too long to even consider such feminine longings. At twenty-six she was a confirmed spinster, and that was the way she wanted it. She relegated the dream to the place of nightmares where she stored memories too painful to deal with.

Yancey roused her for the early morning shift two hours before dawn. Though most cowboys disliked pulling guard at that hour, she preferred it. It meant that she would be in the saddle longer than those who had drawn guard duty during the night, but it was an even swap considering the quiet beauty of the pre-dawn hours.

Still only half-awake she swung into the saddle and settled easily while the compact quarter horse plodded slowly around the perimeter of the sleeping cattle. Belle too knew her job. After a while Charlie began to hum, softly at first, then louder. The cows liked singing and whistling, it kept them settled down, just as it had during the long arduous drive up from Texas. Roundup was little different from that six-month cattle drive, it just didn't last quite so long. In two or three weeks they'd be finished with the branding and could settle back to normal ranch tasks until fall roundup in August when beeves would be cut out for shipping to market. By then yearlings would have fattened on the lush, green summer grasses and would bring a good price.

She let her clear voice rise to meet the gentle night wind, singing the ballad of Lasca, a favorite of all cowboys.

"Lasca used to ride on a mouse-gray mustang, by my side."

Across the way someone began to accompany her on a mouth harp. Off to her left creek water murmured over its rocky bed, adding to the melody.

"She was as bold as the billows that beat. She was as wild as the breezes that blow."

As she continued the song, Charlie thought she heard the steady thud of horses' hooves out of cadence with those of her own mount. She broke off the stanza and listened intently, but there was nothing but the soughing of the wind through treetops and the sweet song of the harp blending with the rush of water. Off and on during the hours before the sky lightened to silver, and long after she finished the heartbreaking tune with *"Does half my heart lie buried, there, In Texas, down by the Rio Grande?"* the prickly sensation that she was being watched wouldn't go away. Still she saw no one.

Mitchell Fallon reined in his horse abruptly. He had been so caught up in the singing that he had almost ridden up on a rider skulking along in the shadows. The man appeared to be following someone, but in the dark Mitch couldn't tell who. The rider continued to give that impression by moving in furtive stops and starts.

The singer halted for a moment, so did Mitch and so did the mysterious rider. After a while the woman began to sing again, a tune that plucked at Mitch's heart. He could practically hear tears in the voice as he made out the sad tale of lovers caught up in a stampede and the woman dying in her lover's arms.

Buried emotions rose in his chest and he used anger to suppress them. What in the hell was he doing out here in the middle of the night in the first place? It sure wasn't to listen to some corny love song. The colonel had said he should be visible, keep an eye on things, get to know faces and habits so he would be useful later when the man put into action his strategy for getting rid of these small ranchers.

Deliberately Mitch rode out into the open so that the rider he was pursuing could see him, and shouted a noncommittal greeting that came out more like a grunt. The cowboy replied with a similar sound and Mitch rode on.

Even when he did bed down he couldn't sleep. The strains of the beautiful and forlorn ballad haunted him, and he knew Charlie Houston was responsible. Her and her ebony dark eyes that wouldn't leave a man alone. It was unnerving to catch sight of her watching him. He wanted nothing to do with a woman, especially not one who was supposed to be his enemy. So why was he lying awake in the dark of night thinking about her? He turned one way, then another, but each time he closed his eyes, there she was asking something provocative and dangerous of him.

Finally he rolled from his blankets and, carrying his boots, crept out of camp. He wore no shirt and a ripple of cool air off the water sent goose bumps skittering over his bare flesh. At the edge of the creek he sat on a large boulder and gazed east across the shadowy plains as they rose gently toward the sky.

In his heart, his dead wife cried softly, and he could find no way to quiet her. The presence of the Houston woman had reawakened his guilt, and that made him angry. There were times when he simply wanted to ride to the edge of a cliff and dive off, join Celia and their child and be done with facing day after endless day with the unanswered question on his lips. Why hadn't the men who had senselessly killed his wife and child killed him too? He had asked it thousands of times, but there was only silence in reply. The absence of reason nagged at him like a forgotten lyric, a faded dream.

Stars winked in the flowing water and he thought again about killing the men who had so brutally murdered his family. For a long while that was all he'd thought about, but he wasn't a killer, never had been, despite the reputation he'd gained after the war. A war did its best to turn a man mean, and Lord knows that one had, but his outlaw ways had been aimed more at something else. Taking back what should have been his. Payback for having been robbed of his family and his life. He had never returned home to his parents and sister in Missouri, and he blamed the war for that too.

Dear God, how he wished things had been different.

During the next few days the roundup chewed away the miles in a slow, distinct rhythm. Riders fanned out into the brushy hills to bring in strays. Men returned covered in mud after rescuing some unlucky animal trapped in a bog. At night exhausted cowboys who had been in the saddle up to eighteen hours snored loudly through a few hours rest. The days became one long blur of backbreaking work that left everyone worn out come bedtime.

Occasionally Charlie caught sight of the gunslinger, but never so that she was forced to acknowledge his presence. He paid little attention to her at all, and it humiliated her to be caught a couple of times staring at him. She did notice that he didn't pull guard and only occasionally rode herd. He was simply there and everyone walked a wide circle around him. He ate alone, rode alone, slept apart from the others like a renegade wolf wary of the pack.

Despite all that, something in his demeanor beckoned to her, made her wish she knew more about him. She wanted to speak to him, to discover what attracted her, but she dare not, for he was the enemy.

Chapter Two

Ever since Charlie had first drawn nighthawk duty she'd had a sense of being watched, but could never catch anyone in the act. It didn't make sense anyway. Why would anyone want to follow her around? Still, the feeling persisted and she kept a wary eye out. The roundup was winding down, going into the last few days as the circling riders scouted out the last of the scattered cattle when she finally caught the man.

That evening she drew early night watch. Under the roan's hooves the ground grew dark quickly, but the night sky shone silver, silhouetting trees and cattle and riders. She let the horse wind lazily around the stragglers yet to be branded. Most of the cows, newly branded calves, castrated steers, and bulls had been released to the vast summer pastures, and the evening was hushed and placid.

From off to her right came the deep-throated cough of a resting animal. She glanced at the dark humps settling down for the night. That's when she distinctly heard the rattle of a horse's hooves in creek gravel where no one needed to be riding. Digging her heels into the roan's flanks, she reined him off in the direction of the sound and nearly rode into Ritter, a green hand she had hired just for the roundup.

Brown eyes wide in a youthful face, he looked ready to spook when he recognized her.

She pulled up the roan, spoke harshly, "What are you doing out here?"

Ritter clawed his hat off his head. Hair struck up like patches of straw. "Sorry, ma'am. Just looking . . . just checking . . . oh, lawd."

"Don't call me ma'am, my name is Charlie Houston. Pick one, or even Miss Houston, but not ma'am."

"No, ma'am . . . uh, no, sir . . . dang it all."

"What's wrong with you?" Charlie glared at the stammering young man, trying to remember why she had hired him. He appeared to be totally inept, this lean-jawed youth who wore a hat so big it rested on his ears, but she couldn't recall watching him work. "Have you been following me around, Ritter?"

He clutched the hat to his chest, then turned it in rawboned hands too large for the rest of him. No answer came.

"Well?"

"Well?" he echoed. "No . . . I mean, I suppose." He gulped noisily. "Yes, ma'am," he bellowed so that Charlie's horse twitched and laid back its ears.

In the herd several cows bawled, horns rattled together. Her shoulders hunched. "Keep your voice down. Want to start them stampeding? Where in thunder did you work before you came here? Couldn't have been on a cow ranch. And tell me again why I hired you."

"Up north around the Marias. I was a jingler."

Charlie snorted, still unable to recall what weakness had caused her to put this young man on the payroll.

"Isn't any wonder you're green," she said. A jingler was the lowest man on the roundup. He saw to herding the remuda and keeping up with all the saddle horses, but he also drew all the dirty chores, like rustling wood and water for the cook, peeling potatoes, and helping set up and tear down camp. Jobs no respectable cowboy would undertake, no matter what.

She slanted a hard glance at him. "Even a jingler manages to learn something. How long did you work for them?"

Ritter dropped his chin down on his chest and muttered into it. "Last fall was my first. My pap was a farmer."

"A sodbuster. Your first was last fall? And tell me, Ritter, did you think that one of your duties when I hired you on at the Double H was to spy on me?"

He ducked his head. "No, ma'am."

"Well, then, why in thunder . . ." She sighed to calm herself. "I don't even remember including you in on this roundup. If I remember right, I left you back at the ranch to lend a hand where you were needed. So tell me, Ritter, what in thunderation are you doing skulking around like some hyena?"

"Mr. Barton . . . he said I should, I mean, he thought—"

"Barton put you up to this? Yancey?" She trusted her ramrod as if he were an older brother and he put this greenhorn on her tail. Yancey had been by her father's side since the day Matt went out on his own to start the Double H when the War Between the States ended in '65. How dare Yancey set some snotnose like Ritter on her trail to watch over her. Who did he think he was?

Charlotte Houston was four years old when Matt Houston took her from her Mexican grandparents and their palatial home and moved onto the King Ranch in Texas. He was ranch foreman there, and considered he'd made a place at last for his motherless daughter after years of trying to start his own spread.

She didn't remember her mother, and until the day her father came for her, Charlie, then called Charlotte by her extended Mexican family, spoke only Spanish, wore beautiful dresses and shiny patent leather shoes, and was doted upon by grandparents and a large number of aunts, uncles, and cousins.

Nowadays Charlie could speak no more than a few words of her mother's language, in fact did not even remember living with her grandparents. Since her father's death she'd experienced flashes of memory, mostly during the dreaded hours when she awoke in the middle of the night and could not go back to sleep.

When she was fifteen Matt went out on his own with King's blessing and some prize stock that included a few head of the newly bred quarter horses of which King was so proud. Charlie began to work beside her father as if she were his son. Together they built a ranch in Texas that while it never rivaled the mammoth King spread was something of which to be proud.

Then along came the cattle glut and the recession that spawned Matt Houston's dream. He'd heard about the cattle drives to Montana and the lush grassland just going begging, and he began to plan for the day when he would drive his longhorns the 1,500 miles into central Montana and build a barony of his own. So in the spring of 1875 Matt and Charlie Houston, along with Yancey Barton, seventeen faithful hands, and Chocco the cook, left Texas and headed north.

Charlie had never faltered in her duties, not even when Matt was killed, and now here stood one of her green hands telling her that her trusted ramrod had actually ordered him to spy on her. She'd be damned if she'd put up with that, not even from Yancey Barton.

"You ride in my place, Ritter."

"Me, ma'am?" He gulped, too late trying to swallow the forbidden form of address.

She tugged Belle's head around, bumping Ritter's

mount and sending it dancing. "That's what I said, and I am the boss, not Yancey Barton. You got that, boy?"

"Yes'm, I do," he stammered.

The horse was surefooted in the dark or Charlie would have been pitched to the ground as she urged the roan back to camp where she dismounted and stomped her way through the sleeping men until she came upon Yancey Barton's still form.

Stripping back the bedding, she grabbed her foreman by the shirtfront and yanked him to a sitting position.

He peered at her owlishly. "What in the hell . . . ? Charlie. Damn, what's happened, girl? You all right? You hurt? What . . . ?"

"You put Ritter on me, and I want to know why," she demanded, her anger throbbing at her temples like thunder.

Yancey closed his hands around her balled fists that still clutched his shirtfront. "Take it easy, sweetheart. Lord, I thought something god-awful had happened. Ritter?"

"The young greenhorn. He's been following me around, says you put him up to it."

The man lying in the bedroll next to Yancey rolled over. "What the hell's going on? Can't a feller get some sleep? Dang."

"Can't we talk about this in the morning, Charlie?" Yancey said in a low voice.

"No, we're talking about it right now."

"Well, I don't understand why you're so all-fired mad, I was just doing my job like Matt told me to."

Charlie squeezed her eyes shut and gritted her teeth. "Matt's dead. Dead. And I'm running the outfit. You don't . . . dammit, you don't just do something like that. I intend to see to Matt Houston's dream, and I don't need some snot-nosed kid sneaking around keeping an eye on me, and I sure don't need you putting him up to it. You work for me, you got that?"

An anger such as she had never experienced came over Charlie, so that she fled from Yancey before she could give vent to it. Cursing under her breath, she stomped her way through the bundles of sleeping, weary cowboys.

Charlie shoved through the double swinging doors of the Powder Keg, took a quick look around, and spotted Cal at the bar. Ignoring a few greetings she elbowed through the crowd of celebrating hands.

He spotted her coming. "Buy you one, Charlie?"

"If the next one's on me."

Cal Malone chuckled. "I reckon that'll be okay."

He signaled Lance, who owned the place and tended bar when he couldn't get anyone else to take the job. The well-fed man laid a meaty palm over the two bits Cal slapped down for the drinks.

Lance eyed Charlie, for ladies weren't allowed in the bar. He had put up with her before, and a glance from Cal told him to do so again. Charlie grinned. She appreciated Cal as a friend. He took her at face value.

They talked about the tally, how each ranch had done, and drank the foamy brew. Charlie was comfortable with Cal, even when he criticized her choice of beeves. Cal favored Durhams and shorthorns and had begun to breed them into his herd. It wasn't an argument, simply a discussion, and things were calm, considering the crowd, when someone bumped Cal's elbow and dumped his mug of beer down the front of his shirt.

The rancher's short temper flared. He roared, slammed the mug down hard on the bar, and swung around with big fists cocked to take full measure of his adversary.

Even though he had to look up at the man who had

bumped him, Cal didn't back down. He was set to pop him one. He'd been like that since Becky and the baby died, and Charlie guessed she understood, but when she caught sight of Mitchell Fallon's flat agate gaze she grabbed Cal's arm. It did no good.

The iron-hard muscles flexed, shaking her loose, and Cal came around in a swing headed for Fallon's jaw. The gunfighter dodged the punch much like a snake striking. His head just wasn't in the line of fire anymore, and it was so quick that Cal, expecting to hit something solid, went stumbling past Fallon and into the crowd around the bar.

Before Cal could make his way back through the men who were doing their best to hold him off for fear the gunman would shoot him, Charlie and Mitchell Fallon just sort of stumbled into each other.

She put her hands flat against his chest and pushed away. "Want to hit me too?"

"Haven't hit anyone yet. Son of a bitch comes back I'll wipe up the floor with him. Got a quick temper for a little man. Could get him killed."

She narrowed her eyes to slits. "You watch out who you threaten, Mr. Fallon. You may work for Colonel Dunkirk, but that doesn't give you free rein around here. If I were you I'd drink someplace else. Someplace where you're welcome."

"I drink where I please, and I work for who I please. Never have asked anyone's permission for either. And don't think because you're a woman you can talk to me like I'm filth. I got as much a right in here as you do."

The rigid tone of his voice, the angry clench of his strong jaw, hit her like a physical blow. He had remained the distance from her that she had created with her earlier shove, but she swore she could feel the fire of his breath directed at her.

Caught up in his unfaltering gaze, she lifted her chin

and squared both shoulders, though inside she trembled so hard she just knew he could see her jittering.

Faced down like that by a woman, Fallon's austere expression softened, and for just the flickering of an instant she saw in his features a sadness so intense that it overwhelmed the harsh demeanor. Before she could be sure, and before she could respond to the encounter, he had shoved past her and out of the saloon. She was surprised to feel a thick lump in her chest, an aching loneliness. Sometimes she missed her father so much it was unbearable, and at such inopportune times. It annoyed her that a run-in with that frightful man could be such a moment. Matt could have dealt with this situation and smoothed the waters in such a way that both men would have gone away feeling vindicated. She guessed she'd inherited her emotions from her mother's family.

She shared another beer with Cal, but both were so upset by the encounter with the gunslinger that they parted company. Cal, she supposed, would find a pretty girl and love his way out of his foul mood in one of the cribs out back. She decided to ride on home to the ranch. Night riding was one of her favorite pastimes especially when she needed settling.

As she headed out of Miles City on the surefooted roan darkness crept across the azure sky, stealing lazily from east to west to swallow the flaring sunset. By the time she topped the rise above the ranch the vast sky was a deep purple awash with millions of stars. She halted there a moment, visualizing more than seeing the ranch buildings spread out below her. Not much yet. Not much.

"It's your dream, Matt. Dammit, why couldn't you stick around to make it come true?" As the spoken words tumbled into the empty night she stared through tears at the flickering stars.

She ought to just ride away, leave behind the marauding Indians, the prowling wolves, and the two-legged snakes who would like to see her fall. Just go back to Texas and her mother's people where she could learn to be a lady.

Between her legs the restless pony tossed its head and whinnied, danced a little two-step. She came out of her reverie, rubbed at the tight muscles along the animal's tawny neck. "Ho, boy. Ho. What's wrong?"

A replying whinny came out of the nested darkness below. The horses penned in the corral back of the skeleton of a barn moved restlessly, their hooves thudding.

In that instant she saw something flash inside the raw log walls of the roofless structure, and nudged her heels into the mare's belly to ride a bit closer. As she did flames erupted in the doorway of the barn and out of the inferno burst a horse and rider. Columns of fire leaped into the sky as the animal raced across the barnyard. She skinned her Winchester from its scabbard and without aiming pulled off several shots at the fleeing figure, hunched low in the saddle. She couldn't really see him except in the fierce glow of the fire, and the surrounding darkness quickly engulfed him.

Maybe she'd hit him, maybe not.

She vaulted to the ground and raced for the water trough. A sickness down inside told her it was no use. What little water she could haul to the inferno would have no effect. Armed with two buckets she made several trips between the trough and the burning barn, but heat and smoke soon defeated her and she sank to her knees. She knelt there for a long while, until the flames consumed the freshly peeled logs, leaving only a smoking pile.

Green timbers wouldn't burn that fast without help, and in a puff of breeze she detected the pungent odor of coal oil. The rider had made sure this one wouldn't be put out.

With a sigh that made her smoke-burned lungs ache, she rose, retrieved the Winchester from beside the water trough, and called for Belle. After unsaddling the mare and turning her into the corral with the others who continued to trot circles and squeal nervously, she trudged to the one-room cabin. Once inside she found the hollow silence unbearable. Loneliness crept its way into her heart and soul, and that in itself was bad enough without the added burden of fury over the deliberate fire.

And so the colonel's war had begun in earnest. Now that winter was over, the roundup done, all the innuendoes and veiled threats spouted by Dunkirk's men would come to pass. In the end he would probably win and get her land, no matter how hard she fought.

After she washed her hands and face, she tugged off the dusty boots and skinned out of her clothes. Every muscle ached, none so much as her heart. What should she do? Despairing of an answer she crawled into bed. Lying in the dark, she thought of the ranch in Texas. The bright and airy rooms in the sprawling adobe house. The young Mexican woman who scrubbed the pine board floors till they gleamed, aired the blankets on the porch railings, and cooked delicious meals that filled the rooms with their savory aromas. How she missed it.

Damn that Dunkirk! He had sent one of his rowdies to burn down her barn even before the hands could finish building it. He wasn't satisfied with stealing all the government land for his own, he had to have what belonged to all the honest, decent folk too. Probably would have burned the whole place if she hadn't rode in when she had. Damn him to hell, how could she fight him?

She thought of Mitchell Fallon and his words of

hate. A brutal man who would shoot anybody who tried to fight back. Could he have been the one who torched the barn? He'd left early enough to reach the ranch ahead of her. Barn burning didn't seem the kind of thing a man like him would do. He was here for much more specialized work than burning barns with that Colt strapped low on his hip and those killer's eyes hard as stone and devoid of emotion. But if he had set the fire, she hoped the bullet she'd put in him festered and gave him gangrene.

After lying in bed for what seemed like hours, she finally gave up. Standing naked in the center of the dark room she shivered and hugged herself. Spring nights were chilly and goose bumps rose up her arms and flitted down across her bare breasts.

She felt her way across the room and started a fire in the cookstove. Once the flames crackled she filled the kettle. A hot bath would help her sleep, and the business of preparing one would keep her thoughts on something besides her troubles.

While the water heated she lit a lamp and, wrapping herself in a quilt, sat cross-legged on the floor. From under the bed she pulled out a small humpbacked chest, opened it, and removed a music box and several metal disks. Winding the crank and inserting a disk, she shed the rough cowhand exterior as easily as she'd removed the Kentucky jeans and flannel shirt and union suit.

The lovely strains of Chopin soothed her soul, and dancing so unencumbered freed her from the rigid restraints of her singular life. She began to dance, bending and turning like a lithe willow in a gentle breeze. She ended the dance by sinking to the floor on the heaped quilt as the melody faded. The utter silence that followed was broken only by her breathing and the muted thumping of her heart.

Far off in the distance she heard the echoing forlorn

howl of a wolf and an almost indistinct reply from another of its kind. With a shudder she rose, poured the hissing water into the washpan, and soaped up a cloth. Eyes closed she began to rub the soft fabric slowly over her bare flesh. Under one arm, along the swell of her breast to the nipple that hardened under the touch.

An image assaulted her: Mitchell Fallon's green eyes sparking fire while he preened like a savage animal. The man continued to bedevil her and she wanted rid of him, in the flesh and in her mind. Shivering, she slipped into a flannel nightgown and extinguished the lamp.

He went to bed with her, no matter how she tried to shut him out, and she curled beneath the quilt, pulling her knees up under her chin. He could come in the night to attack her, or to trail his sensual lips and long fingers over places that might awaken the feelings the tough side of Charlie Houston did not acknowledge.

Mitch Fallon sat astride the skittish black stallion and gazed down at the smoking ruin amid the few poor structures of the Double H Ranch.

Foolish, stupid woman. How could she possibly think she could win this battle, and why would she want to? Even if she'd been a man all the odds were stacked against her. Why didn't she go back where she came from and marry up with somebody, settle down and raise some young'uns and make bread and grow a garden? Why didn't she leave before she got hurt; before she got killed?

He swallowed harshly, thickly. Dammit, he hadn't expected this. The enemy was supposed to be out there. Someone he could kill so he'd feel better. Not some woman. Not someone who made him remember ...

The memories overpowered him. Celia and their firstborn, a lovely little girl as pretty as her copper-skinned mother. He had called the child Fawn because of her doelike eyes, but Celia had insisted on a white child's name because she herself had one, even though she was a full-blooded Sioux. He could not even think about his family without becoming enraged. Everywhere he went he looked for the men who had killed his wife and child.

Annoyed at the unexpected lapse into the past, Mitch lifted the reins to turn the stallion and ride back to Dunkirk's spread. A light went on in the cabin, a feeble glow that brightened the windows and made him hesitate. He wasn't sure why he didn't just ride away, yet he paused a moment longer when a graceful shadow swayed across the lighted square and disappeared from sight.

What the hell? Someone was dancing in there. Whirling and twisting, bending and swaying.

He leaned forward in the saddle, felt the thickness of his manhood, a throbbing heat he'd thought long dead. Drained away from him like Celia's blood in the dusty street of Bismarck.

The stallion shifted angrily, wanting to go, held in place only because the man on his back was his master, with a will stronger and darker than he himself.

Raising to stand in the stirrups, he lifted throbbing loins from the caress of the leather. In the cabin below lamplight outlined the lean, feminine body. The woman raised her arms, turned to reveal a contour of lush breasts; a firm leg lifted so he could imagine he looked into her innermost secret places.

Good God, what was wrong with him? Sitting up here like a peeping Tom, some adolescent youth getting stirred up over forbidden sights. Yet he couldn't move away as the figure twirled and bent and disappeared once again from the window.

In the distance wolves howled, the stallion sawed at his bit and moaned, a gentle breeze picked up to cool the sweat of Fallon's ardor. Still he watched, a man filled with hate enraptured by an unexpected glimpse of pure beauty. A beauty that exacted no penalty from him for his enjoyment.

Soon enough he would go back to the world in which he chose to live, and that too made him very angry.

Hell, if he hadn't been thinking of Celia and Fawn, hadn't been trodding dangerously close to reliving what he could never, never recapture, he wouldn't have been aroused by the magical vision down there in the first place. The unreal occurrence reached inside him and ripped at his tortured soul until he wanted to shout with anguish. He never expected to see such a thing out here on the Montana plains where life was reduced to a harsh day-to-day struggle for survival. It had taken him by surprise, that was all.

How he felt meant nothing in the scheme of things. He had no intention of ever experiencing again the intensified emotion that loving a beautiful woman inspired.

Yanking the stallion's head around he whipped the reins and spurred the taut flanks. He rode as fast and hard as he could away from the sight of the cabin and the images that painfully exposed the futility of his own existence.

Chapter Three

By dawn the Double H hands had returned from Miles City, a bit chagrined when they caught sight of the smoking rubble that had once been a barn.

Ritter clattered up onto the porch as the sun rose and tapped meekly on the door. Miss Houston was mad at him before, and now she would probably jerk his shoulders up around his ears. He figured somehow him not being here for the fire would turn out to be his fault, as if he ought to have known it would happen.

Already dressed in jeans and a flannel shirt, but still in her stocking feet, Charlie swung open the door and gazed up at him. Her eyes were so black the pupils didn't show, her skin the color of coffee with a healthy dash of thick cream added. She was the prettiest woman Ritter had ever seen, tough and sturdily built but at the same time delicately turned so that every movement was feminine.

He gestured over his shoulder at the smoldering mass of ashes. "How'd it happen?"

"That no-account Dunkirk must've sent one of his men to set it. Did a good job too." She shrugged, looked down at her small stocking feet. "Didn't even get it plumb built. Reckon that'll put some of you boys to work."

Belatedly Ritter jerked his hat from his head. He hated what else he had to tell her on top of the fire, hated it so much that he just forgot and spilled out that name she'd asked him never to use. He just kept doing it, like he was dumb or something. Ma'am, ma'am, ma'am. It seemed all he was able to blurt out when he was around her. And here it was, rolling off his tongue again. He screwed up his face and shifted from one foot to the other. By the look she gave him he knew it was too late to try to take it back.

Though she'd said it before at least a hundred times, she repeated with quiet exasperation, "Call me Houston, Ritter. I've told you I don't cotton to ma'am much."

He nodded, uncomfortable more with his piece of news than with the expected request. "Yes'm. I mean . . . okay, fine. Chocco ain't comin' back, ma'am, I mean Houston." He let his voice trail away on the last syllable. How dumb he felt calling her that. It would never do.

The news about their cook jolted her. "Chocco? Why not? What happened?"

"Well, he said . . . he told me to say he liked riding the trail fine, doing the cooking and taking care of the chuck wagon . . . but, well, he said when it comes to ranching, he just ain't cut out for it. Said he's heading back down to the Brazos, hopes to latch on to a herd he can cook for."

The surly Chocco had said little after Matt was killed, even though he had stayed on for the winter. For that she was grateful, but his leaving sure did put her in a bind.

"Any of the other boys cook?" she asked after thinking on it awhile.

He had already backed all the way to the edge of

the porch just in case she got physical, and he began to shake his head. "I don't reckon they can, ma'am. Uh—"

"Never mind, Ritter. Thank you for telling me. I'll get my boots on and ... well, hell, I don't know what. Chocco left the chuck wagon?"

He flinched and raised his shoulders in reply. He wasn't used to a woman who used words like *hell* and *dammit*. It wasn't natural somehow. He hadn't paid attention to much of anything in Miles City but finding him a pretty girl and knocking back some beers, and so couldn't remember exactly everything the old cook had to say before he took off.

When it came to grub, all Ritter knew was spooning beans off his plate. Every cowboy could boil coffee. That wasn't saying much about what it would taste like, plus that didn't have anything to do with cooking anyway. One thing he knew for dang sure, and it worried him a heap more than the missing cook. If those gunslingers of Dunkirk's drew down on him, he'd probably get himself killed because he didn't know anything about one of those fancy sidearms much less how to shoot at someone.

"Tell the men I'll be on down, we'll figure something out." Charlie shut the door before Ritter could reply.

She leaned her forehead up against the cool wood for a moment, then went to get her boots on. Sometimes you reached a point where things could only get better, and she figured she wasn't too far off that mark.

The chuck wagon was parked out back of the bunkhouse, tongue pointed toward Texas, as if the surly old cook had left a final message. On the trail he would have put the tongue toward the North Star each night so the drovers would know the direction in which they should travel the next day. This, though, was a sign of where Chocco had gone, and maybe a hint that she too would do well to go back where she belonged.

Shrugging, she began an immediate search of the contents of the wagon. She lifted the cover from a bowl stuck away in the grub box and took a whiff.

"It's sourdough starter, I know that much," she said aloud. "At least we'll have biscuits."

She puttered around in there quite a spell while the hungry hands moaned and milled about like cattle. She rattled spoons and unwrapped supplies until it finally occurred to her that they would need a cook fire. She put two of the boys to building one.

Belatedly she realized it would be easier to cook breakfast on her cookstove in the cabin, if anything about cooking could be easy. Since she was already committed, though, she stuck to her guns, digging her way through the unfamiliar utensils until she finally located the Dutch oven. Heartened by the find, she dipped flour into an empty bowl and then spooned in some of the gooey sourdough starter.

Ritter watched anxiously. He'd never before seen a woman who couldn't cook, except maybe a soiled dove or two, and of course they'd never had to cook 'cause what they gave their men had nothing to do with a cookstove or satisfying an empty belly. This woman, his boss, who insisted he call her Houston, rolled her shirtsleeves up to her elbows and with a terrible expression on her face stuck both hands right down into that mess she'd made. After a while she lifted them out, long strands of dough hanging from each finger like drool from a suckling calf.

"Pour me out some more flour, Ritter, would you?"

He obeyed but felt foolish, looked around to make sure none of the boys saw him doing such a sissy job. There was a limit to what even a jingler would do.

She finally had this great big wad of rubbery stuff

that she played around in for a while longer, then started making balls and tucking them into the Dutch oven. When she had it layered up pretty good, she covered the thing and nestled it down in one side of the blazing fire.

He couldn't keep his mouth shut any longer. "Ma'am, I think you're supposed to put coals on top and sorta heap 'em up around that thing."

She was so dithered she didn't even make anything of him calling her the forbidden *ma'am*, instead pursed her mouth into a pretty pout that made Ritter wonder why some man hadn't grabbed her up a long time ago.

"Well, yes, of course. I know that," she told him. "You do it, Ritter, I'm looking for something else to cook."

He obeyed. He figured he'd probably do anything she asked him to, bar none.

Eventually she found a slap of salt-cured fatback wrapped in a greasy cloth, sliced some off, and tossed the pieces in a long-handled black fry pan. That too she placed on the fire, jiggling the burning wood around until she made a level place. Flames licked up around the sides of the pan and meat began to sizzle right away, then caught fire. Enormous orange flames, fed by the grease, leaped from the skillet.

"Ritter, dammit, give me a hand here," she yelled. She smelled hair burning and staggered back away from the fire before her head could go up in flames.

He scooped up a double handful of dirt and threw it over the burning meat.

She stood there a moment staring down at the mess, grease and curls of black meat poking up out of the brown earth, then tramped to where the hands were gathered, a safe distance from her and the cook fire.

Blowing singed hair from her sweating face, she addressed the amazed men. "At least the biscuits are cooking. I'm sorry about the meat. If one of you ever says a word about this ever to anyone, I'll send you riding, you understand?"

They all nodded somberly, but she could tell they were just about to bust out laughing.

"That's all right, ma'am," one of the men ventured, and someone chuckled.

"Don't call me that," she shouted.

"Sir, then," came a low voice.

She whirled to see Ritter, thumbs hanging from his pockets and an amused, innocent expression on his boyish face.

"I can make coffee, I know how to do that," he offered quickly before she could come down on him for something. He skittered off to do so, seeing this whole thing escalating into a disaster that might cause all the hands to quit. This woman rode like a man and worked like a man, who could expect her to cook, anyway?

He filled the mammoth pot with water, threw in several hands of Arbuckle coffee, and turned to set it on the fire just as the lid to the Dutch oven lifted with an ominous hiss. He watched fascinated, while swelling sourdough biscuits pushed the heavy lid off into the fire. Then a mushrooming white mass oozed out over the sides of the iron pot. In the hope that what was left in there might accidentally cook into something the boys could eat, he just backed off and let 'er rip.

Charlie scooted for the house, muttering under her breath about men who were so helpless they'd starve before they'd cook a meal. Safely hidden inside she opened a can of peaches and sat down at the table to spoon the luscious golden halves from their thick syrup and onto her tongue that felt like it was coated with smoke.

She would most definitely have to ride into Miles City and see if she could hire a cook, or every man on the place would desert the Double H before she even got the ranch producing.

"I won't fail you, I won't," she said aloud. She'd made the promise to the memory of her father uncounted times during the long winter months. While alone in the cabin night after night, all she'd had to think about were her memories and the raw grief. But it was time she started to live in the present and face her responsibilities.

She would make a go of this place one way or another, and damn anyone who tried to stop her.

Mitch refused the fat cigar Dunkirk offered as well as the leather chair the man indicated. He lazed instead near the wide windows and studied the portly uniformed man who had hired him to do his dirty work. Dunkirk was a bastard, that's for sure, but he had the upper hand in this territory because he knew what it took to win. As for Mitch, he didn't much care. Win or lose was all the same to him.

"We're going to finish up this business this summer," the colonel railed. "I'm tired of these cowboys riding up from Texas after we did all the hard work here in Montana and expecting to cut their slice from our pie. This land is mine, all of it. I broke trail when no one else had the guts. I wintered and froze my ass and figured out how to get enough land to do me any good when the damned government wanted to parcel it out to every lazy sodbuster and soldier who come along. Men who don't know anything but to hold out their hand.

"By God I'll not see it torn down by these three-up outfits who'll steal the water even though they haven't got enough head to hold a decent barbecue, or a bunch of nesters who'll plow up the grass and butcher my cows to feed their snot-nosed kids."

The colonel let his gaze wander around the room,

taking in the half-dozen fighting men he'd gathered there. "I want the water choked off first, and you can start with the Rocking R and the Double H. They're watering on the Porcupine where it makes that great big loop onto their land 'fore it comes back on mine. Come a dry spell they'll use it up. I want it stopped."

His close-set eyes came to rest on Fallon. "You got anything against going after a woman?"

"Woman . . . man. Makes no difference to me," Mitch said. The lie squeezed at his gut.

"You keep an eye on that Houston girlie. She's no ordinary woman, and she can shoot too. I don't aim to see any of my hands gunned down, and especially not by any female, you got that? If you don't think you can handle that, say so now. I got men who won't think twice, but I'm spread thin here. They're closing in on me from all sides, and on top of that, the savages are pilfering horses and cattle every chance they get. I gotta put guards on my herds, for God's sake.

"Hell, it ain't bad enough the government throws all kinds of barriers in the way, they don't even have the gumption to take care of this Indian problem out here, once and for all. What they need to do is bring in enough soldiers to wipe out the bloody savages, make room for us white men."

Mitch turned from the fiery stare in the colonel's little pig eyes. He ought to just ride out. What was he doing here working for this filth, anyway? It was probably the most low-down job a man could have. Still, it didn't much matter what he did anymore, did it? Dying one way was as good as dying another.

The colonel continued to watch him while rolling his cigar around between his lips until he had the end wetted. "I can't spare anyone from ranch chores for a few days. All these other ranchers hiring leaves me shorthanded. I've sent for some more men, but in the meantime I want you to get to know the enemy, Fallon, nose around."

Radine Granville was a professional, and she plied the oldest profession very well. She didn't mind tending bar once in a while, and would do so with good nature because she liked Lance Brannigan O'Shea, owner of the Powder Keg. But they had a deal. If a man came in wanting a poke, she left the bar and did her pleasuring.

She was proud to say that no man had led her down the path to sinning, nor had poverty been to blame. She just plain liked sex and she liked to please men. She couldn't imagine anything better than getting paid for something she enjoyed doing so much.

This particular night had turned out to be quiet. The few drifters who dropped in didn't want much of anything but a mug of beer and to be left alone. Most of the good men were working on the surrounding ranches, coming in so beat at the end of a long day that all they could manage was to fall into their bunks. Come Saturday night they'd all come to town to howl and things would be different. So Radine mopped at the bar top and refilled an occasional mug while Lance did some whiskey inventory and got his next order ready in the back room.

She glanced up at the sound of the batwing doors swishing open. The gunslinger who worked for Colonel Dunkirk came in, like some kind of sleek cat on the prowl. Radine eyed him warily. She liked most men, dirty or clean, as long as they treated her right. Meanness she couldn't stand, wouldn't put up with, and Lance always backed her up on that.

This one wore a gun on his right hip, but that didn't scare her nearly as much as his eyes. Though he'd been in more than once, she still hadn't taken his full measure. He was one hell of a man, that she could tell in a glance.

He ambled to the bar, checking out the few patrons with more than casual curiosity. When he finally stood before her, Radine swept her gaze slowly and deliberately from the top of the bar right on up to the brim of the black Stetson. She'd never met a man yet who could keep his true intent from showing in his eyes, and despite her earlier assessment, wished his weren't now in shadow. Then he shifted just a bit and the glow from the wall lamps illuminated the emerald-green depths of those eyes. For a brief instant she caught a glimpse of a deep melancholy reflected there, and she yearned to reach out and soothe him. Before she could he shut down the vision just as if he'd realized she'd seen into his soul and closed a door.

Nonplussed, she continued her inspection of the rugged features, stopping at the scar. A slash through his left eyebrow looked like a jag of wicked lightning that had spawned a great white streak in his black hair.

She shivered and turned away. "What'll you have?" she asked, and was surprised that her voice trembled.

"A beer ... first." His tone showed he wasn't well pleased with her once-over.

She drew a draft, set it before him, and stared at the foam that dribbled down one side of the glass. "And second?" she asked, amazed that for the first time in her career a man had caused her to go nearly speechless.

He shot her a piercing look so cold that she dropped a glass she had absentmindedly begun to polish. It hit the floor with a sharp explosion, but she didn't flinch, even when a few splinters nicked at her ankle like insect bites. This man she couldn't read and that worried her. Desire and fear stirred together in the pit of her stomach. At first she thought there wouldn't be enough money in the world to put her in a room alone with him, yet in the next moment she wanted to give herself to him for nothing.

He finished the beer without telling her what he wanted second, never once glancing at the bare swell of her creamy breasts. Nor did he seem to notice she'd broken a glass to smithereens.

"And second," she prodded, afraid of his reply. If he wanted her, would she take him upstairs?

Mitch found he had been staring with fierce concentration in the mirror above the whore's head, and it was making her mighty nervous. He shrugged. "I've changed my mind."

Vaguely disappointed that his second wish wasn't for her, Radine considered coming back with a snappy remark, but held her tongue. It wouldn't be wise to rankle this one, and she had decided she didn't want to be in a room alone with him anyway.

Fallon thought she wasn't bad-looking, kind of like a plump, ripe strawberry, with red hair and flushed skin dusted with freckles, her cheeks brightly painted as were her lips. She'd be mighty sweet in bed, he figured, even though she was a bit older than most doves he'd run across. He even considered smothering his growing fire with this little redheaded whore, but changed his mind in the instant it took him to remember what had fanned that fire in the first place. Charlie Houston would not be easily forgotten by going to bed with a whore. Besides his feelings went deeper than that, and once again he wondered why. There would never be a meeting ground for the two of them, even if he did decide to pursue her. Besides, she was just a tough cowpoke who happened to be female. Probably had no use for men, and certainly not for the likes of him.

After he left Radine realized that she hadn't asked his name. He would make an interesting but dangerous lover. She even felt sorry for the man, for she'd seen his like before and he would probably come to no good.

Provoked by her own frustration, Radine ran off the remaining three customers and pulled the heavy wooden shutters over the swinging doors of the saloon. She stood there with her back up against the rough wood for several minutes, waiting for the storm of emotions to quiet so she could get to sleep without being bothered by itches she couldn't scratch.

Chapter Four

The morning after the barn burned Charlie set two of the men to rebuilding it and rode out for Miles City to talk to the sheriff. For a good long while she could hear the distant rhythmic chuck of axes from the wooded slope. Yancey had promised to keep a guard on the place to prevent a recurrence of what had happened the night before. Maybe what she really needed was a gunhand like Mitchell Fallon. Her men were cowboys used to punching cattle, and while they might pick off a rattler or a coyote with a rifle, none were used to shooting men.

During the three-hour ride she had plenty of time to think. It disturbed her that the dark brooding visage of Mitchell Fallon continued to disrupt her plans for protecting the ranch and hiring a cook. Why he should haunt her was a mystery. She hadn't thought seriously of men since her crush on Yancey Barton when he thought her merely a child. And she certainly had no business considering for one moment even a passing interest in a hired gunslinger. Especially not one who worked for the other side in this battle for range land. If she were serious about anyone, it should be Cal Malone. He treated her like a friend, but had made it clear more than once that they might team up. Charlie sensed, though, that he was more interested in combining the two ranches than in a romantic pairing. He couldn't quite get over the loss of his wife Becky. Such a joining would be practical since the two shared a north to south boundary line and butted up against the southwest corner of the colonel's Circle D.

The rumble of approaching hoofbeats brought Charlie out of her reverie, and she reined in quickly. Three Indian braves rode up on her from a wooded gully. She recognized Gray Horse and his son Spotted Moon, both Northern Cheyenne, but the third brave was a stranger to her.

Last fall, she and her herd had no sooner arrived on the Double H than Gray Horse had shown up. Even before they had started work on the bunkhouse, the first of two structures they'd built before winter set in, the Indian had been there, explaining in his elusive way that the two peoples shared this land. She had promptly presented him with a longhorn steer for his tribe to butcher, and Gray Horse had reciprocated by giving her a fine tanned deerskin. Even so, friendship between the white man and Indian on the Montana plains was a touchy situation.

Charlie considered the present danger, and in spite of a thundering heart greeted the three ominous braves.

Spotted Moon leaped gracefully from his small paint, while Gray Horse and the other brave remained mounted.

"Split Skirt," Spotted Moon said. "I am pleased that winter did not chill your heart."

Charlie remained in the saddle. Spotted Moon was a huge Indian, and she felt more secure looking down on him. She smiled at the name the Cheyenne had given her. "And you wintered well too, I see."

He gazed off into the distance beyond her shoulder. "Old Fox passed into the land of the gods."

She suppressed a shudder. Old Fox was the medi-

cine man, so dried and feeble he had seemed to be at
least two hundred years old, though of course she
knew he wasn't. Last fall, a week or so after she presented Gray Horse with the steer, he and Spotted
Moon had carried the old man to her cabin on a tra-
vois. He proceeded to conduct some kind of a ritual
over her and her home. Gray Horse and Spotted
Moon had not explained the ceremony, but they
beamed as if Old Fox was doing her an extreme
honor. She behaved as if she understood the ceremony
and smiled a lot, feeling rather foolish.

Later she had repaid the visit, riding up on the small
family band of Northern Cheyenne in their encampment near the Elk River. She and Spotted Moon's
wife, who spoke no English, had discovered a kinship
that Charlie couldn't explain. She held the woman's
child in her arms, cupped a hand over the downy hair,
and closed her eyes in odd contentment when the
baby nuzzled her breast. The enormous swell of emotion that charged through her at that moment had
remained with Charlie during the long winter. She
often thought of the band out there in their tepees in
the freezing cold. The tiny beautiful child sewn in
thick skins to keep away the ravages of the brutal
north wind.

Remembering that incident, she gazed down at
Spotted Moon from the back of her horse. "And your
wife and child, how are they?"

"Our women and children are hungry," Spotted
Moon said, pride tinged with an undertone of resent-
ment. "The buffalo are few and the iron rails will soon
run them all from our land. If we do not fight soon
we will have nothing left. We would not wish to fight
Split Skirt. Old Fox paid you much honor, and your
cattle have multiplied grazing our land."

Charlie suppressed a smile of admiration. There
were still plenty of buffalo on the vast plains, but

Spotted Moon certainly understood diplomacy. "You would honor me if you rode to my ranch and told my foreman that you are to have two steers."

Before Spotted Moon could react, Gray Horse spat something quickly and gestured with the feathered lance he carried. Everyone looked at once including Charlie. Atop a rise with the vast Montana sky at his back sat a lone rider on an enormous black horse. He appeared to pay no attention to their sudden interest in him, but the third brave sent out a spine-tingling cry that made Charlie's skin crawl.

Spotted Moon gestured, obviously anxious to ride away.

Gray Horse spoke again.

"My father says we must come to the ranch when you will be there. He says we want three beeves, and that we could take the cattle we wish at any time, but we will not." The brave glanced once more toward the rise where the rider had been, and so did she. The man was gone, leaving behind a fine trail of dust that rose from beyond an outcropping of red boulders.

Before she could turn back and reply, the three Indians rode away, the stranger letting loose with another of his shrill cries. She was a little more than uneasy at the encounter, for it hadn't escaped her notice that all three of the braves were painted as if for battle.

That wasn't all that worried Charlie as she headed once again for Miles City. What was Mitch Fallon doing spying on her and what was he up to? She certainly had plenty to speak to the sheriff about when she got to town.

Sheriff Clarence Newton, referred to behind his back as Sheriff Newt, frowned at her when she clattered into his office and slammed the door. She'd worked up a full head of steam just thinking about Dunkirk and his crooked ways.

"Purty day, ain't it?" the laconic sheriff said without rising.

"If it weren't for the smoke coming off that heap of rubble that used to be my barn, it might be."

The sheriff raised gray eyebrows, the only hair for quite a stretch up his forehead. "Someone kick over a lantern?"

Charlie gritted her teeth and slipped off her leather gloves, folding them over one hand to have something to do until her voice would work right. When it did her reply ricocheted around the small office.

"You know damn well they didn't. Some no-account poured coal oil all over the place and lit it afire."

"How do you know that?" he asked, and squinted up at her.

"I could smell it, and I saw him ride out."

"Last night? Who was it?" Sheriff Newt finally showed some concern, but no doubt for the wrong reasons.

She couldn't really blame him too much for his lethargy. Colonel Dunkirk pretty well ran the district and he intended to see things went his way. If Newton didn't cooperate, well, he'd just be run out of town or shot some dark night. Newton knew full well that the colonel wanted her and all the small ranchers gone, and would do just about anything to accomplish that goal.

"I suppose I could wire the territorial marshal, let him come on down and investigate," she said in a tight voice.

"No need in that, little lady. I'll look right into it. Said you saw him? Who was this feller?"

"It was dark. He wasn't real big and he rode a gray, maybe an Appaloosa. I took some shots at him. Could be I hit him."

"Not unless he decided to bleed somewhere besides at the doc's you didn't. No one come in shot up that

I know of." Newton rose and took a new Kalispel Stetson off the hat rack. "Not much to go on, but I'll check around. Anything else?"

Charlie slapped the gloves smartly in the palm of her hand. She was as tall as the graying sheriff and took advantage of that fact by glowering right into his eyes. "He comes back, I won't miss. You might pass that around while you're checking," she snapped, and jerked the door open to stalk from his office.

Out on the boardwalk she swiveled on one boot heel and jigged down two steps where she bumped smack into the broad chest of Mitchell Fallon as he emerged from the alley. He grunted and automatically caught at her, his large hands closing around her upper arms.

His remarkable eyes flared for just an instant, then he said in that mocking voice, "Pardon me, ma'am."

"You shut up," she said loudly, and shoved out of his grasp. "Stop following me around and stay off my place too, or I just might shoot you as well."

Mitch batted his eyes and watched Charlie stride off down the street toward the saloon. He waited until the doors stopped their wild swinging at her back before moving.

"Woman must drink panther piss for breakfast," he remarked aloud to himself. At the hitching post he unwound the reins of his waiting horse and as he rode past the saloon, tipped his hat solemnly. Whoever she was looking to light into next deserved sympathy as well. He couldn't blame the lady considering the tight hole she'd dug for herself. She was apt to be a lot more put out before Dunkirk was through with her. He wished he could just go tell her to go back home where she belonged and be done with it. Probably wouldn't do much good, though. She appeared just ornery enough to put up a good fight, and that was too bad. It would no doubt get her killed.

Charlie's heart thudded at her temples for a full five minutes after she sat down alone at a table inside the half-empty saloon. Her arms throbbed where he had held them and she couldn't get those frosty eyes out of her mind. She glanced around the murky room. It was too early in the day for much more than ne'er-do-wells and the usual three or four poker players in the dark little place. Still, she could leave word here that she was on the lookout for a good cook. She grinned wryly. Perhaps she'd modify that and just say she was looking for any kind of cook. Forget the good part.

Radine came strolling in from the back room, eyes still swollen with sleep, and Charlie hailed her. She liked Radine because she was honest and didn't care a whit what anyone thought. Though there were other doves in Miles City, she was extremely popular. Charlie could only guess why. The woman was a bit too plump and some older than the other girls, yet the men sought her out. Charlie had often overheard them talking about "good old Radine," and how she could fix up a sore body.

Radine fingered at her mussed red hair and laughed merrily as she sat down with Charlie.

"Early day, isn't it?" Her big eyes, bright as dew-touched sloe berries, studied Charlie's somber expression.

"Looking for a cook," Charlie told her. "Thought maybe Lance would pass the word, and you too."

Radine nodded. "Wouldn't hurt if you stuck up a notice over by the bar too." She fingered the ribbon at her throat, glanced up at Charlie. "You see that new guy the colonel hired?"

"He wouldn't make a good cook."

"Well, I wouldn't mind him doing some cooking with me, hon." Radine giggled like a girl, a habit

Charlie found most disconcerting in this woman more than a dozen years her senior.

"Well, Fallon scares me, and he ought to you too," Charlie told Radine, remembering the man's cold regard. "Men like that don't care who they hurt."

"Fallon? Is that his name?" Radine rubbed up and down her arms with both hands as if suddenly chilled. "Maybe you're right. I've pleasured more than a few who thought nothing of belting me around afterward. What happened to your cook?"

"Went back to Texas, and if I had any sense that's what I'd do too."

"Aw, you don't want to leave this wonderful place." Radine gestured around the primitive saloon, the whiskey barrels holding up raw board planks that served as a bar, the crude tables and chairs, the boarded-up window holes that would soon be uncovered for the short, hot summer.

The two women laughed.

"You'll tell Lance then?" Charlie said and stood to leave.

"About needing a cook, yeah." Radine traced through a crack on the table with a chipped nail. "Charlie ... if I ... would you ... I mean, could I come to call sometime?"

The question stopped Charlie in her tracks and she turned to regard the sincere, round-cheeked face, untouched by paint this early in the day. Radine was just about the only woman in town willing to be seen talking to her without glancing around nervously to see who was watching. She was surprised to see the eagerness in the woman's expression.

"Why, I think I'd like that a lot. Please do come out sometime. And the next time I'm in town, maybe we could meet somewhere ... well, maybe somewhere for lunch, or something."

Radine beamed. "That would be wonderful."

Charlie took her leave, repeating her invitation once again. She didn't want Radine to think she wasn't sincere.

After leaving the Powder Keg she posted a cook-wanted notice at every business in town, and spoke to several townspeople about her need, but came away empty-handed. What hands had been laid off after spring roundup had either ridden on or couldn't cook. She was surprised to learn that Dunkirk had hired a lot of those let go by the smaller ranchers. He must be building an army out there at the Circle D.

At the mercantile she studied several samples of barbed wire thoughtfully, stopped a moment to touch a finger to the two-strand Gliddens. How wicked it looked.

"Montana lands are no place for that devil's creation," a voice at her back said. "Man rides into it on a horse it rips his guts out. Him nor his beast can get untangled. He'll die thrashing around there on the ground."

She shuddered at Colonel Dunkirk's implication, catching an underlying threat that had nothing to do with his sorry remark about barbed wire. Before she could bring herself to reply, he'd changed his tone.

"I'd say we all did right well at roundup, wouldn't you, little lady?"

"Don't call me little lady and I won't call you little man," she said back at him.

Dunkirk chortled and patted his amble girth. "Well, now, *ma'am,* I don't hardly think it would be fitting to call me little man, not by any stretch of the imagination." He dropped his glance so that it stopped deliberately at the level of her breasts. Though bound under the loose flannel shirt, her nipples hardened in defense of his visual insinuation.

"You are no gentlemen, sir," she said.

"And neither are you, my dear," Dunkirk replied.

"And you would do well to stop acting like one before I forget that."

The threat was there, unspoken and terrifying. He would give her no quarter despite her being a member of the gentler sex.

"One of your men rides onto my land again, no matter his intent, and I will shoot him."

"Ah, my dear, you do that and I will see you hanged."

"You'll play the devil, sir." She whirled and walked away, a mixture of fear and raw fury churning within her until her throat burned with it.

She headed back to the Double H without having solved any of her problems, the most urgent of which at the moment was someone to cook for the hands. All she had really succeeded in doing was to further alienate everyone she came in contact with.

Soon after she turned her horse into the corral at the ranch Yancey Barton rode in with news that two of the hands had lit out, saying they wouldn't work hard all day and then have only soggy biscuits for supper, not even for Matt Houston's daughter.

"Besides," he confided, "I think they went to work for Dunkirk. He's been nosing around trying to hire up all the men who work for the small spreads. Figures that's as good a way as any to drive us out."

"I heard that in town. And you, Yancey, what about you?" she asked.

"Me? I'd as soon shoot the son of a bitch as talk to him, but I know better."

"No, I mean, how much longer will it be before you ride out too? Forget Dunkirk."

"Miss Charlie, your daddy hired me on when I was green as a pile of fresh manure, and he put me to handling the worst chores around the ranch. Cutting wood for the kitchen, swamping out the barns, milking the dad-blamed cows, and I never quit on him. Not once did I even think of it, and me just a kid who didn't even have good sense. So what makes you think a little thing like exploding biscuits and burning barns is going to drive me off?"

The man's crinkly blue eyes twinkled as he fiddled with the latigo on his saddle, unbuckling the strap with hands as tough as the leather he stroked.

Despite the lump in her throat she grinned at this sturdy cowboy who had held her in his arms while Matt Houston was put under the ground, and patted her back and told her, "Go ahead and cry, little sweetheart." He'd been around the ranch as long as she could remember and when she was fifteen and he twenty-five she'd fallen in love with him. That had matured now into the love she knew she would have felt for an older brother or perhaps a beloved uncle.

She pulled herself from the reverie, said thoughtfully, "I ran across Spotted Moon and Gray Horse wanting some more steers, and that gunslinger was dogging my tracks plain as can be. Then to make matters worse I met up with Dunkirk in town and he all but threatened me if I don't sell out to him. As if that weren't enough, the sheriff just plain said he doesn't intend to do anything about the barn burning.

"It's been a hell of a day. Makes me wish I ... oh, dammit, Yancey, how can I give up Matt's dream?"

He studied her for a long moment, moving his hat round and round in work-roughened fingers. Then he said, "Don't you have any dreams of our own, sweetheart? Maybe it's time you thought of yourself. Matt Houston always did just what he wanted to do, don't you think he'd want his daughter to do the same?"

Grimly she bit her lips together. "I am doing what I want to do. I love this ranch, every bit as much as he did, and I won't let some sidewinding son of a —"

"Whoa, Miss Charlie," Yancey said. "No need in taking a cussin' fit. I didn't intend to rile you. Let me speak to the men, we'll rustle up some grub like we would were we on the trail by our ownselves for a few days till you can get someone out to do the cooking. One thing at a time is what I always say. Maybe we can keep 'em from riding if they know you're trying."

He stopped twisting the hat and looked right at her. "Them Cheyenne show up, you want me to cut out a couple of head?"

"Yes, I do. I can't see letting their women and kids starve, though I don't expect it'll be much longer before they're driven right out of this country. I don't know what they'll do, Yancey, I surely don't, but I can't help them any more than that. I'm afraid no one can. It's like they're destined to disappear from the face of the earth to make way for the white man. Doesn't seem fair when you think about it, does it?"

"They're just red savages, Miss Charlie, don't fret about them so. They'll make out. Hell, they been killing each other for hundreds of years. What you gotta do is keep peace with them, like the rest of the ranchers. And you're right, soon enough they'll all be gone. This land is too precious to be left to a bunch of wild Indians who don't know what it's truly good for."

Tears filled her eyes, thinking of the women and children in the Cheyenne camp. The babe she'd held in her arms would be walking soon, and chattering and laughing. What had he ever done to deserve such a fate, or any of them, for that matter? But Yancey was right, there was only so much she could do.

"See they get four steers. And see if there's a cow that's fresh without a calf. I'm sure those babies could use some milk. If we can't spare that many, then we'll soon go under anyway."

He palmed his hat down on his head and nodded. "One thing's for certain, Miss Charlie, you're for sure your daddy's daughter, and I can't fault you for that."

The next morning at dawn Charlie saddled up and rode out to the southwestern section of the ranch. After roundup and branding were finished they had turned a large portion of the herd into the rich grassland there. It was fed by a meandering loop of Porcupine Creek that left the Circle D to water both her land and Cal's for several miles before flowing back onto the colonel's spread. She wanted to see for herself how the spring calves were faring.

And that's where she rode right up on Fallon. She thought later that it was almost as if their meeting were meant, and there wasn't anything either of them could do about it. The country was so big, the trails so remote from one another it shouldn't have happened, but it did.

As she rode she sang one of her mother's favorite songs, the only Spanish she remembered. The air warmed and the sky shone the color of Texas bluebonnets. The little mare rounded an outcropping and there he was, riding right at her looking as if he were searching for something.

His appearance cut off her song in midstream, and she sputtered out a challenge. "What are you doing out here?"

Belle danced under her and the stallion he rode let out a coarse greeting as they stopped beside each other.

Mitch didn't want to admit that he was looking for the source of the beautiful music because it made him think of the lilt of his wife's lovely voice, the fragrance of her long black hair, the pulse in her throat at his lips. And dear God, the baby softness of their precious child's tiny body.

His reply was harsh and foolish. "Some law against it?"

A smart retort formed on her tongue, but their wandering glances caught and held and she said nothing.

He tried to make up for his earlier stupidity. "That was some pretty song you were singing. A man appreciates hearing such a thing out here in the wilderness. Lets him know there's still gentleness in the world."

Before she could reply to the totally unexpected comment, he touched the stallion's flanks and rode off.

Charlie turned to watch him disappear over the rise. He rode like he moved, with an agile grace. A man born to the saddle. The saddle and the gun.

She scolded herself for what she was thinking, for she was struck by a sudden image, herself at his side, the two of them walking hand in hand through the tall grass, happy faces kissed by the wind.

"What an utter idiot you are," she said aloud, and kicked Belle into a gallop.

Chapter Five

In the middle of the night Charlie shouted herself awake to a room awash in moonlight. Perspiration slicked her body, not from the temperature, for it was cool once the sun went down, but because of a fierce battle with some particularly wicked demons. Yet when she thought about it she couldn't remember the nightmare that had frightened her so badly. She could only imagine she heard the fading thunder of stampeding cattle. Her gown clung to her in wet patches.

The frightening dreams had begun soon after her father's death, the first of them simply a black seething cloud of fury that appeared beside her bed. A threat so real she gasped for air. For a long while she thought she had actually experienced a brush with someone or something from the other side. No doubt it was her father's anger at having been snatched from a life not yet fully lived. But why threaten her, his only beloved daughter? Of course none of it was real, and in the bright light of day she admitted that.

On many occasions since then she had screamed herself awake, and afterward wasn't sure if she'd made a sound or just dreamed that she had. Wasn't even sure she had experienced the dream.

It was always hard to get back to sleep, and so this

night she rose on shaky legs, peeled the damp gown off over her head, and padded to the window to stand bathed in the cool light of night from a half-moon. Off to her right the bunkhouse humped blackly against the glowing sky, on her left the skeletal framework of the barn threw grotesque shadows, and a line of aspen beyond created long dark fingers across the yard.

Idly she traced a hand along the line of her jaw and down her breastbone, then caressed the swell of one breast. She closed her eyes and swayed, feeling giddy and removed from reality, as if still in the dream.

What was wrong with her? She hadn't been so conscious of her own body since the onset of puberty, but now her flesh responded to every touch and even the remotest of thoughts. Leftover fear that followed her up out of the nightmare only served to heighten that sensual awareness.

Fallon's mere presence had lit a fire, would she never extinguish it? She moved her fingers, gasped at the rigidity of her nipples, and cupped both breasts to still their aching. She wanted his hand there, his mouth, the warm satin of his tongue.

The memory of his moss-green eyes probing hers jagged through her mind like a streak of lightning cuts a storm-laden sky.

The room filled with a choking deadly panic that threatened to smother her. She whirled, hands at her throat, and gasped. Just like the dream, only this time she was awake. She had to get out, now, escape the confines of the room and breathe fresh air. She pulled on the damp gown and raced from the house as if pursued.

At the corral Belle whickered a greeting and came toward her. She scaled the fence, caught a double fistful of the roan's mane, and settled on her back, shoulders hunched against whatever invisible terror chased her.

Hair and gown flying, she urged the horse into a run, leaning forward over his neck and hanging on with both knees. She had no idea where she was going or why, only that she had to be out in the open, had to escape the unknown dread.

Propped against a tree, his horse tethered nearby, Mitch stirred when he heard the thud of galloping hooves. He was probably less than a half mile from the Double H Ranch buildings, and had noticed no one standing night guard. Evidently when nothing more had happened after the fire, the foolish woman had begun to feel safe again. She needed someone who knew all the rules of survival to help her out or she wouldn't make it.

Ah, well, it was probably for the best if she didn't.

A thunder of hooves told him someone was coming, and coming fast. He scarcely had time to scrabble back into the shelter of the brush before the horse and rider pounded into sight.

He gaped in disbelief when the white-clad specter approached, riding like the wind. A white gown flowed along behind shapely bare legs that clamped the animal's heaving sides. The apparition rode straight at him so that he thought horse and rider might actually trample him until both turned at the last possible moment. Mitch swore he felt the breath from the roan's flared nostrils. Off to his left Jeb screamed and pawed air, but the ghost appeared oblivious.

The rider reined in at the top of the rise, silhouetted against the night sky. After a few moments the ethereal figure slid from the horse and stood illuminated by silvery moonlight. The horse dropped its nose into the grass and began to graze, as if this was nothing usual at all. For a long while the figure in white remained transfixed, unmoving.

He knew then who it was. What in the hell was the woman up to now? Mitch led Jeb out of the dense underbrush to watch. If he remained in the shadows she couldn't see him. Then his ears pricked. Someone was coming! Several someones.

She heard it too, for she turned just as a band of riders emerged above the rise and off to the right. She scrambled for the horse but made a bad go at mounting bareback. Then the riders were beside her and she could do nothing but face them.

Mitch eased into the saddle and rubbed his fingertips over Jeb's ear to soothe him.

Charlie didn't recognize the young Indians, but thought they weren't the Northern Cheyenne she was used to seeing. Sioux perhaps, renegades who refused to remain on the reservation in the Badlands. And who could blame them? Yancey insisted that one day she would regret her compassion for the savages. Perhaps now, caught out alone and defenseless like this, she should be more frightened, but she only felt foolish. What must they think of this white woman running around in the dark in her nightclothes?

The leader, a boy who looked no more than fourteen or so, slid from his pony. The others shouted and laughed, obviously egging him on to do whatever he might have in mind.

She tried to keep Belle between her and the boy, but he swatted the mare on the backside so that she moved away, and the Indian stood much too close to Charlie. She could smell his excitement, an overpowering animalistic odor, and it awoke in her at last a fear that dried her mouth and made her heart drum. What a reckless thing she'd done, coming out here alone and unarmed in the middle of the night.

She curled her fingers into fists and raised her chin to regard the young man.

He met her gaze with flashing dark eyes that said he was having a lot more fun than she was.

With a quick movement he grabbed a handful of

her hair. The other boys laughed, shouted. Charlie remained very still, forcing herself not to show her fear.

With the other hand he clawed at the front of her gown and tried to rip it open. The tough fabric held and all he succeeded in doing was forcing her to her knees. The tufts of stiff grass and rock-strewn ground bit into her flesh, but she tightened her lips to keep from crying out.

Some more laughter.

Still she refused to put sound to her fear, though she was so frightened her head swam and her stomach churned.

The boy pulled her face toward his crotch and she punched at him, landing ineffectual blows on his iron-hard thighs and belly.

Slowly and stealthily Mitch rode right up on the braves without them sensing his presence. They were so immersed in their fun that not one of the half-dozen boys knew he was there.

He slid out his Colt and thumbed back the hammer with a deadly snick, and then they knew.

"That's enough, boys. Leave the lady alone."

Deliberately he took aim a few yards behind the one roughhousing the woman and pulled the trigger. The .44 shell exploded from the barrel of the Colt with a tremendous roar. The young Indians might not understand English, but they understood that sound.

He could tell right away they wanted to fight despite the gun, so he transferred it to his left fist and snaked the Winchester out, cocking it with one hand in a fluid singular motion. He pointed it directly at the boy on the ground.

"You first," he said and shot the boy in the arm.

The action effectively took all the bluff out of the braves, turned them into the young boys they were.

The one on the ground clutched his wound and rolled around, the others eyed Mitch in fear, eyes showing white.

Charlie scrabbled to her feet, shouting, "Don't kill them. Please don't kill them."

"Stay right where you are," Mitch ordered. "I ain't killing anybody. You all, git. Now. Take him with you." With the revolver he pointed at the boy hugging his bloody arm and glowering at him.

The young Indians seemed happy enough to do so, all the bluster gone out of them.

She watched them ride away, a mixture of terror and fury boiling up in her. Then she swung to confront the man who had rescued her. "They were only boys, you didn't have to shoot him."

"Had to make my point. They could've took us both. While I'm not used to manners it does seem a lady like you might have some. A simple thank you would do."

She spluttered, but knew he was right. She was really angry at herself for being so stupid as to ride into such a dangerous situation.

"You wander around a lot in the middle of the night in your nightclothes?" He reholstered the Colt and slipped the Winchester back into its scabbard.

The stallion danced sideways when Charlie darted for her own mount. "None of your business what I do."

"Is if I have to put my life on the line."

"Nobody asked you to." Not used to riding bareback, her efforts to mount the long-legged horse without a stirrup were meeting with very little success.

"Where the hell did you come from anyway?" He dismounted agilely to give her a hand, had spanned her waist with two strong hands before she could object.

The only thing between his touch and her flesh was

the thin nightgown, but he left his hands there because to do otherwise would have been impossible. The warmth, the pulsing life against his palms, held him fast.

Charlie took in two careful deep breaths and remembered what had sent her flying across the plains in the first place. Nightmares, longings, loneliness. And now this man's hands erupted within her a deep desire almost forgotten, and she didn't want to pull away. No matter what her good sense told her.

Instead she turned slightly and let him hold her close. The hammering of his heart vibrated, challenged the thrumming of her own.

She was naked. Unclothed beneath the thin fabric and she could feel the roughness of his jeans, the cut of his belt, every button of his shirt pressing against her hot flesh.

He put a finger under her chin and raised her face, his mouth so close it was a blur. His warm breath whispered over her cheeks, her lips . . . his hands trailed upward until he spanned the swell of her breasts with his thumbs and fingers.

Raw passion fed by the moonlight and her near brush with violence made her weak and she sagged with his embrace.

Mitch considered taking her, so explosive was his desire. He would lower her to the ground, pull the gown away from her lovely body, and quench his dreadful thirst for her, out here on the prairie in the quiet of night with only the moon as a witness. Her hair smelled like crisp summer apples, and her skin felt slightly moist as if she were touched by early morning dew. He bent forward, lips and tongue at her throat, and tasted tentatively of her sweetness.

She moaned, stiffened, cried out. "What are you doing? Stop, this instant."

Pushing away from his iron-hard grip, Charlie staggered against the mare's side. Where his mouth had been burned like a branding iron had seared the flesh and she rubbed at it. Cool night air filled her lungs with each gasp, until her brain cleared. What in God's name had she been thinking?

Bad enough she had ridden out alone at night so close to the Indian encampments, but to let this dangerous man get anywhere near her compounded the idiocy. She could think of nothing to say to him as she continued to rub at the spot where his tongue had lapped. So without a word she turned and vaulted onto the little horse. The sound of her breathing was harsh in the quiet night. As she rode away, she and Belle cast a grotesque dancing shadow in the moonlight.

He remained where he was until she rode out of sight, then mounted quickly and kicked at Jeb's ribs, trying to ride fast enough and far enough to escape the haunting memories of the life he had lost so horribly and completely. He had to put this woman behind him as well, for he had used up all his chances at happiness. The rest of his life would be payment in kind for his vicious past, and he intended to make a good job of it.

By the time Charlie slid off the roan's back in her own corral, she was trembling violently. It had taken every ounce of her strength to ride away from the gunslinger. What had happened between them had managed to dull the danger she had been in with the Indian boys. Now she thought of that and wondered what the greater threat had been. She had certainly almost given herself to that man in black ... had he in turn almost taken her? She thought so and that frightened her.

Frustrated with the conflicting thoughts, she decided that what she needed was more work to keep her mind occupied, to tire her body until it could do nothing but pass out at the end of the day. Then perhaps the bad dreams would go away, and with them her emotional tangle of feelings toward the man in black, the man who was her enemy.

For nearly a week she worked until she was exhausted, then fell into bed at the end of each day so tired she scarcely took two breaths before she was asleep. The dreams did indeed vanish, and she knew nothing until the sun awoke her each morning.

The danger from Dunkirk's men remained a continued threat as cows were found with their throats slit and strangers were seen continuously patrolling the periphery of the grazing land. Waiting for their chance to do more damage, perhaps even kill someone. They feared it would come to that sooner or later.

Early one morning while riding range Charlie noticed that the creek wasn't flowing like it should. Someone was messing with the water. That damn Dunkirk again!

Most of the men were in the south pasture, so she was headed in that direction when she rode up on Spotted Moon and three young braves taking charge of four longhorns.

"Morning, Miss Charlie," P.J. said. "I fetched up these steers for the injuns, like you said. But this fella here, he don't want no milk cow less'n he gets the calf too."

She grinned. Sly as a fox.

Spotted Moon eyed her closely, the corners of his lips threatening to turn up in an answering grin.

"We are grateful to Split Skirt for the beeves," Spotted Moon said gravely. "She is most generous."

She nodded. Spotted Moon had served as a tracker and guide for the U.S. Army back when there was all the trouble at the three forts along the Bozeman Trail. That had been one time when the Indian had come out the winner, forcing the army to move out of the area and abandon Forts Kearney, Smith, and Reno. A victorious Red Cloud had immediately burned Fort Kearney to the ground.

Spotted Moon had learned well from his white superiors, and was now turning that knowledge back upon the white man who had cheated his people.

She didn't blame him. "Agreed, she is being most generous."

"I too," Spotted Moon said, and nodded toward the boys. "They are becoming men. If they have to they will die to prove their bravery."

A chill washed up her spine, but she stood firm, making a similar gesture toward several of her hands looking on. "They too are brave men. It would be a shame for anyone to die because of one calf."

Spotted Moon looked right through her, his dark eyes reflecting sadness. "Many have already died because of the white man's greed. More will die because there will soon be no land and no buffalo. It matters little if we begin the fight here at your door, Split Skirt." He paused, letting that sink in, then finished, "All because of one calf."

In a flash she saw the meaning of the situation, and it had nothing to do with the cow and calf. It had to do more with pride, with dignity, with the last painful gasp of a people.

"Give them what they want," she said, inclining her head slightly toward Spotted Moon so that he could say he had won the battle in a proper way.

She dropped the reins and let Belle graze while the Indians and her hand P.J. corralled four steers, a milk cow and calf. The young braves cast quick looks at Charlie and she was sure one or two of them had been in the group that had accosted her the previous week. She pretended not to pay any attention as the entourage rode off, but fear warred with compassion within her. As she beheld the huge and beautiful country that surrounded her small kingdom, she was filled with the knowledge that she was taking part in something that would forever be written in the history of this country. The death of one mighty nation and the struggle toward the birth of another. And all she could think to do was cry like some weak woman.

If Spotted Moon was her enemy, then so be it, but she admired him in a way she could never admire Colonel Dunkirk, whose acts had proven him to be the more dangerous of the two. With the Indian, at least there would be honor, hers and his, even if she didn't always understand it.

She wondered why the Indian hadn't mentioned the confrontation Fallon had had with the young braves earlier. He had, after all, shot one of the boys. Spotted Moon was very sly, and would use his knowledge wisely. She could never second-guess him, and so dismissed her uneasiness.

It took several minutes for her to get her mind back on the issue at hand. The lack of water in the creek. She spotted Yancey and went to tell him the bad news.

Legs hanging, Mitch sat on the edge of a drop-off and watched water back up into a basin above the hastily constructed dam. The colonel's men had finished it just before dark the night before.

The thing wouldn't hold long. It couldn't. When all that water backed up behind it, something would give. Or maybe there'd be a gully washer up in the mountains and the sudden runoff would come racing down into the valley and just eat that dam away. It was purely a nuisance thing, but while it held Malone and Houston would have some mighty thirsty cattle on their hands. That would force them to think over their situation. Given time and equipment, the colonel could build a dam that would hold, at least through the dry summer months, and that's when it could hurt the other ranchers the worst.

The greedy old bastard was simply sending a message. For some odd reason, Mitch hoped that the small ranchers downstream ignored it and let nature take its course, but he figured they wouldn't.

Charlie Houston and her men along with some hands from Cal Malone's spread showed up around noon. Fallon rose and turned slowly, gaze gliding along the valley, past the rise and fall of land to the boulders and brush that could easily hide some of the colonel's men.

The crazy woman was just riding right into trouble. And here he was worried about her when he was supposed to take care of the colonel's interests.

Lazily he pulled his rifle from its scabbard and aimed low in front of the woman and her bunch. With great care he placed three shots a good hundred feet ahead of them, chopping up dust and chunks of sod. They reined in, shouting, and soon were firing back, but he had already dropped behind the rise where Jeb waited.

He slid the Winchester '73 back into its scabbard, mounted the black, and rode south along the low side of the ridge until he had flanked the riders. He expected them to retreat and pass his way soon, but when he heard nothing after thirty minutes or so, he picked his way cautiously back in their direction.

The noise of their work reached him long before he spotted their horses, tied in the shade. They were all involved in the brutal task of moving rock and already had cleared a portion of the dam so that water was beginning to trickle through.

Fallon glanced around quickly. Where were the colonel's men? If some of them showed up, they would probably kill someone just because it might be enjoyable.

Damn-fool woman. They were all fools, when you

got right down to it. What could land be worth that
they would risk their lives?

At least they'd had the sense to post three armed
guards to keep lookout while the other men worked.

Fallon watched them awhile, but with each passing
minute grew more nervous. He did not want to see
the woman hurt, and the longer they kept at this
thankless task, the more that became a possibility. He
regarded the Winchester in its scabbard at his knee.
Shooting at them hadn't deterred them earlier, so
probably wouldn't now.

"Well, hell," he muttered under his breath, dismounted, and leading the black walked right up on
the toiling men, most of whom were so involved in
their work they didn't even see him.

Charlie spotted Fallon as she and P.J. grappled with
a particularly stubborn chunk of rock in the crudely
built dam. She turned loose her hold, P.J. shouted and
sucked at a finger that got mashed when she let go,
and Charlie came up the creek bank cursing.

Fallon smiled. She had a right smart tongue on her,
and he admired some of the inventive names she
called him. His amusement only made her more
furious.

The men, unsure of exactly what was going on, since
no guns had been pulled, simply stopped what they
were doing and stared. A few chuckled and made
comments to each other.

"Well, I suppose you're all just going to stand
around like mules at fertility rites," Charlie declared
when she caught them gaping, and went for the rifle
on Belle's saddle.

Of course she hadn't a chance of reaching it, for
Fallon and his stallion blocked the way.

"That's pretty good, mules at fertility rites," Fallon
said so that only she could hear.

"Get out of my way. I'm surprised you just didn't shoot us all. That was you a while ago, wasn't it?"

"Sure was, and you notice you're all still living and breathing. But you won't be if you don't get out of here before some of Dunkirk's men come back. And they will."

"Dunkirk's men? Last I heard you could be included in that group. What are you doing, playing a game with us? Damn you, Fallon, don't you know what this place means to me . . . to us? How can you go up against honest men trying to make a place in this hard country? Don't you think drought and Indians and outlaws are trouble enough without men like Dunkirk and the likes of you?

"Now get your butt out of here and leave us be, you two-legged spawn of—"

He cut her off by touching her arm. "Miss Houston—"

"Don't Miss Houston me." It should have been a harsh demand, but instead came out like a hoarse plea for understanding. Her eyes filled but didn't overflow and she looked up at him, blinking. "How can you do this? You're not this kind of man. You can't be. If my father were alive . . ."

He nodded, and a great pain swelled in his chest. He looked down into her face, smeared with mud, hair plastered to her forehead and cheeks, and thought how absolutely beautiful she was. And then, immediately, what a fool he was.

A rush of water, the rumble of moving rock, interrupted their confrontation. The men began to shout and jump around, clambering up out of the bed of the creek as the dam came apart and water flowed once again onto the Double H.

"Now get the hell out of here," Fallon said harshly, turned from her, and mounted.

Charlie's heart hammered at her ribs. Damn the

man. She ran to Belle, jerked the rifle out, and whirled to aim at the retreating gunslinger. Sight centered on his shoulder blades, she eased her finger over the trigger, and then just stood there till he rode out of sight, the barrel of the gun wavering in her grip.

Chapter Six

An entire week passed without retaliation from the colonel. At odd times Charlie caught herself scanning the horizon for the silhouette of the black horse and rider.

As the weather turned warmer the ranch hands renewed their complaints about lousy pickings for chuck. The men grew so tired of their own cooking they threatened mutiny. Even Ritter complained that if he had to drink one more cup of that brown gargle he was forced into brewing every morning 'cause no one else would go near the coffeepot, he was gonna hightail it for the Marias where he knew of a ranch with the best cook this side of Canada.

Charlie had to admit things were pretty bad. Then the sourdough starter ran out, a sure sign of bad trouble ahead. The worst biscuits anyone could whip up were better than none at all, and they'd all tried their hand at it. The results had ranged from heavy, hard lumps to a flapjack-looking mess that could only be eaten with a spoon, should anyone be so inclined. Anyway, no one knew what to do to keep the leavening working and so they had just kept using it till there wasn't enough left to start a day's biscuits.

Ritter made the remark that perhaps it just grew overnight, but that hadn't happened either.

Charlie was so desperate that she had almost decided to ride into Miles City and pluck someone off the street. Anyone would do. As she considered this while standing near the chuck wagon watching the men fuss and stir around like a herd about to stampede, a full-blown skirmish developed over the coffee, one of the men calling it belly wash.

"You could read a dad-blamed catalog through this stuff," came the next complaint, whereby the one doing the grousing grabbed the pot out of the fire and poured the remainder of the brew over the coals, sending up a column of smoke and ashes that set everyone to coughing.

Charlie turned away in disgust to eye the chuck wagon. At that moment it was mighty tempting to set it afire and have done with the entire episode. Chocco, that traitor of a cook who'd fled back to Texas, had fared well over the winter in a canvas tent, but she'd planned to build a cookhouse before the snow flew. If things kept us this way, it didn't look like there'd be a cook or hands to feed.

The stranger rode in while all the cowpokes were romping and stomping up a cloud of dust, as near calling it quits as they'd ever been. The shabby man dismounted his mangy-looking mule and attempted to introduce himself amid the hubbub. Ritter finally took notice and tugged at Charlie's arm. She was busy yelling into the face of Hank Bledsoe, the man who'd dumped the coffee.

"Looks like you could learn to make your own coffee instead of acting like such an ass," she hollered right up into his red face.

Bledsoe puffed up, turned more crimson. "Now, lookee here, Miss Charlie."

Ritter tugged at her shirt again and she spun around. "What do you want?"

With a large wooden spoon he'd picked up as a

weapon just in case things got out of hand, Ritter pointed at the stranger.

"What do you want?" she repeated in much the same impatient tone, but this time the words were aimed at the grimy bum.

Sweeping his bedraggled hat off, the man began with precisely the wrong word for the circumstances. "Ma'am? My name is Crane Houston, and I come—"

Charlie grabbed the spoon out of Ritter's hand and threw it at the newcomer. "One more man calls me ma'am on this place and you're all fired, and I mean it," she shouted, and trounced off to the house.

"Hell, dressing like a man hasn't done me one whit of good. How did he know I was a ma'am anyway?" she chanted as she marched. "I don't dress like one, I don't look like one, I don't walk like one. Why does everyone call me ma'am?" She turned around, walking backward, even went so far as to shake a fist in the air, much to her chagrin. "You're all fired. Every last one of you. Fired. Do you hear me?"

Without missing a step, she whirled, stomped up onto the porch and inside the cabin, slamming the door so hard it bounced back open.

She sat down at the table, got up and walked a circle, plopped on the edge of the bed. "If I had a dress, I swear I'd put it on about now, let some man take over this mess and straighten it out."

Having come up with the idea amazed her. Stunned, she sat for a while thinking over what had happened. She had acted just like a woman. Men and women were different in their reactions to situations. A man ... her father, would have settled that uprising out there in a split second without flouncing off like a spoiled child. He might even have punched someone in the mouth, but he would have gotten the job done. Six months ago, that's precisely what she would have done too. What was going on?

Someone cleared his throat and she looked up to see the stranger standing in the open doorway, hat in both hands. Why did men always hold their hats right there across their middle, like they were protecting something precious? She giggled and covered her mouth. Again, just like a woman. She threw her shoulders back and stood as tall as she could, an impressive five feet eight in her boots. That's when she realized with a start that the man had said his name was Houston.

"Did you say Houston?"

The man nodded and raised an eyebrow. He was a little taller than her, fairly broad in the shoulders, with a mustache and several days growth of salt and pepper beard. He wasn't handsome, but he wasn't ugly either. Just quite ordinary, very scruffy, and nothing at all like her father, the only other Houston she had ever known, besides herself, of course. This one was disappointingly down on his luck.

"Are you Matt's girl?" he finally asked. He had a friendly voice and his faded blue eyes sparkled like he appreciated the humor in the scene he had ridden into. There might have been a little bit of Matt there, she wasn't sure.

"Yes, I'm Charlie. Charlotte Maria Houston. Do I know you?"

"Probably not, you were very small when I saw you last. When I left Texas. As I said, my name's Crane, Crane Houston. I'm your very own cousin, your daddy's eldest brother's only boy."

The strange man's announced family tie sent an odd feeling of pleasure through her. He was family. A precious link to her father.

"Oh, come in, please do." She strode to the bed, straightened the coverlet, gestured toward the chairs around the table, the only other place to sit unless you chose the floor.

"Where did you come from? I mean, how did you get here? How did you find me?"

The man sat where she indicated, dropped his disreputable hat on the floor, and folded his hands together on the table in front of him.

Black dirt rimmed the nails, but that didn't matter. She hovered over him, suddenly eager to make a connection. "Are you hungry, could I get you something to eat?"

Crane glanced pointedly in the direction of the chuck wagon outside and smiled. "I don't think so, but maybe I could get you something to eat. And them too."

Her mouth dropped open, the announcement rendered her speechless. Surely such things didn't happen. It was like making a wish and having the genie appear.

He went on. "I mean, I learned to cook pretty good when I . . . uh, well, while I was on my own. A feller gets down on his luck he learns lots of things."

"Uh, well, some may," she replied. "Those yahoos out there would starve before they'd learn how to cook. It isn't proper for a cowboy to know how to cook. Cowboys only know how to tell the front end of a cow from the ass end, that's all cowboys know. And how to sit a bronc so they can ride out on a Saturday night and poke every soiled dove within a thousand miles. That's all cowboys know." She neglected to mention her own shortcomings in that area.

Crane widened his eyes and had the decency to look embarrassed. "You're upset, maybe I should just mount up and ride on. I didn't intend to cause you worry."

"Upset? Yes. Don't go, please, Mr. Houston, I mean Crane, I mean cousin."

"Crane is fine," he said. He stood, pointed toward

the door. "Why don't I just go out there and see what I can do? Would that be okay?"

She let out a tremendous sigh. "Dear God, yes, that would be okay ... Crane. And thank you. Thank you from the very bottom of my heart."

He stopped at the door and turned to study her. "Oh, there's no need for thanks. I expect you'll pay me cook's wages, just like any other hand. Won't you?"

There was a look in the man's eyes that she found puzzling. She would remember it later. Right now all she knew was that this man, this cousin, had rescued her in what her father would have called the ginger nick of time.

She followed him to the door, but not out to the chuck wagon. In no time he had donned an apron and started putting things right.

It wasn't long before Yancey Barton separated himself from the cluster of watchful cowboys and strolled up to the cabin. She stepped out and sat on the top step, grinning widely at him.

"Well, you musta been at the cream pitcher, with that look," he said, and sat down beside her.

She hugged her knees and rocked backward. "It's a miracle."

"Well, now, ain't you just too tickled with yourself, Charlie? Who is that, anyway?"

"You don't need to sound so grumpy. He saved our bacon, showing up when he did. And look, he's already got breakfast cooking. Just smell that meat sizzling ... and the coffee boiling."

Yancey eyed her for a long while, shook his head, and crammed his hat down over his brow. "Don't suppose you asked for any references."

"No. And there was no need. That's my daddy's own kin out there. That's Crane Houston."

"So he told us. Looks like nothing but a chuck-line

saddle bum to me. Why didn't I ever hear of this feller? Your daddy tell you of this feller, did he?"

Something went thud in her stomach. Matt had never told her about any kin. All she knew was his long-time affiliation with the King Ranch. Richard King had been her "uncle," and her mother's many relatives in both Texas and Mexico the only family she knew. Was Yancey only trying to stir up trouble or did he have a point?

"You can't get me down, Yancey. You're always looking for the worst in everyone. You're not getting away with it this time. Saddle bums just come begging to belly up at the chuck wagon. Most of them don't offer to do the cooking. Besides, why would the man make up such a story as that? How would he know about me and my father?"

"Oh, yeah? And just what did he know?"

She thought about that for a while. It was true. He hadn't even mentioned Matt's brother's name. Not that it would have helped her any. The realization made her impatient with her ramrod's cynical common sense.

"Never you mind, Yancey, you just go take care of your business and I'll take care of mine. Put those men to work when their bellies are full, and forget all this nonsense."

He rose, hooked his thumbs in his waistband, and said, "Yes, sir, Miss Charlie. Anything else?" But his eyes were sparkling, and she knew he was only teasing. She and Yancey Barton had never had harsh words over anything, just like he and Matt had never argued seriously.

"No, nothing else. Get over there and eat something yourself, you're entirely too puny."

He loped off without saying anything else, but his earlier questions left a stale taste in her mouth, one she was hard-put to wash away, even with a cup of the excellent coffee Crane Houston served up at the chuck wagon a little while later.

Mitch rode to the Circle D Ranch late that evening in response to the colonel's summons. Out in the corral a couple of rough riders were finishing off a new string of wild horses, and some of the hands sat around atop the rail fence shouting and cussing encouragement with a certain flavoring of derision. In reality the men watching might well be ranch hands, but that wasn't what they were hired for. The more men the colonel hired, the more Mitch wished he could just move on. This was shaping up to be all-out war, and he'd almost rather head for the hills as take part. But he was committed, and besides it kept his mind off darker thoughts. Lately he'd been troubled by a terrible yearning to connect with family, be with people he knew. There was only one, his sister Dessa, off somewhere with her husband Ben Poole making tons of money, he'd heard. He had a mighty urge to ride back down to Missouri and rest his bones in the old family home place. Hard to figure what brought that on.

He was surprised to see Colonel Dunkirk seated atop a buckboard that had been pulled up to the fence, watching the horse breaking as if it were pure entertainment.

"Over here, Fallon," the colonel shouted when Mitch swung from his saddle. "A couple more men I want you to meet. So's we don't go killin' our own when the shootin' starts." The fat man held his belly and guffawed.

Mitchell tilted his black Stetson forward a bit to cut the harsh glare of the late afternoon sun and approached the corral. A great shout went up as a rider clawed sky bouncing off a wild bronc bent double and airborne. The man hit the ground on his butt, grunted, and picked himself up. He walked stiffly toward the kicking, screaming horse.

"Git 'im, Utah. Hell's bells, he ain't nothin' but a bolt of lightning," someone shouted.

All the men along the fence laughed.

The colonel ignored the horseplay and gestured toward two men who stood straddle-legged, one hand on the butts of their side arms, steely eyes aimed at Mitch.

"This here is Cross and the other'n is Neddy. Boys, this is Fallon."

Cross nodded in a lank-jawed manner, a lock of dirty blond hair falling down between his close-set gray eyes, as flat and unyielding as gunmetal. He wore a fancy silver belt buckle as big as his hand. His pal Neddy grinned, dimples bloomed, and he looked for all the world like someone's sweet little fifteen-year-old grandson with fat rosy cheeks and a well-fed body. A new and dangerous brand of outlaw was discovering the territories lately, men who had been too young to serve in the war and had purely self-serving axes to grind.

Mitch nodded curtly, didn't offer a hand, neither did they. Hands belonged on the butts of pistols, not tied up in someone else's fist, and he rested his where it was meant to be just like they did.

The colonel stood in the buckboard and nodded as his bodyguard, the ugly, scar-faced man everyone called Wolf because his eyes looked just like a predator's. The man promptly let go a shrill whistle that not only spooked the horses, but brought every man jack on the fence to attention.

"Colonel wants you all in the study, pronto," Wolf announced, helped his boss down from the seat, and escorted him toward the ranch house.

Mitch had never quite gotten over some of the terms the scarcely literate Wolf used when following the colonel's commands. He obviously picked them up from his boss and was proud to show how he could use them. The word *study* wouldn't be in his vocabulary otherwise. To him it was a room in a house. There was a big shiny desk, bookshelves filled with leather-bound books, and plenty of chairs for the frequent meetings the colonel held there plotting how he would steal his next parcel of land.

Some things in this life were hard to figure out, like how come a man like the colonel was allowed to live on to bedevil everyone while someone like his Celia and sweet innocent little Fawn had to die so horribly. There were times when Mitch toyed with just shooting the old son of a bitch and putting everyone out of his misery. Then, provided Wolf didn't gun him down on the spot, the law could hang him and everything would be all done with.

He picked a chair near the bank of windows where he could look out on the yard and corrals. The position also gave him a good view of the approach road to the ranch itself. He always half expected someone to come riding in looking for him. After all those years following the war when he ran from one hiding place to the other, sometimes just a jump ahead of the law and a hanging rope, every holdup in the territory laid at his feet. The dreaded Yank, many times compared to Quantrill, was thought to be dead, though. Some said he had been killed in a gun battle with Sheriff Moohn out at Alder Gulch near Virginia City. And his sister Dessa and her husband Ben Poole the only ones who knew he and Celia had escaped that fatal gun battle. Yank had died, but only in spirit. Mitch became a different man, a loving husband and father. Now he was none of those, now he was nothing. A man with no life, no love, no connections.

Why the hell didn't he just leave Montana and go somewhere else? Well, by God maybe he just would.

For a running dead man, one place was just as good as another.

The colonel interrupted his musings. "What the hell, Fallon, you going to join us or gape off into thin air?"

Mitch swiveled away from the window. For two bits he'd walk away from this crazy man's army, ride out of Montana, and never look back. But he couldn't. Something held him here that he didn't quite understand. It had to do with the woman, and that's all he knew for sure.

The colonel addressed the men. "It's time to put an end to this nonsense. We'll run 'em all out or bury 'em where they fall, either way they're leaving my land. Starting tonight I want hit-and-run raids. Quick and fast, in and out. Make believers out of them. I'd rather they'd pull up stakes and leave, less questions to answer. If they don't, well, the law around here is bought and paid for. There are five small ranches and three families of sodbusters on my land and I want rid of them, once and for all.

"I've found most men are easily scared bad enough to run if you give them the room to do it. Back 'em up against a wall and some will turn and fight. I'd rather see 'em run, but if you can't ..." He hunched his thick shoulders. A tacit and unspoken permission to kill with his blessings.

When no one said anything, he looked straight at Mitch, then shifted to Cross, then on to Neddy. One by one he made eye contact with the men gathered around the desk.

"All right, I think I've made myself clear," he said.

The men all nodded, ready to do his bidding, no matter what it was. He had bought and paid for their guns. Now he was asking for results, and he would get them.

Mitch shifted uncomfortably. It was one thing to shoot at someone who was bound to shoot you, but this ... harassing settlers, struggling ranchers, women, and kids.

Just ordinary folk. Ordinary folk.

Mitch squeezed his eyes shut. Ordinary folk stood by while others like them murdered his wife and child. There was no reason except that they were Indian, different, frightening to white men who were stealing land that rightfully belonged to the Sioux.

He'd tried to wipe the blood from her face, tenderly unfastened the board that held the silent Fawn, knelt beside them, clutching their limp bodies to his chest, rocking and screaming like a mortally wounded animal.

And the men, their horses prancing around the bloody sight, good men and true. Innocent men. White men. Men just like Cal Malone and Matt Houston and Duffy McGrew and all the rest.

"Git yourself another squaw, squawman. Before we kill ever' last one of 'em, wipe 'em off the face of the earth. Bloody savages."

Mitch ground his teeth and opened his eyes. So real had been the images that he was shocked to find himself in the colonel's study. The stench of death and sweat and anguish followed him into the room, and it took a moment to orient himself. What difference did it make who he killed? What difference indeed? There were no innocents in this land.

Then why ... dear God, why did he say what he did and put himself up against it? "I'll take care of the Houston place, and I won't need any help."

The colonel produced a malicious smirk. "See you do. I'm spread thin, surely anyone can take care of a woman and a few scraggly hands."

Charlie padded around in her socks, glancing out first one window, then the other. The music box tinkled, but her enjoyment was lost to a restlessness she couldn't quite explain.

She went to one of the windows and loosened the tanned deer hide stretched over the opening to let in some night air. There were only three windows in the small cabin and over each she had stretched the beautiful deer hides, tanned fine by the Cheyenne women so that the lamplight glowed through them. Spotted Moon's wife had given them to her the winter afternoon when she had held the woman's child close to her barren breasts.

Things were going well, the ranch had a cook, Dunkirk had backed off, so she couldn't explain the way she felt. On edge, as if waiting for something wonderful or frightening to happen. When the music disk stopped playing she put the music box away. In another moment she moved from the window and twirled through the room on her toes, making three graceful circles before coming up against the bed.

How she missed Matt. The winter had been tough but she'd thought that once through it she would be okay. Now that spring was here the loneliness had deepened into a steady burning ache that no amount of hard work would soothe. She missed working at his side, sensing his manly strength, sharing his love for a hard day's labor.

With a deep sigh she stepped out onto the porch, leaving the door ajar at her back so that a pool of light lay around her.

It was pure carelessness that got him caught. Mitch had ridden fairly close to the cabin and was sitting there taking in the view as shamelessly as some kid when that young man he'd seen around the ranch walked right up on him.

Jeb sensed the man's presence and tried to telegraph it to his master, but Mitch ignored his antics.

The gruff order, "Stay right where you are, mister," was the first Mitch knew anybody was around except him and the lovely Miss Houston, who liked to dance when alone, it seemed.

He wasn't too worried that the man would shoot him, but he felt foolish all the same. Besides, he wasn't too sure about Charlie Houston. She might just as soon shoot him as look at him, especially after he'd been caught sneaking around in the dark.

"Now you climb down off a that there horse and if you even have to sneeze, don't, 'cause I'm not very good with this old rifle and sometimes it goes off when I'm not looking."

Mitch kept his hands high and swung agilely off Jeb. It was pretty dark, but not so much so that he could get away with anything.

"Miss Charley. Yancey. Get yourselves out here, I done caught me a coyote."

The man's shouting caused Jeb to bolt into the darkness. "Traitor," Mitch muttered.

"Shut up, mister,"

Yancey arrived first, waving around a rifle. "Well, Ritter, good work. What was he up to?"

"Just sitting his horse looking in at Miss Charlie. He wasn't doing anything."

"Probably fixing to, though. Come back to finish what you started and burn us out?" Yancey glared at Fallon.

Charlie had stomped into her boots as she clamored off the porch and came on the scene late. When she saw Fallon under the guns of both Ritter and Yancey she yelled at them without thinking. "Don't shoot him, for God's sake."

Yancey turned toward her. "I don't reckon we had that in mind exactly, Charlie. The thing is, what do you want us to do with him?"

She stepped closer so she could look up into Fallon's face. "Why is it every time I turn around I run into you? You're the dangdest excuse for a gunslinger I ever saw."

"He was watching you through the window yonder," Ritter said and gestured toward the cabin.

Charlie glanced in that direction and felt heat creeping up her throat. He could see her right through those hides with the lamps lit. "You mangy coward, you double-butted, red-eyed—"

"Now, Charlie, whoa now," Yancey said. "Don't go getting yourself in an uproar. You'll only say something that'll embarrass you when you go to thinking on it. This here fella ain't worth that. Think what your daddy would've done."

"He'd have thrashed him soundly and made him walk home bare ass naked," she said.

"Sounds good to me," Ritter said. "You hold the gun, Yancey, while I take care of this matter."

Fallon made a rude sound down in his throat and Charlie darted a quick look at him. It would take more than two men to accomplish such a feat, she was sure. Perhaps even Matt Houston couldn't have gotten the job done. Besides, she didn't like the idea, miffed as she was about him skulking around.

"I apologize for staring in at you, Miss Houston," Fallon said, the first words he'd uttered since he'd climbed down off Jeb. "I came by to warn you that the colonel is going to step up his attack on the small ranchers. I'm sorry but I caught sight of you through the shade and couldn't help but look. I never saw a rancher dance quite like that before. It's a rare sight out here on the plains."

She caught a hint of humor in the gruff voice. "Don't you dare laugh at me."

"I meant nothing but to pay you a compliment."

A strange emotion filled her throat and she turned away from the three men. "Let him go. Get out of here, Fallon, and don't come back. The next time you're liable to be shot for the thief and killer you are."

"But, Miss Charlie," Ritter said.

"Aw, hell, Charlie," Yancey added.

"Shut up, both of you. And you, Fallon, you shut up too. No more fawning and skulking around. Stay out of my sight, forever." She walked away and didn't look back.

Chapter Seven

For a while Cal Malone was content to consider the ruckus a part of his dream, so it was several minutes before he awoke enough to realize that the shots he heard might be real. When a bullet whined through the ranch house and shattered a lamp before thudding into the wall beside his bed, he knew.

This was no dream!

He kicked away the tangled blanket, leaped from the bed, grabbed up his Spencer. Disregarding his lack of proper clothing—he preferred to sleep in his union suit bottoms—Cal burst onto the porch in time to see two riders disappear into the darkness south of the ranch house.

Damn that colonel! If the man was bent on war, then by God he would oblige him.

Racing barefoot across the yard, Cal vaulted up top of the corral fence and over onto the bare back of one of his cow ponies. Without considering the futility of chasing after riders in the dark, he bumped loose the top rail of the fence, urged the pony over the bottom one, and headed south in hot pursuit of the fleeing raiders.

Odd they hadn't ridden north back toward the Circle D, but Cal didn't stop to ponder on that too long either. He would catch them if he had to ride till sunrise. Could be they were going to hit every rancher in the area in one night. He rode for maybe half an hour without seeing anything but silent stands of juniper and pine. Finally he reined in the chuffing, sweating horse. No sense killing a good mount. He'd never catch them in the dark anyway. Having ridden away most of his anger, Cal decided he might as well go home.

Disappointment at not catching at least one of the riders in his gunsights rode with him as he headed back toward the Rocking R. He'd like that colonel to meet him face-to-face like a man. The dirty rotten coward, sending out gunhands to harass hardworking men who were doing nothing but trying to make a living.

Be damned if he'd give up the land that he and Becky had toiled over, sacrificed everything for. His beloved wife had even given her life, and he wasn't about to let a bunch of paid-for guns drive him off. They would bury him on the hill at her side before he'd let that happen.

Thus engaged, Cal didn't hear the shot or feel the bullet that caught him in the throat. Surprise flooded over him as he toppled off the horse and landed on the ground flat on his back.

What in God's name was he doing staring up at the night sky?

There was no pain. In awe, he watched a soft glow fade into the darkness, and wondered just what kind of strange dream this was, anyway.

"Becky," he murmured. "Becky, don't cry."

And she smiled and held out her arms to him.

The next afternoon about four o'clock Cal's fore-man Zeke rode into the yard at the Double H. Charlie was swamping out the new barn because all the men were out on the range except Ritter, and he was off somewhere gathering firewood. At the thrum of hoof-beats she dropped the shovel and went to meet the rider, expecting more trouble just because that's the way things were going. Chickens scattered around her feet, squawking and pecking at the ground. On the move she pulled her gloves off and rolled her shoulders to chase away a cramp. When she saw the morose face of the Rocking R's ramrod, goose bumps trickled after a trail of sweat down her back.

"What is it, what's happened?" Her dry throat caught at the words.

He dismounted with the horse in motion. "It's Cal, ma'am. He's been shot."

A familiar jag of pain lanced through her and she covered her mouth to keep from crying out, then asked, "How bad is he?" Without waiting for a reply she ran for the tack room.

Zeke trotted along beside her. "Bad. Real bad. I'm sorry to say Cal's dead. We found him around dawn. The colonel sent some men to hurrah the place and Cal rode out after them. Damndest thing, he was only wearing his drawers and carrying a Spencer. Didn't even saddle up. In all the commotion I never even seen him ride out. Damndest thing."

Tears burned at her eyes as she pulled a bridle, saddle, and blanket off the rack. "Oh, poor Cal. Isn't that just like him? He's dead? How did it happen? I mean, where ... how ... who?" she knew what she was really asking was did Mitchell Fallon have anything to do with her friend's death. Did he ride from here directly over there and shoot Cal?

She would kill him, lie in wait behind some rock and put a bullet between his eyes. Hate lurked dark and ugly inside her, the taste bitter in her mouth.

At the same time her lips wouldn't form the question of Zeke. Did you see a man all dressed in black, riding a wild black stallion? Did he then follow Cal and shoot him down? No, she couldn't ask. She desperately didn't want Fallon involved, wanted him to be innocent. His touch tamed her soul, and that was enough of a reason.

Zeke rattled on. "Out by Butcher's Holler, there where them big rocks are? We figure they laid in wait for him, gunned him down from ambush. He never fired a shot. His horse come in is why we rode out looking at all. Otherwise, you know, Cal would sometimes ride off a mad. Since Miss Rebecca died he's been that way. Ride half the night just staring off in the distance, like he might could catch up with her if he went far enough."

Charlie slowed in her trek to the corral and threw the foreman a look. Sometimes men said the most surprising things. You'd go along and go along, thinking they were just hard-riding, cussing, spitting, drinking, simple men, and then one would say something insightful and catch you unawares.

The man eyed her back, then looked down at his feet. "Reckon he finally did, huh?"

Tears poured over her cheeks as she hurried to the corral to saddle up. Poor Cal. Those sons of bitches would pay. Whether it was Fallon or someone else, this time they would pay. They'd gone too far, shooting Cal Malone, and by God, something would be done if she had to ride to Virginia City and fetch the territorial marshal herself. Someone should have done it long ago and not waited for one of the best men she knew to get gunned down. Who would have thought, though, that the colonel would go this far? As it turned out, he hadn't backed off after they dynamited the dam, he had simply reconnoitered and come at them again, in his own time with his own rules.

Tightening the cinch on the prancing roan, Charlie said, "Ride to the other ranches, fetch Duffy and Lester Burris and that dandy Basil Hawthorne and the others. I'm going to town to see what can be done about this. Tell them to meet me there at the sheriff's office."

With the man trotting at her heels Charlie went to the house and fetched her Winchester. She hesitated just long enough to make sure it was loaded, then hurried back to her saddled horse.

"What about Cal, Miss Charlie?"

She mounted, tugged the mare's head around, and stared down at him. "What about him? He's dead."

"But he'll need a burying."

"Yes, he will indeed need a burying, but not right now. It'll wait till tomorrow. I'll stop at the undertaker's and arrange things. Cal would want to be buried with Rebecca on the ranch."

She kicked the horse and rode off, the wind drying her tears so that her cheeks grew stiff.

Most of the colonel's ranch lay to the north of the Double H, but the ranch house itself was built in the crook of the Porcupine Creek after it flowed off Charlie's land and back onto a section of the colonel's land. Her ranch house and his weren't far apart as distance was judged in the sprawling Montana Territory.

Miles City lay to the south on the Powder River before it ran into the Yellowstone, but she detoured to the colonel's first because she could do nothing else. Grief at the loss of a friend, anger that one man could get away with such a terrible thing as murder, the stubbornness she'd inherited from Matt Houston, all teamed up on her to prevent her doing the smart thing and riding straight into Miles City.

The ranch was unusually quiet when she rode in. The roan slowed, blowing from being galloped hard, and she left her at the hitching rail by the porch. In the eerie silence her boots thunked noisily when she crossed the wide planks.

She pounded on the mammoth door with the flat of

her hand. "Colonel, you better git yourself out here." With the toe of one boot she kicked the door a couple more times. "Open up, now, you no-good, back-shooting son of a—"

"Whoa," a voice said right at her shoulder.

She whirled to see Mitchell Fallon leaning up against a pillar, a frown creasing his broad forehead.

For a moment neither spoke, just studied each other like hunter and prey.

Finally she broke the silence. "Where is that murdering bastard?"

Something flashed in his eyes. A threat? "You ought to ride on your way. This could get you killed."

"Like it got Cal Malone killed? Is that how, Fallon? Did you pull the trigger on my friend, shoot him down in cold blood? All because he wanted something to call his own? Tell me, what makes a man like you able to live with himself? How do you sleep nights? How do you even get out of bed of a morning, knowing today you're going to go out and murder someone else? Just how does that work?

"Dear God, I wish I'd have let Ritter and Yancey at you last night. You don't know how I wish that. I should have shot you myself."

His green eyes batted as if she'd slapped him, and Charlie could have sworn she saw a hint of compassion before his features closed down. He straightened and rested the heel of his right hand on his pistol butt. "Like I said, ride out."

As he spoke a handful of men rounded the corner of the ranch house, all headed in their direction.

She glanced at them, anxiety leaching away her fury. "Oh, I will. And you tell your precious colonel that I intend to bring in the territorial marshal. This is murder, pure and simple. There'll be no self-defense. You've gone too far this time."

Mitch watched Charlie walk away, her gait stiff and

unnatural. He wished she hadn't mentioned the marshal in the other men's hearing. She was barely holding it together, and he wanted to chase after her, tell her he had nothing to do with this. The hate smoldering in her incredible dark eyes, the way her soft, full lips tightened into a sneer of disgust, pained him. He didn't want her feeling that way about him.

That arrogant Cross and his murderous sidekick had done precisely what Mitch had been afraid of and killed Cal Malone. A range war was one thing, but out-and-out laying-in-wait killing quite another. Only in war had Mitch done something so loathsome, no matter the target. Whatever happened now would serve the colonel right.

Ignoring the gunhands and their questions about what was going on, Mitch hurried to the bunkhouse where he threw his meager belongings into his canvas poncho, cinched it up, and headed for the corral. There he saddled the stallion, tied on the bedroll, slid his Winchester into the scabbard, and mounted up. Out of sight of the ranch house he hesitated for a moment, unsure of which direction to ride. Then he headed west, following the trail that meandered alongside Porcupine Creek.

He had seen a stubbornness in the Houston woman's eyes that reminded him of something he'd struggled to forget. He'd seen that same harsh determination in Celia's eyes more than once, a hardheaded resolve that had finally gotten her killed. He hadn't been able to stop her from doing the things she simply had to do. Like walking openly in the streets of Bismarck with her half-white baby, while her people ravaged the Badlands slaughtering the white men who were destroying their way of life for the sake of railroads and gold.

He should never have brought his wife and child back into the territories after they'd fled to Canada.

But she missed her family so, longed for the Dakota land from where she'd come, dreamed of presenting a grandchild to her mother and father. All those years of running with the outlaw bands after the war had made Celia tough and unyielding, and he couldn't stand up to her once she'd made up her mind. Hell, he'd loved her, so how could he deny her such a simple request as to go home to her people? The pain in his heart cut so cruelly that he wished he could forget those few years he'd spent with a woman who adored him, who bore him a child, who gave him hope. Just slash the memory out of his brain as viciously as Cross had slaughtered Malone. Then maybe all he'd have left would be an empty loneliness and no expectations of anything better.

This woman, this Charlie Houston, who dressed like a man and acted like one, had a stubborn streak that he judged would get her killed too. He wasn't going to stay around and watch it happen, and he sure as hell wasn't going to be a part of it.

He rode on, shutting out everything but his need to be gone. Before all hell busted loose he could ride right into the sun as it set in the west. He could be in Idaho Territory before Charlie Houston died, if he rode hard.

Charlie sat outside the sheriff's office on the end of the boardwalk, waiting for the other ranchers to show up. The sheriff wasn't around, nor was his crazy deputy everyone called Acorn because he was so squirrelly.

The colonel was right when he said the only law in Miles City was what he himself allowed. How could the small ranchers hope to get anything accomplished? Why did those filthy killers have to go and shoot Cal? To scare the rest of them, maybe? To say that if they didn't give in and sell out to the colonel, this is what would happen to all of them?

She smacked the edge of her fist down on the weathered wood. Well, it wasn't going to be so easy. It wasn't going to happen because she wouldn't let it.

The men she'd sent Zeke after rode into town some time later. Her own ramrod Yancey Barton was with them, his face a picture of concern.

It didn't take long to weed out those who would fight for their land from those who wouldn't. The snobbish Basil Hawthorne would sell out and return to England, the rest would stay, but a couple were on the fence. Charlie sensed that when it came to push and shove, they'd sell too. She was pretty sure the rest would stick it out.

When she brought up the territorial marshal, the men scoffed.

"And when was the last time you seen him around Miles City?" McGrew asked. "It'll take a while to find him, I'd wager. In the meanwhile we need a plan."

And so it was finally decided that McGrew would send a man to hunt down the marshal, the rest would draw their battle lines. Together they would stand hard against Colonel Dunkirk and his hired guns the best way they knew.

Zeke decided to ride to Virginia City and claim Cal Malone's place before the colonel beat him to it. Zeke had been ramrod for Cal from the very beginning. Everyone agreed and Zeke left. He would miss Cal's funeral, but the rancher would have understood the need for haste.

Charlie sat on the porch long after dark that night, the rifle lying beside her. Yancey had sent two men in off the range for night guard, one was in the loft of the new barn, the other in the bunkhouse. At dawn they would sleep and two more would take their place.

To keep the men from growing careless, all pairs would rotate watching the ranch and riding the range, with everyone getting his share of sleep and range work mixed in with guarding. Yancey had devised a fair schedule.

Sleep proved illusive, and the later it got the more restless she grew. She had ridden in hot and dusty, needing a bath. After a late three-quarter moon crept into the sky she rose from the porch, went inside for a bar of soap and towel and her nightgown. Then she strolled down to the creek breathing deeply of the pine-scented air and the lingering animal aroma that told her she was exactly where she belonged, even in the face of all the trouble.

Mitch's trip to Idaho had gotten him as far as the banks of the Porcupine within hearing distance of the Double H Ranch. There he bedded down for the night. He was in no particular hurry to get to Idaho. He had set up a cold camp and chewed on jerky and hardtack from his pack, then settled back where he could see the light in the woman's cabin through the dense thicket.

Her silent passage through the brush alerted his sensitive hearing, and he crept on his hands and knees toward the sound.

It was late and a beautiful moon crept up from the eastern horizon to illuminate the land. A stand of willows threw umber shadows down the rise to her left, and ahead, thick poplars and box elder stood in silent, dark splendor. Leaves rustled underfoot and the brush crackled as she made her way to the water's edge.

Far off, the bawling of cattle had faded to low, soothing moans as the herd pastured nearby settled for the night.

On his knees, Mitchell gazed in awe through the branches heavy with pungent foliage. At the edge of the creek Charlie Houston shed the trappings of her tough cattle-droving life. She tossed the wide-brimmed dusty hat over a skeletal branch, gleaming in a splash of moonlight, removed the sweat-stained bandanna, and draped it nearby. The stiff-dried Kentucky jeans slumped like discarded skin against the tree's thick trunk. She stood naked, a gentle breeze stirring goose bumps along the curve of her back where it rounded into supple hips and long, lean thighs.

Crouched in silence he caught his breath at the vision that emerged from her cowpunchers cocoon like a moon moth.

Golden light splintered across the still water, reflected around her to caress erect nipples, a tight, flat stomach, the shadowy secret nested below. Tendrils of white curled from the water's surface into the chilly air and she waded deeper into the creek, disturbing the rising mist. Her face remained in darkness, the shoulder-length hair reflected bits of gold like a shattered halo.

Whatever gods ruled over his life were once again tantalizing him, and he wanted to cry out. A savage "No" ripped from deep in his gut but made not a sound.

He couldn't have this woman, he shouldn't want her, yet he couldn't stop his desire any more than he could ride away from her troubles. No woman was more vulnerable than when she was naked, and he was ashamed of spying on her yet he couldn't turn away. For an instant, though, he closed his eyes, and when he opened them her supple buttocks were sinking into the silvery surface as she lowered herself until only her shoulders and head were above water.

How silken and soft that skin would feel beneath the roughness of his fingertips. How sweet her flesh would taste and smell. When he held her, the fine strands of hair would spill over his chest and tickle his nose as he bent to kiss the top of her head. He knew how she smelled, how she felt, what it was like to hold her, and he felt a great loss because she wasn't in his arms. A moan surged from his throat and he suppressed it for fear he would frighten her away and be alone again.

Graceful hands clutching a bar of soap, she massaged up her throat and across both shoulders. He imagined smoothing the fragrant bar over her back in gentle circles until she broke out in goose bumps, turned, and came into his arms.

Her bare breasts would press against his chest, the firm nipples tantalizing him until he lowered his head and took first one, then the other into his mouth.

Dear God, what was happening to him? Had he gone crazy, round the bend crazy like he'd heard about when men remained too long alone in such a empty expanse of land?

It didn't matter that he might be going nuts, he couldn't budge. He remained frozen in time and watched while she washed her hair. She lifted both arms so that her breasts floated on the water, the nipples peeking right at him where he hunkered in the brush like some kind of primitive animal.

As she laced fingers through her hair a pleasant but very disturbing heat swelled between her loins. A tickling sensation tiptoed over her breasts and she was filled with a profound desire such as she had never known.

Disturbed by the wanton feelings and a small sound from the brush, Charlie scampered from the water, dropped her gown over her head, and hurried back to the cabin.

She thought of Mitchell Fallon and how he'd lurked out in the dark and watched her. No man had ever looked at her quite like he did. He seemed to be trying to puzzle out some great dark secret with a gaze that penetrated her very soul. Every time she was caught up by those magnetic green eyes though, they would frost over like glass on a cold night.

Mitchell had watched the woman drift across the moon-splashed meadow grass like a ghost in the ethereal white gown. He waited awhile after she went inside the cabin, hoping she would light a lamp and he could catch a glimpse of her shadow crossing the window openings. But she didn't, and after a while he crept silently back to his camp. He remained very quiet, stealthy even, for he hadn't missed her acknowledging wave that told him someone was keeping lookout besides himself. He'd have to watch his step or they might shoot him for the trespasser that he was.

Chapter Eight

Thunder woke Charlie, sending her scurrying out of bed to tie down the window coverings that flapped in a brisk wind. She thought of Cal and his funeral planned for this morning. For some reason it never failed to rain on a burying.

Just like that horrible day on the trail when they'd buried her father, the howling wind, the icy pellets of rain, men huddled around in ponchos like hovering specters, rivulets of water pouring into the yawning hole before they could shovel the mud onto the canvas-wrapped body.

She shuddered, forced away the memory, and climbed back in bed to snuggle deeper under the covers for a few minutes. Death came on such awesome feet and at the most inopportune of times. But then, when was a good time to greet such an unwelcome visitor?

Outside horses whinnied and men shouted as the ranch came awake for another day. With a sigh of dread she rose, dressed quickly, and stepped out onto the porch. Before moving through the water cascading in sheets off the roof, she pulled the poncho tight around her neck. It was time to say good-bye to Cal.

Standing around the grave, the men kept their hats on to shield themselves from the worst of the deluge.

The rain looked like it had settled in for a long stay. That was the way of this country. Dry as a bone till you thought you'd choke, then it'd come a toad strangler that floated everything away. The month of June was moving on. When this rainy spell passed, there wouldn't likely be another all summer. Charlie welcomed the moisture for the pastures, but she couldn't help wishing the sun had shone for Cal's funeral. A dreary send-off to offer such a fine man. Even the distant mountains wore somber shrouds.

Around the grave, someone said a few words. She paid little attention to them. What mattered was her own farewell to her friend, and she closed her eyes and offered one of his favorite poems as a going-away gift, spoken so softly that each syllable was muted by the patter of rain on hat brims and bowed shoulders.

"Go with God, dear friend," she added at the end, then watched woodenly as the men lowered Cal's casket on ropes. After flipping the lines clear, two cowhands with shovels began to toss the mud and rocks in on him. The dull thuds bruised her heart until it was painful to breathe, and so for a long moment she didn't.

Someone tugged at her arm and she turned to see Ritter squinting from under his hat brim, rivulets of water cascading off the edges. "Come on, it's done. You're soaked. Why don't you just go back to the house and stay there today? Another day won't hurt, and this don't look like it'll let up anytime soon. Only a fool'd go out on any kind of business in this. The colonel and his men'll stay in today, you can bet your bottom dollar."

She shook her arm free. "Don't be ridiculous. Since when does a little weather keep hands from working? There're chores to do and a ranch to run. Part of that is seeing to its safety. I'll be riding out as soon as I can get saddled."

Ritter shook his head and stomped off, leaving her to trail along behind. Stubborn woman, hell, he'd never seen the like. Now he supposed he'd have to tag after her, see she kept safe. Yancey Barton would skin him alive if he didn't. Well, so much for staying by the fire and trading lies with the hands. She was worse to work for than any man. Still and all, he sure did admire her.

Inside the shelter of the new barn Charlie heaved a saddle on her favorite roan Belle, tightened the cinch, and lowered the stirrup. Ritter came from the corral leading an iron-gray gelding that stood at least sixteen hands high. The mount's wide back was steaming and darkly splotched with rain. The pungent aroma of horseflesh mixed with that of the green pine smell of logs in the newly built structure.

She glared at the young hand with a baleful eye. "Where the thunder do you think you're going?"

"With you."

"Nope, you're not. There's plenty to do around this place, and you know that well."

"Dang it all, Miss Houston, I might as well ride out for Texas if I let you leave here alone. Barton'll horsewhip me."

She stepped into the stirrup and swung her right leg over the saddle. "He'll do no such thing. I still run this ranch, not Yancey Barton. He's not my daddy. He's not ..." She gazed a moment at the young man through a sudden gush of tears that blurred her vision. Then grief hit her like a blast of north wind off the prairie, so hard that she swayed in the saddle. First her beloved father, now Cal. Who would be next? What payment did this vicious land demand before it gave in to be tamed?

"Oh, Ritter. Dammit," she said, and slipped from the roan's back. Her wobbly knees gave way and would have dumped her to the ground had the young man not been handy. He scooped her into his arms and carried her through the driving rain toward the house. All strength drained from her, and she allowed his action without comment.

For a long while after Ritter left, closing the door softly and silently, Charlie lay on the bed where he had placed her, his face red with embarrassment. Then she rose, woodenly removed her muddy boots that had left two big wet brown spots on the quilt, and brewed herself a cup of tea. A small fire crackled in the stove and she tossed in a few sticks from the woodpile against the wall before sitting down at the table to sip at the fragrant brew.

Memories of Cal washed over her. The way he used to scribble his poems on brown wrapping paper from the mercantile, hand them over to her so she could put music to the words. And then she would sing the tune for him until he had it memorized.

"Oh, Cal, dearest, how I'll miss that."

She finished the tea and leaving the cup on the table went to the bed and pulled out the music box. Winding it, she inserted a metal disk and snicked the lever. Chopin's Étude in E Major filled the room, and she closed her eyes, tears squeezing out from between the lids.

Bright, warm light struck the side of her face and she blinked into long rays of sunlight that had broken through the heavy clouds. Peering out the window she saw that the sun hung on the rim of the mountains to the west in a wide slat of blue sky.

Near sunset already. How had it gotten so late? Her reveries had put her in another world so that the dreary afternoon passed without her noticing it.

She gazed in silence as the orange ball slipped behind the purple peaks. Bright silver linings flared along the edges of a spatter of rain clouds; shades of lavender, pink, and gold frosted their bilious bellies and darkness crawled across the prairie. Frogs set up a chorus of song and an owl called to a distant echo.

Suddenly the cabin felt small and empty, and much too lonely. She opened the back door and leaned against the frame breathing in the cool clean night air. Moisture hung in spirals of fog, making Charlie think of one of the sonnets Cal had written about warm rains and riding trail. And how cowpokes living out under the wide, dark sky had a true appreciation for living that no one else could even imagine.

She had to get out, go somewhere where she could recapture that feeling, maybe sing a farewell to Cal.

Once it got dark Mitch circled a good distance from the ranch itself and doubled back to the ridge above the scattered buildings. He'd holed up during the rain and hadn't gone near the funeral. Anger over what had happened dwelt in him like a confined beast, eager to escape and wreak havoc. His supper of deer jerky grew thin so that his stomach growled an empty protest. He longed to sit at a table and tuck into a steaming plate of stew, chase it down with hot black coffee. He dismounted there on the ridge, his thoughts roaming like stray ponies, and dropped Jeb's reins to the ground.

Below in the cabin a figure passed by the lighted window.

He had to stop lurking around watching her like some kind of green kid. Better if he rode up and announced his intentions to lend a hand in this war with the colonel. He grinned at the thought, tried to imagine her reaction. He'd be lucky if she didn't hand him his head. And even if she didn't, she'd never believe he had changed sides. She would just think the colonel had sent him to worm his way into the enemy camp.

Approaching her had seemed the thing to do after

last night. He wanted to be the one she called upon, wanted to stand beside her and fight for her dream.

After a while she started playing that haunting, melancholy music that made him think of things best left alone. Of caressing soft, dew-moist flesh, of loving a woman who loves you back, of happy times long past.

To get under his skin even more she began to sing to the music that floated in the black stillness. Amazing how sound carried in these high meadows.

The moon had yet to rise, but the night was far from dark. Some nights out here were like that, and others were like someone had dropped a black velvety blanket over everything. It was the clouds, he reckoned, for they skittered across the sky dragging stars in their wake.

At first it wasn't Charlie he watched, but a furtive figure sneaking from the back of the bunkhouse. He couldn't make out who it was, but the sneaky critter was real careful not to be seen by the guards and was soon hightailing it on foot for a stand of pines just below where Mitch stood watch.

Going careful, Mitch sneaked in for a closer look and was scarcely in place behind a boulder before the sound of a walking horse disturbed him. The mysterious rider reined up and dismounted before he came into Mitch's sight, and then walked directly to where the other man waited.

Mitch dared go no closer, and he could only hear the murmur of their voices. Someone from the Houston ranch was up to no good, it would seem.

After several minutes of quiet conversation, the man who had ridden in led his horse away from the rendezvous and passed so close by Mitch on his way out that he couldn't help but see the silver belt buckle gleaming. He'd seen a buckle like that on only one man in these parts; the gunslinger Cross that the colonel had hired only days before. The same man Mitch was pretty sure had a hand in the killing of Cal Malone.

Now who from the Houston ranch would be fool enough to meet with this killer? Somebody making a deal? But what would they have to gain? The answer of course was money, pure and simple. The colonel had someone working inside, feeding him information, and he was paying him to do so.

But who? Not the foreman Yancey Barton, surely. And probably not that young wrangler. He was so crazy about the Houston woman he followed her around like a puppy dog with his tongue hanging down to the ground. Course that left quite a few men to choose from. He could tell enough about the man to know him if he saw him again.

Mitch was so deep in thought that he didn't see him leave, only realized he was gone when he heard someone else coming and peered out to see Charlie Houston picking her way along the path. Christ, what was this? A Saturday night barn dance?

Mitch stayed right where he was. He hoped the stallion didn't take it into his head to come looking for him. He should have tied him instead of just dropping the reins like that. But Jeb didn't take to being tied and sometimes tore up Ned getting loose.

He grinned. He'd do the same, he reckoned.

Charlie Houston meandered into the clearing, capturing his attention once again. Was that all she had to do, wander around in the middle of the night? And suppose that idiot Cross doubled back and saw her, decided to have himself a little fun.

He lost sight of her for a moment as she picked her way around an outcropping of sprawling juniper brush and melted into the deep shadows. Then he heard her singing in a clear and exquisite voice that seemed to come from a stand of spruce off to his left. He stepped cautiously into the heavy darkness beneath several of the giants, but despite his care dry pine needles crunched under his boots. Abruptly the song cut off. He could almost feel her listening and he remained still for a long time, until the muscles in his legs began to quiver from the stiff position. At last she started to hum, then went back to the ballad about some trail hand pining for his lost love and finding her in the stars.

He listened until she finished, afraid to approach her but unwilling to leave her there alone. Didn't she have any good sense? Out here making so damned much noise that anyone passing by would know right where she was?

Charlie stopped singing and wiped tears from her cheeks with the backs of both hands. Too much dying, too many tears. She sighed and rose from where she had perched on a boulder. As she turned to head back for the cabin, she caught a glimpse of someone darting between tree trunks just at the periphery of her vision. Quickly she judged the distance between her escape route back to the cabin and the threat. Perhaps it was one of her own men, circling the ranch on foot.

More than a little miffed, she stopped and shouted out. "Who is that? Ritter, is that you lollygagging after me again? Answer me now, you're scaring me. Come out and show yourself."

Mitch stepped from the darkness into the clearing. He could have remained hidden, but if he had she'd probably have kept hollering till the noise brought her guards. Then he might have gotten shot or been forced to shoot someone. It was better to show himself only to her.

He took off his hat and she recognized him immediately from the flare of white in his hair, as he'd hoped she would. The recognition didn't gain him the silent acceptance he'd counted on, though. Instead she called out his name in a wild, unsettling way, whirled, and ran directly into a massive clump of brush that completely entangled her. She yelped and fought, and that only got her in more trouble.

He was beside her immediately, grabbing at her. "Stop, stop struggling. You're only making it worse."

"Take your hands off me. Back away. What are you doing out here sneaking around? Ouch, dammit." A thorn ripped at her arm and she cried out. The more she struggled the more caught up she became.

"It's gooseberries. If you don't hold still they'll rip you to pieces." His hands fumbled at working her clothing loose from the vicious thorns.

Despite the gunslinger looming over her, Charlie stopped lunging about. Both sleeves of the flannel shirt were enmeshed, a vine clung tightly to the fabric across her breasts, more wrapped around her buttocks and thighs. Every movement brought sharp, biting pain somewhere else on her body, and she panted from the struggle.

"That's better." His voice hummed in her ear he stood so close. His fingers traced the vine across her breasts, knuckles brushing at her taut nipples.

She sucked in a breath, but remained very still. "Why do you keep bothering me?"

"I could stop, but then you'd be sort of caught up in things." He grunted and plucked away a thorn, feeling for another with fingers that trailed gently over her body.

A shiver darted through her stomach down low, and she caught her lower lip in her teeth. Much as the thorns hurt, his touch upset her equilibrium even more. The teasing tone of his voice surprised her too, for he didn't seem the sort. His nature was more harsh, uncaring, cold, or so she had thought.

His touch moved from one breast to the other and sent unwanted and thoroughly unexpected waves of longing straight to her core.

He felt the trembling shudder and mistook it. "Sorry, I know it hurts like hell. Almost through." He leaned down to get a better look at his work in the darkness and his hair brushed at her chin.

She sucked in a light breath. "Oh, dear goodness."

He stopped for a moment, leaving his hand where it was, the fingers lying ever so gently against her rapidly rising and falling breast.

"Please, take your hand away." Meant to be a command, the request came out delicately and not at all demanding.

He raised his head so that their mouths were on the same level, practically breathing each other's air. "Sorry. Am I hurting you?" It was a whisper, vague and raspy, like it wasn't what he really meant to say at all.

No answer would come to her, for the thorns that remained buried in her flesh didn't cause near as much discomfort as did the desire that exploded in her. She had only to move a scant inch and their lips would touch, and she did, disregarding a thorn that plucked at her arm.

Their mouths brushed for a split second that was so heady Mitch momentarily forgot what he was doing and leaned closer for a better taste. The shift put tension on the branch of thorns that had wrapped itself around her right arm and they dug in unmercifully.

She moaned, as much from the lost chance as the pain, and he went back to work with renewed concentration. At last he had the front of her shirt freed and went to work on the sleeve.

"One thing at a time," he muttered.

"What?" she asked.

"Never mind. There, okay, now turn this way." His voice trembled, but he managed to get a hold on himself to go to work on the length of a vine stuck firmly across her butt.

"How'd you get yourself in such a mess anyway?"

"Well, I didn't exactly do it to myself. If you hadn't come lunging up out of the dark like some night creature I wouldn't have run in the first place." She wiggled tighter against him when he reached around her.

"Hmmm," he said, and circled her waist with his other arm to hold her tight.

"What are you doing?"

"You don't know what I'm doing? It seems we've been at this long enough for you to have figured it out."

"Well, don't hug me so tight."

"Have to if I'm going to ... there, I think you're free." His voice sounded gruff and angry all of a sudden.

She lurched to get out of his reach only to find that one pant leg was still held firmly in the grasp of a thorny branch.

He clasped her once again around the waist. "Hold it, you're just going to make it worse. We're almost there."

"I can get loose myself now, if you'd just let go."

He did and stepped back. "Fine by me." The anger was definitely there now.

The hat he'd crammed back on his head kept her from seeing his face, even though her night vision let her make out his size and shape pretty well. She bent over to untangle her leg and a row of thorns planted themselves firmly across her buttocks, sticking deep into the jeans fabric to bite at her skin once again. She tried to jerk away and raked the back of her hand over another cluster of the vicious thorns.

Crying out as much in frustration as pain, she gave up and stood there trapped.

He did nothing.

"Well?" she said.

"What?"

"Help me."

"Oh. I thought you said—"

"Help me is what I said."

"Sounds like an order to me."

She sighed and pretended ignorance. "And you don't take orders except from our illustrious colonel. Look, I'd appreciate it if you would give me a hand here."

"I'd be pleased, Miss Houston, to give you a hand if you'll stop squirming and shouting like some sissy female."

"I am not . . . never mind, never mind. Go away entirely if you wish, leave me hanging out here till some wolf comes along and makes a meal out of me. That'd be more to your way of doing things, wouldn't it, Mr. Fallon? And just what are you doing out here anyway. Ouch, dammit!"

"You said that already," he said. "You ready to hold still, or do you have more to say? I'm here trying to save your . . . uh . . . well, your skin, and all you want to do is criticize. I haven't even heard a thank you, not one."

"Thank you? Thank you? I have no more to say," she replied, and tightened her lips together. If and when he ever got her loose from here, she would take great pleasure in smacking him good. She would double up her fist and hit him right in the mouth, see how he liked that, the smart-ass. But first, let him untangle her from this mess.

"Well, that's better. Being polite never hurt anyone."

She took a deep breath and closed her eyes. Damn smarty pants.

His hands worked all over her backside, loosening one thorn at a time. Leaning this way and that his body brushed up against hers, muscles lean and hard and enticing, and she was certain he was doing it on purpose.

When he shifted to one side to free the final thorn from her backside the slant of his jaw touched her ear and a puff of his breath stirred her hair. She shivered. He smelled like campsmoke and the deep woods, a whiff of leathery saddle mixed in, and his touch was definitely doing things to her she hadn't expected, especially under such extreme circumstances. She was furious with the man, scared of what had happened, suspicious of what he was doing out here so close to her home, and yet the gentle touch of his fingers, the patient way he went about extricating her from the thorns made her anything but frightened.

He kept uttering little syllables that weren't really words but were meant to be reassuring. Then she felt his hand under her arm so that the palm and thumb cupped the swell of her breast. An amazed "Ohhh" escaped her lips.

"Sorry," he murmured. "Dammit, if you'd hold still."

She squeezed her eyes shut. "I would if you'd stop ... if you'd stop." But she didn't want him to stop touching her, even disregarding the circumstances. She held very still, for the thorns had gouged deeply into the very tenderest of her flesh and the wounds were beginning to hurt badly. Tears ran from under her closed lids.

For an instant he stopped moving. "Don't cry."

"I'm not."

"Your tears are falling on my hands," he said very softly.

She sniffed, bit her lip. Deep down in her belly, where the fiery caress of the gooseberry thorns could not go, a longing stirred like coals fanned by a night wind. This man, this frightening man who seemed so gentle and so harsh all at the same time, threatened her sensibilities like none ever had.

He wanted to gather her up in his arms and tell her it was okay to cry when she hurt. He suspected all the pain wasn't coming from the thorns by the way she'd been singing so sadly earlier. He cupped her buttocks and pulled her gently toward him and away from the damaging bushes. She came close to him without objection. Her firm, soft breasts pressed against him. He drew in a deep breath and held her for a moment, forgetting the task at hand.

Dear God in heaven, if he didn't turn her loose soon he'd make a complete fool of himself. He wanted to kiss her not pry thorns out of her behind.

"What are you doing?" she asked, but he heard no reprimand in her tone.

Without answering he remained pressed against her, both arms holding her in a firm embrace. He closed his eyes and took a very deep breath, then stepped back. Letting her go left a hollow spot near his heart that ached with emptiness.

"Okay, if you don't start flailing around again, you'll be free at last." He spoke in a deliberately harsh tone. Damn her anyway, butting her way into his life when he'd had it all figured out.

Despite the tone, she didn't reply or offer to battle with him over his attitude. Her lack of fight caused him to feel sorry for her. A woman like her, put more or less at someone's mercy, must be awful uncomfortable. She was probably itching to lash out because of all the evil deeds she thought he'd committed. About some of them, she was right, but how could he convince her that he wasn't her enemy? And what the hell did he care, anyway? Caring was a good way to get a quick kick in the teeth. He wanted no part of that kind of pain, ever again.

With a tight grip on her upper arm he led her carefully out of reach of the wicked gooseberry bushes, then dropped his hands away as if they'd been burned.

She stood there for a long moment, regarding the hulking shadow whose face she already knew well even though she couldn't make it out. She rubbed at the fire burning her flesh, caused as much by his proximity as the long scratches dug by the thorns.

"You're fine now," he said hoarsely.

"Thank you." She began to shiver violently. "Please, I . . . I want to go to the house."

"I'll take you," he said, and grabbed her arm and began to drag her out of the shadows and into the open. There was no question of breaking away from the iron-hard grip. She just stumbled along beside him.

The moon peeked through racing clouds and illuminated everything: the umber dark trees, the stretch of meadow laced in pale ivory, a black horse that moved up on them seemingly from out of nowhere.

She stumbled again, tugged at his shirt. "Please slow down. What are you so mad about?"

He stopped and turned toward her. In that moment when he lowered his head to look down at her, she thought she saw moisture gleaming in his eyes. But surely not. She dismissed the idea.

"What are you doing out here alone in the middle of the damned night anyway? Is that all you've got to do? Traipse around in the middle of the night taking baths and causing Indian uprisings and getting yourself all caught up in thorns?" In one swift motion he swung her up in his arms and resumed the long stride, carrying her along easy as could be.

In her head she shouted at him to put her down, that she could walk by herself, but in the depths of her soul she embraced his warmth, his strength, his solidity. The beating of his heart in her ear, the male aroma, the touch of skin where his shirt parted down his chest, eased the pain buried so deeply within her.

There was no place to put her arms except around his neck where the softness of his hair whispered over her flesh.

He spoke no further, but kept right on walking. The black horse followed, his head nodding up and down right beside her feet. Neither master nor beast appeared to pay her any mind at all.

When he had deposited her at the back door from which she'd exited earlier, he broke the silence gruffly, "There, home without harm. Well, at least without much. You'd better put something on those scratches or they'll be sore in the morning. Good night, Miss Houston, and you're welcome."

"Fine, sir. And I'd like you to stop ... stop following me around." The lie tumbled out weakly, both of them knowing she didn't mean it at all.

Without honoring her with even a grunt for a reply, he mounted the horse with agile grace and rode away.

Chapter Nine

She slept in the arms of her lover, and awoke once in the middle of the night wondering who she was and where she lay, but his lips were at her breast there in that dream, and so she drifted back to him on mounds of pink clouds.

He held her in exquisite passion, one hand cupped between her thighs, lips tasting the sweet bud of each breast as if it were coated in honey.

She did not know who he was, perhaps he had no face, for he would not turn it to her, but kept it pressed to her flesh so all she could see was a fan of black hair spread over her like a dark angel's robe. There was a streak of pure white running through it. She wrapped her legs around his waist and he rose from their downy bed taking her with him into the ebony sky where he made love to her until dawn and then was gone, leaving her to caress silver moted beams of light.

She awoke to an empty bed crying huge tears that splotched her pillow.

The dream, though a vast improvement over nightmares of stampedes and death, left an unsettling longing she couldn't fulfill. She found herself wishing Mitchell Fallon would come through the door and finish what he had started when he carried her from the tangle of gooseberry vines.

To make matters worse, and despite the star-studded night, a dreary rain moved once more over the valley the next morning. Once she dressed and had breakfast, two leftover biscuits from the night before, she left the cabin and its lingering dream images and went to the barn. Today she would not be dissuaded from riding the range, and the ensuing argument with Ritter echoed much the same conversation they had carried on the day before when she had given way to her grief and let him win.

It would not happen this time, for she had to be on the move, not closed up in the cabin with desires she didn't understand and couldn't consummate.

When Ritter finally glared at her in helpless disgust, his every objection shot down, she took some pity on him.

"Don't trouble yourself about what Yancey will do to you. I give the orders around here, no matter what he and you might like to think. You'll stay here and mend tack, it's in horrible shape. And when that's done, there's stove wood to chop. And Crane could use some more firewood too, while you're at it.

"I'll ride the circuit, just like I told you. Yancey comes in, you tell him so." She stepped lithely into the saddle, tugged the roan's head around, and urged it forward into the dismal weather.

"Fool woman. I'm a blamed cowboy, not a greenhorn jingler." Ritter continued to mutter under his breath and turned to fiddle with the gray gelding's bit. "Her orders is everyone rides out in pairs, but she rises out alone pretty as you please. Can't blame me if she's scalped or hung for a rustler or gunned down by the colonel's men."

There would be hell to pay no matter what he did, and Ritter knew it. He figured the choice he had to make was to look out for her, so he remained back in the darkness of the barn until the thick soup of mist, fog, and rain swallowed up her lone figure, then he mounted and urged the gelding to follow.

Sometime later a third rider joined the bedraggled parade. Mitch Fallon had spent the night in his camp under the thick stand of spruce, and kicked his heels into the stallion's sides soon after Charlie plodded past him. He heard the second rider coming, the footfalls muted on the saturated ground, and retreated into the shadows to wait for his passage. It was that young boy everyone called Ritter. The one that dogged her every step. Mitch recognized the overgrown Montana Stetson that nestled low over his forehead. She had her a guard of sorts, and he admired the young man for his bulldog determination. The woman would probably hogtie him to a tree if she caught him following her. Mitch feared Ritter would not be able to protect her from the likes of a killer like Cross, though. When the huge gray horse and its diminutive rider disappeared into the murkiness, Mitch fell in at the rear of the procession. If she caught him she'd tie him up with the same rope as she used on Ritter, but it couldn't be helped.

After what Cross and Neddy had done to Cal Malone, and then watching the gunman's midnight rendezvous with one of her hands last night, Mitch wasn't taking any chances that the pretty owner of the Double H might be the next target.

Odd how he felt about her, and with no stake in this whatsoever, he still couldn't just ride away. That had all been settled the night before when he'd untangled her and then carried her to the cabin. Their lips and their bodies had touched, her tears had fallen on his flesh, and he had looked into her soul. It had taken every ounce of willpower he had to ride off and leave her at the door. What he had wanted to do was follow her inside and fold up around her on the bed, hold her close all night. Immerse himself in her bouquet of leather-scented sweetness, breathe the very air she did, caress her delicate wildness. Find out who she was, really. Explore the being that lay hidden deep down inside her. Maybe even show her his true self if she cared to look.

The fiery ranch owner had wormed her way into his life, and he couldn't dig her out with a spade. Maybe, just maybe, he didn't want to, even though thinking about the sheer impossibility of it tended to make him mad. There was certainly no percentage in sticking up for the underdog, he'd learned that a long time ago, yet he could do nothing else. It was much too late. He should never have laid a hand on her, nor gotten close enough to exchange breaths, to look into those cavernous eyes, to brush lips with her. God almighty.

Charlie paused several times to get her bearings in the gloom, other than that she kept moving at a pretty steady pace. Once she heard the harsh cough of a cow and realized she had ridden into a herd of grazing longhorns in the low-hanging mist. Each in turn raised a head, balefully regarding the intruder while they chewed the sweet green grass.

In spite of the poncho and wide-brimmed hat, she was soon wet clear through. Cold seeped into every pore so that she shivered. Better put up at Cal's ranch for the night and get a fresh start in the morning.

She expected no one to be at the ranch. There hadn't been time for Zeke to file a claim in Virginia City and return, yet a saddled pony stood hipshot at the hitching rail out front.

Surprised and a little cautious, she drew closer and saw that the saddle and bedroll were soaked as was the poor animal. His head drooped and rain drizzled from his velvety chin. The cow pony carried the Rocking R brand, and she recognized it as one Zeke was fond of riding. How had it gotten here? Maybe Zeke rode another mount. That still didn't explain this one.

Something was very wrong. No cowpuncher leaves his horse standing out in the rain until it's this wet, not with a barn so near. The black window openings of the small ranch house stared balefully at her. Empty places exuded a peculiar sense of abandonment, this one even more so, and she could almost hear Cal's ghost warning her to beware. With all that had happened recently, she feared dismounting and walking up on the place without taking a few precautions.

Her heart slammed into her throat as she imagined someone inside taking a bead on her, and she remained mounted thinking about what this could mean. Something had to have happened to this poor horse's rider. Something dreadful.

At last she swallowed hard and dismounted. Her heart wouldn't stop its thumping, and for good measure she took the Winchester out of its scabbard and jacked a shell into the chamber. Tying Belle beside the bedraggled cow pony, she crept as quietly as possible up the path to the porch. On her toes she went up the steps and slipped along the front of the house to a window to peek inside. Raindrops pecked incessantly on the roof and dripped onto the saturated ground, the only sound but for her own breathing and the thundering of her heart.

Easing to the door she reached out with one gloved hand to push it open. It creaked and she hunched her shoulders, waiting and holding her breath. Not the slightest movement or sound issued from inside. That was worse than a noise.

"Zeke?" she whispered through the open door. "You in there?"

Foolish thing to ask. There was no reply, and she gingerly put a toe against the door to swing it open farther. Inside something ran across the floor, squealing and making a terrible clatter. A shout escaped from between her clenched lips and she jumped backward, almost toppling off the porch.

"Holy cow," a man hollered from out of the mist at her back. "What the tarnation's going on, Miss Houston?"

Hands clutching at her throat, Charlie whirled. "Ritter, what are you doing here?"

The young cowboy vaulted from the tall gelding and double-timed it to her side. "What's going on? What happened?"

"Ritter, I thought I . . . never mind. Look, it's Zeke's horse, and he's been here a long time. Oh, Ritter, what do you suppose has happened?"

"You stay here. I'm just fixing to find out." He started to go in the door, then turned and pointed at her. "And I mean it, if you'll excuse me. Stay put!"

In this case, she was only too glad to obey.

Ritter shoved at the door, but something was holding it and he had to lay a shoulder into it hard to force the thing open enough to squeeze inside.

Zeke lay crumpled on the floor, blood drying around him in a great wide pool. His head was cocked back at a crazy angle and what Ritter could see of his face was covered in blood as well. He took hold of the dead man's shoulder and rolled him away from the door. When the body came to rest Ritter saw that Zeke had been scalped.

Foul-tasting bile poured into his mouth and he made a fist over his lips. He stayed hunkered there for a moment until his belly quit heaving, then he stood and removed his hat. Dirty savage Indians. As if they didn't already have enough trouble with the colonel and his rampaging, now they had the Cheyenne on the warpath. He knew some families of Northern Cheyenne were camped out over toward the

Bighorn River, Indians who thought nothing of venturing into range land to cut out a few cattle once in a while. A couple of them had even had the nerve to beg some beeves off Miss Charlie. Some of the hands had reported sightings of Sioux lately, renegades off the reservation in Dakota Territory.

"Ritter, what is it?" Charlie called from outside. "Ritter, please, answer me."

Before he could reply he heard approaching hoofbeats and a man's voice. "Miss Houston, you okay? What in hell's going on here?"

"Fallon! What is this, a camp meeting? Ritter, if you don't come out this instant, I'm coming in, orders or no."

"On my way," Ritter said, and his voice broke crazily so that he had to swallow and try again. "I'm coming out now."

He stepped onto the porch to see a tall man dressed in black striding forcefully up the walk, one large hand resting menacingly on the butt of a Colt .44 in a low-slung holster.

Ritter grabbed her arm and yelled, "Dammit, run, Miss Houston, that's one of the colonel's men."

She shook off the young man and swung around so that the barrel of her rifle pointed toward the intruder even though she held it loosely at her side. She regarded Fallon with cool disdain, not at all like the inner turmoil she felt.

Ritter darted a glance from one to the other. If he'd been armed, he would have drawn down on the scoundrel and shot him on the spot, but Miss Charlie just stood there with her Winchester dangling.

The gunman mounted the steps and ignored Ritter to question Miss Charlie. "Are you hurt? Who's in there?"

"Of course I'm not hurt, and I don't know yet. Let's

ask Ritter, shall we?" She turned and gave Ritter such a look that he cringed.

He hated to tell her about Zeke, but more than that he dreaded her wrath. It would all probably be directed at him, and he'd had nothing to do with Zeke's death. And why was she taking the appearance of the gunslinger so casually?

Miss Charlie and the stranger glared at him as if he had something to do with Zeke lying dead in there. He gulped, unable to say anything.

"I'll just go see for myself," she said, and started to push past him.

Ritter grabbed her arm. "No, no don't." He appealed to the gunman, not sure whose side he was on, but then the man took her other arm.

"It's probably best you don't go in there," he told her softly. "What is it, boy?"

"It . . . it's Zeke, Mr. Cal's foreman. He's been . . . he's been scalped." Ritter shivered uncontrollably and ran off the porch to upchuck in the bushes. He felt more than a little miserable, and wished he were back in the bunkhouse wrapped in blankets instead of standing wet in the rain and puking.

Charlie ignored poor Ritter. "Oh, dear God, dear God, no. What's happening? Why would they do this?" She tried to envision savage Indians, knives at the ready hacking away at the bloody scalp, but all she could think of were the soft brown eyes of Spotted Moon's wife, the child sleeping in her arms. This would mean trouble for the Indians, for sure. And the women and children would suffer the most.

She stumbled as if dizzy or disoriented, and Mitch wrapped his arms around her. Her breath came hot through his shirt and little tremors passed from her to him. He wanted to gather her up and carry her away to a warm, dry place where he could soothe her grief. He could think of nothing to say, so he patted at the back of her head and leaned his cheek down into the tangle of dark hair.

Dear God, he'd forgotten how good it felt to hold a woman in his arms. How soft and sweet they were. How helpless they could be.

"You probably did this." She hauled off and kicked him in the shin.

He let out a surprised "Ow" and stumbled away from her.

Whirling, she tried to push past and go inside the house.

Ritter grabbed her. "No, Miss Charlie, don't go in there. He didn't do it." He gestured toward the gunfighter. "You don't want to go in there. It was Indians, I promise you."

Fire in her eyes, she pointed a trembling finger at the cow pony still tied to the hitching rail. "When did you ever see an Indian leave a perfectly good horse behind? White men did this, and you can bet they're tied in with the colonel."

She was nearly sputtering with fury when she darted her gaze toward Fallon. Somehow, he was to blame for this. She just knew it. How could she have let him put his hands all over her the other night? How could he be so helpful and soft-spoken knowing what horrible thing lay in there?

"You'll do anything, won't you? Anything. How can a man like you live with himself? Well, you didn't have to kill Zeke. He was no threat to anyone, he just wanted to stay in the saddle and do his job. An honest man, he was an honest man, just like Cal."

She tilted her head to look up into his face, shout, "When are you going to kill me?"

He studied her intently, absorbing the hate that emanated from her like heat boiling from a prairie fire. He didn't blame her much, but he wished she didn't feel this way about him. He'd observed her in her most private moments when she thought she was alone. He'd held her nearly naked body in his arms, he'd picked thorns from that sweet flesh. What could be more intimate? He felt as if his soul was completely lost to her. There had to be a way he could make her believe that all he wanted was for her to be safe.

She had grown ominously silent, standing rigid with one hand clenched around that rifle and her shoulders thrown back. Though tears continued to run down her cheeks, she kept her eyes on him, not flinching or backing down. If he had been the man she thought he was, he would have killed her and the foolish boy right on the spot and ridden off. But she didn't yet realize that.

Damn her for getting inside him and making him feel he owed her or any of these other fools anything. And then turn around and accuse him of the killing.

With furious control he said, "No, I didn't kill the man inside, I didn't kill your friend, and I will not kill you. No matter what you think. You and this boy get yourselves back to your ranch before something happens you can't stop."

He nodded curtly and strode across the porch, the jingles on his spurs ringing merrily in the sodden air. Shoulders hunched, he waited for the bullet she would send into his back, but none came. He would only go so far as to be out of her sight, but no farther. Whether she liked it or not, he would not leave until this was over.

Without asking permission, he untied the poor drenched cow pony, led him into the bran, and unsaddled him. Before turning him loose he rubbed him down with a gunny sack. The tough little quarter horse made snuffling sounds and nudged Mitch on the back with his nose in a gesture of thanks as he worked.

"It's okay, boy. No one deserves to be left out in the cold and wet, not even a poor old horse." Finished with the chore, he strode out to his own mount, climbed into the saddle, and rode off.

He didn't look back to see if she watched him leave, but he had a hunch she did, damning him every step of the way.

Charlie's teeth chattered but she remained where she was, not moving an inch while the lowering mist swallowed Fallon. Maybe she could have shot him if he'd come at her with hate and malice in his green eyes. Gunned him down for the monster he was, but not this way, not a back shot. Those eyes had transmitted nothing of a killer. Sorrow perhaps, melancholy, confusion even, but no threat.

"I was going to stay here the night," she then told Ritter in a sad voice.

"Well, you can. I'll just move the body. I can put him in the barn." He was eager to please, do anything to help her, she looked so forlorn and lost with her hair all smashed down by wearing the hat in the rain all day and her skin gray with shock.

"Oh, no. No. I couldn't stay in there now. Not with . . ." She broke off and waved a limp hand toward the open door.

"Well, the barn then. It'll be dry in there and you'll be fine. I'll keep watch."

She reached out and touched his arm. "Thank you, Ritter. You're very nice, even though you do trail around behind me like some hound." Glancing around quickly, she went on. "You know I'd rather the Indians had done this than those awful men who work for the colonel. At least they have a reason for killing white men. Reckon he . . . I mean, he got here awful quick. Could have been just hanging around after . . . you know." Her head nodded in the direction in which Fallon had ridden off.

"Well, maybe, I don't know. I just can't figure a

white man doing something like that, but then a man will do some pretty awful things sometimes."

"What are we going to do . . . I mean, with the body?"

He raised his shoulders. "Maybe I ought to bury him. I could put him up on the hill with Mr. Cal." He arched his neck and stared up into the heavy clouds. "This looks like it ain't gonna quit very soon, and I hate to think of him just laying in there like that."

"Well, I guess that's best. I'll give you a hand."

She took a deep breath, dragging in the clean wet air that tasted of pine and mountain snows. She was through crying, it was a weak and feminine thing to do, and like Ritter had once said, she didn't do womany things. Before he could stop her, she jumped off the porch and ran to the barn, forgetting that her hat was still lying where it had fallen when Mitch Fallon wrapped her in his arms. Thinking of that, she felt hot all over. For just a moment, when Fallon had pulled her to his chest and laid his cheek against her hair, she'd almost lost all sense and forgotten who the man was.

It seemed every time they got together he did something for her.

Hair dripping she ran inside the barn and began looking for a shovel to dig Zeke's grave.

When the bolt of lightning struck later that night she was dreaming about the stampede that had killed her father. With tight fists she knuckled away the nightmare vision of St. Elmo's fire crackling across the horns of the charging cattle herd that had trampled him. Even after she came awake, the smell of burning hair lingered.

Despite the storm, the air in the barn was warm, and she could smell the steam off the horses, hear them breathing and snuffling in sleep.

The lightning strike appeared to signal the passing of the storm, for the rain on the roof let up and the intermittent flashes of light and rumbling thunder faded into the distance.

She sat in the hay for a moment, stretching her aching muscles, then crept through the velvety darkness to the door. A heavy bar held it shut, and she hoisted it, careful not to make any noise that would awaken Ritter. As the door swung inward she saw fire licking into the sky, throwing a crimson reflection onto the low scudding clouds. For a moment she was terrified, then as she stepped out into the rainwashed night, she realized that a huge Ponderosa pine had been split in half. The enormous jagged trunk left standing shot fire high into the sky. The heat from the flames touched her face and lit up the barnyard. Eerie shadows played with orange reflections in puddles of rain.

She felt strangely removed from reality, as if she walked within the confines of a dream in which she could do anything she wished without consequence. And indeed, perhaps she was still lying asleep in the hay.

He emerged from the shadows, appeared to simply materialize out of the intense blaze that leaped and danced at his back, and she fought an intense desire to go to him. He wore no hat or shirt. A gust of wind lifted his hair, whipping the white streak upward as if to join the flames.

Mesmerized, she waited for him to come to her. There was no fear in her, even though she thought there should be. She watched with amazement as her trembling fingers reached out to him. His eyes shot tiny flecks of red and yellow and he reached out a hand to meet hers, fingertips touching fingertips. She gazed into his face until a dark shadow fell over it as he came away from the firelight. This man with such acute sadness in his eyes quivered as he touched her.

Without hesitation she moved closer, into the emanating heat he'd absorbed from the fire. It washed through the cool air between them, encompassing her. He lifted her hand toward his mouth. She thought he would kiss it, but instead he placed her knuckles along his jaw and held them there.

She swayed, closed her eyes a moment. Dear God, she was so very tired of being alone.

He put his arms around her, gently at first, then enfolding her in an eager lover's embrace. Her fingers played through his hair, slightly damp from the rain and warm from the fire. His mouth on hers was hot and wet, the desire that shot through her as vivid as bolts of lightning left from the storm.

Groaning, he lifted her off her feet, held her so close she could feel the laddering of his ribs, the rise and fall of his breathing.

Perhaps she was indeed imagining it all, lying in the barn dreaming, but for the moment it was real. For that brief, ecstatic moment, she clung to a man who had come to her from a bolt of lightning, and she wanted nothing more in life than to be with him, experience in all its glory the extraordinarily keen sense of gratification. The world could have disappeared and she wouldn't have cared one bit at that moment. The ache in her heart eased at his touch and she wanted it all. Everything he had to offer, all he ever had been and ever was.

"Charlie Houston," he whispered into her mouth, his tongue lapping the velvety softness of her underlip.

He lowered her back to her feet then, took away his arms, and stepped backward. She blinked, and he cupped her face in both hands, leaned down, and with a feathery touch brushed her lips with his, then pulled away so quickly she had no time to react.

She said nothing, but only because she was
dumbstruck to find him gone as if in a pouf of dust-
devil cloud, leaving her to stare at the destructive fire
that rose like a pillar of flame into heaven. It might
well have swallowed him up, for all she knew. His
departure left her feeling as if she'd lost something,
and she stood there for a long time, tongue licking at
his taste, a faint pungency that reminded her of new
grass drenched in early morning dew.

The anger came almost as an afterthought, and she
wasn't sure who to aim it at. The man who had entered her life like a dark angel to steal her soul, or
herself, for being so dim-witted as to let a gunslinger
kiss her. Had she gone mad?

She turned her back on the crackling fire and raced
into the barn, her looming shadow dancing hugely in
front of her like an uncanny companion trying to warn
her of some dire destiny she had not yet dreamed
of herself.

Chapter Ten

With the barn door closed at her back, Charlie remained very still, allowing the darkness to soak up the pounding of her heart. Ritter snored softly, a small animal skittered into the far corner, and her heart continued to thump wildly in her ears. She wondered if it would ever slow down again.

A desire to lie with this dark devil of a man, feel his mouth caress her most sensitive, secret places, nearly overpowered her. She would open herself to his need, his manly, exquisite, frightful desires. She shook her head so hard lights flashed behind her lids.

"Stop this, stop it now! This is not a man you can trust. Foolish, foolish woman. Wake up."

She remained still until her eyes grew accustomed to the inky blackness inside the barn, then made her way back to the bedroll. Instead of sleeping, she greeted the man in black who returned to haunt her.

Gently she moved the tips of her fingers along the ridged scar above his eye, opened her mouth eagerly to his, tasted the flavor and felt the texture of his sensuous lips. So real, so like life that she shivered and slipped her cold hands between her thighs to warm them in the heat gathering there.

Mitch sat on the porch of the ranch house after Charlie Houston vanished into the barn. He could still feel her mouth under his, satiny smooth and slightly open in surprise. He could have had her then if he'd wanted, but hell, he didn't even know why he'd kissed her. Bedding her should be the furthest thing from his mind, yet in that storm-charged instant he'd almost swept her up and carried her inside the barn to lie with her, take her by force if need be. Some things were not meant to be taken roughly, though, and a man had to know when to use brute power and when not to.

He wished again that he had ridden off to Idaho when he had the chance, then immediately changed his mind. By now he would be in the mountains, and she would be rushing headlong toward disaster. The colonel would have what he wanted.

He gazed into the night sky a long time, thinking about that. He could stop this. And what he would have to do wouldn't be much worse than anything he'd done in the war. Celia had done her best to make a peaceful man out of him, driving away the demons. But they returned in full when he held her bloody body in his arms. Not much in his life had ever made any sense, and it seemed that each time he came close to fulfilling a desire, it was snatched away.

All he had to do was eliminate Charlie Houston's enemies. He slipped the Colt from its holster and ran a thumb over the cylinder, cocking back the hammer so it would roll freely. He could kill every one of them, these men who wouldn't stop this madness. He could do that for her, and then ride away.

Gently he let the hammer back down and sat for a long while with the gleaming pistol lying across his lap.

If he allowed his feelings to rule, he would love her and lose her, and he couldn't bear that to happen. He might have to die to protect her, and that he could do, but he couldn't watch a woman he loved die. Not again. He just couldn't.

With trembling fingers he touched the ridged scar above his eye. In the darkness flashed memories of that dreadful day, Celia and the babe sprawled in the street in Bismarck. Throwing himself at first one, then the other of her attackers, beaten until he was bloodied and on his hands and knees. There were too many of them, and those good citizens who stood by simply watched. Groggy, dizzy, out of his mind, he gathered his dead wife and child into his arms. Covered with their blood and his, he rocked and moaned and cursed his own weakness, his inability to protect them. Only then, when he could fight no longer, had one of the men put him out of his misery, sending him into oblivion with a vicious blow from his gun.

He came to much later lying on a table in a saloon in that horrid town. A man who said he was a doctor leaned close and stitched at the wound above his eye. In the background a piano tinkled, a woman shrieked in delight.

The doctor quieted Mitch's desire to get up and put his fist through a wall or someone's face. "Hold still while I sew your head back together. Wonder they didn't kill you, son."

When Mitch struggled, cried out her name, the doctor called for help to hold him down while he finished. He wet a cloth with whiskey and cleaned around the wound that ran from his patient's eyebrow up into his scalp, then wrapped a bandage firmly around Mitch's head.

"Lay there awhile before you move around." The doctor nodded at the two men, and they let go Mitch's shoulders and glided out of his sight. He felt disoriented and weak, his vision blurry. No one paid any more attention to him, just left him draped over the table like a hunk of meat.

And how he'd railed at them all, like some kind of madman, finally struggling to his feet to stagger around in the dismal place, bumping into tables and chairs and customers until they just sort of herded him outside where he stumbled to his knees in the dusty street. No one gave a damn what happened to him.

"Where are they?" he screamed then, and raised his arms toward a distant, uncaring sky.

But he never found out what the townspeople had done with the bodies of Celia and Fawn. He didn't remember much about the next few days. He awoke one morning lying beside his horse in a ditch out in the Badlands, and didn't know how he had gotten there or what had happened. It was weeks before any of the memories came back, and when they did he wished like hell they hadn't.

Sitting there on the porch steps, he dragged his thoughts away from those awful days to think about the woman he'd held in his arms only minutes earlier. He gazed into a night sky ablaze with starlight. Cool air from the mountains chased after the passing storm and kissed his cheeks. Tomorrow would be a pretty day. Too pretty a day to die. For a good long while every day had been a perfect day to die. He examined his newfound feelings, his desire to live, and was awed.

He rose, stretched both arms high above his head, and took a deep breath. Something passed from him, no stronger than a sigh, a touch of night wind, but it left behind a refreshing release from the bondage of the past.

The band of Cheyenne came just at daybreak, when silver and gold streaked the rainwashed sky into a gleaming pearlescence. A tall and impressive brave led them—there were no more than a dozen, some of them very young.

Mitchell had dozed propped up against the porch post, and stumbled to his feet when he heard the muffled hoofbeats. Both arms out away from his body so they could see he wasn't going for his Colt, he waited.

The Indians were painted for war, as were their horses, and Mitchell's mouth grew dry. Word was that Custer and his Seventh Cavalry were in Montana to take care of the Indian problem. Once and for all, some said. There'd been a skirmish up on the Little Powder River early in the spring while snow still dusted the ground. Mitch dreaded what would eventually come of the army's plans. Would Celia's people, the mighty Sioux, at last be driven from the face of the earth forever?

He greeted the Cheyenne with cool politeness. Perhaps one of them spoke English.

His "Good morning" was considered before the Indian in the lead raised a hand and halted his pony. The rest drew up just behind him and spread out in a jagged line.

"I am Spotted Moon."

"I am Fallon."

The Indian tilted his head toward the ranch house. "We heard that this man was killed by the whites."

For a moment Mitch was confused. His thoughts were on the murdered and scalped Zeke, but immediately he realized they must be talking about Cal Malone.

"The man who owned this ranch is dead, yes," he said.

"No man owns land. Land is for The People, as far as the eye can see." Spotted Moon paused a moment to consider. "We Cheyenne, the Dakota, the Absarakas, the Crees and Shoshones, the Burned Thigh Assiniboines, the Waist and Skirt People. If we fight it is among ourselves for coup. The whites have no right to the honor of battle with The People."

Mitch nodded. "Yes, I understand."

The brave went on in his deliberate English, as if Mitch had not said anything. "Long Hair drove us from our land, and now he is coming here. Soon we

will fight with *Hi-es-tzie,* but do not think he will win
this last great battle. Our Chief Lame White Man joins
Crazy Horse and Sitting Bull. There will be no more
white man on our lands as long as the sun rises."

Mitch knew the Cheyenne was referring to George
Armstrong Custer when he spoke of Long Hair and
Hi-es-tzie. And he dreaded what would happen. The
vast tribes of the Sioux, whom this Indian referred to
as the Dakota, had moved with these people from the
Black Hills reservation to the Powder and Bighorn
River country a couple of years back after Custer
blazed the infamous Thieves Road that led to the dis-
covery of gold in Dakota Territory. Custer had tangled
with the Indians on more than one occasion, had
fought with Sitting Bull twice back in '73.

Who was at fault really mattered little, for Mitch
judged that the Indian would soon be destroyed. It
was the only way the white man could survive. And
survive he would.

But he didn't deny Spotted Moon's claim, he simply
stood there regarding the proud and fearsome Cheyenne brave and waited for what would come next.

Just at that moment, the thing he had prayed
wouldn't happen did. The barn door burst open and
out came Charlie and Ritter.

"Spotted Moon," the woman called, and ran to the
Indian at the head of the band.

"Split Skirt, it is good to see you."

"What are you doing here?" Her quick eye took in
the war paint and she thought of Zeke and his hideous
death. Had the Cheyenne finally decided that peace
would not save them and scalped poor Zeke in there?
Perhaps they had killed Cal, the braves were armed
with breechloaders and magazine rifles. Though she
doubted her wandering suppositions, she felt a tingle
of fear standing there gazing up into the fathomless
dark eyes that reflected the bravery of a mighty na-

tion. At the same time, she was cannily aware of the presence of Fallon, though he hadn't spoken directly to her.

"You are a friend to The People," Spotted Moon said. "We wish to tell you that we will soon join together over there." He raised his arm straight and stiff and pointed across the rolling plains toward the timbered mountains of the Bighorns and the river the Indians called Greasy Grass.

"I wish you would return to the reservation, Spotted Moon."

"We cannot. They take our ponies, they take our guns, and we have nothing, and now they ravage our land. It is enough. We will fight, and you must not get hurt. Split Skirt, you have fed my people, not because you were afraid but because you have a spirit within you.

"Once I helped the white man to find his way, and he taught me to speak his words. Now I tell you that this is the last time I will allow the white man's words to roll from my tongue."

The Indian crossed his arm over his chest, fist touching the place where his heart beat, as if saluting her, then he emitted a bloodcurdling yell. The entire party replied in kind, kicking her ponies into motion.

For a long while after the braves rode out of sight Charlie stood with her hands held stiffly at her sides. Finally she said, "They will die. They will all die."

"They deserve it," Ritter muttered. "Look what they did to old Zeke. And who knows, maybe they even killed Cal. There's going to be a lot of bloodshed. Miss Charlie, I wish you would just ride back to the ranch."

While Ritter spoke, Mitch studied Charlie, awe-stricken by her compassion for a people she scarcely knew. She kept her eyes on the departing braves until they were nothing but a lingering cloud of dust, and he saw the sadness in her features. If she became too deeply involved in this Indian problem, then she would face more danger than she already did from Colonel Dunkirk.

He struggled to tell her so. "The Dakota are a proud people, I think they've been pushed as far as they'll push. Old Crazy Horse and Sitting Bull aren't gonna back up anymore. At some point, they're going to turn and fight. I hope that idjit Custer realizes that.

"We'll see plenty of blood shed here by the colonel and his bunch too. For that reason, Miss Houston, I think your hand here is right. You should go back to your ranch and hole up if you refuse to sell out and leave. I'm afraid the colonel is out to destroy you and all the others like you. And he's only just started."

Charlie listened to his words with a heart heavy as death. This man, her enemy, her nemesis, both attracted and frightened her. She whirled, eyes swimming in tears. "And why would you care? Your gun is paid for by the brute. For all I know you're just following me around to keep track of me for the colonel."

Mitch settled his black hat down carefully on his head. "Nope, that isn't so. Not anymore, but I don't expect you to believe that. I'll just get my horse and ride, if you'll excuse me. I quit the colonel when that animal Cross killed your friend Malone. I don't much care if you believe me or not, but I do wish you'd believe me when I say your life is in great danger.

"Someone on your ranch is dealing with Cross, and if you don't find out who and put a stop to it, you don't stand a chance. You may not anyway.

"Why don't you go back down south to your people, Miss Houston? This is no place for a well-born lady like you. Go before this land is drenched in blood, and some of it yours." He turned on his heel and took great long strides toward the barn.

Charlie shouted after him. "I won't leave, this is where I belong. We've sent for the marshal."

Mitch raised his shoulders and halted. She was one stubborn woman. He gave it one more try, turning to face her. "Listen to me. The territorial marshal has more feuds and fusses to see after than can be handled in this country. Hell, it'd take two months just to ride over half of it. For the most part they'll let the vigilantes take care of justice in these parts, and you and I both know who controls the local vigilantes. As for the army, they've got their hands full fighting the Indians right now. You can expect nothing from them. What do they care about a small range war? The colonel has hired men who are nothing but wild animals running on instinct."

Trapped by a sudden inexplicable anger, Charlie ran toward Mitch. "And what are you, Fallon, but an animal?" she hissed.

The heat of her wrath washed over him like a brutal summer wind off the prairie, and he batted his eyes. He was surprised he didn't stumble backward under her attack. Instead he turned and strode briskly to the barn where he saddled the black and rode out, paying little attention to the direction in which he headed. It happened to be north, and it wasn't long before he came upon a herd of cattle carrying the Circle D brand. Reining the black's head to the right he swung back toward the east and the Double H Ranch. He might just manage to save Charlie Houston in spite of her bullheadedness.

Despite earlier plans to the contrary, Charlie rode back to the ranch after her disturbing meeting with Mitchell Fallon and the band of Cheyenne at Cal's ranch. The ever-faithful Ritter tagged along.

They rode on in silence for a while, Charlie contemplating the morning's happenings. Finally she asked,

"Do you put much stock in what Fallon said about someone at the Double H being in cahoots with the colonel?"

"Nah. I figgered he's just trying to draw attention away from his own self. We might have asked him just how come he showed up so quick after we found Zeke's body."

She nodded. "Or for that matter how come he's always conveniently around when something happens. You'd think a man working for the colonel would ride with the colonel's men, instead of hanging around my place all the time. Every time I turn around there he is." And sometimes in a most startling way, she thought but didn't say, remembering the night before when he'd literally walked out of fire.

Ritter studied her overlong. "Oh, is that right? Like when?"

Quietly she changed the subject. "Do you think the Indians are really going to fight?"

"I wouldn't be surprised. And I reckon it's time we done something about the problem. It don't seem to be possible to live side by side with them. They just keeping stealing cows and horses and ragging folks."

She reined in and gazed out across the rolling valley toward the distant peaks, shadows of purple and deep blue in the dusk. "Can't much blame them for wanting to keep this beautiful land."

"Nor us either," Ritter replied. "We might ought to get moving. If it's true what them braves said, there'll be war parties about. It wouldn't do to get caught out after dark."

Yancey Barton rode into the Double H late that same evening not long after Ritter and Charlie arrived. Ritter's version of Zeke's death, that the Indians had done it, and Charlie's vehement denial, were met with some ideas of his own.

"Now, Miss Charlie, you know you've always been

a mite partial to the red man. You sure you ain't giving him the benefit of the doubt."

All three had gathered eagerly around the cook fire to fill their plates with helpings of Crane's delicious rabbit strew. Charlie ate in silence and waited for Yancey to continue.

He did. "Ritter saw him scalped, plain as can be. It was some of them wild Cheyenne, no doubt about it. They've been off the reservation from over Dakota Territory for years now. And it sounds to me like it's all about to come to a head. They've got their backs against it, they'll turn and fight, and if you ask me it's about time the army took care of the problem once and for all."

She eyed him critically. "And you've always hated the Indian. He couldn't do anything right, as far as you're concerned."

"It's a known fact they ain't any good Indians less'n they're dead, and you know that. This country'll be better off when they're wiped out."

"What about the women, Yancey, and the babies? Little babies? How can you say that?"

"Those little babies grow up into big bad Indians that'd just as soon scalp you as look at you. Besides, it don't look like we'll have to worry overmuch too long. There's a lot of talk that the army is moving on them. They're coming up from Fort Fetterman and from out west at Fort Ellis. That foppish Custer will be in on it, you can bet. The government's fed up with dealing with these red savages breaking the law. They belong on a reservation or, better yet, dead."

A shudder passed through her and she stopped eating. Even the delicious stew didn't stand a chance against nightmarish visions of the massacre of families such as those she had visited in Spotted Moon's camp. It would be bloody and brutal and she hated to think about it. She hated too the way Yancey spoke of those people, as if they weren't even human, though it did echo how most white folks felt.

The more she thought about his words, the more upset she became. The idea that little Indian babies would soon be massacred by a bunch of soldiers armed to the teeth was too much to bear.

She decided to ride over and speak to Spotted Moon's family, try to talk them into going back up into Dakota Territory to the reservation before something terrible happened. It would be best not to tell Yancey or Ritter where she was going. She finished her meal, then went to the house.

Just before dawn, with the sky glowing a metallic silver not yet color-washed by the sun, she sneaked out the back door. She had staked Belle out in the scrub pine the night before so Ritter wouldn't spot her leaving and tag along. The way he felt about Indians, he would be no asset and might actually cause trouble for her. She left a note that she had gone to visit the McGrew and Burris ranches to the north to discuss the threat Colonel Dunkirk posed.

The day unfolded serenely in lavenders and pinks and golds and found Charlie well on her way. A gentle breeze stiffened as the sun came up, blowing from the southwest to caress her cheeks. A few times she thought she smelled smoke, but for the first few hours of her trip saw nothing but an occasional skittery rabbit, some distant high-flying birds, and a scurrying lizard. Along about noon she stopped for lunch near a spread of juniper thick with blueberries.

Mitch almost rode up on her out on the little rocky flat, but her roan kicked up some loose stones that warned him just in time to keep that from happening.

When she rode on he was not far behind. Where in God's name was she going?

During the afternoons the roan climbed a long, steady rise that topped out abruptly, the panorama below bringing Charlie to a halt. Across the wide expanse of rolling valley cut by the Little Bighorn River was camped the biggest gathering of Indians she'd ever seen.

Dear God, what were they up to?

She remembered what Spotted Moon had said, the words of war that she had taken almost lightly because she never truly believed the Indian would turn and fight when he saw the huge army of the white man. She'd always thought they would just pick away at isolated groups of whites, and eventually those that were left would settle peacefully on the reservations. But this. This was an army of Indians, thousands of them. They were certainly not just a few Cheyenne families like she'd seen in the spring. It was a camp of gigantic proportions, the settlement sending up a pall of smoke that hung thick in the valley.

This time Mitch did ride up on her.

She jerked her mount's head around and confronted him. "What in the Good Lord's name are you doing still following me around?"

Mouth open to reply, his glance moved beyond her shoulder and he said in hushed awe, "Oh, dear God."

The admiration in that uttering caused her to turn once again to behold the magnificent sight.

Black dread then struck him speechless. Here they were, the last of a magnificent people, finally pushed as far as they would push. Ready to fight, ready to die. His gut tingled with the fearful knowledge. He wanted to ride out across the prairie, waving his hat, shout a warning that they must leave, go back to the reservation where they would be safe. But all he could do was stare in total fascination at the mighty force.

Finally the spell was broken, and he nudged Jeb with his heels. It was as if he no longer even knew Charlie was there. He rode to the very rim of the rise and stood in the stirrups to get a better view.

"That Cheyenne was right, I guess," he said then, so softly she had to strain to hear him.

Haranguing him about following her would do no good, Charlie decided, so she asked, "Are those Cheyenne?"

"Lord, no. Well, maybe some, but you are looking at the biggest gathering of Sioux you'll probably ever see in one place in your lifetime, maybe ever. I'd bet Crazy Horse himself is down there, and the Hunkpapa chief, Gall. Aren't they magnificent?"

She dragged in a breath, trying to see what he saw. And yes, they were magnificent and quite terrifying.

Fearful of taking her eyes off the Indians she cast a quick look toward him. "How do you know so much about the Sioux?"

"My wife . . ." He didn't finish, but turned to meet her gaze with the same profound green expression she'd seen before. Like looking through moss into a bottomless pool of icy clear water.

"Wife?" She whispered the word and wet her lips, suddenly wanting a drink from the canteen hanging near her knee, but she couldn't look away from Mitchell Fallon. For he stared past the Indians into a place she sensed no longer existed, and whatever he was thinking eased the harsh lines of his rugged face into response. The expression softened the definition of his lips so they were no longer drawn tight. He was thinking about someone he loved.

A bright memory struck her, of that full lower lip, moist and insistent against hers when he came at her out of that fire like some apparition. It had been almost like being seduced by the devil. But now, catching him in this unguarded moment, she remembered only the pure, intense pleasure. She felt herself flush and tried to cover the embarrassment with a question.

"What do you suppose they're up to?" she asked

in a whisper. She wanted to say, tell me about your wife, but didn't.

"What?" He came away from wherever he'd been, once again the hard-bitten Mitchell Fallon. Tense, somber, and ready to face the enemy. "Waiting for the army, I'd say. Waiting to fight and die."

"Well, shouldn't we tell someone?"

"Who? God, look at that."

"Well, someone. They'll butcher them."

"They're ready for battle, no doubt about it."

"Fallon, listen to me. We can't let the army ride into this."

"Why not?" He spat out the words. "This is their last chance, don't you see that? Why would we want to ruin it for them? Let them have what little glory there is left. Let them die in an honorable way without our interference, not starve to death on some damned reservation."

"There are so many of them. You're talking as if the Indian will lose. How can you think that, with so many of them down there? And what's honorable about dying?" Charlie's horse danced sideways and she gentled her.

"What's honorable about stealing their land and sending them to live in some godforsaken place that we'll take away from them soon enough if we see fit?"

She opened her mouth to argue some more before she realized that he was voicing her opinions, the ones she'd come to Montana with, the ones her father had espoused, the ones she'd only yesterday been using against Ritter and Yancey. Why should she argue with Mitchell Fallon just because of who he was?

"I'd always hoped we could all live here," she said, and spread one arm wide so that the roan half stepped again. "There's so much land. So much. Just look at how much."

He laughed, a brutal, hard sound that grated on her

ears. "White men can't even get along with each other. We just fought a war, brother against brother, because we couldn't get along.

"And them down there. Hell, they fight with each other all the time over one thing or another. What makes you think we can live side by side with an entirely different culture? Best to get it over and done with, not prolong the agony. They'll meet their destiny just like we'll one day meet ours."

She gaped. A man like him, speaking of destiny and scruples. She'd never expected it.

"Well, I'm going to ride down to ... to ..."

"Leave it be. You don't even know if the army is on its way. That idiot Custer wouldn't believe you if you could find him and warn him."

"Yancey came back last night, he said Custer is riding in with troops, and some others too."

He shrugged. "We could stay and watch. It'll be a fine battle."

"How can you be so cold?"

"Cold? I watched my Sioux wife die because there wasn't a white man in town who would stand up for her, nor me when I tried to save her. Why in hell should I care what happens to a few soldiers. If they'd done their jobs, this wouldn't be happening in the first place.

"Now, I'd suggest if you don't want to somehow get caught up in this mess, you'd better just ride away." Green fire flashed from his eyes that were no longer peaceful or still.

She took up her reins in one hand. Fallon's wife was dead, and he had loved her. "And is that what you're going to do too? Just ride away?"

"No, Miss Houston, I think I'll ride on down there and join the Indians. Might be fun to see how many whites I can kill before one gets me."

"You're mad, stark raving mad."

"Probably," he said, then rose in his stirrups and whacked the huge black stallion across the rump.

Tears filled her eyes as she watched the man and horse tear down the incline in a straight, unwavering line toward the encampment of Sioux. She wanted to follow, she wanted to shout at him not to go, not to die, but all she could do was swallow past a dry lump in her throat and watch a trail of dust follow him across the rolling prairie toward the camp. It was only later that she thought she never did find out what he was doing following her, but by then it didn't seem to matter.

He found Celia's brothers in the camp, the two of them painted for war in brilliant streaks that disguised the amiable natures he had always known in these men. Across their stoic faces slashes of black and red somehow made of them brutal savages, just like the white men believed they were. Mitch knew better, but he found his brothers-in-law far past caring about anything but this one final encounter.

Though they spoke of destroying the white man once and for all, Mitch sensed beneath their words of bravado the knowledge that this would simply begin their own destruction. He thought, though, that they had no idea of how bad it would get before it was over. Perhaps he didn't either.

He bid them farewell just as night fell, embracing each in turn and saying the words Celia had taught him, the words that had no translations to the white man's tongue. He would meet them again in another place, where the spirits guarded his wife and child at this very moment.

When he rode away, the taste of futility lay on his tongue like ashes from the cold fires of another time.

Chapter Eleven

Word about the massacre at the Little Bighorn reached the Double H Ranch Monday sometime before noon. Tim Lawrence, one of Duffy McGrew's hands, raced in on a lathered horse, leaping off before the animal came to a full halt. Charlie was down at the corral watching Ritter work with an unbroken bronco. The sound of pounding hoofbeats raised goose bumps across her shoulders. The way things had been going she expected the worst. Someone else must be dead.

Even as she and Ritter ran to meet the man, she dreaded to hear what he had to say. Nothing could have prepared her for the horrible news.

"It's them savages. They've done killed the army. Custer's dead, they're all dead. My God, you should see it. Dead soldiers and dead Indians and dead horses, all piled everywhere, and this one lone horse standing in the middle of it. Just standing there like he didn't know what happened. Leather Norse from the Burris ranch rode up on it. Says he could still hear the blasts of gunfire echoing in the air. Me, I doubt that, but you know old Leather.

"Army's got the rest of them savages pinned down, or vice versa, who knows. Leather, he didn't stick around to find out. He lit out, you can bet he did, soon as he seen it. Plumb turned his stomach, and him at Bull Run too."

Her knees wobbled, threatened to buckle, and she grabbed Ritter's arm for support. She couldn't speak as the boy put his hands on his knees and gasped for air so he could go on.

"The rest is coming," he panted.

She shot a look of panic toward Ritter.

The young man grabbed the lanky rider's arm. "What do you mean, Indians are coming? Are they going to kill us all?"

"No ... no. The army, a whole 'nother column of 'em riding south down the Bighorn," he said. "Goin' to finish them Sioux off. Ever' last one of 'em. So Leather said. Word is they're gonna kill the Indians till they ain't a one left, not man, woman, nor child. They massacred Custer and the Seventh. What do you expect? It was Gall, they say. Gall and Crazy Horse."

She remembered Fallon mentioning both names. She wondered if he was still at the Sioux camp when it happened. And everyone dead. Surely that wasn't right. All those families, women and babies. Dear God in heaven. Spotted Moon's child, the child she'd held in her arms, kissed the soft cheek, nuzzled the soft down of his dear head. Tears rolled silently down her cheeks. She wanted desperately for someone to put their arms around her, comfort her. It was hard sometimes to be strong.

A shiver passed through her, and she straightened, turned back to the issue at hand, and tried to quiet the boy.

"Settle down, that's enough. Somebody, take this man's horse to the barn and cool him off."

While one of the hands who had raced up to hear most of the story led the horse away, Charlie and Ritter took the excited young man to the porch steps, sat him down, and fetched him a cool dipper of water.

Tim swallowed a few gulps, shook his head. "You shoulda seen it. My God." He drank some more. "A bunch of us rode on down there first thing this morning. Lord, I ain't never seen nothing like it in all my borned days."

The boy was all of seventeen, and the remark under other circumstances would have been humorous. But uttered thusly in the midst of such heartrending news it only served to sound poignant.

"Well," she said after a moment. "I guess they got what they wanted." She tried not to think again of the innocent victims of such senseless violence.

"What?" Ritter asked vaguely.

"Oh, just something someone said to me about the Indians dying honorably in battle rather than starving on some reservation."

Ritter made a rude noise and went to refill the water dipper.

Nervous chatter finally muted, Tim hugged his knees and stared off into space, as if contemplating the horrific scene he'd witnessed.

"Did you know Mitchell Fallon?" she asked, and tried to keep her tone noncommittal.

"Who?"

"That gunslinger Colonel Dunkirk hired. The one with the white stripe in his hair."

"Don't reckon I did, ma'am," Tom said in a trembly voice. "Heard talk of him, though. Why?"

She gazed off in the direction of the Little Big Horn. Dear God, suppose he had meant what he said and had remained with the Sioux and been killed? But then the boy said it was Custer and his men who were all slain. Some of the Indians survived, at least till the rest of the army caught up with them. Well, it was useless to worry. After all, there was no reason for her to have an interest in the fate of a gunslinger. Was there?

She got up from the step and walked out across the dusty yard hugging herself. Tears filled her eyes once again and she let the warm drops run unheeded down her cheeks. Oh, the stupidity of it all. Men and their deadly games.

Ritter caught up with her before she reached the barn. "Miss Charlie? Tim there, he's plumb tuckered and no one has rode to tell the rest of the ranchers hereabouts, just them up north. I think someone should ride out. Tim says that Leather wanted him to ride on to Miles City, see what news there is of the army."

She lowered her head, keeping it turned away from him while she wiped her wet cheeks. "And you want to do it?"

"Yes. Well, I mean, someone should. It's not like I'd be leaving you here alone. There's Slate and P.J. and Crane in case something happens."

She chuckled bitterly. "If those Indians decide to massacre every white man in this territory, no two or three cowboys will stop them. You know what? I think I'll just ride with you. Let the boys watch over the place. We can ride back out tomorrow. I'm curious too just what's going on other places. Let's get saddled up."

For once, Ritter didn't object like he usually did when she made her own decisions. He just nodded and went with her to the corral to fetch a couple of horses. They wouldn't, after all, be riding anywhere near the battle. Ritter wished he could ride out and watch awhile, and he might just do that once he got Miss Charlie safe in Miles City. This idea of hers was a good one. For a change, he wouldn't have to watch every move she made to keep her safe. Wonder she didn't want to ride out and watch the army whip them red savages. She clearly had something else on her mind, though.

It was late before they arrived in Miles City, though they didn't tarry at any of their stops to warn sodbusters and ranchers along the route. The town was crowded and afire with the wildest of rumors.

They tied their horses at a crowded hitching rail and Charlie went to see if she could find a place to spend the night. Ritter headed for the Powder Keg, which was bulging so that he could hardly shove his way through the swinging doors.

Bits and pieces of conversation bounced around as he made his way to the bar, dodging an occasional elbow or boot heel or sloshing beer mug.

"Hear tell they massacred every white from Dakota Territory all the way here."

"Man ain't safe in his own bed when a whole army can't stop a few piddling red savages."

"Few. Few? Some say they was ten thousand of them out there, hiding and laying in wait, and Custer, that idjit who can't find his own behind to put on his pants, just rode right into it. Him and fifty men."

"Fifty? I heard more like three hundred and fifty."

"Well, I ain't gonna go count the bodies. Are you?"

"Guess they got back at him for Sand Creek, huh?"

"And the Washita too."

"Them was Cheyenne."

"Well, fool, they's Cheyenne with them Sioux. Been here awhile, just waiting."

Ritter ordered a whiskey and leaned on the bar.

The town was a beehive of activity. The excitement of the battle between Custer and the Sioux had sure brought everyone running. Charlie wondered how long it would take to get something to eat and headed up the street. If nothing else, she'd buy something in the general store, if there was anything left.

Mitchell Fallon hadn't joined the crowd at the Powder Keg Saloon. When word had reached Miles City of Custer's defeat at the hands of Gall and Crazy

Horse and all those Sioux and Cheyenne, he had spent some time riding the trail alone under the vast dark sky.

It was a warm, sensuous night, the kind of night created especially for speaking to the spirit world. He'd never had much of a religion before Celia, and she hadn't ragged him about it. Just demonstrated her own beliefs in a quiet and peaceful way that made him envy her. Once she grew large with child, she began to talk to the unborn baby, explaining her gods, and Mitchell finally understood her serenity. He never was sure he believed, but he did learn to understand. Perhaps that's all that kept him sane when she and the baby were killed, if indeed he was sane. Sometimes he thought himself quite mad.

He rode on into Miles City Monday evening, searching for word of what the army would do. All anyone learned was that the battle raged on, with Major Reno and Captain Benteen's forces pinned down by the surviving Sioux and Cheyenne. He considered riding out and joining the battle, but he was too white for the Sioux to accept, and he couldn't raise up arms against his wife's clan. So he waited and watched.

Late in the evening he saw Charlie riding out of town all alone, and he tagged along. Where her shadow had got to he had no idea. She probably took off when he wasn't looking.

Dark found Charlie making camp a little ways out of town near the river in a small clearing surrounded by thick box elder and sandbar willow. After unsaddling Belle and staking her out in some grass nearby, she rustled up some kindling and dead wood, built a fire, and tossed down her bedroll. Spreading it near the crackling fire, she sat, dug a Barlow from her pocket, and tackled a can of peaches.

She had speared up the first sweet golden piece of fruit when she heard the rider approaching. She dropped knife and peach half back in the can and grabbed up her Winchester from where it rested beside her against a log. In the excitement she kicked over the can of peaches, but came around just in time to point the weapon at Mitchell Fallon's midsection.

Though relief poured through her at seeing him alive, she yelled at him anyway. "Damn you, Fallon. You made me spill my peaches. I thought you'd be dead."

He stood beside his horse, holding the reins. "You going to shoot me with that thing, or just point it at me?"

She put the rifle down and grabbed up the can. All the juice had run out, but some of the fruit remained. She tried to concentrate on eating, wishing she could ignore his presence entirely. But her heart thumped hard against her chest, and she didn't think it was from fear. She had truly been afraid that he had died in yesterday's battle, or maybe been wounded badly. Relief at seeing him alive and in one piece poured through her, a surprising, palpable emotion. He looked perfectly okay, now that she had a chance to check him out.

While she entertained all these thoughts Fallon had let his horse's reins drop and hunkered down by the fire, making himself at home just like he belonged there.

"Hoping you'd have come coffee."

"Well, I don't."

"You've got some peaches," he said, and grinned quite suddenly and unexpectedly.

She liked what it did to his features. The corners of his eyes and mouth lifted, dimples broke the severe angularity of his cheeks, nicely even teeth flashed, and his green eyes sparkled an intriguing fire all their own.

As if he had her in some kind of spell she held out the can. "Have some. It was all they had left in the store. We'll be hungry in five minutes." The double meaning didn't escape her.

Nor him, obviously, considering the lustful grin he displayed. "Thank you, I believe I will." He moved closer, picked out the knife she'd left standing in the can, and stabbed out a half. Without taking his eyes off her he gingerly slid the fruit onto his tongue. Sweet juice glimmered on his lips. His throat rippled when he swallowed and he handed her the knife and then the can so that she had to touch his warm fingers.

"Thank you kindly," he said, and his tongue flicked out to lick away the juice.

She watched with fascination, overcome with a powerful urge to kiss those sticky sweet lips. Heat swarmed up her throat and into the roots of her hair. Fallon took off his hat, leaned back on the log where she'd propped her rifle, and sighed.

"Thank you," he repeated, and closed his eyes.

"You said that." Her voice broke and she had to search for it again before continuing. She almost forgot what she was going to ask him, then she remembered. "What are you doing? Why do you turn up everywhere I go?"

"What? Me?" He didn't open his eyes. "Right now trying to get some shut-eye."

"Here?" She forgot that he hadn't answered her most important question. Why he kept following her.

He let his eyelids drift open languidly and pinned her with an amused stare. "Public property. Doesn't belong to anyone in particular."

She studied him for a long while. "You're awfully unconcerned considering what happened to your friends."

"What happened to my friends?"

Surely he knew. "Well, a lot of them died yesterday, and more are going to, I'd guess."

"They counted a lot of coup. They killed that bas-

tard Custer, they won their battle. And it's not uncon-
cern, it's a harmony of sorts. What I am sorry about
is that it won't last. You're right, by this time tomorrow, the tide will probably turn, but at least they will
have honored their forefathers."

She sighed. "I don't understand."

He sat up, looked at her intently. "I know, but you
don't have to." He heaved himself to his feet. "Well,
if you don't want me here, guess I'd better ride on."
Raking back the long black hair he settled the hat on
his head.

"Don't go," she said in a whisper.

"I didn't hear you," he replied, and leaned down
close.

She cleared her throat and looked up at him, eyes
reflecting orange flickers of flame from the campfire.
"I said, don't go."

He nodded. "Ah."

He wanted to take her in his arms, throw her on
the ground, and rip those stupid britches and shirt
from her body, reveal the true woman that she was.
A full-grown, healthy woman. He wanted to teach her
what that body was really made for, and it wasn't
busting broncs and riding herd on some stubborn longhorns. It wasn't trying to hang on to land so rough it
would kill her long before her time. It would dry her
up, wear her out and kill her, if some terrible disease
or crazy Indian or whiskey-soaked cowboy didn't do
it first.

Instead he knelt on the ground very close to her so
that he could smell her hair and her skin, her breath
sweet as the peaches they'd shared. And he put one
hand up to the side of her face and rubbed her cheek
with a thumb.

She didn't expect the sudden gesture, but she remained very still, wanting badly for him to take her
in his arms. Her breasts tingled with the desire and

she licked her lips. He bent forward quickly, captured the tip of her tongue between his lips, and held her like that an instant, moaning softly, waiting for her response. She opened her mouth to him, and he laced the fingers of one hand through her hair, holding her close, tight, lips locked to his.

She put one arm around his neck, the other along his shoulder, and he lifted her so that her aching breasts pressed tightly against his chest.

The inside of his mouth was soft and moist and peach-flavored, and his tongue did things that nearly drove her mad before he moved to lapping and kissing down across her jawbone and to the sensitive flesh below her ear. His hat tumbled off bouncing on her shoulder, and then he had her on the ground, lying beside her. At her back the warmth of the fire did not even compete with the heat of her desire.

His hungry mouth searched past the collar of the shirt, then he ripped it away, buttons popping off. She wore a light undershirt and her nipples were rigid against the fabric, rising and falling with the gasping of her breath. He took one in his mouth, wetting the thin cotton and exploding an exquisite pain within her that spread from far down in her belly and filled her body with bright wonder. Her head swam with intense pleasure and she reached out for him, fingers pushing up his shirt so she could span the taut muscles with spread hands. Life pulsated beneath her palms, vibrant and warm.

He grabbed the hem of her undershirt, tugged it up to kiss her belly just above the belt of her jeans, then fumbled with the buckle. It didn't budge. Frustrated, he grunted and got on his knees astraddle of her, turning her so that she lay on her back looking up at him.

"Oh, Mitch. I've never . . . oh, please, just . . . I can't."

The buckle was loose now. "Help me. Undo these

buttons. Hurry," he said, and kissed her bared breast, his tongue playing around the nipple until she cried out in ecstasy.

How could anything feel so good? She writhed, moaned when his lips left her breast so he could go back to work on the buttons of her jeans.

Dragging in several deep breaths, she put her hands flat across the front of her pants. She wanted him, wanted him desperately, but she couldn't let this happen. Not now, and not this way. This wild, untamed outlaw would get what he wanted and ride off. Then what would become of her? Oh, dear God, all she wanted was him inside her.

"No. You've got to stop. I can't ... we can't. Oh, please. I'm sorry. I can't."

He panted, tried to push her hands aside. "You what? You can't? Of course you can. It's easy, just close your eyes and make a wish. It won't hurt, you're strong. I won't hurt you, I won't."

"But I've never ... never before ... I can't just do it like this. Please, Fallon. This is crazy. I want you too, but ... dammit, stop!"

She struggled, slapped at him ineffectually, rolled her head around. All she wanted was to be in his arms, to enclose him within her pulsating loins, feel his mouth on hers, his tongue doing all those wild things to her. And he seemed to sense it so that she couldn't stop him.

The crazy desire fueled her anger. This was wrong. She'd be sorry and so would he, then he would be gone and then where would she be. Where was love? No, she'd never find love. This ... this was simply raw, unbridled lust.

All of a sudden, she realized he had stopped trying to undo her pants. He still knelt over her, but his hands were resting on the ground on either side of her while he breathed raggedly, his head hanging down so that his hair tickled at her cheek.

She touched his face tenderly, held away the hair so she could see his green eyes, smoky with passion. "I'm so sorry."

He took a deep breath, moved imperceptibly away from her touch. "Yeah, me too."

He took his time getting off her, as if hoping she might change her mind and they could go on. But he didn't push it and when she lay stiffly, not saying anything more, he dragged in the night air once, twice, then leaned back against the log. She could hear the rasp of his heavy breathing.

The shirt wouldn't button back up, he'd torn off all the buttons, so she tied it at her waist, extremely conscious of the wet spot on the undershirt where he had sucked at her breast through the cotton fabric. A cavity deep down in her belly throbbed with heat and dissatisfaction.

They both watched the fire till he finally threw a couple of sticks on it and said, "Why didn't you tell me you . . . I mean, a woman your age, I just thought . . ."

Miserably she shook her head. "Yeah, well, you can just think something else. And why would it have been all right if I'd had a man before?"

"I didn't mean it that way. I just meant . . . oh, hell, I don't know what I meant. We haven't got any business messing around with each other anyway."

"My feelings exactly. That's why I stopped you, not because I've never . . . never made love. Nothing could come of it, and I don't want to let you think it could. And I certainly don't want to let a man have me who's just going to ride away."

"Trouble is," he said with a wry grin, "if I stick around it's bound to happen again. You see, I can't seem to keep my eyes or thoughts off you. Not ever since I saw you dancing that night, graceful as a white dove."

"Saw me dancing? When did you—?"

He interrupted as if she hadn't spoken. "God, you are so beautiful, and you keep yourself hid in those ugly clothes so no one will guess what you've got there." He pointed in the general direction of her chest.

She spread her hands over her breasts, imagining him spying on her in those most private of moments. "You've been peeping in my windows, spying on me? How could you do something like that? Even you?"

He raised an eyebrow. "Even me? Oh, you mean a man with no scruples, a man who goes around shooting people? That kind of man?"

"That's exactly what I mean. I guess I shouldn't be surprised at anything you'd do."

He gazed at her. A look of sadness came over his face and he reached out a crooked finger, ran it down her bare flesh in the gap of her unbuttoned shirt. "Well, maybe I would do just about anything, but I didn't . . . I wouldn't ever do anything to hurt you. I'd like you to believe that. Don't ask me why it matters, but it does."

She remained very still, though doing so took every ounce of her energy. He'd become in her mind no longer a bloodthirsty gunfighter, but a man seeking her approval, courting her in some odd sort of way. Not the kind of courting that offers up the live-happily-ever-after fairy-tale ending, but a promise of mutual trust, of friendship.

She found herself wishing he were someone else, then immediately thought that wasn't right, for if he were he would have no appeal for her. He had a tough inner strength and she liked to think she did too. Both had been scarred but surely not irrevocably.

Without hesitation, she cupped a hand around his

fingers, still trailing languidly down the front of the open shirt, and lifted them to her lips.

Transfixed, he kept his eyes on her, unsure what to expect. First she said yes, then no, now was it yes again? He waited, desire for her growing once more. This time, maybe they wouldn't stop.

She lifted her head, gave him back his hand. "I'd like it if you would stay here tonight. It was foolish of me to come out here alone, considering what's going on."

Hope erupted from deep down in his gut, but then he looked into her eyes, like great black marbles shining in the firelight. And he saw there sorrow, regret.

"Just that?" he asked softly.

She nodded.

"Fine. You're right about it . . . us . . . being foolish, but I don't expect you'll change your ways anytime soon, and from what I've seen you're an expert at foolish."

"Now you're mad at me."

He chuckled grimly. "Hell, yes, I'm mad at you. If it weren't for you I'd be halfway to Idaho right now."

"I don't see that as very desirable. And how did I keep you from going to Idaho?"

"By being so stubborn, that's how. Why don't you sell out and go back home? What in thunder is wrong with you, woman?"

She cringed at the term. "Woman? Woman? I'm not woman, I'm me, Charlie Houston. I don't call you man. And I won't sell out, I'll never sell out. My daddy sacrificed his life for his dream, and if you think I'm going to give it up, you're crazy."

He nodded and leaned back on the log, staring into the fire. "And what is your dream, Charlie Houston?"

She opened her mouth to answer, the automatic reply that had always come so easily before she'd met this man. That her father's dream and hers were the same, but she didn't get the words said. Things had happened to make her think about that.

All she finally said was, "I don't know, Fallon. I guess I just don't know anymore."

Chapter Twelve

The Indian trouble put an end to the range war. Yancey said it was because of all the activity with the army. The colonel was no fool. He'd bide his time.

Charlie missed Fallon, who'd ridden off soon after he'd spent the night at her campfire outside Miles City. It surprised her how many times she would look up expecting to see him astride that enormous black stallion of his and be disappointed to find him not there.

The extra hands not needed on the range had built a cookhouse and Crane appeared happily settled in. He'd taken to joining her in the cabin of an evening after supper to talk about Matt and his memories of their childhood. She found herself looking forward to his company.

Even an infestation of screw worms in a herd of cattle on the western range north of the Porcupine didn't cause undue concern. That was just normal to ranch life. Charlie and a few of the men rode out to do some doctoring. The entire month of July had been hot and dry; rabbit brush and sage crackled beneath the hooves of the ponies as they rode. Several times she raised her face to the blistering wind and thought she smelled smoke, but saw nothing. God help them if the range caught fire in this hot, dry, windy weather.

They worked late into the evening doctoring the cattle, spreading a mixture of axle grease and carbolic acid into the wounds left by the fly that laid eggs beneath the thick hide of the beasts.

In the midst of choking dust and bawling cattle, Charlie heard the dreaded words "Fire, fire," and felt her stomach clench.

She mounted Belle and quickly scanned the horizon. Hungry flames and a column of smoke to the southwest ran ahead of the wind straight for the herd.

She interrupted the jabbering of the excited hand who had ridden up with the news. "Has it jumped the Yellowstone and the Bighorn?"

The man's eyes were wide with fright. All he wanted to do was get on his horse and ride. She grabbed the horse's bridle. "I asked you . . ."

The man fairly screamed his answer. "She come right cross the river and ain't nothin' gonna stop her . . . nothin' in this wide world." He cut at the horse's flanks with his spurs, the jumping animal's shoulder bumped the roan's and she danced nervously.

Charlie calmed Belle and shouted orders. "Listen to me. We can save these cattle, pick up others as we go. Head 'em south and east. We can't outrun it, but we sure as hell can outflank it. The whole world is not on fire, not yet anyway. We'll just run like hell out of its path."

Concern for Yancey claimed her attention. He'd taken some of the men to the north pasture to check on the herd there and could be trapped by the inferno. No time for that now.

"Ritter," she shouted, reining in the prancing roan.

"Right here."

"Round up as many as you can, let the strays go

Flank 'em over there." She pointed, and Ritter took two men and rode.

Circling in the opposite direction with three other hands, she rounded up a fair-sized herd and started them moving east. At the Porcupine south of the ranch house where it bent back to the north and onto the Circle D, they would turn the herd down toward the Yellowstone. If the wind didn't switch, it would wipe out the ranch houses at the Double H, the Rocking R, and maybe even Dunkirk's Circle D, but this herd would be saved.

The half-dozen hands drove the herd hard, down through a draw and over the next ridge. Beyond in a flat meadow, Charlie spotted some more grazing cattle. Each in turn raised their heads to point long spreading horns skyward, bawled, and galloped along with the thundering herd when it overtook them.

They had a jump on the fire, maybe all they needed, and she didn't look back. It took all of her strength not to ride directly to the ranch and try to save the buildings, but she knew that was useless. The wind might shift. Or it might rain. Neither possibility seemed very likely. She tried not to think of Yancey.

Save enough cattle to survive the winter. That's what she had to do, all she could think of doing.

It seemed like an eternity of eating dust before the herd finally reached the Porcupine. The lead cattle slowed, milled in the water till it turned muddy. She drew her rifle and fired several shots in the air. The other hands followed suit and rode into the creek, forcing the cows through.

Ritter caught up with her on the far bank. "Miss Charlie, I believe we're out of its path. Look yonder."

He was right. The fire had continued to move to the northeast. The ravaging beast would miss them, but not the ranch, unless something stopped it.

"Okay, start turning them down toward the Yellowstone," she shouted, and he passed the word.

They were off Double H property. Though Colonel Dunkirk used this land north of Miles City for grazing, he didn't legally own it. He had run ads in *The Post* that he held possessory rights, and that made most believe it was his, but she knew better. All the same the man wouldn't be happy about her putting her cattle there. He was bound to try to do something about it and use the law to back him up.

Soon after they turned the cattle and let them meander into the river to drink, she asked Ritter's help to get a head count.

When they'd finished the tally, Ritter asked, "You reckon Yancey Barton'll see that fire a-comin'?"

"Well, if he don't, he's blind as a shedding snake," one of the hands piped up. "Lookee yonder at her burn."

They paused to stare in awe as flames and smoke highballed it across the dry prairie. Off to her right, crossing the path of that inferno, rose a growing pillar of dust. She scarcely believed what she saw then as a herd of longhorns emerged from waves of summer heat like specters appearing from nowhere. And riding flat out, two horsemen, one on each side.

She lit out for the galloping herd. "Whoopee. Let's give 'em a hand."

The far rider was Yancey Barton, and coming right at her, covered in dust and bent over in the saddle, rode Mitchell Fallon. He looked about as much like a gunslinger as Ritter at that moment. As she rode past him to bunch up the rear of the herd, she took off her hat and waved it in a circle above her head, shouting an enormous whoppee. His answering yee-hah brought laughter from deep down inside her. It felt good.

The hands at the river helped slow the running cattle with shouts of their own. As they mixed in with Charlie's bunch there was a great deal of celebration among the men.

Charlie held back, embarrassed to approach Fallon who, surprisingly, was right in the middle of the celebration. Instead she dismounted, tied the mare, and walked a ways uphill from the drinking cows to watch the smoke on the horizon as it continued to race up-country. On its way to the ranch. At least they'd saved some cattle. Others would be spared simply because they were not in the path of the fire.

She wasn't aware of Fallon until he spoke. "Wind's dropping. If it lays at sundown the fire might burn itself out along the banks of the Porcupine."

She lifted her face into the wind so that it dried the dust-coated sweat. Removing her hat she rubbed gloved fingers through her hair, then peeled off the gloves and doubled them over her belt. She tried every reason she could think of not to look at him, but none of them worked.

He grinned and poked at her cheek with a finger. "Muddy face."

The familiar voice and the tone he used filled her with longing. God, how she'd missed him. "Yours too," she said, but didn't touch him like he had her.

He quickly pulled his finger away, looked down at his boot toes. "Both could use a wash, I reckon."

What were they doing talking about dirty faces? She thought of plenty of other things she wanted to say, but didn't. They just stood there for a while staring at each other.

Finally he grunted, took off his hat, and blotted at his forehead with one arm. The wind caught at his hair, twisting the white streak through the long dancing tresses. Peering out of the grime, his eyes gleamed like summer rain, and she couldn't help but remember what it felt like to be in his arms.

"Thought you were gone," she finally managed, but only after she pulled from the trap of that intense gaze to look down the slope at the watering cattle.

"Nope." He put his hands on his hips and that's when she noticed he wasn't wearing the Colt.

"Where's your gun?" she asked.

"Been working cattle. Rifle's enough."

She raised her brows. "Oh? For who?"

"Burris needed a hand, thought I'd stick around."

"He wasn't afraid to hire you?"

"No, in fact he liked the idea, once I convinced him I no longer rode for the colonel." He grinned again, showing his flashing teeth and erasing the sternness. "Kind of peeved I wouldn't wear the Colt, though. Thought he'd hired him a gunhand."

"Didn't he?"

He was quiet for a while, then turned to stare at her until she finally looked back at him. "Only if needs be. Sometimes any man'll fight, given enough reasons."

"Or woman," she added. Without saying any more she placed her hat back on her head and left him standing there, hands still on his hips and long legs spread wide in the dusty black britches, hair whipping in the wind. She turned once to look and saw he hadn't watched her walk away, but was gazing out across the prairie.

Like Fallon had predicted the wind laid at dusk. By dark they could see the line of fire stretching for miles, not wild and wicked now but burning lazily. They watched until it reached an arroyo, or perhaps the trickle of Porcupine Creek, and then it just burned itself out. Soon the stars were brighter than the dying embers, and there was left only the pungent smoldering odor in the night air.

"Well," one of the hands joked, "I prayed for rain, but guess the Good Lord figured I just didn't know what I was asking for."

Chuckles worked their way around the campfire. Everyone sat on their bedrolls, chewing on jerky or hard biscuits most carried when they were out on the range and conversing in soft voices. Augurin', the old-timers called it.

"Miss Charlie, whyn't you sing us one of your'n Cal's songs?" Ritter asked.

She picked up a stick and drew lines in the dirt. She hadn't sung for anyone but herself since Cal Malone's death. The hands had all at one time or another heard her singing to the cattle as she stood guard, either on the drive up from Texas or out here on the range. Only a few knew Cal wrote the poetry that she put to music.

She began to hum softly and everyone grew quiet. The fire crackled and popped, and off in the distance wolves set up a conversation. She sang them a song about a Montana lady who fell in love with a back east dandy who broke her heart when he went back home to marry his sweetheart. One of the boys accompanied the tune with a mouth harp, hesitantly at first till he got the rhythm, then sweetly, sadly.

A knot formed in her throat as she finished the song. It made her voice husky.

"And high on the hill where the wild wind blows, she sits her strawberry roan. And cries to the wolf in the moon's white glow, her heart turned hard as stone."

The plaintive last notes from the mouth harp faded and no one said anything for a long while after the notes died away.

Then Ritter said, "That old Cal, he had him some poet's soul, didn't he?"

Tears surprised Charlie and she wiped them with the heels of her hands. "I think he had Robert Burns memorized," she reminisced.

"Robert Burns?"

"A poet," she said.

"I knew a fella once could quote poetry," someone across the fire said. "But not me. I can't even read it good, too many odd words."

"Them ain't odd words, Quigley, they's just longer than *the* and *but*."

Everyone chuckled.

She sensed someone moving up on her from out of the dark and swung around. It was Mitchell Fallon, all washed clean, his hair wet and curly around his face. Firelight shone on his high cheeks and broad jaw, reflected in the glade-green eyes. He reached a hand down to her without saying a word and she took it, rising easily to her feet.

The savory tang of burning wood scented the still air. She walked beside him still holding to his hand, and they strolled away from the glow of firelight. Below them the river reflected dancing points of starlight, scattered and blurred as if unreal.

"What will you do?" she finally asked.

His thumb roamed over the back of her hand. "Do?"

"Once the soldiers are gone the colonel will start up again. He'll fight till he takes all the land away from us. He'll pick us off one at a time till the ones left are too scared to stay and light out. Then, what will you do?"

He tightened his hold on her hand, stopped walking. "I'm not going to let him do that to you." His voice was hard as flint, scary, and she could believe him very easily. He could be a frightening man.

"You mean just to me, or to all of us?"

"I meant you, I guess. It's you I care about."

She looked up at him. "I don't understand why." But inside she did and her heart knocked around like it had broken loose and didn't have a place to go.

He lifted her chin with the other hand, the one he wasn't already holding on to her with, and bent to kiss her gently. She flicked her tongue out to touch his warm lips, surprising him. His eyes widened and he wrapped his arms around her, deepening the kiss.

When they finally pulled part, he said, "Damn if I know what to do about you."

Snaking her arms around his waist she said softly, "There's nothing you can do about me."

He laughed into her hair. "Blamed if that isn't true."

"Come to work for me," she said, and lay her cheek against his chest so she could hear his heart beat. "Together we can make the Double H what Matthew wanted it to be."

"Matthew?"

"My dad. I worked with him so long I just called him Matthew like all the men on his ranch. I was five years old when he put me astride my first horse. Quite a shock to a little girl who'd been raised in drawing rooms wearing stiff dresses and patent leather shoes. But I took to it." She rubbed her cheek against the fabric of his shirt.

"I loved him so much, and you—"

"I am not Matthew, not your father." He stiffened, thinking of a little girl he had failed to protect. A little girl to whom he was a father. "I can't make you any promises, Charlie."

"So far, I haven't asked for any." She felt as if he had struck her, or at the very least withdrawn from her once again.

"But you will. You have to. The only promise I've made was to myself, and that was to see that you don't get hurt. I'll break it only if they kill me."

A chill washed through her. He spoke of his own death so casually. Yet he still held her in his arms, hadn't pushed her away, even though she'd sensed his retreat. "Wouldn't it be easier to keep your promise if you were living on the Double H? The Burris ranch is a long ways off."

"That's why I was on my way back down here when I saw the fire. It occurred to me that I needed to be closer to you."

Charlie wiggled up tight against him, felt his muscles quiver in response and his arms tighten. "Is this about close enough?" She felt breathless, on the brink of something important and arousing.

Fallon lowered his mouth to the hollow of her throat. She vibrated with desire, slipped her hands up under his shirt. Beneath her palms his smooth warm flesh pulsed with life, and she wanted him desperately and completely.

"Come, come with me. Hurry," she said breathlessly.

Pulling from his embrace, she took his hand and led him partway down the riverbank to a secluded spot beneath a thick stand of willows. In the dark shadows they were well away from the campfire and the cattle.

Tense and on the edge of a passion that threatened to smother all his senses, he could only think of her naked in his arms, between his legs consuming his urgent need. Yet he knew, back in a dim-lit corner of his mind, that if he did this he was setting his path in a way he might not wish to go. A way in which she might regret going. He could not pledge himself to this woman, yet his desire for her verged on lunacy. He blocked out a dire foreboding from that hidden place where he stored his doubts about life and death, his fears of his own inadequacy.

If she were a man he would know how to handle her. He would pull out his gun and shove the barrel into her soft belly, say leave me be or I'll put a bullet in you. That's how threatened he felt, yet he wanted her in ways he'd never dreamed of wanting a woman.

She challenged even the most formidable of his resolves.

She dragged him down to the ground. It was so dark he couldn't see her, could only hear her quick breaths, feel her fingers fumbling with the buttons on his shirt, making their way down to his belt buckle.

A white-hot flame of desire grew everywhere she touched him, and he helped her loosen his pants. They were both on their knees, her head bent so that fine strands of her hair tangled with the dark curls on his chest.

He captured her hands in his for a moment to give him time. Time to calm the wild surge of passion; time to make sense out of this unexpected fierce tenderness uncoiling like a sleeping beast within him. He had thought love gone from him forever. Where had this come from, this renewed perception of self and needs and caring, of life itself?

"Charlie, Charlie, are you sure?" He could scarcely breathe out the question for fear she'd say no, for fear she'd say yes.

She answered him in a fierce whisper. "I'm sure. I've waited so long, and you're going to go away. If I don't love you, if you don't love me now, you'll be gone and I'll never . . . you'll never . . . we won't know what it would have been like. What it will be like. I just want to love you. One time. I just want you to love me. One time. Then it won't matter, nothing will. Because I'll know. Don't you see? We'll both know forever and always what it was like to be so totally absorbed with such . . . such freedom of spirit, such ecstasy.

"Oh, do love me. Please do."

She wrung her hands free of his grasp, tugged at his pants, got them open and down past his hipbones. She lowered her head and kissed his belly button. Her tongue darted out, flicking at his quivering flesh like little bites from the sun.

He tried to reason with her, senseless words that climbed from coarse to ragged, but she wouldn't stop unless he hurt her and he couldn't do that. So he lay down on the ground as she lowered his britches over his hips and spreading his hands at her waist lifted her so that she straddled his thighs.

She still wore her clothes and felt awkward sitting on him that way. Rising to her knees she began to undo her pants.

"No, wait. Wait a minute," he said.

"I can't. I want you . . . want you inside me. You do too, I can tell." She squirmed around on his bulging manhood, teasing just a bit, but nevertheless very serious about her intent, plucking and tugging to get rid of the jeans she wore.

He dragged in a deep, jagged breath. "I do, yes, I do. But what you said. You're right about what may happen. I run away. I like to run away when things get too tough. And Charlie Houston, you're too tough."

Softly, "I'm not so tough," then she went on with renewed vigor, "well, anyway, we agreed. It won't matter, we'll know what it's like to love one another. We can keep the memory forever."

"We didn't agree on anything. And this isn't loving one another. This is . . . well, this is . . ." He grabbed her with both hands, pulled her head down to his chest and held her tight, his voice hoarse, raw with desire. God, how he wanted her. This very minute. He imagined plunging into her, the hot wet silkiness, the burning, pounding surging release. "This is not what you deserve. You deserve a man who will stick with you love you, and take care of you."

"No, dammit," she cried and tried to shove away "I don't need someone to take care of me, I need someone to love me."

Fighting her, holding her. "Okay, okay." Suddenly he was quiet, hugging her close and breathing against her cheek. "It's not me, Charlie. I'm sorry, it's not me." He closed his eyes, wanted to cry for the loss of all he wanted, but it was better. Better to lose it now while he could still bear it.

She hammered at his chest. "Damn you, damn you," she cried, then tore from his arms and leaped to her feet. Infuriated, depleted, she stumbled away from him.

After a while he rolled to his knees, pulled his pants on, and fumbled around in the dark until he found his hat. Pain so intense it took away his breath cracked through him like rage, and he knew all about that. Rage he could deal with and he fed it with every vengeful thought he could muster.

Fallon stayed on at the Double H Ranch, and Charlie just tried to pretend she didn't notice. She wanted him to leave, wanted him to stay, did nothing about either, for she couldn't look into his eyes or speak to him for fear the pain would kill her. Yancey finally came to Charlie about him.

"This new hand, this Fallon, when did you hire him?"

A hand squeezed at her heart and she gasped, looked away from Yancey's squinty gaze. "I didn't, not really."

"Then what's he doing sleeping and eating here?"

Lips dry, tongue sticking to the roof of her mouth, she managed, "Is he working?"

"I reckon. He just kind a pitches in when something needs done. I ain't never told him to do anything. It's a strange situation, if you don't mind my saying so."

"You don't have to tell me it's strange." If he knew the truth, this friend, what would he then think?

"You want, I can get rid of him. He did work for

the colonel, you know. Strange how he just sort of showed up." At that Yancey eyed her in his thoughtful way, and almost grinned, like he knew a secret she might wish to be let in on.

She wanted to tell him it wasn't what he thought at all.

"What did you say to him ... when he just kind of showed up?"

Yancey scratched up under his hat. "What do you mean, what did I say?"

"Well, I mean when we hire someone new, don't you introduce him around, show him his bunk, tell him his job? You don't just let him sort of fall into things, do you?"

"Not generally. But I have to admit, that's what I did with this fella. He's the falling in kind of man, you know. He acted like he knew where he wanted to sleep and where he wanted to work, and so I figured you'd hired him. I just let him."

"Without even asking me. Sounds like just about anyone could ride in off the trail and go to work here without either one of us hiring him."

Yancey laughed. "Well, now, Miss Charlie, not many men would just ride up and go to work like this one did. To tell you the truth, this is the first time it's ever come up in all my years of ramrodding for your daddy or even before."

She couldn't help chuckling, though bitterly. It was an unusual situation, and if she hadn't been so blindly furious at Fallon for rejecting her advances, she might have seen even more humor in it. As it was, whether she liked it or not, the Double H had a new hand, and she'd just have to learn to live with that. She certainly wasn't up to confronting him about it. Be damned if she'd tell Yancey to take care of it. He'd think she wasn't up to really running the ranch, just like some of the men already thought.

The best she could do was discuss her pent-up feelings with Radine every chance she had to go to Miles City. They had become friends, and she guessed that's what friends did. Share their innermost secret feelings and desires.

Chapter Thirteen

Fallon waited until the lamp went out in Charlie's cabin to assure himself that she had retired for the night, then he came out onto the porch of the bunkhouse. It was a bright night and he had no desire to let anyone see him.

Crane had snuck off earlier, and he intended to catch him coming back, find out what the hell the man was up to. He didn't trust him and his sneaky ways, and he particularly didn't like the way he nosed up to Charlie all the time. Since seeing him meet up with Cross in secret that night in the clearing, he had kept a close eye on the man. He was definitely up to something, and it didn't bode well for Charlie Houston. Wasn't the cook supposed to be her cousin or something?

It was a long time before Crane returned. Fallon snoozed sitting slumped up against a porch post, hat tilted down over his eyes to keep out the bright moonlight. He heard the soft clop of hooves, though, and was instantly alert. Crane came into the brightly lit yard leading his horse slowly to make as little noise as possible. His furtiveness was evident in the way he took his mount into the barn and unsaddled him, came back out a few moments later after having turned the horse into the corral out back.

Stretching lazily, Fallon rose, but Crane didn't see him until he had started up the steps to the bunkhouse.

"Evening, friend," Fallon said.

Crane yipped, sounding just like a dog that had been kicked. He recovered quickly. "What do you mean, scaring a man like that? Good thing for you I don't carry a side arm, I'd a shot you for a thief."

"Or maybe I'd a shot you," Fallon said, his hand going unconsciously to his bare hip. The Colt lay stored in the chest at the foot of his bunk, his way of divorcing himself from the gunhand Charlie knew him to be.

"Don't know why you'd want to do that."

"Oh, I don't know. A man rides out in secret, sneaks back in the wee hours of the night, making sure no one sees him. Must be up to no good of some kind, I'd wager. What would you think?" Fallon slouched against the post, glaring at Crane but unable to see his expression in the shadow cast by his hat.

"I'd think that it was his business entirely, what a man does on his own time."

"Unless that business has to do with betraying the brand he rides for."

Crane jerked as if he'd been socked. "Why would you think that? You crazy or something? I love Miss Charlie; hell, she's my own cousin.

"If anybody'd be up to no good around here, I'd guess it'd be you. Come riding in here with a gun on your hip shooting up the place, and next thing we know you're riding herd over Double H cattle. Now, I don't know about some, but I take that as mighty suspicious."

Fallon straightened. Crane had leaned forward so that he felt the heat and moisture of his breath as he spat out the last words. Fallon definitely didn't like anyone coming that close to him, but he'd be damned if he'd back off.

"Move away, mister."

The old savagery rose in Fallon's chest but he held back. Charlie might not understand if he maimed her cook. He'd heard the stories of her cooking escapades. Anyone who shot down a perfectly good cook, and on the steps of her bunkhouse to boot, would not be held in very high esteem by Charlie Houston. In fact, she might do some disabling of her own.

Crane shrunk away when he caught sight of the dark figure on the porch.

Fallon grabbed his arm. "I want to tell you something. I can't figure what you and that bastard Cross are up to, but you do anything to hurt Charlie Houston and you've got me to deal with. It won't be pretty, but I promise you this, it'll be quick. Got that?"

A ray of moonlight on Crane's cheek cast great dark hollows around his eyes when he stared up into Fallon's face. His voice trembled when he spoke, but he got the words out. "I don't know what you think you're gonna do with her, but you can be assured no Houston would have any dealings with the likes of you. She'd die first. Now, take your hand off me and let me pass."

Fallon felt the man's arm quiver under his grasp, but he let him go. He had some grit, and that worried him, for in a pinch he might actually show enough courage to do whatever it was he and Cross had planned. He'd have to keep a real good eye on this one. To discover a wolf living in your midst didn't bode well for survival, especially if other wolves were circling to attack.

Fallon waited until all sounds of Crane's retiring were silenced, then he went inside. Before crawling into his own bunk he retrieved the Colt and slipped it under his pillow.

*   *   *

Something awoke Charlie in the predawn hours. She suspected it was only the excitement of fall roundup beginning. After tossing in the bed awhile, she got up and dressed. She would sleep better on the trail, and there was no point in fighting the restlessness any longer.

She stepped out on the porch and dragged in a deep, sweet breath. Birds waking in the brush along the perimeter of the yard warbled inquisitive soft music in the predawn air. A tingle of excitement walked up her spine and radiated across her shoulders. Roundup, the most exciting time of the year.

Crane came down the steps from the porch, didn't see her, and headed for the cookhouse to make breakfast. It wasn't long before the smell of burning wood from his fire tinged the first pale glow of morning.

The place came suddenly alive as if someone had rung bells or blown wake-up call on a horn.

She watched the men and their good-natured horseplay around the washpans for a few moments, then started across the wide yard. She could smell bacon frying and bread baking and so wasn't paying much attention to where she was going. That's how Fallon got right up on her without her seeing him. Or at least, that's what she told herself later. Her hunger had let down the careful guard she'd put up against him ever since that night on the riverbank when he'd refused her advances.

He swept off his black hat, a little the worse for wear since he'd started cowboying. She guessed gunslingers weren't as hard on their clothes as cowboys, for since he'd taken up the latter occupation his jeans had become worn, his shirt faded, and the boots well used. He looked not at all like he had the first day she'd seen him, all dressed in black sitting atop that prancing stallion, so remote, so fascinating. She

stopped and faced him, her chin up so she could look
into his face.

"Good morning, Miss Charlie. Looks like you're
ready for roundup." He didn't sound cheerful, exactly,
but he sounded different than he used to. A little less
threatening, and more relaxed. That was the only
word she could think of. Relaxed. Like he enjoyed
what he was doing.

Well, maybe he did. She'd give him that. She smiled
at him, determined to enjoy this day to its fullest.
"Good morning to you, Mr. Fallon. I hope you're as
ready as I am. I expect my men to work till they drop,
just like I will."

She laid a heavy accent on "my men," and looked
him right in the eye, no matter that it cost her. A
shiver of delight coursed through her when he met
her gaze with a smoky one of his own.

"I'll do my best to keep up with you, boss." Fallon
screwed the hat back down on his head, cocking it
slightly so that it shadowed the scar above his
eyebrow.

She didn't notice until he walked away that he had
strapped the Colt .44 back on his right hip, low and
ready, just like he'd worn it the first time she ever
saw him.

Mitch had never ridden a roundup as a cowpuncher,
but he had no intentions of sitting this one out. Wher-
ever Charlie was he intended to be too, keeping an
eye on Crane Houston.

The black took well to hard riding, so Mitch set a
fast pace to keep up with the other drovers. Yancey
had seen to spare mounts for the Double H men and
they joined those from other ranches behind the chuck
wagon in the care of a wrangler. Whatever job a man
was assigned, there'd be a horse trained to do it. His
stallion didn't exactly qualify as a cow pony. By the

end of a punishing day's ride, the caravan of men and horses and equipment reached its destination.

The rolling land, dotted with spruce and pine, roughened in places into canyons, and it was in one of these that the herd would be held during the process of gathering the scattered cattle. Mitch could see the reasoning as soon as the wagon boss and his circle riders began to lay out plans for the next day's roundup.

The "canyon," if it could be called that, had a wide, flat entrance with plenty of grass and was flanked by brushy hills. At the other end it narrowed and became boulder-strewn and rough, forming a natural corral big enough to hold all the cattle they'd gather from these sections. Obviously they'd used the place before.

Crane immediately went about setting up the chuck wagon beneath some lodgepole pines well clear of the entrance to the holding pen. The bed wagon was parked alongside. Several springs fed a small creek nearby and plenty of deadwood lay scattered about.

Luke Awhile, the wrangler from the Bar S, would also hold that job for the roundup. He corralled the remuda of more than a hundred horses and started gathering wood for the cook fire. Assigned all the chores the real cowboys were loathe to do, such as hauling wood and water and cook's helper, Luke could expect to be razzed by the cowboys. They didn't disappoint him.

"Hey, Luke," one of the men hollered at him, "don't you go picking up one of them cow chips afore you check under it. Scorpions do love to bed down in that stuff."

A round of laughter followed as Luke went to work turning over the dried cow chips left from spring roundup to use in the fire.

Fallon remained aloof from the horseplay, preferring to unsaddle his stallion and give him a good rub-down in privacy. He was surprised that the colonel hadn't sent Cross and Neddy to ride along and be their usual troublesome selves, but they were conspicuously absent. Some of the Circle D's regular cowboys eyed Fallon suspiciously, and he knew this meant the colonel would soon know that he was riding for the Double H brand, if he didn't already.

That evening he took his tin plate of stew and cup of coffee to a spot where he could keep an eye on just about everyone, most especially Charlie Houston.

The object of his attention stood in line at the chuck wagon with the rest of the men and then took her steaming plate to a table-size boulder a ways back from the campfire. Some of the men gathered in groups, others paired up, and she listened in perfect contentment to their joshing and teasing. This was what she liked best about ranching. The roundups, the getting out and riding free and shouting into the wind and sleeping under a raven-black sky sprinkled with stars.

It was at times like this that she missed her father the most, and feeling a little lonely, she finished her meal. After scraping the last few bites of stew out of her plate on the ground for the night critters she took her dinnerware to the washtub where the wrangler would scrub everything clean before retiring for the night. As she turned and started around the back end of the chuck wagon, she spied a lone figure at the crest of the rise, a dark silhouette against the silvery evening sky. Standing out there staring down at the campfire, alone and removed from everyone, he made her think of how she'd been feeling herself. Someone else lonely like her. The sight brought a thickening to her throat.

She wanted . . . she wanted something, an unnamed something, and seeing that singular cowboy outlined against the fading daylight made her almost sick with the need for a thing she couldn't even put a name to. She climbed the rise toward the man. She'd speak, remark on the day, talk about tomorrow, and if he didn't respond, well then she could always walk away. It was possible that he wasn't lonely at all, but simply wanted privacy, in which case she would leave him alone.

As she approached the mysterious figure, he turned to stare out across the valley, and too late she realized that it was Mitchell Fallon. She should have known. He never took up with anyone, always set himself apart. Well, perhaps she had known it was him and chose this way to break the long silence that had held between them since that fateful night on the riverbank.

"Beautiful, isn't it?" Surely she could have thought of something better to say.

"I heard you coming, wondered if you'd hightail it when you figured out who I was. Yes, it is beautiful, but only when it sleeps."

"Why should I run from you? I'm not afraid of you. What do you mean, only when it sleeps?"

"Life here. It's so harsh that sometimes the beauty gets lost in the demands the land makes on us, in our striving to endure. Sometimes it's just so damned hard to get from one day to the next that nothing is beautiful enough."

"That sounds like self-pity to me," she snapped, angry at him and not sure why.

He snorted but didn't reply right away. Charlie was afraid he'd hear the thumping of her heart, and wondered why she couldn't be anywhere near him without feeling tumultuous and giddy.

He finally spoke, so softly she had to strain to hear him. "I guess it does. I just don't know how to get on with it, and so sometimes I get to feeling sorry for myself. I know I'm not different from lots of others who've lost all they love, but that doesn't make it any easier."

She scarcely breathed as he talked, for he had never spoken in such revealing terms to her. She wanted him to go on, let her inside the world in which he survived so tenaciously, so angrily.

He startled her then by turning toward her, grasping her upper arms, and looking down into her face. "I couldn't save her, no matter what I did or how hard I tried. And you're as stubborn as she was. But I will not let anything happen to you. I promise you that. I promise."

Then he turned her loose as if she were a demon, and before she could react at all, he strode away. She wanted to go after him, make him explain what he meant, make him talk to her so she could learn what kind of man this was. But she couldn't move from the spot, and so she stood there rubbing her arms where he had held her. And she watched him until his shadow blended with the other shadows in the canyon. It was like watching him disappear off the face of the earth. She wanted to howl like the coyotes she could hear as night encompassed her. Howl and howl until Fallon turned and answered, came to her call and carried her off somewhere and they could make love in the woods like wild things until she would at last be sated. And maybe he would tell her what he was all about.

By dawn the next morning the wagon boss had left with a dozen circle riders. They would remain in the saddle eighteen out of twenty-four hours driving cattle from their assigned sections for miles around.

Though Charlie wasn't a circle rider, she did work the herds all day, and took her turn nighthawking as well. She had chosen her favorite roan Belle for that task, leaving some of the less surefooted animals for day work. She and the little roan got along well, they understood each other because they'd always been together. Matt had given her the foal even as it stood wobbly and wet at its mother's side. She had broken Belle herself, and loved her as only a young woman without friends can come to love a pet, with all her heart and soul.

The wolves came on the fifth night, spooking first the horses in their rope corral, and eventually the longhorns. The pack dashed and darted at the fringes of the herd, picking calves as their natural target. Before anyone could react the cows began to mill and bawl, tossing their heads so their immense horns cracked together like rifle shots.

She and Belle had started around the wide mouth of the canyon when the remuda began to cut up. Belle lifted her ears, snorted, and whinnied. Charlie swung her around so that she was facing the milling cattle straight on, and in the same instant came the ominous low rumble as the cattle started to move. Back deep in the herd, waves of panic spread outward, like rocks tumbling into an avalanche.

She stuck her spurs in hard and got the roan out of the way of the chaos, then rode hard alongside, anxious to contain the stampede, put a stop to it quickly. Other night riders did the same.

The ground shook. Charlie bent low over the roan's neck, heard the valiant horse's breath chuffing in and out as she raced to outdistance the cattle so they could be turned in upon themselves.

In the darkness she made out shadowy clumps of boulders as she and the horse raced through the night. Cowboys yipped, and it sounded as if someone had reached the front of the herd, for several shots resounded from that direction. They were ahead and trying to turn the lead cattle, stop the stampede.

She blanked out memories of another stampede, lightning and pouring rain, balls of dancing fire and death. Matt's death. She mustn't think of anything but stopping the herd. Hooves pounded, dust boiled, her heart kept a beat with the cacophony, and then the cattle turned, swinging around so that she and the roan were caught in the center of the vortex.

The drovers must not see her, must not know she was there!

The roan screamed, shuddered, and screamed again, then went down into the maelstrom of pounding hooves and bawling, panicking cattle.

Kicking free of the stirrups, Charlie bounced literally onto the heaving back of a broad-shouldered steer, slid down his side, and was swallowed up by the herd. She rolled into a ball, tucked her head low, and covered it with both arms. A sharp hoof cut into her thigh, another kicked her into a tumble among the churning legs.

Involved in a nightmare of choking dust and the stink of fear, she only had time to think how ironic that she should die in the same way her father had, before strong arms swept her up and out of the deadly stampede.

Wild with fear for her life, Fallon had urged the powerful black right into the herd as soon as he saw her go down. The cattle were turning, slowing, and God help him, maybe he could get to her in time.

He just kept thinking that over and over. Get to her, get to her, save her, for God's sake.

And then he had a firm hold on her, swooping her up off the ground and into the saddle before him like a bundle of rags. By that time the cattle were no longer in headlong flight, but still confused and very dangerous. The black shouldered his way through them as if born to the task, escaping with only a shallow gash across one shoulder.

At first Fallon couldn't tell if Charlie was breathing, or if she was all broken up, the life stomped out of her. He carried her to the campfire, where the cowboys gathered around, murmuring among themselves, some shocked and totally mute. Yancey tried to take her from his arms, but Fallon just kept walking, his features like hard cut stone, his eyes haunted.

Ritter and Crane made her a bed near the fire where they could tend to her wounds and Fallon put her there, but he wouldn't release her hand, and they had to work around where he knelt beside her, the limp hand clasped against his chest. None dared challenge the warning in his glittering eyes. Crane, charged with administering first aid as the cook usually was, brought out his box of supplies and went to work cleaning the blood and dirt from her face. Immediately she began to make mewling sounds down in her throat, and Fallon lifted her hand to his mouth, bending over it to taste the reassuring warmth.

If she died ... no, he wouldn't let himself think such a thing. If she lived, that's what he would think of. If she lived, he promised her in silence, if she would just live he would take her in his arms and make love to her, just like she had wanted. My God, how could he have denied her and himself that? Life was so fleeting, death so furtive and sneaky. He thought he should have learned that by now.

No, dammit, no, he would not let her die.

He rocked on his knees. "Don't die, don't die," he whispered against the battered knuckles of her fingers.

She stirred, moaned, and began to thrash around.

"Hold her still," Crane ordered, and Fallon took her by the shoulders. Ritter captured her legs and stopped her from flailing. "Don't feel like any ribs are broken," Crane announced. He went on to check her entire body with capable hands, acting as if he knew what he was doing. By the time he finished, looking a bit chagrined because this was a woman he was laying hands on, Charlie had fully regained consciousness.

The first face she looked into was Fallon's, because he still hovered over her, refusing to move. Crane simply had to do his doctoring around him, and so that's what he did, him not being the kind to confront a man who held death by such a loose rein.

Eyes going wide and rolling, Charlie screamed, "Matt, Matt, no."

"Ssh, ssh, you're fine," Fallon whispered. He cupped her face with both hands to stop her throwing her head back and forth. "Charlie, everything's okay."

His breath exploded out of him with relief as he uttered the words. Yet he worried. She could be hurt inside, and they wouldn't know it right away. She really should be checked out for wounds all over her body. He rose and bellowed at the gathered, worried faces.

"Git. All of you git. Can't you see we need to give her some privacy. Go on."

The men darted glances at Yancey and at the wagon boss, who had come in during the melee. Both nodded. They understood that this woman couldn't be stripped naked in front of everyone.

They all pulled back into the shadows, turning away as if ashamed.

Fallon leaned down over her and began to unbutton her shirt. "Goddammit, why didn't you stay where you belonged?" He spoke so softly that only she heard him, if she was capable yet of understanding what was being said.

Her eyes shifted quickly back and forth, then lit on him and stayed there a moment. She frowned in puzzlement and formed a name with her lips, but he couldn't tell what it was. Surely not his.

"You know, a doctor ought to see her," Crane said to Yancey so that Fallon could hear.

"I agree," Yancey said.

"'No, no. I'm okay," Charlie said very clearly.

She struggled to sit up, but Fallon held her down, pulled the shirt back to inspect for bruises, swelling, and breaks in the skin.

Yancey stepped forward. "I'm not sure you ought to be doing that," he told Fallon.

Fallon glared at him, slid his spread hands beneath her rib cage to feel around on her back. She strained to sit up.

"No, no, not yet, just lay there," he murmured. "Do you hurt anywhere?"

She chuckled grimly. "I hurt everywhere."

After checking her neck, back, and front, Fallon reached for the buckle on her belt. "And it's bound to get worse too. I'm just going to take a look at your stomach, okay?"

She gazed up at him a moment, then nodded. Yancey sighed in disgust.

Fallon slipped her pants down past her hips and palpated her stomach gently with the tips of his fingers. "Tell me if it hurts."

She nodded, watched him intently, lower lip caught in her teeth.

Ritter, who had stood a few feet away watching without embarrassment, said, "I'm riding to the ranch to get the buckboard."

Yancey blew out an explosive breath and turned away from the sight of the gunslinger with his hands all over Charlie. "Good idea," he told Ritter. "We're closer to the Rocking R. Cal's buckboard should still be in his barn, no reason for it not to be. Take two horses out of the remuda. We'll try to keep her down till you get back."

Ritter nodded, stared worriedly down at Charlie for a few seconds, then took off on a run. "I'll be back by dawn," he promised.

"Belle, where is she?" Charlie asked hoarsely.

Fallon, who had found a blanket to cover her with after he removed her jeans, pulled it up under her chin and swung around to stare toward the distant spot where he'd pulled her from the trampling hooves. No one had thought about her horse.

She grabbed his arm. "Don't let her suffer, please."

"I won't. I'll go see to her right now."

"Please do. Please." There were tears in her voice, choking her.

He pulled his Winchester out of the scabbard and walked the quarter mile or so to where the roan lay. He needed the break, time to think about what had almost happened to Charlie, and to him too. The walk out and back would give him that. Help him settle some of his rocketing emotions. When he reached the forlorn lump in the churned-up grass he saw immediately that there was no need for a bullet, the little horse was dead. Poor Charlie, he'd seen how she loved that roan, and he hated like hell to tell her Belle was gone.

On the way back to the campfire he got to thinking about how he'd worried that the colonel would send someone to hurt Charlie. All the time it would be something else that would bring her down, something no one could have prevented. A cowboy riding herd expected to one day be killed in a stampede, or gored or stomped or flung off a cliff in some wild night ride. Death came on many feet, it only seemed more tragic when man added to the risk by doing some killing of his own.

She appeared to be sleeping when he returned, so he took the black to the rope corral and spent some time rubbing him down after he pulled off the saddle. The grooming kept his mind and hands occupied, but it also gave him time to think about how he felt. So much had changed for him since he rode down out of

Canada scarcely two years ago so his wife could visit with her people. Perhaps the biggest change, though, had occurred right here on this range after he met Charlie Houston. For before that all he'd wanted was to die. Now all he wanted was for her to live.

He strode back to where she lay and knelt beside her. "You can't die on me." He grazed his fingertips over her forehead and down one cheek. "I won't let you."

Her eyelids fluttered and she looked up at him out of those ebony eyes. "Did you take care of Belle?"

"Yes, yes I did. Everything's okay now."

She let her eyes drift shut, and he bent to kiss her tenderly, first on one cheek, then the other. "I love you, Charlie Houston. I just hope I have the courage to tell you when you can hear me, when we can do something about it."

He fetched a blanket and lay down nearby where he could keep an eye on her until Ritter returned with the wagon. He would be going back to Miles City with her.

Chapter Fourteen

Mae and Lige Sample, owners of the general mercantile, put Charlie up in their spare room right down the street from the doctor's place. When she'd been in bed four days she decided enough was enough. Everyone was at roundup except her and Fallon, who hovered around her like an old setting hen.

Stretching her sore legs gingerly beneath the covers, she smiled at visions of him sitting beside her, holding her hand as if she might break. With a grunt born of exasperation at being bedridden, she threw off the covers and eased both legs over the edge of the bed. The flannel nightgown hitched up over her knees as she slid forward.

At that instant there came a rap-rap on the door and it swung open. Fallon stood there, hat in both hands, gaping at her. "What in thunder do you think you're doing?" He came across the room in two great strides and plucked her up into his arms just as she hefted herself to her feet.

"Never mind what I'm doing, what do you think you're doing?" she replied.

"Hmmm," he said, and nuzzled her neck.

"Fallon, stop that. What in the world has gotten into you?" Despite her protest, she thoroughly enjoyed being held in his arms. His energy and vibrant masculinity gave her strength. She purely tingled with anticipation.

"As I recall," he said into her ear, "you once wanted me to do more than this."

"Don't remind me." She locked her arms around his neck, concentrated on the clean line of his full lips for a long moment, and then kissed him softly.

He responded by opening his mouth in welcome, but she had pulled away already.

"Now put me down before you bring disgrace on my head."

At that moment, with Fallon nibbling at her ear and making silly animal noises that she protested to only meekly, Mae Sample bustled into the room. Because she was carrying a clean towel and washcloth with a bar of soap balanced on top in one hand and a pitcher of water in the other, she was almost across the room before she noticed the hanky-panky going on right under her nose.

"Oh. Oh, my. Well, I do declare. I mean, what is the meaning of this, sir?" The soap plunked to the floor, followed by the towel and washcloth and a big dollop of water from the brimming pitcher. "Dear me, oh, dear me."

"Fallon," Charlie warned sternly.

Laughing, he set her down on the bed and recovered the items from the floor, presenting them to Mae Sample with a broad bow. Then he retrieved his hat where it had fallen to the floor when he entered, held it poised above his head, flashed a smile, and said, "Ladies, good afternoon," and left.

Charlie stared after him, her mouth hanging open.

"Are you all right, Miss Houston?" Mae asked, so flustered she had turned beet-red beneath her fuzz of graying hair.

"Yes, of course I am. Mr. Fallon is ... well, he's

quite exuberant at times. He doesn't mean anything by it."

"Probably didn't have a proper raising," Mae muttered. "But that's no call to act so ungentlemanly. The very idea, entering your room and you in only your nightclothes. Let alone . . . well, I mean . . . did he have you in his arms?" Mae patted at her bun, tried to tame the escaping frizz.

Charlie muffled a giggle. "I don't think so, no," she lied. "He was just helping me. I'm going to get out of bed today so I can go home, and he was just . . . just . . ." She let it drop, for she could tell by the woman's expression she was getting nowhere.

It occurred to her that she was acting pretty silly herself, giggling and making excuses for her actions like some schoolgirl. That was not at all like her.

She hugged herself. She could still feel his arms around her, pressed up against his chest, the beating of his heart, thump-thumping against her breast, his warm, sweet breath feathering her tingling skin.

Oh, dear God, Fallon, where will we go from here?

The practical answer, of course, was nowhere. To leave it be would be best. But she didn't feel very practical. In fact, she felt flushed, excited, expectant. She had asked him to make love to her once and he had refused. What would he do if she made that same request again? More importantly, would she ask again now that it clearly would mean commitment?

When it was time to leave Fallon embarrassed her by carrying her out of the Samples' front door, down the path, and into the street where he placed her with a flourish on the wagon seat. "Would you rather ride lying down?" he asked.

"No, no, this is fine," she replied and smoothed her skirts. Skirts. Ye Gods, the man was mad. He'd gone to Sample's mercantile and bought her a dress to go home in, and she had put it on, fingers trembling as she buttoned the smooth fabric up over her breasts. Of course, he hadn't thought to bring her a corset and Mae had come running over with one, along with a chemise when she'd learned what was going on. And long stockings and lace-up shoes. Lord, her feet ached already, longed for the supple leather of her well-worn boots. She'd begged him to let her wear the boots under the dress, but he was having none of it and had already bundled her slightly tattered things and put them in the buckboard.

She waited until they were well out of Miles City on the way back to the ranch before she tackled him.

"All right. I want an explanation of all this, now while we're alone and you can't go running off when the questions get too hard."

"All what?" He slapped the reins smartly on the horses' rumps so that they broke into a trot.

"This"—she gestured at the dress—"and this," she said and puckered up her lips to make a loud kissing sound. "All of it. I think you know exactly what."

"Are you angry?" He angled a glance at her, saw she was hanging on and making faces, and slowed the team. "Are you sure you don't need to lie down in the back?"

"I'm fine. Just fine. Thank you for slowing down, though. My tail is still sore."

"Oh, Charlie. Dress you like a lady and you still talk like a—"

"Talk like a what? I talk like Charlie Houston, not some simpering city-bred female."

"Okay, okay. You're right. I love you the way you are."

"Then why in thunder did you make me get all gussied up in this . . . this . . . oh, God, I can't breathe. How do women wear this getup? No wonder they get the vapors all over the place all the time." Suddenly she stopped chattering and stared at him. "Wait, wait. You love me? Is that what you said?"

He nodded and grinned, turning to look at her adoringly.

"Stop this wagon, this instant," she said.

"What? Now, right here?"

She looked around. "Well, no, up there in those trees."

"Yes, ma'am," he said.

Neither of them spoke until he had pulled the wagon deep in the stand of spruce.

Without the protest of the wagon wheels, the clanging and rattling of the double tree, the day was peaceful. Birds chattered among themselves high in the trees and a soft breeze touched at Charlie's loose hair, blowing a strand across her cheek.

He slid over toward her, slipped off his glove, and twisted the fine hair in his fingers. "Beautiful, the way you let it blow loose like that. Not all knotted up on your head like you're ashamed of it or something. It shines like polished wood."

"Fallon," she said softly, and turned so she could kiss the inside of his wrist.

"I want to love you," he said. "I do love you."

She blinked her eyes, surprised that a tear slid from beneath one lid and ran slowly down her cheek.

"Aw, don't cry." He put a finger at her jawline, caught the tear, and put it between his lips. "I don't want to hurt you."

"You aren't hurting me."

"I guess I never understood why a woman cries when she does."

"It's okay if you don't understand, as long as you care."

"I care, darlin'. I do care."

"Let's go home, then. Now. I've got to get out of

these clothes and back to work. I'm going to Cheyenne with the herd."

Fallon's mouth dropped open. "You're not." Not really an order, but more a statement of amazed disbelief.

She tilted her head and smiled sweetly. "Yes, I am. You might as well learn before we even start this, and I am anxious to start, you know." She took one of his suspended hands in both of hers. "I'm not going to do what some man tells me. For too long I've made up my own mind. Matt believed every full-grown person had that right, and so do I."

For a long moment he was totally speechless. Finally he let loose on her. "I'm not 'some man.' And you were just dragged from under the hooves of stampeding cattle. Someone has to have some common sense. How can you think of making that ride so soon?"

"It'll be a few weeks before the herd is ready to go. By then I'll be fine. I've looked forward to going all summer, and I'm going. I hope you'll come along too. But not to take care of me."

"Not to take care of you," he repeatedly woodenly. "I can still see you bouncing around in the dirt under all those cows like some danged rag doll, all limp and looking dead."

"Oh, I know." She kissed the hand she held, leaned her head on his arm. "You saved my life and I'm grateful. But not because you're a man and I'm a woman. Because you saw someone in trouble and you helped out. Anyone would do the same for a friend. I mean . . . well, you know what I mean."

This time he couldn't say anything. He squeezed his eyes closed, hoping the visions wouldn't come, but they did. Celia being kicked over and over by the vicious boots of her attackers. The baby, strapped to her back, cries cut off brutally before he could reach them. Then, abruptly, Charlie lying wan and still on the blanket beside the fire, and him thinking she would die.

"No, I won't. Dammit, no. I can't." His stern denial cut hard into the soft summer air, his fists clenched until cords stood out in both arms. "This will not happen, I won't let it."

She stiffened, shoved herself out of his reach, but he only smashed at the buckboard seat, hitting it with one fist, then the other. The sharp thunks echoed off across the valley. A flock of birds rose from the nearby trees like a twisting cloud, squawking into the blue sky.

For a brief instant she had thought he would hit her. Maybe it was the granite set of his rugged features, or the shadows that clouded his green eyes. Whatever it was, her heart had leaped into her throat and she threw her hands up to ward off the expected blows.

The gesture registered belatedly, and he touched her arm gently with the back of one hand. She jerked involuntarily.

Without a word, he unwound the heavy leather reins from around the brake lever and set the team in motion.

They must have gone five miles before he spoke in a deadly flat tone. "I just can't watch another woman I love die and me not able to do anything about it. You belong in the kitchen, in the bedroom, in my arms, not out taking your life in your hands every day."

Miserable, she nodded. She understood why he felt the way he did, yet wasn't able to agree to such a thing. "And you? I can sit at home and wait for someone to shoot you down because you wear that dreadful gun hanging on your hip. Or maybe you'll get ground to bits under a stampeding herd and it's okay if I have to wait for that to happen. What's the difference? Tell me, please. What's the difference?"

He shook his head, glowering. "I wouldn't have hit you, you know. Back there. You were afraid."

She bit her lip, admitted it. "Yes, for just a split second, I thought you would. Some men do things like that to women."

"Not this man."

"But how could I know? We don't know each other yet. It takes time, and I want us to have that time. But not if you're going to tell me what I can do. Not if you're going to try to change me from what I am, from what you love, into something I'm not. Into a pampered, protected little helpless female. If you can't make peace with that, well, I'm sorry."

"You said you loved me." The last she uttered in such a forlorn voice that he turned to her.

"Oh, God, I do. You don't know how much. I love you more than anything in this world or the next. I cherish you. You are more precious than the breath I draw, all that out there, the sky, the sun, the wind. If I had more words I would use them. I can't even tell you how much I love you because not all the words have been invented for that. You are why I am still alive, do you know that?"

"And you are why I'm still alive, Mitch, and I do know that. You literally dragged me away from death's reach, and I was so afraid until I felt your arms I thought I would die of the fright, even if those cows didn't kill me."

"Then why?"

"Because I won't hide from life anymore. I think ... well, I guess I really do know that after my father was killed I hunkered down into this little dark place where nothing could get to me. I was too tough, mean sometimes. Hard, so hard. But I'm lonely and it's no way to live. And so I've let myself love you. God knows why." She laughed, harsh little choppy sounds.

They rode on for a long while, both staring straight

ahead, the space between them much wider than the physical gap on the seat.

After a while he asked, "You okay?"

"Yes, thank you."

"When will you leave?"

"I don't know yet. I may just ride on out and check on the roundup in a week or two, then go with them from there." She paused, glanced at him. "Will you be going?"

He squeezed the reins so tightly his hands tingled. "I guess not. I may ride on out to Idaho Territory." Going back, back to the way it was before. The long rides into nothingness, accompanied by only painful flashes of memory, never the good times, always the bad. Standing on the edge praying a strong wind would push him off.

He glanced at the woman beside him, chin held so high, so proud, despite the bruises. His heart swelled, his vision narrowed until all he could see was her battered body at the far end of a long, long tunnel. Unreachable. He would ride away and disappear, try to forget her, be no more successful than he had been forgetting Celia and Fawn. But knowing that would be far better than watching her go to her fate. He could almost see her death, so vivid was the apprehension.

At the gate to the ranch, he turned the team, letting them move along at their own slow pace to prolong the inevitable.

She felt as if her heart were breaking, as if she could hear the cracks and feel the wrenching apart of each blood vessel, of each cell, the living flesh ripped and torn. This couldn't happen, she wouldn't let it.

The ranch house and barn, the bunkhouse and the new cookhouse, grew to life-size before them. This was her home, where she belonged, riding free. She turned and looked at the man beside her, the man sh loved. How could he ask her to make such a choice? Whatever happened with the ranch, her father's dream transpired into her own, she must remain who and what she was. Couldn't Mitch see that?

Yet, there was more to life than taking, there was giving too. It would break her heart, her spirit, if he rode away from her. There must be no more lonely nights. With a sigh she asked, "Would we have children?" She hadn't guessed she would ask that question until it was out.

He hauled up on the reins, dropped them, moved toward her. Relief burst through him like spring sunlight, a joy so supreme he wanted to shout to the heavens. "Oh, Charlie" was all, though, that he could say before enveloping her in his arms, burying his nose in her silken hair. "Yes, yes, we'll have children."

She clung to him, squeezing so tightly it made her arms ache with the effort. "I won't give up the ranch. Not that. The other, maybe, but not the ranch. We will live here."

"Of course, here. Oh, Charlie, I love you."

He kissed her throat, her jaw, nibbled at her chin and nose, then opened his mouth over hers, drawing in her sweet essence.

When at last they drew a little apart to gaze at one another, it was as if a new day had dawned, separate from all the rest, with promises of its own. Everything would be fresh, all the old scars healed. They believed that, each of them, fervently and absolutely.

She felt a stirring, a dark nameless menace uncoiling from the very depths of her soul, but she pushed it down to bask in the light of their love. Nothing was ever perfect, and she was foolish to expect it to be so. You took the most of the good and the least of the bad and made the best out of it you possibly could. That's what her father always said, and he was right, of course.

With trembling fingers she traced the scar into the white streak of hair. He closed his eyes to memories of the past her touch evoked. Too long he had worn the mark like a symbol of his failure, the emptiness in his life. He captured her hand, pulled it down to his mouth, and sucked at each finger, then traced the lines in her palm with the tip of his tongue.

"You are my love," he murmured into the flesh there, "my life."

She shivered with desire, a wanton sensation that shocked her with its intensity.

"Let's go, let's go home," she finally told him shakily.

He nodded and took up the reins. She wrapped her hands through the crook of his arm as they rode into the yard and toward the barn.

Settled cozily in the cabin that no longer seemed so empty, so lonely, they chatted, sitting close together so they could touch. The wedding would not take place until after everyone returned from Cheyenne, they decided. It would be the biggest celebration the territory had ever seen. In their happiness they even agreed to invite the colonel. He would see that they were forming a strong union and stop this ridiculous range war. He would learn they could all live in peace in this vast country.

It was as if speaking of the colonel, even in such an abstract way, somehow brought the man himself to the Double H, for he arrived that very afternoon in a fine black and gold buggy pulled by a spirited red mare. Wolf was with him, doing the driving, and he hopped down and went to the other side to assist the large man down from the single seat.

For a moment she remained in the doorway, then squaring her shoulders walked out on the porch, followed by Mitch. For some reason she didn't want the colonel in her home, and hoped to prevent that by speaking with him on the porch. Not very hospitable, but considering the circumstances, she thought it forgivable.

The colonel tilted his head to gaze at her standing at the top of the three steps and removed his hat.

"Miss Houston, I see you are on the mend."

She nodded and that's when Mitch stepped out of the deep shadows under the sloping roof to stand at her side.

The colonel showed little surprise. "Mr. Fallon, I had heard you were a hand over here, but surely they could use you on the roundup, or was the Double H able to hire more hands?"

"What do you want, Dunkirk?" Mitch said, and stepped down so he was standing between the colonel and Charlie.

The colonel held his ground, not at all intimidated. "I came to talk to Miss Houston. Business. In private. If you don't mind."

"As it happens, I do," Mitch said.

"And as it happens, do you have that right?" the colonel asked, smirking.

Charlie stepped out from behind Mitch. "As it happens, Colonel, he does."

Mitch had studied this man closely in the several encounters he'd had with him, and never once had he seen him show surprise or doubt. It flickered through his close-set eyes now.

"Ah, well I suppose I shouldn't wonder. A fine-looking woman like you, all alone to run this . . . well, this rather shoddy place. It follows that the first smooth-talking good-looking man who comes along could get himself a profitable toehold.

"I should be most careful if I were you, dear lady. Men like Fallon here are experienced at deceit. He will have his hands on all your . . . uhm . . . assets before you can look twice."

Mitch tensed at her side, the bodyguard Wolf responded in kind, but remained a few steps away in the yard.

"Why, Colonel," she said sweetly before Mitch could react further, "I'm surprised at your concern. All along I thought that was *your* intent."

Nothing fazed the uniformed man, and he merely smiled and spent some time glancing over the outbuildings, as if he had come to buy. "Not much of a place, is it? But then, it's the land that counts, isn't it? And you have how much?"

"I'm sure you know exactly how much. My father and I each claimed the maximum allowed by law. Of course, we didn't hire anyone to get any illegally for us."

"Ah, but you, like the rest of us, run your cattle on free range, dear lady, technically claiming it as your own."

"What do you want, Dunkirk?" Mitch asked again. "Cut the bull and get to what you came here for."

"Yes, well. I came to make the lady one final offer for the Double H before ... well, before—"

"You burn it to the ground?" she shouted, incensed. "Get out. I don't want to sell, not to you or anyone else. This is my place. My father died for it."

The colonel eyed her savagely for a moment. "And, my dear woman, you may do the same."

Mitch was at the colonel's throat before Wolf could move or Charlie could cry out. He wrestled the fat man out into the yard and punched viciously at his face.

Wolf let out a savage growl and landed on Mitch, hooking a thick arm around his neck from behind and dragging him off the heaving colonel. Mitch was a big man, but Wolf stood two or three inches taller and probably outweighed him by forty or fifty pounds. He pitched Mitch halfway across the yard with seemingly little effort. Mitch skidded and rolled, but amazingly was back on his feet like a supple animal and charged Wolf, who had turned to help the colonel up off the ground.

Mitch's hurtling body hit Wolf low, just as the man pulled the colonel upright. When he smashed into the huge bodyguard, all three went down into a pile that for a moment looked all arms and legs and one large belly.

Charlie waited no longer, but ran inside to fetch her Winchester from the corner, jacked a round into the chamber, and hurried back outside. By the time she stumbled down the steps into the yard, the colonel sat dazed and bewildered while Mitchell Fallon beat Wolf bloody. The man had already stopped fighting back, but Mitch kept pounding him, pulling him within reach, hitting him, and when he staggered as if to fall, propping him upright for another round.

For a moment she stared, transfixed by such sheer brutality. She had expected to come back out here to save Mitch's hide. God knew, she wouldn't have shot anyone, or at least she didn't think she would have. Now what did she do? Wait till Mitch beat the man to a bloody pulp, or make the gesture anyway and put a stop to this ridiculous situation.

The decision was easily made, for she hated watching anyone get beaten so badly. She pointed the gun on a slant into the air and fired off a shot, jacked another round into the chamber and fired it too. Mitch hunched his shoulders, hesitated for a moment without looking back at her, and Wolf fell, first to his knees, then flat on his face. With a roar Mitch bent down, grabbed the unconscious man by the collar of his shirt and the back of his belt to drag him over to the colonel, who had finally managed to stagger to his feet.

"Take your filth out of here before I kill him," Mitch said through gasps. "You stay away from here and from her." He whirled and pointed at Charlie where she stood holding the Winchester down at her side. "Or I'll let her shoot you, you son of a bitch."

Her mouth dropped open. As amazed as she'd been at the fury Mitch had displayed, at his obvious intent to actually beat the man Wolf to death, she was even more amazed that he could say such a thing in an almost humorous tone.

The colonel retrieved his hat from where it had fallen in the grass and sparing only one glance for his bloody bodyguard huffed out to the buggy and climbed aboard.

With disdain he spat in the dust, then said, "I'll send someone for him. If you decide to kill him, let me know and I won't waste my time. I've got more where he came from. More than you can imagine. If you're smart you'll take what you can get for your shipment of beeves and light out, because nothing is going to stop me from having all the land. Certainly not one burnt-out gunslinger and a female who can't shoot straight."

Chapter Fifteen

For several moments Charlie gaped after the colonel's buggy and the thin trail of dust it left.

"I ought to show you how straight I can shoot, you old fool," she shouted into the wind, but didn't raise the gun, for she had remembered Mitch.

He stood staring down at the unconscious Wolf, and she went to him. "Are you hurt?" She pulled him around to inspect his face. Other than a trickle of blood from a small cut on one cheekbone he didn't have a mark on him. She put an arm around his waist and he squeezed her shoulder, grimaced.

"I think I broke my damned hand," he said.

"Come on inside, I'll clean it up, we'll see. It wouldn't be any wonder. I thought you were going to beat him to death."

Mitch shrugged. "He was going to do the same to me. I just did it first, that's all."

She glanced nervously up at him. The violence he'd unleashed was an awesome thing, and she wasn't sure she liked it. This man kept a lot more hidden than she would ever have guessed.

"What shall we do with him?" She gestured toward Wolf, who showed no signs of coming to.

Mitch touched him with the toe of his boot. "Poor bastard."

"Poor?"

"He did what he was paid to do and that no-good Dunkirk just leaves him lying here like a discarded carcass."

She grinned.

"What the hell is so funny?" he asked, and began to inspect his swollen, battered knuckles.

"You are. You beat the man senseless, then feel sorry for him. I don't know what I was worried about."

They went up the steps together and crossed the porch into the house without speaking. Inside, she made him sit in a chair while she immersed his hands in a pan of cold water to take down the swelling.

He concentrated on her ministrations for a while, then asked, "What did you mean, you didn't know what you were worried about?"

"Oh, nothing really."

"Yes, you did. Tell me."

"I was . . . well, a little unnerved when you . . . when you wouldn't stop hitting that man. It was so violent, so brutal, and I guess I'd never actually seen that side of you before."

He nodded, waited while she tore strips of cotton feed sack to bind his right fist. Tongue between her lips she gently wrapped the battered hand and tied off the bandage.

"I'm sorry if I scared you," he said when she'd finished.

"Well, you did."

"But then?"

"Then what?"

"You said you didn't know . . ."

"Oh, yes. That. When I saw the pity in your eyes and you actually felt sorry for your victim, well, I guess I realized I had nothing to worry about."

He circled her neck with his left hand, the one that

had only delivered a few blows and hadn't suffered drastically from the fight, and pulled her toward him. "The only thing you've got to worry about, darlin', is feeding me before I starve to death."

Her eyes grew wide, her mouth pursed. "Oh, dear."

"What?" he asked softly. He leaned close, kissed her lightly under one ear.

"Well, I can't . . ." She shivered as he nibbled down the side of her neck.

"Go on," he said and took a big love bite.

"I forgot to tell you, I can't . . ."

He pulled the collar of the dress down as far as he could, fiddled with some buttons at her throat, and kissed her in the vee, his hot breath washing down between her breasts. "Can't?"

"Cook," she blurted. "I—can't—cook. Oh, dear, Mitch."

She collapsed into his arms, while he worked the dress open with one hand, slowly, awkwardly. His mouth followed the parting of material with such leisurely passion that Charlie gathered handfuls of his shirt and yanked, trying to make him move faster.

He stopped abruptly. Hot breath in and out, moistening the skin where his mouth waited.

"What? What is it?" she asked, almost frantic with desire.

"You can't cook? You can't cook? My God, what am I thinking."

With that he abandoned breaking trail between her breasts and lifted her into his arms. He carried her to the bed. "Well, that does it, woman. I can't make love to you if you can't cook." He lay her on the mattress very carefully and stood over her, looking down, shaking his head woefully. "Too bad too. You're a fine-looking woman, even if you do dress kind of funny."

He turned from her, fetched his hat, put it on, and went out the door. She lay there for a moment, not sure whether to take him seriously or not. She waited for him to return, hands lying across her quivering stomach.

After a minute she called, "Mitch?" No answer.

Surely he'd been teasing. Was just lying in wait for her outside the door. "Mitch, where are you?"

He stuck his head around the doorjamb. "Ma'am, I was just thinking maybe I'd better pour a bucket of water over this poor fellow. I'd hate for him to lay out here and die while we're having all this fun. Wait right where you are, don't move. I have a feeling we're going to have to discuss this cooking thing." He pointed a finger at her, grinned, and bounded off the porch.

In a little while she crawled carefully off the bed, still favoring her sore muscles, and went to the door. Mitch had revived Wolf and both were sitting in the yard side by side deep in a very serious conversation. Quietly she closed the door and took off the dress, stripping right down to the buff, immensely relieved to be rid of the long stockings and hateful lace-up shoes. Then she pulled on her BVDs, jeans and chambray shirt, thick white socks and a pair of boots, not the ones she'd worn on roundup, for she couldn't find them anywhere.

Then she went out to sit on the porch. Wolf and Mitch were nowhere to be seen, but she wasn't worried. It wasn't long before Wolf rode out of the barn on a mustang, one of hers no doubt, and Mitch came walking across the yard. She rose to go meet him, and when he saw her in her range-riding clothes, he raised an eyebrow but said nothing.

"Still hungry?" she asked.

"A lot of good it'll do me."

"I've got some canned peaches."

"Well, I suppose I can live on canned peaches . . . and love."

"Do you think so?"

He stopped right there in the middle of the yard and pulled her close. "I know so."

Someone rode up in the yard in a big hurry, shouting for Charlie, for anyone, in a loud frantic voice.

It was Ritter. Heart in her throat Charlie turned to face the man.

"Oh, Gawd, Miss Charlie. Thank God you're here. And Fallon too." He stopped to get his breath. Under him, the horse danced and snorted.

"What? Ritter, what in the world—?"

"It's Mr. Yancey. They've killed him. Blasted sons a bitches have killed him. And P.J., he lit into one of 'em and got his arm broke for his troubles." Ritter stopped again, dismounting from the excited horse. It ran off toward the corral whinnying.

"Who? For God's sake, Yancey dead?" She stared through tears.

Mitch put an arm around her shoulder. "Who did this, Ritter?"

"One of them blamed gunsels of the colonel's. Rode up on us out of nowhere. Started in on Yancey, you know how he was. Couldn't rile him if you tried. Knew better than to outright shoot him, so they just kept picking and picking. Finally set him off and he went for his rifle. Never got it out of the scabbard. Just shot him. Dang it, it was murder, pure and simple."

She staggered into Mitch's grasp. Not Yancey. Not dear, sweet Yancey. "I knew him all my life," she cried into Mitch's chest, the world swirling blackly around her.

"Are you sure he's dead?" Mitch asked Ritter, holding on to her tightly.

"Wasn't when I left, but they shot him right through the chest with a .44. Ain't nothin' would save a man from that."

She grabbed Mitch's shoulders. "We've got to go to him, now, before it's too late."

He nodded, a dread rising in his throat. He wished he could just take her far away to some safe place where nothing could harm her, where no one could get close enough to bring her pain. But he knew that would never happen, because there wasn't any such place. Not for this woman, and certainly not for him.

Despite Mitch's objections, Charlie insisted on riding out to see about Yancey.

"Just let me hitch up the buckboard at least," he pleaded, even as he saddled a mean-tempered buckskin for her. The choice horses were all in the remuda with the roundup.

"You know I can do that myself. And I can ride. I'm only sore, not broke."

Mitch yanked the latigo through the cinch. The buckskin grunted and kicked out. Mitch exploded. "Dang knothead. Charlie, dammit, you've got no business riding this half-broke mustang."

She shooed him away and stepped her left toe into the stirrup. "You just take care of yourself, Mitchell Fallon, and I'll do the same." Swinging deftly into the saddle, she hauled back on the reins just hard enough to let the horse know who was boss. "Settle down before I take a board to you," she said, then scratched the fractious horse behind one ear.

The mustang darted sideways and tossed his head trying to dislodge the bit. She kicked him into a gallop, leaving Mitch and Ritter staring after her. The half-wild buckskin wasn't Belle, nor did he give the smooth easy ride of the poor little lost roan, but she rode him wildly and at full tilt out across the field, turned, and rode back into the yard. The ride set all her muscles to aching and she was reminded of her near miss under the stampeding cattle.

She smiled grimly down on the two men. "He's fine, he'll do. You coming or not?"

Dusk closed around the trio as they reached camp, and every muscle and bone in Charlie's body cried out for relief. She tried to hide her pain from Mitch, but he guessed and insisted on helping her down off the mustang. That she allowed such a thing told him all he needed to know, but he didn't try to stop her when she broke into a run on spying Yancey lying beside the fire.

P.J. spoke first and loudest when she sank to her knees beside her beloved ramrod. "I tried to stop 'em, Miss Charlie. But they just flat out shot him. Throwed me off my horse and busted my arm." He cradled the arm close to his body, sitting there beside his boss and staring into the fire because he couldn't bear to look at her.

"He's still breathing," she said softly. She laid a hand on Yancey's forehead and his eyelids flickered.

The sound he made wasn't exactly a word, though it apparently was intended to be.

"Hush, now. You'll be fine." She looked up and around at the men, some of whom had just wandered over. Most of course were out gathering cattle. "Has anyone sent for the doctor?"

"We did that, Miss Charlie. Soon as it happened."

"Crane done what he could too," another added.

"And the doc, he ain't in town. Trent come back just a while ago and said he had gone to a place up on the Missouri. Some feller fell out of his loft and broke his back. A nester."

She turned back the blanket to inspect the hole in Yancey's chest. His shirt had been ripped away and a crude dressing applied to the wound. It was soaked with blood. She removed the cloth with a grimace; the blue-black hole, about the size of her middle finger, oozed blood.

"Did the bullet go clean through?" she asked.

Crane appeared from the cluster of men. "A .44 Winchester, at close range. Must've missed every bone he's got in there. It come out the back all right. Left him an even bigger hole. I covered it up best I could. You know chest wounds, Miss Houston. If he's lung shot, well, then we can just wait for him to die."

"Or not," she shouted at the man. "He can hear you."

The cook shrugged as if it made no difference, then dissolved back into the small gathering of men.

She found Yancey's clammy, feverish hand and held it in both hers. "Now you listen to me, Yancey Barton. You will not die and leave me with all this. Not after all we've been through together."

Yancey moved his lips into a grin that looked more like a grimace of pain. "Couldn't . . . couldn't face old Matt . . . if I did that," he gasped out. "And I'm sure headed the same place." What might have passed for a chuckle turned into a groan and the man fell silent.

"Well, you're just not going to die. I won't let you. Crane, get me some hot water and clean rags and something for bandages."

She had Mitch turn Yancey gently so she could wash and bandage the wound in his back, then carefully folded a clean blanket and lay it on the bloodied one before easing the groaning man down. Mitch held the washpan close so she could clean the chest wound, then tore strips from the cotton fabric to tie the bandage on.

After giving Yancey some more whiskey to help him sleep, Mitch and Charlie found bedding of their own for the night.

"I wish you didn't have to sleep out on the ground so soon after our accident," Mitch told her when she lowered herself very carefully. "I'm going to go rustle us up some supper. Crane's got a pot on the fire.

Whatever's in it will beat what we've had so far today."

"Mitch?" She looked up at him gratefully.

He turned, waited.

"Thank you."

Jaw clenched, he nodded. Damndest most stubborn woman he'd ever met in his life. As he looked down into her glistening dark eyes, a fist took hold of his heart and squeezed until he gasped. How he loved her. Dear God, if anything happened to her he couldn't live, and he'd probably be so insane with grief he'd take half the world with him when he went.

Fetching food for the two of them had only been half the reason Mitch left Charlie's side. Within him had swelled a bitter hatred, a need for revenge against the men who had struck once more at the woman he loved. He wanted to ask some questions out of her hearing. He signaled P.J. to follow him away from the campfire, and the young cowboy did so, despite the obvious pain of the broken arm.

Together they stood near the chuck wagon.

"Now, I want to know who those men were that shot your ramrod."

P.J. frowned. "Two of those gunslingers the colonel hired. I don't know names."

"Then tell me what they looked like."

"One was big and ugly, wore a right fancy silver buckle and leather holster. The other was a fat little runt, looked like a damned kid not dry behind the ears. He kept giggling like his wheelbarrow wasn't fully loaded. Might not have been, but he could use a gun just the same.

"Mister, I did my best to stop what happened. I even took a shot at them after they knocked me off my horse. It was no use. Hell, I'd fight for Miss Charlie, but I ain't no gunslinger, I'm a dang cowboy."

Mitch patted the man on his uninjured shoulder.

"Hey, I know. You did all you could. It's that Cross and Neddy that's to blame for this, not you."

P.J. pointed at him. "Yeah, that's it. That tubby feller called the other'n Cross, and I forgot till you said it. Cross, that's it. The ugly one's name was Cross."

Mitch nodded. "I'll be riding out later tonight, after everyone is asleep." He glanced quickly toward Charlie, who sat near Yancey staring into the fire. "I don't come back, you see Ritter takes care of her, you hear?"

"I'll watch her myself too," P.J. declared. "She's a plumb brave woman, good as any man I ever saw."

"You do that, but tell Ritter to keep an eye on her till I get back, and not let her do anything too foolish. And tell him to be careful of Crane, you understand?"

"The cook?"

Mitch nodded, picked up two tin plates, and began to fill them both with beans from the kettle hanging over the dying fire. "Just tell him, he'll know what to do, take my word for it."

Carrying the steaming plates of beans seasoned with fatback, Mitch tried to envision the life he and Charlie would have together, the happiness they would find, the children they would bring into this vast Montana Territory once this mess with the colonel was cleared up. The kids would be stubborn and pretty like her, mean and strong like him. They'd whip the world, they would.

"What are you grinning at?" Charlie asked when she took the plate.

"I was just thinking of our kids. What they'll look like with you and me for folks."

"Oh, Mitch," she said, and wiped her eyes on the back of her hand.

"Hey, he's going to be fine. Eat up. You need to

get your strength back if you intend to keep on traipsing around, and I reckon you do."

They both cleaned their plates before retiring side by side. He held her in his arms until her breathing evened out, little puffs of air flowing over his face tucked down against hers. Then he eased carefully from the embrace and went to saddle the stallion.

At his approach the black nickered and pulled at the rope tying him to the corral. Horses around him whinnied and trampled the ground, but quieted after Mitch led his mount away. He waited until he was out of view of the camp before he mounted up and rode toward the Circle D and a showdown with Cross and Neddy. It had been a long time coming.

When Mitch hadn't returned by the time the doc arrived at camp the next day, Charlie, as Ritter put it, "had a wall-eyed fit." He thought for a while he was going to have to tie her up to keep her there. If it hadn't been for Yancey, she would have ridden out in search of Fallon. As it was, she chose to ride with the wounded ramrod back to Miles City in the back of Doc's wagon. She was afraid he wouldn't live, and she refused to let him die alone with no one holding his hand.

She couldn't find Mitch anywhere in Miles City, but didn't have much of a clue as to where to look. She did, however, catch up on news about the Indian troubles. After General Terry pulled the fat out of the fire, saving Reno and Benteen who had ridden in on the heels of Custer's defeat, the tide of battle had shifted. The army had the Indians on the run. She grieved for all those who had died on both sides and most especially the innocent victims. But there was nothing she could do and she had Yancey and Mitch to worry about.

As the days passed without word from Mitch, her heart turned to ice. Despite all his words, he had left her. It was obvious. On the fourth day of Yancey's confinement, when he began to show some real sign that he truly would recover, she rode out early and headed for the Circle D Ranch. If anyone there had seen Mitchell Fallon they probably wouldn't tell her, but she had no place else to look.

When the colonel greeted her before she could dismount she didn't know what to say to the man. He was responsible for so much heartache that what she wanted to do was yank her Winchester from its scabbard and shoot him between the eyes. Instead, she held her fury in check and played the game by his rules.

"Why, what a pleasant surprise, Miss Houston. You honor me. Light awhile. Would you like a cold drink?"

She licked at dry lips, removed her hat, and blotted sweat from her forehead with the curve of her arm. Much as it galled her to accept refreshment from the man, she couldn't resist, and swung down from the horse.

"That would be nice, thank you." Her tone was scarcely civil.

They sat on the porch, the colonel looking well pleased. "Now, tell me, what brings you out to the back forty on such a day? Are we ready to make a deal?"

She played with her hat a moment, then put it on the floor beside her, tented her fingers, and, without looking at the colonel for fear of what she might see there, remarked as casually as she could, "I wonder if you've seen Mitchell Fallon lately?"

The colonel threw back his head and laughed. Before she could react, a man she had never seen before came out carrying a tray with a pitcher and two glasses. He wore guns on both hips, and she couldn't help but think about how silly he looked serving them drinks, as if he were a maid.

After the awkward gunman poured them each a glass of cold lemonade, the colonel lifted his as if making a silent toast, then took a sip. She stared at him.

"I could have warned you the man wasn't trustworthy. So now he's left you in the lurch as well. That's too bad. Well, of course, he does still owe me some time. Some men, my dear, realize who the winner will be and that's the side they wish to fight on. Mr. Fallon is one such man, I can assure you."

Heat flushed up her throat and her head throbbed. She drank thirstily from the glass, then thunked it back in the tray and stood up.

"You, sir, are not going to get away with what you are trying to do to all of us. I promise you that. We will stop you. You should never have sent your men after my ramrod, because frankly, Colonel, I don't care much what I have to do to bring you down now.

"My father worked for one of the biggest and best cattlemen Texas ever produced, and he never did the things you have done to earn his fortune. My father, sir, would have spit in your eye and cut you off at the knees, and that is exactly what I will do, sooner or later. You can count on it.

"And if you do see Mr. Fallon, tell him for me that it goes double for him should he choose to stand against me."

The colonel simply opened his arms wide as if to say, *here I am, do what you will,* and then he smiled.

She scooped up her hat, hitting the edge of the table so that the pitcher and glasses rattled. One toppled to the floor, shattering in hundreds of glistening pieces that crunched under her boots as she strode across the porch.

Weary and sad, she rode on over to the Double H, expecting to find no one there. An extra horse browsed in the corral with the few unbroken mustangs. She turned her buckskin in with them, planning on staying overnight before riding back to see about Yancey.

Carrying the Winchester she went up to the house to see who was there. The sun sat on the lip of the mountains far to the west and the air had begun to cool somewhat. She wanted a bath and a long night's sleep in her own bed. Instead she would have to deal with a visitor. A drift of smoke came from the fireplace chimney at the cabin. Someone had settled into the place, a drifter perhaps, or maybe even a squatter who thought the place abandoned.

She jacked a shell into the breech and crept quietly up the steps, staying to one side of the door.

"Whoever's in there, come on out, hands where I can see them." She lifted the rifle to her waist.

The door creaked slowly open and Wolf filled the doorway. He held both hands out away from his hips, but he wore no gun.

His pockmarked, lupine face lit with what passed for a grin. "Sorry, ma'am. I worried about the place. Decided to look after it. I'll get my stuff, get out of your way."

She grinned a little herself and sighed with relief, lowering her rifle barrel so it pointed at the porch floor.

The man showed no signs of the beating Mitch had given him, even the worst of the cuts and bruises had plenty of time to heal. She insisted he stay, and he moved his stuff to the bunkhouse with what appeared to be pleasure. With Wolf it was difficult to tell.

"I'm afraid I can't offer you supper," she said from the doorway of the bunkhouse. "I'm only going to be here overnight."

She watched the man arrange his things beside the bunk, and then he looked up shyly. "I been here since,

well, since the fight. Didn't have a place to go. I hope
. . . I mean, I'll leave."

"Nonsense. I'm shorthanded. The colonel surely
won't welcome you with open arms."

"They come to burn you out. I run them off."

"My God," she said. "When? I mean, thank you."

He nodded and sat on the bunk, his long legs
splayed. After a moment's silence, he looked at her
as if to say, what next?

"Have you seen Mitchell Fallon?" she asked, misery
and shame in her voice. She hated what his leaving
had done to her. How long could she chase around
after this man who obviously wanted nothing more to
do with her.

"He the one . . . ?" Wolf ran a curved thumb above
his own eyelid into the hairline.

"Yes, him."

"Did they get him, you reckon?"

The possibility hadn't occurred to her, and she
flinched as if struck. "My God, do you think so? I
mean, I never thought, he is . . . well, so capable. He's
survived so much. He talked once about riding on to
Idaho, but dear God, you don't suppose?"

Wolf unwrapped his legs and arms and stood, the
top of his head almost touching the low-hung log raf-
ters. "Hey, no, you're probably right. The way he handled himself." He wryly fingered his own jaw. "And
I know for a fact no one could take him in a gunfight.
The man was fast and mean as a snake when he
wanted to be."

Feeling some measure of relief she nodded. She
couldn't decide which would be worse, Mitch leaving
her or Mitch shot down by some other hard case. She
didn't want him dead, no matter what he decided to
do.

They had no more to say to each other, so she told
him to stay as long as he liked, added that she would

appreciate it and would see he was compensated come payday.

"I think I'll just go to Cheyenne with the herd," she said over her shoulder. "Make yourself at home." She took her leave then, and trudged to the empty cabin.

Chapter Sixteen

Charlie, Ritter, and Crane returned from Cheyenne in early October to find Wolf and Yancey Barton at the ranch. Yancey was stove up some, but on the way to a full recovery. Every time he had to sit and rest a spell he would nearly foam at the mouth with impatience. Neither he nor Wolf had seen hide nor hair of Mitchell Fallon, but it was common knowledge that he had gunned down both Cross and Neddy in a gunfight and then disappeared. Word was that the sheriff, under the colonel's prodding, was looking for him for murder.

With a heavy heart, Charlie settled down to the business of readying the ranch for the coming winter. While happy to learn that Mitch hadn't left her deliberately, she could hardly bear the thought of him being hunted like some wild animal, and hoped that he had indeed ridden off to Idaho Territory.

As for the range war, the shooting of Cross and Neddy seemed to have taken some of the wind out of the colonel's sails. No one expected that to last long. Now that everyone was back from roundup, he would, as promised, get serious. The colonel had ordered the ranchers to take their profits and leave the territory. A few did, but most swore to stay and fight. So the next round was sure to begin, and soon.

With the prospect of another lonely winter stretching ahead of her, Charlie missed Mitch dreadfully, but she was fully prepared to do her part in holding off the colonel and his men.

Radine spotted Duffy McGrew in the crowd at the Powder Keg. Word was his wife had left him and gone back to Denver to be with her parents. The Stallings had bankrolled the ranch, everyone knew that, and Duffy was furious and drinking heavily.

As she delivered a round of beers, she overheard something that made her fear for her friend Charlie Houston.

"That son of a bitch Fallon ain't nothing but a no-good Yank," McGrew said to his cronies gathered around the table. "Give me half a chance I'd shoot that cowardly no-good. I know things about him he wouldn't want told."

Bending across the table, Radine deliberately let her full breasts lie on McGrew's arm. She wanted to learn more, and knew only one way to do it.

The rancher peered down the front of her scanty chemise, then stuck a folded bill there.

"Come on, baby," Radine said and took his hand.

The already staggering McGrew followed her upstairs.

Her only fear was that he would pass out before she could worm the information she wanted from him. But it was easier than she had thought, for he obviously needed to talk to someone and all she had to do was bring up the gunslinger's name.

"Damn traitor," McGrew said. "I was with him in the war and woulda followed him anywhere and did. We had a gang and was doing just fine till his sister led the vigilantes to our hideout." He paused and fumbled at her naked breasts. "Pretty things. My wife don't like me to touch her there."

Radine smiled seductively. "What did he do?"

"Left us. Run out when the dang sheriff and his band of killers showed up. Most of us was killed, but not me ... no, sir. And I know where there's others too.

"Oh, honey, come closer and let old Duffy have some of that."

"I will, baby. I will."

She snuggled up against the man, who was so drunk he couldn't perform, but he could talk.

"Kill him, hang him up in some tree for the buzzards. Teach him to run out on us, leave us for the wolves. Everyone can come spit on the sumbitch. Sent my man for the marshal, but he never come back. Neither one of 'em. Injuns probably got him."

"The marshal?"

McGrew snorted, but didn't reply. "Jest wait, you'll see."

He took a deep rattling breath and his head lolled away from her. She slipped from the loose embrace of the snoring, drunken McGrew, sat on the edge of the bed, and slipped into her robe. She was worried about the things he'd said. Worried for that handsome devil with the white streak in his hair and her friend Charlie Houston. The two of them had been mighty cozy, and then that awful gunfight. Radine had visited with Charlie a few times while she was laid up after her accident, but hadn't seen her since all the ranchers had ridden back from Cheyenne. She wondered if it would be considered proper for her to ride out for a visit before the winter storms cut them all off from one another. Good women friends were hard to find for someone like her.

Thinking of all the man on her bed had said, Radine decided she didn't care if it was proper or not. Charlie needed to know what she'd heard. First thing in the morning she would borrow Lance's buggy and ride out. She hated horses and never rode one. She had other uses for those particular parts of her body than getting them chafed raw by a leather saddle and the plodding of some dumb animal.

"This is really nice," Radine remarked when Charlie enthusiastically welcomed her into her home the next morning. The neat and cozy little cabin sure beat the dump she lived in, and she thought what it might be like to have something like this.

"It's okay for one person. We had plans for a bigger place, my father and I, but then he was killed before . . . before we got here." Charlie swallowed hard over the words, then smiled. "I never expected you, but it's wonderful to have a visitor. I'll make us some tea."

Radine nodded and sat where Charlie indicated, one of two straight-backed chairs at a small square table in one corner of the single room. A bed was shoved against another wall, and a stove used both for cooking and supplementing the heat of the fireplace sat across from the front door.

Charlie pulled a kettle onto the stove where a small fire crackled. The nights had grown chilly and she'd built a fire every morning now since returning from Cheyenne. Winter would soon be upon them.

"Would you like some music? I have a music box. Let me get it." Charlie started toward the bed.

"I came to tell you something. Music would be nice. Maybe later. This is important."

Charlie twisted around at the serious tone in Radine's voice. Her cherub face carried a frown that took away its usual gaiety. She forgot the music box and went to sit in the chair near Radine.

"What is it? You look so . . . so intense."

Radine nodded and fiddled with the hem of her best shawl worn specially for this occasion. She did not go calling often and felt unsure of herself. "It's about . . .

about that man, the tall man with the white streak in his hair?"

Charlie's heart tumbled around until she had to catch her breath. "What about him? Tell me, have you seen him? Is he all right? Is it true what they say about him being wanted for murder? Oh, Radine, please."

"I remembered how you felt about him, that's why I came all the way out here. I thought you might get a message to him. If he's still around he needs to light out. Go far and fast."

Charlie nodded. "But I'm sure he knows that. He must know the sheriff is looking for him."

"Oh, no, it's worse than that. The sheriff is the least of his troubles. That old fart couldn't scare anyone with both guns drawing a bead. He can't see across the street.

"No, this is someone else. Someone who'll do a lot worse than arrest him for murder."

"What are you talking about?" Charlie felt as if her life were seeping out of her through tiny holes, and she would never get it back.

"That McGrew fella, owns the ranch up north near the Missouri?"

Charlie nodded, waited.

Radine told her what Duffy McGrew had said as their tea grew cold in its cups.

By the time she was finished Radine was practically in tears.

Charlie gaped at her. The only sound in the room was the sizzling of water in the kettle until she dragged in a deep breath. "My God. Is everyone in the world crazy? Did he say ... does he have any idea where Mitch is? I mean, I haven't seen him. He could be anywhere.

"That's probably it. Mitch is probably not even

around here anymore. He's gone, I'm sure. Long gone where no one can find him."

She clasped Radine's fisted hands in hers and gazed into her wide eyes, a racking pain shooting through her chest.

Outside the wind kicked up, rattling the golden leaves in the aspen trees along the ridge behind the house, and on the stove the water continued to boil, untended.

Mitch led the black through the falling shadows of night, pausing a moment before venturing into the open between the draw and Charlie's cabin. A cold wind cut through his shirt, and he wished again for a good thick mackinaw.

She was in there, he could see a glow through the deer hides tacked over the windows to keep out the cold night air. He didn't dare approach for fear someone was watching the house.

Shivering, he leaned against the warmth of the stallion's quivering shoulder. He should have left the territory days ago, weeks ago, even before he'd hunted down that devil Cross and his crazy sidekick Neddy. Now he didn't know how he was going to protect her against what was sure to come. If he revealed himself anyone could shoot him and get away with it. Colonel Dunkirk and the sheriff had seen to that with the bounty they'd put on his head for murder. It would be paid for his dead body, no questions asked.

A clattering sound caught his attention and he raised his head into the wind. Something furtive had rattled through gravel; a man, an animal? He listened, checked the stallion for signs he'd heard it, but the horse remained docile, too weary to act up. He just stood hipshot, hindquarters turned to the wind, head down.

Both of us sort of feel the same way, old buddy, Mitch thought without speaking aloud.

Bits of icy moisture struck his cheeks and the brisk smell of high country snow rode on the wind. He pawed around in his saddlebags, dragged out a blanket and canvas poncho. He wrapped up in both and settled down to keep an eye on the cabin. Soon the airborne pellets turned to flakes. The first snow of the season and him without home or hearth. The light in the cabin, her invisible presence nearby, tugged at him, and he wanted only to hold her in his arms while they lay together near a warm fire.

Did he dare? No one would see him, surely. There were no lights in the bunkhouse, and she would probably have let all the men go except Ritter and Yancey and that sneaky Crane. He'd been on the verge of figuring out what to do about the traitorous man and his obvious connection to Dunkirk when Yancey was shot.

A shadow flitted across the window shade at the back of the house and he hunched deeper into the shadows. The back door cracked open, letting out a thin wedge of light. Then she was standing there, door thrown open. She stepped out into the blowing snow, leaving the door wide so that he could see her plainly. He gasped with the beauty of her shapely long legs, supple curves to a narrow waist, and uptilted breasts hugged by the gossamer windblown gown.

Dear God, how he wanted to hold her, smell her, feel the silkiness of her skin.

He stepped out into the open, called her name softly, realized that she couldn't hear him for the wind, and called out again.

She stood in the snow for a moment, face tilted upward so that flakes caught at her eyelashes and melted on her cheeks. Riding the wind her name echoed like a vaguely recalled dream, and she opened her eyes, peered into the blowing snow.

"Mitch? Where are you?" She didn't expect a reply except in her wishful imagination.

Out of the darkness and wall of hurtling flakes appeared a shadowy figure, and again her name repeated. "Charlie. Charlie."

It was clear and real this time.

Joy exploded through her like sunlight on a spring day. It was Mitch. Ignoring bare feet and the frozen ground, she started to run, and at that precise moment a rifle shot rent the storm-swept night. A horse screamed and the shadow pitched forward without making a sound.

She shrieked and ran to the fallen man, oblivious to the prickly shrubs and rocks and tough sprigs of dried grass that chewed at her feet. She ignored the frigid wind and the icy pellets, felt only the searing pain in her heart. Kneeling beside him, she brushed a fan of snow-crusted hair from the side of his face and leaned close.

"Mitch? Oh, Mitch."

He moaned, tried to move. "Charlie?"

"Yes, oh, yes. Darling. We've got to get you inside."

He moved one arm, raised himself on that side. "Horse, get my horse."

She glanced around. It was so dark, she could see nothing but what was illuminated by the light coming from her open doorway. "I don't see."

"There, back there. Call . . . call him."

That turned out not to be necessary. The stallion emerged out of the darkness, nosing his master and snorting.

She reached for the reins, but the black tossed his head high and danced backward.

"Ho," Mitch said raggedly. "Ho down, there."

She darted out a hand, grabbed one dangling rein, and led the nervous animal to Mitch's side.

"Put my arm in the stirrup. Help me."

She could barely make out the weak plea, hurriedly positioned herself under him, and hoisted him up until his crooked elbow threaded through the stirrup. Then she led the horse slowly to the back door, dragging Mitch along. His arm slipped out once and they had to do it all over again. The stallion, skittish at first, finally seemed to understand what was expected of him, and he dragged his master literally to the door. Mitch was unconscious, the upper half of his body sprawled inside, the rest hanging out onto the ground.

Leaning against the huge stallion, she shoved him out of the way, then went inside and began the task of dragging Mitch the rest of the way into the house. It was as tough as wrestling with a thousand-pound steer, but all she could think of was getting him into the warmth. He couldn't die, she wouldn't let him. By the time she had sweated and grunted and strained to lug him inside, she was covered with perspiration and the warmth of the cabin had been replaced by a bone-chilling cold.

She slammed the door, filled the stove and fireplace with wood, then quickly dragged the heavy quilt off the bed. Kneeling beside Mitch she wiped his face gently with both palms. Hot tears of anguish poured down her cheeks. He was pale, tinged blue, and so cold.

Lips covering his, she breathed into his mouth as if she could give him some of her warmth. He made a small, weak sound down in his throat and shuddered.

Quickly she removed his shirt and boots. The blanket and poncho he'd had around him had fallen off in the effort to get him to the house, and she bundled the quilt around him tightly. Getting him warm had to come first, even before seeing to the wound, which wasn't bleeding profusely.

The small room heated up fast, the snow caught in his hair melted and formed a tiny puddle on the plank floor. Her own bare feet began to ache, but she ignored the pain to huddle over him, rubbing his hands briskly. Though some color returned to his cheeks he made no sound. He was breathing, though shallowly.

With trembling fingers she traced his features. The high, rugged brow, the eyes, sunken now, the wide cheekbones and square jawline, the fine nose and full, firm mouth; she touched the jagged scar that ran up into his dark hair and fragments of the pain he had endured shot through her fingertips straight to her soul.

"Oh, Mitch, don't you die. Don't you dare die. Where have you been, my darling? Where?"

She kissed him softly, then rose and poured boiling water into the washpan, fetched soap and a cloth, and sat down beside him on the floor to clean the wound. She prayed the bullet had gone all the way through, for she had no idea how to dig it out, even if she dared try.

The bullet had caught him high in the right shoulder and torn an ugly hole in the fleshy muscle where it came out. It was bleeding front and back, but not spurting. At least he wouldn't bleed to death. He remained unconscious all the time it took her to clean the two wounds and wrap them tightly. She was relieved because she had no whiskey to give him for the pain.

When she finished she put more wood in both fires, slipped hurriedly into her clothes, and went to take care of his horse. Only then did she begin to wonder who had been skulking around close enough to have seen Mitch in the darkness and shot him. By the time she returned from the barn, a full-fledged blizzard blew flat across the land, snow so thick she could hardly see the light from the cabin. No telling when it would stop. Maybe a piece of luck for Mitch, maybe not. No one could get to them for a while, and that would give him time to mend before facing the law, but should he need a doctor that could be bad.

Back inside, she found him just as she'd left him.

Kneeling there she skinned out of her clothes, except for the thick socks and underwear, and crawled under the quilt on the floor beside him. Snuggled close to the man she loved, she soon fell into an exhausted sleep, his heart beating firmly against her cheek.

Sometime before dawn he cried out and tried to roll over. She caught him about the waist with one arm.

"Shh, it's all right, you're okay."

"Charlie, is that you?"

"Yes, darling," she said.

"What happened?"

"Shh, be quiet. Go back to sleep." She kissed him, eased him back down. "We'll talk in the morning. You need to rest."

He was quiet for a while, breathing harshly. "Charlie?"

"Yes?"

"Are you sure it's you?"

"Oh, yes, it's me."

"I'm not dead?"

"No, you're not dead. Now go back to sleep."

He nodded, wrapped his good arm around her shoulders, and pulled her so close she could scarcely breathe. "Okay, I will. That's what I'll . . ."

She lay very still, ear pressed against his chest, but he had no more to say. For a long while she listened to the wind moaning around the eaves of the little cabin, then she too dropped off to sleep.

Mitch opened his eyes and found himself looking at log beams. He hunched, in preparation for climbing to his feet, but an intense pain slammed him flat before he could much more than wiggle.

"What . . . where . . . ?" He remembered nothing, his mind empty and black as a cave.

With a great deal of care against the fire that raged in his right shoulder, he rolled his head to one side. Saw the legs of chairs and a table; carefully turned the other way to gaze at the bedstead and one side of a potbellied stove. He tried to lick his lips, but found his tongue so dry it only clung to the top of his mouth.

What in the hell had happened to him? He couldn't even remember what he was doing last . . . night? morning? whatever. Nothing made sense.

Someone clattered across the floor, stomping hard with huge boots. A giant.

His head hammered. "Could you . . . could you quiet down?" he thought he said, but his ears told him different. It was more like gurgle, cough, grunt, gurgle.

She came into view then, kneeling beside him, her face flushed from the cold, her eyes bright and shiny as berries, her fingers touching him. The tips made cold little dots on his cheek.

"Charlie?" he croaked. He would have sung the name if he could have managed.

"Oh, you're awake." Tears poured down her cheeks but she laughed, and he thought he must be going crazy. "Oh, Mitch." She kissed him full on the lips, her mouth warm and sweet, the tears salty. With the one arm he could move he grabbed at her, ran his hand up and down her back to make sure she was real; all the while he drank of her kiss, keeping his eyes open so he could gaze at her wonderful face.

She cupped his cheeks in both hands, pulled back long enough to babble some words he wasn't sure he understood, then began to kiss him all over until his face and neck were wet.

He tried once again to say her name in a voice dry as husks.

"Oh, darling, I'm sorry. Wait, wait just a minute." She pulled away, despite him thinking he had a death grip on her, and was soon back with a dipper of water. She lifted his head and gave him a few sips, holding back when he tried to gulp too quickly.

"I thought you were dead. When I saw you fall I was so frightened. Did you see who shot you?" All this poured out as she fed him the cold, delicious water.

He drank and took in her every expression, the delicate lift of the fine brow, the wrinkle of her exotic nose, the sweep of the long black lashes. When he had enough, he pulled back from the dipper and swept it away with one hand, spilling the last few drops on himself and pulling her close again.

"Don't go. Don't leave. Ever, ever again," he said into her fragrant neck. Then he was falling, reaching up to hang on. Falling into blackness.

"I didn't leave you, Mitch. You left me," she whispered, but he couldn't hear her.

When he awoke again later in the morning, together they were able to get him into the bed, where he remained the rest of the day, taking only sips of water occasionally and sleeping the rest of the time.

Ritter came up along about noon and brought her some soup Crane had made from a tough old hen. She asked him in to tell him about Mitch, going into great detail to explain what had happened the night before.

"My God, Miss Charlie. Storm must have covered the sound of the gunshot. Who would have done a thing like that right at our doorstep?"

"Anyone. You know that. But most probably one of Dunkirk's men."

"He's wanted for murder. Could have been anyone who wants the bounty."

She studied him thoughtfully for a moment. "Maybe, but if so why didn't they come on down and claim the body?"

"Probably didn't want to face you," Ritter quipped.

"Smart. I'd a shot the bastard, no matter who it was."

"See what I mean?" Ritter said. "How is he, will he be all right?"

She shrugged. "It's clean. Who knows? You know what bullet wounds can be like. Some live, some die, even after you think they're okay. Oh, Ritter, I couldn't bear it if he died."

Ritter stared down at his boots, soaked from the snow he'd waded through. "Well, one thing's for sure, with the snow drifted like it is, it's liable to be a while 'fore anyone can show up for him."

"I won't let anyone take him."

"Even if it's the sheriff?"

She snorted. "Sheriff. That's a joke."

"Still, he is the law." Ritter watched her closely, believing she meant what she said. She was obviously in love with the gunslinger who lay there in her bed. He had watched them together, knew something was up, but hadn't thought it quite this serious. Miss Charlie seemed old enough to know better than to fall for a man like that. But, as he well knew, you didn't get to pick who you fell in love with. It just sort of happened. Sadly, sometimes there wasn't anything you could do about it, either.

"What are you going to do?" he asked.

"As soon as he can travel, I'm getting him out of here. Somewhere where no one will ever find him."

He nodded. Somehow he'd expected that. "And what about you?"

"Me?" she asked, gazing at the sleeping man in her bed.

"You can't go on the run with an outlaw."

She gritted her teeth and didn't say anything else.

After a while Ritter excused himself. "I'll bring up some more soup later on, maybe you can get some down him. It'll be good for him."

"Ritter?" she said when he swung open the door.

He waited.

"Don't tell anyone he's here."

"Not even Yancey?"

"Not even Yancey. This is between you and me. Promise?"

He fingered his hat a minute, then screwed it down on his head in preparation for going out into the bitterly cold, cloudy day. He twisted to look her in the eye. "I promise, Miss Charlie."

He stepped out onto the porch and pulled the door shut firmly behind him. He'd promise her anything. He'd do anything for her. He couldn't help loving her any more than she could help loving the outlaw. It was just the way things happened sometimes. The god-awful way things happened.

Chapter Seventeen

I t was long after dark when Mitch came awake, strangely alert and rested. Charlie lay curled into his left side, her warm backside tucked against the curve of his hip, her head on his arm. He rubbed his nose in her hair and thought about loving her forever, just like this. Waking up every morning to watch her sleeping next to him. Entering her as she slept, making slow, warm, easy love while daylight broke around them like some kind of bright magic.

He dragged in a harsh breath and held his eyes closed on the vision a moment longer. They would never know each other's bodies in such an intimate way. It was too late. Too late for both of them. He had to get away from her. Far away, before someone came and she was caught up in his guilt. Painted with the same brush that blackened his future.

She murmured and stirred, twisted in the bed so that when she opened her eyes they stared into his.

"Good morning," she said, and kissed him as if it were the most natural thing in the world. As if she were used to finding him in her bed.

He held her, squeezed his eyes shut. "Oh, God, Charlie. God." It was not a curse but a hopeless prayer. He knew better than to expect an answer.

"I love you, Mitchell Fallon," she whispered against his mouth, and ran her warm tongue over his lips.

He moaned and a deep-down ache nearly made him cry out. The agony of losing her might well be his undoing.

"Does it hurt?" She had misunderstood, and he let her.

It hurt all right, but the wound in his shoulder was not the cause of it. He flexed his right arm gently and found he could tolerate the jab of quick, slicing pain.

"It's better," he said, and turned away from her expression of devotion. "Is it still snowing?"

"Ah, so you are back among the living." Her tone rang oddly, as if he had hurt her.

Better a little now than a lot later.

When he didn't look back at her, she unfolded herself from the bed and went to put wood in the stove. It was chilly in the cabin, the fire only a cluster of glowing embers.

"You need to nail shutters over the windows for the winter."

"Yes," she said absentmindedly. "I didn't expect it to snow so early."

"That's the way with this country. You never know what to expect."

She stood near the fire, hands spread in the welcome warmth as the logs crackled to life. She hated what was going on between the two of them. The sudden coldness, the conversation that meant nothing. He hadn't truly returned to her after all.

"What is it, Mitch? What's wrong?" she finally asked when she could bear it no longer.

He avoided her gaze, stared at the wall beside the bed. "Wrong? What's wrong? Just about everything, I reckon." His voice was still weak, but harsh nevertheless.

"We'll figure something out. I meant between us. You and me."

"There is no us. No you and me. There's only you."

"We were going to get married, and then suddenly you're gone and the next thing I know you're wanted for murder and I don't even know where you are. If you're dead or alive. I love you, Mitch. You love me, I know you do. You came back. We'll go somewhere where they can't find you."

He snorted, made as if to rise, and groaned. "Dammit, that was a mistake, coming back. I've got to get out of here."

She rushed to the bed. "If you want out of here so bad, why did you return in the first place?" She glared down at him, wanting to pound on him and to hold him close, all at the same time.

"To make sure you were safe. To see you one more time. Hell, I don't know. I just keep coming back, don't I? If I'd followed my inclinations in the first place I wouldn't be within a thousand miles of here . . . of you. We'd both be better off."

"Then why are you? Why don't you just leave?" She clenched her fists, settled for beating on the mattress where she had lain at his side only a bit earlier. Dreaming of him, of his mouth and his hands and all of him surrounding her, enveloping her, soothing her. "Damn you, why don't you just leave?"

She threw herself at him.

He grunted at the agony that lanced through his wounded shoulder, then he had his arm around her, holding her close while she cried.

After a few moments her sobbing quieted and she moved her head to kiss his chest, sliding one hand down past his belly button to rest in the curly hairs below.

He gasped sharply and she nibbled at his throat, at his earlobe.

"Charlie, please don't."

"I will, I don't care." Her warm breath sent shivers through him, and then her seeking lips found his, her fingers caught in his hair so that he couldn't have pulled away if he had wanted to.

She shifted without breaking the kiss, and hovered over him, her firm breasts, bare beneath the night-gown, brushed at the hairs on his chest.

He cupped her round buttock with his good hand and urged her to straddle him. The quick frantic movement pulled their mouths apart, but she bent forward so that one breast touched his cheek. He shifted only slightly and took the taut dark nipple between his lips, flicking his tongue against the tip.

She rocked in ecstasy, locking her knees tight against his waist. She couldn't bear it if he stopped kissing her like that. Nothing had ever felt quite so wonderful, ever. Wave after wave of sweet warmth radiated from his mouth deep into the very core of her. Pulsating so that she desired it all, everything he had to give, but couldn't stand the thought of taking her breast from his mouth.

He pulled away and she cried out.

Placing his hand flat across her belly he gently shifted her up and back until he could slip inside her sweetness.

And then she was all hot and cold, wet and smooth, joyous and sublimely content, but with a wildness that possessed her, took her out of herself. The world opened, swallowed her into brilliant sunlight and velvety darkness as she rode a shaft of fiery pain that slipped away into an ecstasy that enthralled her with its beauty and passion.

When she came to her senses, lying facedown on his chest, his hand splayed in her tumbled hair, she thought she must have injured the shoulder wound. He breathed in great jagged gulps that sounded like sobs, and when she was able to rise from his grip she saw tears running from the corners of his closed eyes.

"Oh, Mitch, what's wrong? Is it your shoulder? We shouldn't have ... Oh, baby." She played her fingertips gently over his flesh, then wiped the tears where they ran down to his ears.

He opened his eyes, still drenched so they looked like mossy woodland pools, deep and dark and green pools, hiding all manner of secrets. His silence frightened her and she ran a finger over his full lips.

"Please say something, darling. Anything."

He swallowed, licked his lips. "I can't. There aren't any words. We are alive and I love you. Even if I never take another breath, I am complete at last." He pulled her down and kissed her so tenderly, so sweetly, that she herself wanted to cry with the beauty of it.

She lay with him until he fell asleep, too exhausted to speak further. Then she rose very carefully, washed in hot water from the kettle on the stove, and put on the dress he had bought her so long ago, when they had been planning their life together. Just wearing it made her feel closer to that time when they had thought happiness awaited just around the corner, closer to a life with him. A life, she saw now, that would never be.

She had no idea what would happen next, but whatever it was, it would happen to the both of them. She would not let him leave her again.

Charlie dropped another stick into the stove, shut the door, and turned in time to see the back door swing inward. Crane stood there staring right at her with wide shocked eyes.

"What do you want?" She ran toward him, tried to shove him back outside before he could spot Mitchell asleep in the bed. "What are you doing? Get out of here!"

He might as well have punched her in the stomach when he pulled the pistol and pointed it right at her. "Here, girlie. Stop acting like that." He jerked a quick look around the room, saw the man in her bed. "Just like I thought," he yelled and brought up the gun.

She screamed and swung on his extended arm, ruining his aim so that he shot through the floor. The gunshot boomed in the small room, black powder smoke burnt her eyes and nose.

Startled, Mitch came awake and lunged to a sitting position, grabbed his arm and yelled out in pain.

Nearly deaf from the gunshot, Charlie continued to wrestle with Crane.

He backhanded her, but she came right back at him, swinging an uppercut that caught him on the point of his chin and almost knocked him silly. It did loosen the gun from his grasp so that she was able to wrench it away.

She backed off, holding the pistol out in front of her with both hands. "Now. Now, you. You just don't move. What are you, crazy? What's gone wrong with you? We're kin. How dare you bust in here shooting up the place. No, no, don't you move. You just stay right there where you lay."

"What in the hell is going on?" Mitch yelled, staggering to his feet. Amazingly, he remained upright, though he swayed. All he wore was the bottom half of his union suit.

Feet pounded up the porch steps and someone hammered on the door. Voices yelled:

"What's going on in there?"

"Miss Charlie, you okay?"

"Open this consarned door before I kick it in."

She kept her eye on Crane, who showed no signs of rising from his position on all fours. He'd obviously never expected her to fight back so desperately and was now having a hard time getting over being belted in the jaw. She backed toward the front door, yelling out at the same time.

"Quit making so danged much noise. I'm coming, and we're all right. Hold your horses, dammit."

By then she had unlatched the door and in tumbled Yancey, Ritter, and Wolf, the latter making as if to kick the now helpless Crane, the other two panting and cussing under their breath. Snow flew from their boots and pant legs that were crusted in the white stuff. A jab of icy air came in with them and continued to come in until Charlie finally convinced them to shut the "damned door."

"What in thunderation is going on in here, anyways?" Yancey boomed. "Crane? Miss Charlie? Fallon? What the hell?"

"I can explain," she began.

Her cousin interrupted. "I was just trying to pay a visit, and she ups and—"

Wolf aimed a kick at the prone man's butt and he howled.

"Shut up, Crane," she ordered and gestured toward him with the gun. "What he was trying," she said to Yancey and Ritter, "was to shoot Mitch, and him already wounded and lying in bed asleep. He's crazy. And if he twitches one more time, I'm going to put a bullet between his ugly eyes, kin or no kin."

"Want me to take him out and throw him off a bluff?" Wolf asked in his low-down, husky voice.

Ritter held out a hand. "Now, take it easy, Wolf, and you too, Miss Charlie. No call to go shooting anyone or throwing him off no damn bluff."

She whirled toward him. "Don't you go trying to cajole me, I'm not your maiden aunt. I'll shoot the son of a bitch if I'm a mind to."

"She will too," Yancey said with some admiration.

Wolf made a sound that she supposed was amusement.

"And you just keep quiet too," she told her ramrod. "Let me think."

Everyone shut up, and all eyes turned toward her. She did, after all, have the gun.

After a moment Mitch groaned and sat down on the side of the bed, hard. Charlie poked the gun toward Yancey. "Here, you watch him," she said and went to Mitch's side.

"I can explain if anyone would just let me," Crane whimpered, acting brave now that no one was pointing a gun at him and Wolf had quit trying to stomp him to death.

Yancey cast Charlie a dark look. "Looks like to me there's a lot more explainin' than yours due around here. But we'll start with you. Speak." He glared at Crane and slammed the S & W on the table.

"I got the stew on the fire, and then I got to thinking it would be nice to . . . well, to visit with my cousin there. Having not seen her to talk with in a while. She used to enjoy my stories of her father and me as boys. Well, anyway, that's all I was doing. Being cooped up all the time is no fun.

"How was I to know she had . . . a man . . . well, in here in her bed, and would have such a mad fit when I caught them. How'd I know she wasn't a hostage?"

"A hostage? Caught us? You dumb little runt." She dragged her angry gaze away from Crane to check out Mitch, who was pale, but otherwise seemed fine. She said softly, "Why don't you lie back down."

"I'm fine. It's time I got out of here, anyway."

"Oh, you're not going anywhere in the shape you're in." That order issued, she turned her attention back to her visitors. "He didn't catch us doing anything, and even if he had, what business is it of his, or yours either?"

"No one said anything," Ritter muttered. She was wearing a damned dress! And had a man in her bed, and looked all sweet and self-satisfied. It was perfectly obvious what had been going on. And it was painfully obvious that it was none of his business, and she would be the first to tell him so if he brought it up. So he didn't.

"Why are you looking at me like that?" she demanded. He might not have said anything, but from the expression on his face, he was thinking it.

He shrugged and glanced at Yancey. "Like what? I didn't say a word, and I didn't look at you anyway."

A little shame-faced, Crane hauled himself to his feet, but kept one eye on his gun on the table and the other on the silent Wolf. He didn't think Yancey had it in him to shoot him in cold blood and Wolf kept looking at Charlie for a clue, so he inched over to the other chair and sat down opposite the man. "Whew, who'd of expected something like her just grabbing me as I come in the door and socking me like that?"

Yancey grinned broadly. "You socked him?"

Wolf issued his amused snort again.

"I did, sir. I most certainly did. And I'm about to sock somebody else too." She glared at each of them in turn.

Crane eased his hand across the table. "If nobody minds, I'm just going to take my gun and go back to the bunkhouse. This whole thing has upset me, and I don't think I want to stay here any longer. I suppose you'll be firing me from my job now," he said to Charlie as his fingers closed about the gun butt.

She studied him awhile, then thought of all the good stews and bread the man was capable of cooking up. "Oh, I reckon not. That is, if you behave yourself and mind your own business. Don't come sneaking around on me anymore. Come up to the front door proper-like, knock, and get invited in or not. Anyway, it wouldn't be right to throw you out in this dreadful weather."

Crane stuck the gun in his waistband and nodded. Next time he would he more careful, and he wouldn't worry if he had to shoot her as well as her outlaw friend. She'd pay for humiliating him in front of everyone. He dredged up the sweetest smile he could manage and went scuffling out the door.

"I'll keep an eye on him," Wolf said, and left too.

Yancey and Ritter stared at Charlie and Mitch, who sat side by side on the edge of the bed, then both broke out into laughter. In retrospect the situation was funny, but she realized that sooner or later they would want to know what Mitchell Fallon was doing lying wounded in her bed. For now they could all laugh about it. It would be a long hard winter, with few humorous situations, she would wager. It was best to take them where you could get them.

"I'm going to help him get away," Charlie told her two friends some time later after explanations concerning Fallon's presence were out of the way. "And if you're thinking on stopping me, then just leave. Get off this ranch and don't come back."

Ritter studied his boot toes; Yancey picked at the edges of an old cut on his thumb. Neither would look at Charlie. She had talked Mitch into getting back in bed, but he was wide awake and alert, holding her hand as she sat beside him.

"Think what you're doing," Yancey mumbled.

"I am thinking."

"If you take his side you'll lose everything you've worked so hard for, that Matt gave his life for. He's wanted for murder, Charlie."

"He didn't kill anyone, though," she insisted.

"Yes, I have. Plenty of times in the war," Mitch said, surprising them all. "I reckon that wasn't murder or there's a whole bunch of killers running free. I did go after Neddy and Cross for what they did. They shot you, Yancey. And worse. They've done worse. They killed Zeke and Cal too. But I called them out fair and square. Both of them at once, and they drew down on me and I shot them. Last I looked, that wasn't considered murder. Maybe in New York City, but not in Montana Territory.

"The colonel wants rid of me, and he's got that so-called sheriff in his pocket. It's simple, but I can't beat it."

He squeezed Charlie's hand. "It's long past time I left this place anyway. I won't have her in trouble for me. I can get out on my own."

She shook her head angrily. "No, you can't. Look at you. You're helpless as a baby rabbit. You wouldn't get five miles in this weather without help. Yancey, they killed Cal, those awful men. We've got to do something."

"All right," Yancey said, slapped his thighs, and got to his feet. "I'll get him out. How's that? I'll take him into high country, he can hole up in a line shack up there. They won't go looking for him, not in this weather. He can finish mending, then take out when he's recovered, when the weather breaks." Yancey watched Charlie for a reaction.

She held Mitch's hand to her lips for a moment, then looked back at Yancey. "You'd do that for us?"

"I'd do it for you ... and for Cal and Zeke," the ramrod corrected. "He don't mean nothing to me, one way or the other."

"No," she said firmly. "Then, no."

"What? Why?"

The men echoed the questions and pinned her with three sets of eyes.

"Because if something happened you'd let him die. Or you'd let someone shoot him if it came to him or you. I wouldn't."

"You mean to tell me you'd go up there with him

and protect him with your very own life? You'd die before you'd let someone hurt him?" Yancey practically roared the questions.

"I love him," she said so softly the declaration was almost lost in the aftermath of Yancey's shouted words.

"Love him? You love him? How in the hell did you come to that conclusion?" the ramrod asked. He was fairly jumping with anger. "Lying in the bed with him? That ain't love, Charlie, dammit, that ain't love."

"Get out of here," she said. She leaped to her feet. "Out, out. Both of you. Now, now. Go do whatever it is men like you do when you've got nothing better to do. And leave us alone."

"Miss Charlie, dammit."

"No. Even if you were my father, I wouldn't let you treat me like this. And he wouldn't have. He would've understood about love."

Yancey grew red in the face. "Yes, Matt Houston did know all about love. He loved your mother and he loved you. And you're wrong. He wouldn't put up with your shenanigans with no two-bit outlaw. He had good reason for that too. He was a good man, was Matt Houston. And you should try to live up to that goodness. Not go wasting your life on a no-account who can do nothing for you but give you misery."

Though he drew breath for more ranting, he didn't get the chance. She went at him with both fists, punching and kicking so that he had to protect himself by grabbing her wrists and holding her out of reach.

She stopped the physical attack, but not the verbal. "You shut up. I'm a grown woman. I have a right to choose my happiness without you throwing my father's love in my face. You don't know what he would have thought, and it's not fair for you to put the words there."

He turned her loose. "He charged me with your

well-being. I'm sorry if I hurt you, but it's for your own good I say this. Get him out of here. Let me take him out of here and out of your life before it's too late."

Yancey swung to face Mitch then, appealing to his good sense. "If you love her, then do what's right. Leave before you get her hurt bad, killed maybe."

Anger grew so dense within her that her ears pounded with a thunderous heartbeat. She balled her fists once again and shouted, "Stop, you stop this instant. This is my life, not yours. Stop running it. Let him be. Let us both be."

Mitch struggled to his feet and went to her, encircling her shoulders and holding her close. She was so angry it frightened him, and he could feel her trembling even as she allowed him to put his arms around her.

"You'd better get out of here," he said to Yancey. "I'll talk to her. Go on now, leave us be. Come on, Charlie. Come on, darlin'. He's afraid for you. Don't you worry. Everything will be all right. We all love you, we'll work something out."

She buried her face in his chest, sobbing as if her heart were cracking into bits. She felt as if it were. How could she give up the only true love she'd ever known? It wasn't fair, and she was weary to the bone of being alone.

"I said get out of here," Mitch repeated to Yancey without raising his voice.

The tone may have been soft, but its intensity sent Yancey from the room. He left the door standing open for Ritter to follow, which he did, and pulled it closed so quietly it made no sound above the crackling of wood in the stove and her frantic sobs.

It was a long time after the two men left before she would talk to Mitch, and he gave up soothing her with words that sounded empty and useless in the face of what was about to happen. They would part, they must. And his heart ached as badly as hers at the prospect. He held her, caressed her, kissed her; it was all he knew to do.

Later he tried to get her to eat a can of her favorite peaches he'd found in the cabinet, but she wasn't interested. So he took his time and made a pot of coffee, heated up the leftover chicken soup and ate as much as he could. He would soon need all the strength he could muster, for he couldn't remain on the ranch much longer. Another day of sunshine and someone would be beating a path to her door looking for the notorious killer. Him. He had to be gone by then. And the trouble was, he felt as wobbly on his legs as a newborn colt.

Chapter Eighteen

It was a fact that working in the Powder Keg, Radine sometimes heard much more than she wanted. But when that McGrew began bragging and making his plans to go after Mitchell Fallon, snowstorm or no, her ears perked up. He was actually going to do it this time, not just drunkenly talk about it. He was going out the next day to the Double H and he had some men agreeing to go with him. They were in the mood for a lynching, and her friend Charlie was in danger.

Later that night she crept from bed and dressed warmly in several layers of clothes. Wearing an old pair of boots she'd found discarded out back of the mercantile, she sneaked from the room and down the outside back stairs. With luck no one would miss her. They'd just think she had decided to spend the night upstairs with a man.

At the livery she charmed old Clutter into loaning her a horse and saddle and set out for the Double H. The snow covering lit the night so she had no trouble seeing her way.

The horse plodded slowly but steadily through the drifts. Several times Radine drew up to check landmarks. She knew if she headed directly toward the highest of three peaks in the far distance and kept the red bluffs always off to her left, she would come to Porcupine Creek. Charlie's ranch lay just above the creek on the far side. She could ride north for a while, and if she didn't find it, double back, keeping to the creek. With luck she would reach the Double H by daybreak. Without luck, she'd either ride off into infinity and freeze to death or be caught by renegade Indians fleeing the army. Dunkirk's men could even catch up to her, if they were foolish enough to be out in such weather.

Head down, she rode on into the bitterly cold night, remembering that Charlie Houston was the only woman anywhere she could call friend. The woman had always been nice to her. Once Charlie had brought her a whole box of sweet milk chocolates. Said some young dandy had given them to her. Radine had never had a friend who wasn't a whore, she had to do this for Charlie. Had to warn her that come dawn Duffy McGrew and his vigilantes would leave Miles City with only one thing in mind. Hunting down the man Charlie loved and killing him. The mood McGrew was in, God only knew what they would do to Charlie before they took out in search of the gunslinger they called Yank. McGrew had been in rare temper since his lady wife left him; in fact, he'd turned downright ornery, not at all like the gentleman rancher everyone had taken him for. Course word was his father-in-law was dickering with Colonel Dunkirk to sell him McGrew's ranch, and he held the paper, so he could. Radine didn't blame the man for being upset, but she wished he wouldn't take it out on Mitchell Fallon and Charlie Houston.

Through the pair of thin linen gloves, the cold air stiffened her fingers quickly, but she hung on to the reins. Ice had formed in low spots where the afternoon sunshine had melted the snow and the night's plunging temperatures had refrozen it. But the shaggy little

mare was surefooted and every bit as stubborn as its
rider. Skirting the highest drifts and doubling back to
stay on course, she and her mount reached the Porcupine while it was still full dark. Dawn hovered just
beyond the horizon, quieting the wolves in their
night song.

After crossing the creek, the horse's hooves cracking through the ice so that she was jostled roughly
about in the saddle, Radine paused a moment. To her
right, north, if she missed the Double H she would
come to Colonel Dunkirk's place. But she had no intention of riding that far.

The insides of her legs were chafed even through
the union suit and cotton bloomers she wore, and she
remembered once again why she hated to ride horse-
back. No decent lady would ever subject herself to
such misery on purpose. She moaned and the little
horse stopped.

"No, honey. I didn't say whoa. Come on, giddup."
She nudged the mare's sides with her boots and the
valiant little horse moved on. By the time the sky
turned an icy silver at the eastern horizon it was obvious that she had chosen the wrong direction. Her fingers had no more feeling and she was cold all the way
up her legs. Insides quivering from the cold she re-
versed direction and headed back. She was beginning
to feel frightened. Maybe she wouldn't make it.
Maybe they'd find her body frozen into some snowdrift come spring thaw. Until then everyone would
wonder what had happened to her. They'd go around
supposing this and supposing that. And only old Clutter at the stable would know she had ridden out that
night. It would be an almighty mystery and become a
story folks would tell for generations.

She giggled at her active imagination and rode on,
sagging in the saddle, the warmth emanating off the
horse all that kept her from freezing to death. She

came upon Charlie Houston's cabin just as the first rays of sunlight burst across the snow-strewn land like a magnificent explosion.

Someone peck, peck, pecked at the back door, and the persistent noise finally brought Charlie grumbling from the warm bed. Her eyes were swollen from crying, but she was dry-eyed and quietly furious as she crossed the boards in her stocking feet.

She leaned against the panel. "If that's you, Crane Houston, just take yourself off from here. Go away, whoever it is. I'm not of a mind to deal with any of you."

"Charlie, Charlie, it's me. Radine. Open up, I'm freezing. Hurry."

"Radine? Where in the world . . . ?" She swung open the door, reached out to support the woman who sagged to her knees and reached out almost blindly.

Her breath had frozen in crystals on the muffler wrapped around the lower half of her face, and the skin around her eyes was blue from the cold. She could not stand on her own, and Charlie supported her to a chair where she knelt and quickly removed the boots and heavy socks from the woman's tiny feet. They too were blue.

"My goodness, honey, what possessed you to come out like this?"

Radine rocked with the pain in her feet and hands, her reply muffled by the frozen cloth around her face. Charlie unwrapped that and fetched the spare quilt that she quickly bundled around the poor woman.

"Let's move you over by the stove and I'll stoke up the fire."

"You've got to listen to me," Radine gasped, while Charlie guided her toward the stove and stuck the chair under her. "They're coming after him. They're coming here to find out if you know where he is, and they'll find out too."

The noise the two made awakened Mitch, and when he propped himself up to peer in their direction, Radine caught sight of him. "Oh, he is here. Oh, no. They'll kill you both. Oh, you've got to get him out of here. Listen, listen to me."

Charlie tossed another stick of wood into the stove and went to put her arms around Radine. "Shh, it's okay. Who's coming? When?"

"Last night. In the saloon. McGrew and a bunch of other men ... they talked about ... about him." She raised a stiff arm, pointed at Mitchell. "How they're going to kill him 'cause the sheriff is too much a coward to ride out and hunt him down."

"Aw, hell," Mitch said and sat up on the edge of the bed. There he paused, grimaced, then lurched to his feet. "I'm leaving. Now. I won't have you hurt by this."

Charlie paused in her ministrations. "Not without me, you're not."

"Listen, you've got to let him go," Radine babbled. "They'll kill you if you go with him."

"It doesn't matter," Charlie said. She rose and went to Mitch. "I love him, he loves me. Nothing else matters. How can I live without him, Radine?" Her voice rose an octave with the question.

Mitch took her shoulders. "Charlie, don't."

"Oh, Charlie. Oh, poor Charlie," Radine said.

"Well, it's true." Charlie put her arms tightly around Mitch's waist. "I love you, and I won't sit here and watch you ride off to be gunned down somewhere, and I won't even know where."

"This is your home, you have to stay here and be safe."

"I don't care about ... this ... anymore. It's not

my home, and it's no longer even safe. It belongs to Matt Houston."

"It belongs to you."

· "I know and I promised him. It was his dream forever, mine too. But, Mitch, what I do know is that I don't have anything without you. Empty, I'd just be an empty shell."

Mitch cupped the back of her head with a big palm and pulled her close to his chest. "Oh, Lordy, girl. I know, I know. But I can't let you go with me. I know how that is, and I won't do it. Not again."

"Mitch," she said into his bare chest. "Do you love me?"

"Oh, dear God, girl, you know I do."

"Then don't leave without me. Don't leave me here alone. I'll not be alone anymore. I'd rather die with you than stay here alone and always be without you. I swear I would."

"No one is going to die, Charlie. No one. But you've got to let me go." He cleared his throat, gazed down into her dark, tear-misted eyes. "If you go with me they'll catch us. You'll slow me down. I'll be too afraid for you. It'll get us both killed." He swallowed hard, turned away to keep her from reading the truth in his eyes. He expected to be killed and didn't want her to see it.

She sorted her thoughts. If she went to him later, after he was safe, that would work.

"All right, get dressed," she said at last. "Yancey will do what he said in the first place, take you to the line shack in high country. There's food and water there, and wood and a place to sleep. Then he'll come back here, like nothing had ever happened. We'll all say we don't know where you are, haven't seen you. I can make them believe me. Everyone respects me.

"And then when they don't find you, and they won't, I'll come to you. The weather will get worse and they'll give up looking after a while. And when they do, I'll come to you and we'll go away somewhere. Start a new life. It's the best I can do, Mitch. I won't just tell you good-bye and never see you again. And you can't go alone, not in your condition. You wouldn't get there. You'd never make it alone."

He sighed, glanced once at the poor waif wrapped in a blanket by the stove. She gazed back at him with wide moist eyes, shaking her head up and down, up and down. He read her promise there, a promise to see to the woman he loved.

"Yes, all right. But I'd rather Wolf went with me. That's best. He's tough and mean and single-minded. Dammit, Charlie, don't put your life at risk for me. If something happened to you because of it I'd never be able to stand it."

She tilted her face up to look into his eyes, bottomless with anguish, regret, pleading, and saw what she was doing to him. "Oh, my love," she said and touched the scar.

He leaned down and kissed her, and transmitted in that kiss all the longing and devotion she'd waited a lifetime for. She felt a tear fall from his cheek to hers and knew she would have to be stronger than she ever had been. She had to do it for him because she loved him more than herself and because he loved her more than life.

Reluctantly she pulled from his embrace. "Get dressed. Quickly. I'll fetch Wolf. We'll have you long gone by the time those vigilantes get here. They'll find nothing but me and Yancey and Ritter and our poor old cook, waiting out the winter storm. Now hurry, Mitch. Hurry, please."

In the barn while Ritter saddled the black for Mitch, Charlie rattled instructions to a solemn-faced Wolf, who had agreed eagerly to help.

"After he's safe, you can ride back out the same

trail. Drag out your tracks as you come. If you're not back soon and anybody asks, we'll just say you're on a hunting trip. Up in the mountains. For elk or something. I don't know."

"Wolf," Yancey pitched in. "Just tell 'em he went hunting wolves. Everyone knows how them sons a bitches drag down our calves. We sent him wolf hunting, if anybody asks."

She nodded. "And nobody here has seen Mitch, not for weeks and weeks. Not since before we left for Cheyenne." She glared at Ritter who nodded grimly.

"Charlie, honey," Yancey said. "Calm down. Everything will be all right. He'll take care of him. Ain't nothing going to happen." He hesitated a moment, gazed at her with love in his eyes. "I'm so sorry. About yesterday ... you were right, I had no call to treat you like a child. It's just, well, I love you."

She touched his arm. "I know. It's all right. And I love you too." She turned to the silent big man who was busy saddling a large gray for himself. "Please take care of him. Please. He's ... he's my life. Do you understand?"

Wolf nodded.

Yancey patted her shoulder awkwardly. "I think I do too, honey. Matt loved you with all his heart. And he loved your mother even more."

"Never mind that now. This isn't the time. It's Mitch who is important here, not me. Wolf, I trust you to take good care of him."

All the while they talked, Mitch stood straddle-legged in the wide-open barn door, his back to them while he stared out into the distance. He might as well not have been present, the way they discussed him. Charlie had a habit of taking charge that might rankle some. Mitch found it oddly soothing, for it told him she could handle most any situation without falling apart. He certainly hoped that to be true, for she would need that strength in the upcoming days and weeks when his past was bound to come to light. He wished now they'd had more time together, that he had told her all the things she was bound to hear from others who wouldn't know the whole story.

Wolf yanked at the latigo and tightened down the saddle, dropped the stirrup and climbed aboard.

Mitch turned to see Charlie standing there looking at him with an expression of sadness so intense he wanted to grab her up and take her with him. Kiss away the hurt, love away the pain he'd caused her. He reached out, went to her.

"Mitch," she cried in a small voice and threw herself into his embrace, hugging him so tightly he winced.

She kissed the tip of his chin, his cheeks. "Take care, don't you let anything happen to yourself. I'll come to you as soon as I can."

"Charlie, I don't—"

"Hush," she said and covered his lips with trembling fingertips. "As soon as it's safe, I'll be there. Don't you go riding off anywhere else, you hear? You wait for me."

He nodded.

She stood on tiptoe and kissed him once more quickly, then squeezed her arms fiercely around his neck and buried her face in his warmth for a split second. When she backed off so he could mount she noted that despite his wound, he managed to climb on the stallion without help. It made her feel better about his chances.

Wolf had spurred his horse from the barn and waited outside. Both men carried large bedrolls and double saddlebags loaded with food and water. They would be fine. Charlie just kept telling herself that as she stood in the open doorway of the barn and watched them ride off, headed west toward the Big-horn Mountains. She held her fingers tightly over her mouth to keep from crying out until they disappeared into the thick grove of pine and were gone from sight.

Ritter shuffled a foot on the dirt floor. "I reckon we'd better git Miss Radine hid real good 'fore that bunch gets here. They'll suspect if they find her here. And make sure you clean up all sign of Fallon in the cabin."

She nodded. "Yancey, why don't you ride out behind Wolf and Mitch and obliterate their prints if they leave any. We don't want anyone following them right off this place. What about Crane? Will he talk? He was pretty put out at me yesterday."

"I'll cut his tongue out for him too," Ritter mumbled. "No, he won't talk. I believe Yancey had a little talk with our friend Crane last night. Made a believer out of him. You ought to get rid of the man, Miss Charlie. There's something about him I just don't cotton to either."

"But he cooks a mighty fine biscuit, Ritter," she said in an attempt at humor.

Ritter only nodded, and neither smiled.

"They'll be okay, won't they?" she asked outside the barn.

"Wolf will see to it. And that Fallon. He's one tough fella. He's survived more than this, a lot more. I don't think you need to worry about anything but dealing with that bunch of vigilantes. And I'll be right here with you for that.

"Now, you go fetch Miss Radine and we'll hide her out here in the root celler till they're gone."

They stood there a moment and watched Yancey ride out to do some trail muddying, then Charlie went to get Radine.

As it turned out, the first visitor that day was not the gang of vigilantes that Charlie had expected. Along about ten, Colonel Hulbert Dunkirk showed up accompanied by a new bodyguard even bigger and uglier than Wolf.

She met them in the yard with a loaded Winchester, pointed the thing up at him in his fancy carriage. "Don't bother to light, Dunkirk."

With the wave of a pudgy hand the colonel signaled the ugly man to stay put and addressed her.

"I think you'll welcome what I have to say. I've come to make you a final offer on the ranch. A very generous offer, I must say. Get you out of this hellhole and back to civilization with cash to spare."

"I'm not interested."

"Now, look here, Miss Houston. You and I both know you just barely broke even in Cheyenne. It's liable to be several years before you make enough for a new dress."

"Why, Colonel, I thought you noticed. I'm not much for dresses. Now git. It's cold and I'm tired of standing out here."

At that moment came the thunder of hoofbeats, and they all turned to see a handful of mounted men headed for the ranch.

"Looks like the thaw has brought out all kinds of vermin," Dunkirk remarked. He stood and hailed the leader. "You men ride in from Miles City? How's the trail?"

"Dunkirk, what the hell you doin' out here?" Duffy McGrew shouted and vaulted down from his horse.

"I might ask you the same. Shouldn't you be seeing to your own place? Or has Stallings stole it out from under you already? Perhaps he's considering my offer as pretty fair, since he's saddled with a son-in-law like you."

Charlie welcomed the exchange, aware that any delay of the vigilantes meant Yancey, Wolf, and Mitch were that much farther away. Finally she interrupted.

"Gentlemen. Gentlemen, excuse me." They continued to argue and she pulled off a high shot aimed at the distant trees. The resounding blast gained their immediate attention.

"That's better. Now, this is my place, and if you've got a bone to gnaw I'd appreciate you're doing it elsewhere. Could I ask what you want, McGrew? Surely you didn't ride out to argue with Colonel Dunkirk here, seeing as how he's trespassing too."

"We're on the trail of that outlaw. The sheriff don't see fit to do nothing but prop his feet up on a table in the Powder Keg, and so we figured we'd just do his job for him. There is a bounty on the man's head. Time we cleaned up the territory, we figger."

"And what outlaw might that be?" Charlie asked, her tongue thick and dry.

"That Yank fella. Mitchell Fallon, the one marked like a skunk. He's wanted for gunning down Dunkirk's men. Cross and Neddy. Cash bounty on his head."

"Sounded like a fair fight to me," she said. "It's not usually the law's affair when a bunch of gunslingers go at each other. So why the bounty?"

"Because the man is a war criminal."

Colonel Dunkirk sputtered. "He's a what?"

"Wait a minute, here," she shouted. "First off, I haven't seen hide nor hair of this Fallon since I went to Cheyenne. He lit out over a month ago for Idaho. Second of all, where do you get your information? A war criminal? If that were true the army'd be on his trail, not a bunch of ragged tails like you. So why don't you just ride on about your business."

"I believe we'll just search the place."

She shifted the barrel of the rifle so it was pointed at McGrew's midsection. "You'll not search my place, sir. I don't harbor criminals."

"Yeah, and you don't lay with them either, do you, Miss Charlie?" McGrew said with a sneer.

The men riding with him guffawed loudly, but the

noise was cut off when she fired a shot between McGrew's feet. Snow and ice sheared off in all directions and Duffy hopped backward.

In an even, tightly controlled voice, she said, "Not because you say so, but because I want you to be satisfied I'm not harboring any criminals, I invite you to search every building on the place. In my home, you will kindly wipe the mud off your boots and keep your filthy hands out of my things. It's one room, you can see real quick that no one's there. Now, git busy so you can git off my place."

She trailed along with smug satisfaction while the men went from barn to bunkhouse to cookhouse and finally to her cabin. Idly she wondered where Crane had gotten to. There was no sign of him anywhere.

After McGrew and his men left, she faced the colonel. "I don't know exactly what you're hanging around here for. You might as well ride on your way. I've told you, my place isn't for sale. And even if it were, I wouldn't sell it to you if I were starving. I'd give it back to the Indians first. So you and your hired killer get off my land and don't come back. Next time I see you on my property I'll put a bullet in that fat gut of yours just to see if you bleed red blood."

Dunkirk's mouth dropped open with astonishment. He nodded curtly to his driver/bodyguard and they were off in a flurry of ice and snow and mud.

When she turned to go back toward the cabin she saw Crane lurking in the doorway of the cookhouse. Where had he gotten to earlier?

She dismissed all thought of her cousin when Ritter brought Radine back to the house in a few minutes, straw clinging to her hair and clothes.

"They never even found the trapdoor to the root cellar. Good idea to put her down there," he told Charlie proudly.

"Thank you very much, Ritter," Radine said

sweetly and patted the young man's cheek. He blushed furiously and stammered his way from the cabin.

"I believe that fella needs a woman to teach him a few things," Radine said as she settled once again close to the stove.

"He is a shy one, but I don't know what I would have done without him. He understands things the other men don't."

"And he loves you," Radine added.

"No."

"Yes, indeed. But you don't need to worry. He's so in awe he won't ever try to do anything about it. He'll just worship from afar."

"That's so sad," Charlie said softly. "To love someone and not be able to . . . able to do anything about it."

"It happens to a lot of us," Radine said.

Charlie swallowed over a lump in her throat. Somewhere out there in the drifts of snow and bitter cold rode the man she would always love, going farther and farther away from her with every passing hour. Would she ever see him again? How would she live without him? It appeared that yet another cold and lonely winter awaited, with little hope for happiness. This was such a vast country. Its wide-open spaces, the infinite miles of land and mountains and sky lent to the feeling of her own tenuous existence. And yet she knew that she and Mitch, Radine, Yancey, Ritter . . . everyone . . . were important bits and pieces of the whole, threads in a fabric that held this immense country together, for better or worse.

She sighed and went to sit beside Radine. Sometimes she just got much too sentimental for her own good.

"Can you cook?" she asked Radine.

"Some. I'm not fancy, but I can stir up meat and potatoes, beans and coffee, corn pone and biscuits."

"Well, then. Would you teach me? It seems we have some time on our hands."

"I would be delighted," Radine said. "But I really ought to go back to Miles City. Lance will be wondering what happened to me."

"You won't get fired if you stay awhile, will you?"

Radine threw back her head and laughed. "I never was hired, far as I know. We have a . . . well, a working arrangement. He don't pay me, I don't pay him. It's a bargain that fits both of us."

"Well, then. Stay awhile. Teach me to cook and I'll see you have room and board with me. How would that be? Oh, please do. I'd love having you. It's so lonely out here, and the men have their own things to do." Charlie pondered what she'd said for a moment or two. "Funny, there was a time I'd a been down there in the bunkhouse playing cards and matching the men tale for tale while we sat around the stove. I don't have much of a hankering for that anymore."

Radine smiled "Maybe you're turning into a proper lady. That's what love does to you. Makes you think of birthing babies and cleaning house and . . . and cooking." She eyed Charlie from under half-closed lids. "And of course, the very best part. The loving part."

Charlie felt a flush, but joined her in easy laughter. How good it was to relax and enjoy company, even if just for a short while.

Chapter Nineteen

Someone knocked loudly on the door and Charlie picked up the rifle from its niche before opening it. She'd heard no one ride up. Slipping the latch she poked the barrel through the crack and peered at Crane Houston.

"What do you want?"

He smiled. "To visit, that's all."

"What about?"

"Wasn't that long ago you enjoyed my telling you stories about your dad when we was kids." He waited.

"That what you want to visit about. My dad?"

"Well, that and something else. It's real important. It's about your mother and something you might want to know. We all want to know about family. I figger ... no, I know you're no different."

"You knew my mother too?"

He shrugged. "In a manner of speaking."

She let the door swing wider. Even Matt hadn't been too forthcoming about her mother. Besides, Crane wasn't armed and she was.

After she let him in she propped the rifle in the corner nearby. Handy just in case. Then she seated him at the table and took the other chair for herself, without offering coffee. The house smelled of good cooking, and she was proud of the bread and spice cake Radine had helped her create the day before. She didn't offer any to Crane. She was still pretty mad at him.

He picked nervously at the tip of a callused thumb, finding it hard to get started with whatever he'd come to say.

"Well?" she finally asked, a bit curtly.

"Well? Well. Your ma was a pretty woman, young. Sixteen, I believe when you were born."

She nodded. That she knew. Where was this going?

He turned his head and slanted his eyes at her slyly. "He ever tell you how they met?"

She searched her memory, Matt's flowing descriptions of the Florez hacienda, her own recollections that were merely tiny flashes that she couldn't ever put together, she'd been so young when he came to take her away from her grandparents. Then she shook her head.

"That dirty little shack in El Grande, and her huddled back in the corner, dirty and near naked?"

She blinked and stared at the man. "What are you talking about? My mother was a lady from a fine, rich family. Dolores Maria Ramona Florez. Do you think I'm stupid? What is this?"

On her feet, she was ready to do battle.

He held up a hand. "Hold it, don't go getting snippety on me. It was your mother all right, and she'd been raped until she was of no more use to the *banditos* who left her there. Your daddy always was a bighearted son of a bitch. He felt sorry for the poor dirty little waif.

"Imagine his surprise when he gets her cleaned up and finds out who she is. Where did you think he got his bankroll to leave King and go out on his own?"

She nearly spat at Crane. "That's a filthy lie. You get out of here and off this ranch. Now." The order would barely pass over her dry tongue. This man was infuriating.

He rose to face her, barely tall enough to look her in the eye. "You were the baby she carried in her belly. Sired by some no-account white border bandit who never looked back. Not a child of the almighty Matt Houston at all."

Burning tears filled her eyes, and her heart thumped so hard she couldn't breathe properly. "You lying devil, you evil ugly little man. How can you spout such filth?"

His close-set eyes sparked and he grabbed her arm viciously, swung her around, and popped her soundly on the jaw with his fist. It knocked her to the floor, where she crouched on her hands and knees, shaking her head to clear the flashing lights and a falling curtain of darkness. She gazed at the rifle, just out of reach.

The sound of his oily voice fell all around her. "We're going to talk some more about just what your rights are here on your 'daddy's' ranch. I think we can come to some sort of agreement. What do you suppose people would think? Even if that outlaw Fallon didn't care, which he just might, there's all the other ranchers. Bastards don't have any rights to inheritance, and especially not if they're women. The law won't look kindly on this."

Jaw aching she swung her head, glared up at him. "I don't give a damn what people think. Who's going to listen to your lies, anyway? You get out of here. Mitch will kill you when he finds out. You poor little fool."

"It's you who's the fool, cousin. The next time I'll aim better and your gunslinger will be dead."

"You shot Mitch?"

He nodded, a sardonic grin revealing yellowed teeth. "Who'd you think? That fat toad Dunkirk? He has to hire everything done, but I'm tired of waiting to be paid. We're going to do it the easy way, and the colonel can eat worms."

She struggled to get to her feet, but he shoved her with the toe of his boot so that she tumbled to her butt up against the wall.

"I think we need to discuss a few things here."

"I'm not discussing anything with a liar."

"We'll see who's lying. Where were you living when your ... when Uncle Matt came to fetch you?"

"With my grandparents, my mother's parents." She let out the reply before realizing that she didn't want to discuss this.

"And how old were you?"

"Five, no four. I'm not sure."

He held his tongue between his teeth a moment. "What happened to your mother?"

The question didn't deserve an answer and she didn't give it one.

"She killed herself, didn't she?"

With a quick flick of her eyes, she measured the distance to the rifle standing in the corner near the bed, then glared at him. He mustn't guess her intent.

"I don't suppose you remember her at all, but then you really should. I do and I'm only a couple years older than you."

What was he getting at? She tenderly massaged her throbbing jaw.

"Oh, your 'daddy' married her all right, but only for the money. They paid that no-account Matt Houston to marry their precious daughter and claim her bastard. You. And then there you were, and for a while Uncle Matt, well he just took off. Oh, he come back all right, after she was dead. It was big talk in the family. My dad ranted and raved about his only brother taking that Mexican bastard on just so's he could get the money he needed to start out on his own. Uncle Matt had learned all he could from Richard King, but he never saved enough money for a spread of his own. He had too much liking for high-stakes living at the poker tables in San Antone."

Nearly blind with fury, she used the energy of the adrenaline surging through her veins to catapult from the floor and leap for the rifle. The tips of her fingers skinned across the polished stock just before he grabbed her and tossed her aside.

Standing over her, he shook his head. "Naughty, naughty. Why do you think you never went back to visit your grandparents, or they never came to see you in Texas? Because they wanted nothing to do with their daughter's shame, that's why. She killed herself, your mother did. Out of humiliation for what she had done. Leaving them you to look at day after day. A terrible reminder."

"She did nothing, nothing," Charlie screamed. "Even if it was true, she wasn't to blame."

"Ah, but it is true, and you're beginning to believe me, aren't you? It all fits together, doesn't it? Daddy suddenly buying that big spread, the cattle and horses and fancy house and servants. Did you really think he earned that kind of money working as a lackey for Richard King?" Crane shook his head pityingly. Then he leaned forward and took her chin in an iron-hard grip.

"Pretty little Mexican bastard. A Texas bandit for a father and a whimpering little Mex for a momma. You're not a Houston. Look at you. Just look and tell me you see anything of Matt Houston there. Hell, all the white blood in the world won't make you anything but a no-account greaser."

She gritted her teeth against his painful grip on her jaw. Though she wanted to spit in his eye, all she could do was stare at him through a misty haze of hatred. He was lying, he had to be. She couldn't think.

Everything was blurred, his hateful face, the bed, the stove, the table and chairs, the Winchester out of reach in the corner. What was going on here, what did this man want? All she knew for sure was that if he ever took his eye off her for a second she would grab up the Winchester and blow him to kingdom come. She might even laugh as she did it.

But Crane wasn't about to give his cousin that chance. "Where are the papers on the place?"

She shook her head, then wished she hadn't, for everything went fuzzy again. "What? What papers?"

"The deed on this place. The Double H. By rights it belongs to me, the only heir of Matt Houston. You're gonna sign it over to me."

"No, I won't. You mangy, no-good liar. I'll never do that. You'll have to kill me."

"Oh, no. If I could get it by killing you you'd be dead already. But Dunkirk would have it then, faster than I could say brown mule, and I wouldn't see a dime. I want it all legal and proper."

"Legal and proper? You call this legal and proper, forcing me? Coming in my home and knocking me around like the low-life coward you are? You're crazy, that's what you are."

He shrugged. "I guess I could beat you till you did what I wanted, but that might look suspicious if you went to the law. So I reckon I'll just have to play my ace in the hole, my draw card, the one I've kept up my sleeve. Uncle Matt would appreciate this, he truly would."

He pulled back the tail of his coat to dig in the inside pocket. He was distracted just enough for her to scramble away from him. Grunting she clawed her way to the rifle.

She whirled, both hands wrapped firmly around the breech. Crane shouted and pounced. But she had moved just out of his reach, and this time she had a better grip. The barrel punched him right in the belly. He grabbed it, wrapped his hands around hers, and as they struggled, fingers clawing around the trigger guard, the gun went off.

The explosion kicked her backward into the wall, its blast slamming into her eardrums; thick acrid black powder smoke choked off her breath, tears poured from her burning eyes. For a moment she stared with disbelief, the blast echoing around the tiny room.

He didn't let go of the rifle barrel, just stood there hugging it while he let out a low bawling sound like a downed steer. He tottered there for what seemed an eternity, then crumpled to the floor where he lay motionless, a look of stark amazement frozen on his features.

She'd killed him! She did nothing for the longest time but stand over him and gape. Her eyes blinked, adrenaline pumped through her system like boiling acid; her mouth dried to paper around the remaining taste of black powder; her heart boomed like echoes of the gunshot. Still she couldn't move from the spot.

Blood spread in a thick pool around the body before she finally came to her senses. She tugged at the stock of the Winchester until his death grip gave up the barrel.

With frantic choppy moves she went to her knees beside the bed, dragged out her father's metal box of important papers. In it was the deed to the Double H Ranch. Her fingers bumped up against the music box and she pulled it out too, making a double bundle out of the two with a blanket from the bed. She had to run, get away, go to Mitch. Quickly she put together a bedroll of her heaviest clothes, filled a cloth sack with food from the larder, and picking up the Winchester headed for the barn. She spared not even a glance at her dead cousin.

Just like Mitch, she would be judged a killer and an

outlaw. She would find Mitch and they would go away together. Far away where no one would ever find them. What else could be expected from the bastard child of a bandit?

Snow began to fall late in the afternoon, spitting at first, but then saturating the air in a thick impenetrable blanket of fat flakes, some as large as wild plum blossoms. Charlie hunched deeper into her woolen coat, stopping once long enough to shake out the canvas poncho and wrap up in it. Surely this early blizzard wouldn't continue through the night. That reasoning soon proved to be a fallacy, for the farther she rode, the sorrel picking its careful way as they climbed into high country, the harder the snow fell.

It most certainly could snow all night. Could she find the line shack if it kept up? She had always been proud of her unerring sense of direction. As afternoon darkened into evening she began to look for a place to make camp for the night. Not even the best Indian trackers would ride on in a blizzard after dark.

Yet nothing mattered but that she catch up with Mitch. Not the horror of what had happened in the cabin, nor the terrible stories Crane had spouted about her father.

The first night she camped under an overhang that extended almost deep enough to be a cave. She was safe from the worst of the raging wind, but not warm enough to be comfortable. The shelter was big and would shelter both her and the sorrel. Once she had a fire going and the blanket, coat, and poncho wrapped around her, she felt safe from freezing during the night.

What would Ritter do when he returned to the ranch to find her gone and Crane gut shot? Suppose Yancey returned as well. Was Mitch already safe in the line shack?

Before she found answers a weary sleep pounced

on her like a hidden beast. She dreamed then of Mitch, his lips nibbling her fevered flesh, passion smoking his green eyes, and of Matt Houston, the fair skin and aquiline features, sandy hair and brittle cobalt eyes. She thought he pointed at her, but saw that instead he shook his finger at a hazy, dark-skinned man whose teeth were bared in laughter. When she whirled to get a better look the man became her. Her face, her naked body, sprawled on a dirt floor, mouth opened in a soundless scream.

She cried out and awoke herself, startled the sleeping horse so that he snorted and pawed.

The snow had stopped and the sky glowed like polished gunmetal. False dawn. She could sleep no longer and rose, rubbing her tingling muscles and stomping the ground to bring feeling into her legs and feet. She filled a tin cup with snow and pushed it into the glowing coals, stacking more dry wood on the fire at the same time. When the water was hot, she sprinkled its surface with dried sassafras bark and let it steep. She would need energy, and so added a healthy dose of dark sugar for good measure.

Standing hunched over the dying fire she washed down a slab of spice cake with the tea. After doling out a ration of feed to the horse, she packed up and moved on. A need to reach Mitch drove her relentlessly so that she ignored the cold wind that cut eerie shapes in the new snow and brought tears to her eyes, exposed above the muffler she'd wrapped around her mouth and nose. Beyond the scudding clouds the sun broke through and glared off the white drenched land in shards of painful light that almost blinded her.

She squinted, spotted the familiar gap ahead that would lead her into the hills and ultimately to the line shack. Beyond the rising land the indigo and purple mountains stood like giant guardians. She halted the horse a moment, twisted in the saddle, and glanced back the way they had come. Her past chased her, reached out and grabbed at her, urging her to return to where she belonged. She gasped for air and pulled the muffler away from her face. Great clouds billowed from her mouth, were caught by the wind and dissipated. She could die out here, frozen to death, and maybe never be found.

She considered that for only an instant, then turned back toward the rugged hills thick with towering ponderosa and lodgepole pine and blue-green spruce.

To break the uncanny silence, she spoke aloud. "Oh, God, Mitch, I love you." The words bounced around in the cold air, darted back at her in echoes that faded away to nothing. High above her a hawk screed in reply, and she shaded her eyes to search the pale blue sky.

McGrew had called Mitch a killer, but it wasn't true, it couldn't be. What Mitch had done, he had done for good reason, and she would never believe him to be a cold-blooded killer. Not any more than she could think of herself that way because of what had happened to Crane. But folks would all say it was so. How easily a thing like that could happen. How quickly life could explode around you, so that nothing tangible and dear remained. Nothing but the man in the line shack up there somewhere, a man who was all she had left in this world to cling to.

The weary gelding cut the trail to the line shack by late afternoon, but they would not make their destination before dark. That meant another night spent out in the open. The heavy snow had slowed their passage, they had waded drifts so deep that at times she had dismounted and led the valiant horse. With relief she saw that the trail was blown clear in most places. It snaked around the outer perimeter of the ridge with a sheer drop off to the left, and was still treacherous, with icy patches and loose shale. It was there, as the animal picked carefully through the clattering rock, that he lost his footing and fell. Hooves rattling for purchase in the slick gravel, he screamed and lunged, trying to keep all four legs under him. But his hindquarters went down. She kicked loose of the stirrups and bailed off just as he plunged over the edge.

Frantically she crawled to the rim and peered down, heart hammering thickly in her throat. The horse lay several hundred yards below on a wide shelf. He kicked once, nickered, and then didn't move again.

She had to get down there. Without her bedroll she would never make it through the frigid night. She would freeze to death. Before she could lose her nerve, she twisted around on her stomach, let her legs dangle over the precipice, and poked around with her booted toes until she found a solid foothold. With gloved hands she latched on to a sapling pine and lowered herself another few feet. Slowly, agonizingly, inch by inch, she worked her way down to where the sorrel lay. Once or twice she slipped in the snowy terrain, but always dug in and held on.

It was dark by the time she touched both feet to the wide ledge where the horse lay unmoving. Panting and exhausted she gazed at the gelding through tears she told herself were from the cold. But down deep inside she knew they were for Mitch and herself, for the poor animal, and for the loss of her father and Cal. So much death, such sadness. She slipped off one glove and touched the cooling flesh of the horse. Dead. She'd known that already. Anger and a stubborn will to survive brushed away her tears.

No time now, dammit, no time for weakness. It could get her killed.

The blanket in which she had tied up the strongbox and the music box weren't on the horse, they must have come off in the fall. The rifle too was missing. She would search in the morning. The bedroll she unfastened and tossed up against the cliff face. One of the saddlebags was caught partway under the heavy body and she strained and heaved, muscles bulging, before she finally yanked it free of the animal's dead weight. Sweat had soaked through her clothes by the time she set up a makeshift camp against the cliff behind the body of the gelding. She made a small fire of pine branches scrounged from the bluff's face and snuggled down in her wrappings, chewing on a piece of mangled spice cake from the saddlebag.

The next morning she crawled stiffly to where she could stand and tilted her head to gaze up the sheer precipice toward the trail. Hard to believe she had come down that, and now all she had to do was climb back up.

When he returned from taking Radine to Miles City Ritter drove the team straight into the barn and unhitched them. The house appeared deserted and still, and he decided to check on Charlie. The door to the cabin fell open under his fist and his heart thudded heavily. The overpowering stench of gunpowder and a pitiful groan greeted him.

He found Crane sprawled in a pool of thickening blood and hurriedly knelt beside him. "What happened? Where's Miss Charlie?"

"Shot ... me. Shot ... gone."

The rattle of hooves outside heralded another arrival, and Ritter postponed the questions to hurry to the door and greet Yancey.

Disregarding the cook's obvious pain, the two greeted each other.

Yancey stomped inside and glanced around. "What in thunderation's goin' on in here? Where's Charlie?"

"If I know'd I'd tell you," Ritter said. "This son of a bitch, he knows. Now help me beat it out of him."

Yancey slammed the door and knelt down opposite Ritter. "Who shot him?"

"He says Miss Charlie."

Crane nodded, then groaned some more.

"If she did, well then I reckon she had good reason," Ritter said.

"Blamed well told she did," Yancey said.

"Aw, he ain't hurt bad. Dang bullet just barely cut through the flesh. Too bad it wasn't a tad to the left, we'd a not had to worry none about this one. I reckon this here blizzard helped you wipe out them tracks just fine. Where you been?"

Yancey shrugged, stared out the window for a while. "Had to hole up till the worst blew over. I come the long way around so I wouldn't run across any of them yahoos. It was snowing my tracks full most of the way. Don't figure there's any danger anyone can follow them to the line shack at Redrock—it's rough country."

Before Ritter could chastise Yancey for saying anything in front of Crane, the thunder of approaching horses sounded.

"Well, dang," Ritter muttered, and went to peer out the window. "It's that Duffy McGrew and his crew of vigilantes, and he's got some of the colonel's men with him, and, aw hell, there's the sheriff too."

"Fine pairing," Yancey said. "You reckon they're looking for Fallon?"

"I expect they are. They rode off after all of you yesterday not long after you left."

Yancey grunted. "Didn't get too far, did they? And where was you when this happened?" He gestured toward the man on the floor.

"I took Miss Radine back to town and the storm come and so I stayed till today. Hell, I couldn't have got back. Who would have thought her own cousin couldn't be trusted to look out after her?"

"Well, you shouldn't have left her alone with him. I figgered that Wolf would be coming back in by now, but he must have laid out the storm too."

Ritter scowled. "Can't tell about him. Want me to go see what them yahoos want?"

"I expect you'd better, but watch what you say."

Ritter bit back a reply. Yancey ought to know he had better sense than to misspeak in front of that bunch of mavericks.

As it turned out, though, Crane Houston spilled the beans, with Ritter and Yancey trying hard to stop him, while the sheriff and Duffy McGrew stood there taking it all in.

"Well, I expect we need to go after them, then. Fallon and the girl both. These sissies have wasted enough time holed up in town for the storm to blow over," the colonel said after Crane finished his blabbering about Red Rock Canyon and the line shack.

"Figgered we'd find the two of them nice and cozy right here. This storm and all. I reckon it's too late to start today," the sheriff said. "It'll be dark in an hour. We'll leave out first thing in the morning. Everybody pack plenty of food and clothes and ride your best horse."

"Old fool," McGrew muttered where Ritter could hear him. "Think he was the only one who knew this country. He'll probably fall off his horse drunk 'fore we even get out of sight of Miles City."

"You two men can go with us," the colonel said to Ritter and Yancey.

"Not me," Ritter said. "I ain't tracking down Miss Charlie."

Yancey punched him in the shoulder, shook his head. "Course we're going. Wouldn't miss watching you durn fools chasin' your tails all over them mountains for a few days. It oughta be good fun. Now, who's gonna take this fool back to town to the doc's? Won't be me, I'd as soon he died as not."

With one leather-gloved hand Charlie clung to the exposed root, her cheek pressed tight against the bluff. The pungent odor of wet earth and sap invaded her nostrils. She wished she could look up, but didn't dare for fear of falling. Instead she peeked down and tried to gauge how much farther she had to climb. Maybe she'd come halfway. It was hard to tell.

Feeling above her head with her other hand, she grabbed on to another slippery root, tugged hard to test its strength, and then patiently knocked new toeholds with first one foot, then the other.

Only a few more feet and she would be able to see over the rim. She rested a moment, then began the process once again. It was rough going, especially with the bedroll strapped to her back. She hadn't found the rifle, nor the bundle holding the music box and Matt's strongbox. The saddlebags she'd had to leave behind. No way to carry them. But she figured if she could climb to the trail by noon, she could walk to the line shack before dark.

As she struggled for yet another handhold, she imagined the expression on Mitch's face when she burst through the door and threw her arms around him. His presence and the warmth she imagined would pour from the mud fireplace in the tiny shack became so real as she climbed that heat played on her face, his taste touched her lips, her flesh trembled with his imagined caress.

She shivered and inched painfully upward, grunting and clutching at anything she could find to hang on to. Kicking at a loose spot to make yet another toehold, she raised upward and one hand felt something different. A flat spot, smooth rocks.

Was she there?

She patted around a bit and must have moved too quickly, for one foot slipped free and dangled out in space. She skidded down, scrabbled and grabbed at something, anything, cried out as she slid, imagined plunging back down beside the dead gelding, or worse falling all the way to the bottom of the canyon.

In her crazy descent, a root she grabbed held, and she hung there by one hand taking shallow breaths that burned down into her lungs.

With one foot she carefully felt around for a toe-hold, found it, and stood upright so that her shoulders were above the trail. The bundled blanket lay right in front of her, still tied around the music box and strongbox. It must have fallen off before the sorrel pitched over the edge.

Nearly sobbing with relief she bent forward and squirmed onto her belly on the trail, legs still dangling over the rim. The chant became a silent prayer of thanks.

She had made it!

Chapter Twenty

The sun dropped below the jagged cut of mountains off to her left as she rounded an outcropping of sienna boulders and spotted the line shack, nestled back in a grove of pine. It overlooked a vast meadow that stretched out before her, a lake nestled in its midst like a tiny jewel, shoreline iced and sparkly.

Smoke trailed from the chimney of the shack in a thin spiral that flitted among the green-needled tree branches.

She panted out Mitch's name with every step she took. The expression on his face when she burst inside told her all she needed to know.

With a whoop he kicked away from the chair and wrapped her in his arms before she could even close the door at her back. He smelled of wood smoke and strong coffee. His hand on the back of her head felt strong, gentle, caring.

"Oh, how I missed you," she breathed into his chest. "Are you okay?"

He hugged her so tightly she gasped, his mouth at her ear, then searching across her cold, cold face to find her lips.

She tasted him, touched him all over, fingers in his hair, along his shoulders, over his back. At last their mouths locked as if starved for the nourishment each could give the other.

"Ah, dear God, you're so cold," he said, and began to undress her.

The hat and bedroll first, then the gloves, poncho, and coat. Rubbing at her arms, pulling her closer to the fire, all the while planting hot quick kisses wher-ever his lips could reach.

She closed her eyes, gave herself up to his care, exhaustion and cold fading. He seemed then to notice the door ajar, the bitterly cold air invading the small space.

"Wait, don't move. Stay right there." He held out both hands toward her, as if he could fix her in place with some kind of invisible lines. He never took his eyes off her as he closed the door.

She saw at last the clarity of his features. The drawn, haggard look of him, as if he had undergone some terrible and tragic experience. Holding out a hand she beckoned him to her side where she sat coiled beside the fire. And he came down to her, gath-ering her close.

"I thought I'd never see you again. You're here, really here." He touched her face with the tips of his fingers, quick little fluttering touches, then hugged her up close again, shuddering.

After a while he asked, "All this time I hoped you wouldn't come, but prayed for you to with every breath. Why did you? How . . . ?"

"Don't ask, not yet," she begged and turned her face up to study him. "You look so tired. How's your shoulder? Are you eating, looking out for yourself?"

"Yes. No. I don't know. It's all right. It was bad when I first got here, but I slept . . . I must have slept a long time. I don't know what day it is. I haven't been awake too long, I don't think."

"And Wolf. When did he leave?"

"Lit out right away, tried to beat the storm. I couldn't get him to stay. Odd fellow, fits his name to a tee. Let's not talk about all this." He dropped his head to her shoulder, sighed, and together they lay down in front of the fire. "I just want to hold you. Hold you forever."

"Yes," she said into his neck. "Yes."

She awoke wrapped in his arms, his breath soft and sweet in her hair. "Oh, Mitch," she whispered. "What are we going to do? I love you so much. Oh, Mitch."

He slept on without a reply.

Again she dozed off, and the next time she awoke he was watching her. Lying just as they had been when she fell asleep, but watching her with moss-green eyes that spoke volumes.

The fire had burned low, and he rose to put a few chunks of pine on the flames. They sparked and cracked and lit the room with dancing golden light.

When he lay back down beside her and took her in his arms, their lips touched, lingered, broke away, and came together once again. They uttered little sounds of pleasure that rippled through the silence like pebbles dropped in a still pond.

Hands found bulky clothing, buttons popped, shirts came away, jeans loosened and peeled down, leaving them both in their underdrawers.

He stopped for a moment, studied her lithe frame, brushed the back of his knuckles over her breasts. The nipples puckered beneath the woolen material. Keeping his eyes on her face he began to slowly unbutton the top, stopping after each button to kiss her, first through the woolen, taking little nibbles at her breasts, then on the bare skin as the cloth came open down the front. His moist breath heated her skin and she pushed into the love bites, moaning with pleasure.

On his knees, hands at her waist, he buried his face in the taut mound of her belly. "I only knew how much I loved you when I had to leave you. It hurts so much to be without you. All I want to do is hold you forever."

She took his face between her palms and tilted it so that he was looking at her. "It's all right, we won't have to be apart again. We've got plenty of time. All the time in the world. I've so much to tell you."

He shushed her lips with the tips of his fingers. "Not now. Not this minute. I want you first, I want every inch of you, I want to be in you and around you and with you completely. Now, this very moment. Please. Later we'll talk, later." He groaned and ran his hands over her, at the same time nibbling on every inch of exposed skin he could find.

Despite her weariness and despair, her body knew what it wanted. This man, his touch, his kiss, his love-making, was all her frenzied flesh desired. Everything else could come later. Much later. His desire, his passion, had chased away everything but their mutual needs. He was alive and so was she, and it would be enough for now. They should celebrate.

As he got rid of her union suit, she removed his, and soon they were lying naked on the floor in the eerie golden glow from the fire. He raised to one elbow, gazed at her with the firelight sparking in his green eyes, and she touched the scar above his eye. His dark hair tumbled over her hand. He closed his eyes a moment, as if to shut out unwanted memories. Then he pulled her hand from the scar, kissed the open palm, and gently placed it low on his belly. She caressed the heat and rise of his desire, and he lowered his mouth to trail his tongue over her lips, darting its tip in and out in a matching rhythm to her touch.

The warm kisses moved from her mouth down across each breast beyond the gentle mound of her stomach, heated her longing so she lifted her hips to welcome the sweet deep search.

In her eyes the fire leaped higher and higher, consuming their slick, naked bodies, carrying their ashes into the darkness of night and beyond, shooting their souls into the frigid black sky beyond the stars.

He gathered her then, into his lap facing him, and entered her with a smooth and tender grace, nudging the core that exploded as they rocked together, crying and laughing and sobbing in ecstasy. He shuddered and stopped moving, holding her close and breathing great gasps against her throat, unmoving except for the rhythm deep inside.

Then he let out a gentle "aah" and somehow they were lying side by side on the floor once again. She wasn't sure how they had gotten there, spooned as she was, butt tucked up against the curve of his stomach and thighs. Perhaps she had passed out for a moment or at least lost all conscious thought.

Around and within her rested a serenity as if she had been soothed by an angel, and she tucked his hand close to her heart and slept.

Mitch awoke with a shooting pain through his injured shoulder, and seeing that he and Charlie were sleeping on the hard floor, didn't wonder.

He'd thought it all a dream, the lovemaking and ecstasy of having her, but waking with her hair tousled beneath his chin filled him with an extreme joyousness. It had, after all, been real. No dream could have given that much pleasure. He grinned and shifted, trying to get rid of the ache in his shoulder muscles. Foolish of him to act in such a crazy fashion. Foolish but oh, so wonderful.

He eased his arm from around her and stretched out the worst of the kinks, but couldn't help groaning.

She came awake instantly and sat up, her bare breasts tilted toward him, her eyes wide and frightened. That went away almost immediately when she took in their joint naked condition.

"I thought I was dreaming," she said, and smiled so sweetly he sensed a gentle cracking around his heart.

"I love you, Charlie Houston, with everything I have to give. And I always will."

"Oh, Mitch, I . . ." Her eyes filled.

"But if I don't get up off this floor I'll be crippled for life. And another thing . . ." He struggled to his feet, using the back of the only chair for help. ". . . what the hell are you doing up here, anyway?"

Sitting there on the floor, looking up at his totally naked, beautiful body, his face attempting to scowl away the satisfaction from the night before, she couldn't help but laugh.

"It's not funny, Charlie. You came up here alone, I presume, and you could have been killed. My God, what were you thinking?"

Everything that precipitated her flight came back in a rush that sobered her quickly. "I have to have clothes on for this," she said. "No more questions till we're dressed, please."

He nodded in agreement, and they both dressed, strangely shy in the small room with no privacy for either. He finished first and stepped outside to gather up some wood for the fire. It was snowing again, great fat flakes that had already filled her tracks to the door.

He fanned the coals to life and added a few sticks of kindling. "I'll put on some coffee." Suddenly he wasn't so anxious to have this talk with her, she seemed so upset. What could have happened now?

With his back to her, shoving the pot of water and grounds into the fire, he didn't get a good look at her face when she blurted out her news.

"I killed Crane Houston. Oh, Mitch, he's dead and I killed him."

The announcement left him speechless. He turned

to take her in his arms. "Surely not. What did that scum do to you, did he hurt you?"

"No ... well, yes. I guess he did, but not the way you mean."

"I don't understand."

"He said that ... that I'm not ... that Matt wasn't my father. That my father was an outlaw who raped my mother and ran off. Oh, Mitch, do you think that could be true?"

"Aw, honey. Aw, dammit, I'm sorry. Don't worry, he's probably lying. He's a worthless piece of crap, that Crane. Even if he is your cousin. Hey, did you ever stop to think, he might be lying about that too? Being your cousin, I mean."

"It doesn't matter, I killed him. When they find him they'll come after me too. Do you suppose it's my real father's blood in me and I'm nothing but a killer? Oh, Mitch, now they're going to be after both of us."

He held her out away from him and studied her tear-stained face. "Don't talk nonsense. You're the same person you always were, Charlie Houston, Matt Houston's daughter, and don't you ever believe any different. And as for running away together, that isn't a good idea. Honey, I've been on the run, I know what it's like. You wouldn't like it one bit, believe me. No, I won't run off with you. Absolutely not!"

"Mitch, dammit, we don't have a choice." She jerked from his grasp. "I don't have a choice, and neither do you. There's a reward out for you and now I've committed murder. What do you suggest we do, wait here for them to ride in and shoot us down. Or hang us?"

He chuckled wryly. "They don't usually hang women, especially not women like you. You're well thought of, and Crane Houston is a nobody. They'll believe you when you tell them it was self-defense."

"With Colonel Dunkirk just slobbering for my

ranch? No, they won't. That sheriff of his will do just what he wants, and that means they'll send me to jail at best. Mitch, what's wrong with you?"

He shook his head, then took a long look at her. "What's wrong with me is that I love you and I know the value of life, of loving. I'm not going to let this happen to us. I've lost everything I loved once, and dammit I won't let it happen again. We'll figure something out, but we're not running. Not another step. I've run as far as I'm going to, and I sure as hell ain't letting you start."

Frantic, Charlie begged Mitch to listen. But he was acting like a crazy man. Haphazardly packing supplies, throwing things on the table, ranting on about dragging a woman around the country so she could be killed.

He threw a tin cup and plate at the table and both bounced to the floor with a loud clatter. She grabbed his arm and he whirled away from her, but then, as quickly as he had begun the madness, he stopped to stare at the floor, shoulders heaving.

She lay a hand on his back, the shirt soaked with perspiration and clinging to muscles so tense they quivered.

"Mitch, please talk to me."

"I can't."

"You have to. I won't leave you, and that's that. And I won't let you leave me either. Say what you want, think what you want. It's not going to happen. No matter what we decide to do, it will be together."

He waited, ramrod stiff, as she moved around him, hands lingering, not losing touch, until she stood squarely in front of him. Head drooping, he swayed as if all energy had been drained from him. She inched up close until their bodies curved together, tried to get him to look at her.

"You're exhausted. You need a lot of rest before

you go on. For goodness' sake, Mitch, you were shot ... what, a week ago? Why must we make a decision now?"

He heaved in another breath, pushed past her, and swung open the door. "Then I'll leave, right this minute. If you won't listen to reason, if you won't admit that I know what I'm talking about ..."

Conversation abruptly cut off, he gaped at the thick blanket of falling snow, so dense it had already piled a good foot up against the door. The drift leaked tiny wet puffs onto the floor at his feet.

She ran to stand beside him, then couldn't help but laugh. "Well, Mitch, go on. Leave."

The words were nearly childlike in their relief. He had no recourse but to remain there with her, indeed, they neither one had any choice but to remain snowbound and together in the cabin.

No one could get to them and they couldn't get out. This would give her some time, time to convince him, time to love him. "Oh, Mitch, look, isn't it beautiful?"

His clenched fists loosened at his side, and he raised his head. "How can you tell? You can't see through the stuff."

"Yes, isn't it wonderful?" She put her arms around his waist, laid her head on his chest, and stood there hugging him, until finally his arms lifted and encircled her.

A tired chuckle grew deep in his chest.

"What, Mitch? What is it?"

"My horse left."

She waited a moment for him to go on, to tell her something amusing.

He didn't.

"Mitch, why is that funny?"

He slumped and she felt the weight of his exhaustion.

"I couldn't have left if I'd wanted to. Only a fool would walk in this."

As she led him to the small bunk, she replied, "Only a fool would even go out in this." She coaxed him to lie down.

He didn't object, just mumbled something about that traitorous Jeb and how he should have known he couldn't trust the crazy horse. "Just like me," he said twice, his voice dying away on the end.

Before covering him to his chin with a blanket she gave him a kiss on lips that responded for a second, then went lax. His breathing evened out and he was asleep instantly. He must have been going on sheer courage alone. The fire crackled pleasantly behind her as she sat there for a long time holding his hand. Then she rose, put on her coat, and plowed her way through the deepening snow to bring in an ample store of wood from the pile Ritter and P.J. had cut and stacked that spring.

The storm swept down out of the mountains, catching the posse far from Miles City and any ranch. They holed up the rest of that day in a stand of lodgepole pine.

Wolf showed up just after dark, scaring the bejeebers out of Ritter, lurching into the firelight like some furry animal.

Ritter stared aghast. The last time he'd seen Wolf was when he rode off with Fallon. Where in thunder had he been? And what had happened to Fallon? He wanted to ask, but didn't dare, for fear someone might overhear.

By the following morning the posse found themselves hopelessly snowbound, and it wasn't long before two of the deputies lit out for town, several of Duffy's pals right on their heels.

One declared that making a try for town beat the

thunder out of hanging around there getting frostbit or heading off up into those mountains where they'd sure freeze.

McGrew stomped and hollered and turned red in the face till Ritter thought he might bust a gut.

Truth to tell Ritter agreed and he told Yancey so, but the ramrod insisted they stick around. "Someone's got to look out for Miss Charlie's interests. If they do run her and Fallon down, I want to be on hand to make sure it goes all right."

"They're gonna shoot that gunslinger, Yancey. You know they are, and no way can we stop 'em," Ritter said.

"Could be, but we can't let them harm Miss Charlie."

"Shooting Fallon will harm her," Ritter muttered, but didn't think Yancey heard him. At least he made no show of it.

As Ritter walked away he noticed Wolf standing nearby, close enough to have overheard the conversation.

"He's right, kid," Wolf said in his gravelly voice, startling Ritter for he spoke so seldom. "You need any help, I'm with you. Them two could use an even break, I figger we're it. Don't say nothin', but Fallon's big stallion showed up sometime last night."

Struck speechless, Ritter watched Wolf stride away before he could question him further. The man did talk when he had something to say, but what in the hell could it mean that Mitch's horse was out wandering around? Had the two of them tried to ride out on him and something terrible happened? Things just went from bad to badder, and he felt helpless to do much but watch.

The posse now consisted of Sheriff Newton, Duffy McGrew, a couple of men deputized in town, and four of Duffy's men, plus Ritter, Yancey, and Wolf. There

was also, of course, the very unhappy Colonel Hulbert
Dunkirk and his unhappier bodyguard, whose name
no one had ever heard. The colonel merely summoned
the man with a look, when even that much was necessary. It was a mystery where Dunkirk found such
loyal servants.

Ritter didn't like it at all, but he wasn't the kind to
keep complaining, and besides, he was worried about
Miss Charlie. Truth be known, he'd just as soon have
had his butt turned to a warm fire back in the bunkhouse of the Double H. It was somewhat consoling
that Yancey Barton and Wolf remained for the same
reason. The safety of Charlie Houston. Things could
be worse, but then they could be a hell of a lot better too.

From where he lay on the uncomfortable bunk
Mitch watched Charlie with thinly disguised amazement. She had wound up that music box and was actually cooking, dancing, and humming at the same time.
It looked like she had some notion of what she was
doing and might be enjoying it. He had slept several
hours and awakened refreshed if slightly befuddled at
their predicament. The snow now reached halfway up
the door. He hated being left with no choices that
made sense, but there was a sort of calmness all
around, what with the music and Charlie and the
knowledge that they were cut off from a world that
offered them only a brutal reality.

Brown beans bubbled in an iron pot that hung suspended over the fire; there rich aroma permeated the
small shack. Deftly Charlie stirred up some cornmeal
and spooned out the thick batter into cakes on a cast-
iron lid shoved onto the coals she'd raked to the front
of the fireplace.

Whoever had built the snug line shack had meant

its occupants to survive weeks at a time in total isolation. There was food, water, and plenty of firewood.

As if in reply to his wandering thoughts, she interrupted her singing to say, "Thank goodness Yancey had the foresight to have the men build some of these line shacks when we first arrived last year. I was upset at the time he took away from the ranch. Soon as he had me a cabin, he put up several of these. Said it would mean the difference in life and death for the men caught on the range in bad weather. Now, here it is saving our lives."

Fascinated by her actions rather than her words he barely nodded. "Who taught you to do that?" He pointed toward the johnnycakes puffing in the heat from the coals. "Last I knew you were living on canned peaches or bumming from the hands' cook fire."

She glanced at him with an embarrassed grin. Her cheeks glowed a rosy red from the fire and a lock of hair tumbled over one eye. A lump rose in his throat. How on God's earth could he leave her?

"Radine ... she spent some time with me after you rode out. I asked her to teach me, so I'd make a good wi—" she stumbled, stopped, and stared at him. Her dark, wide eyes filled and she wiped angrily at them with her fingertips.

"Aw, dammit, Charlie, I'm sorry," he said and held out his arms to her, wincing at the movement. "Come here."

For a moment he thought she wasn't going to move. She held her arms rigid at her sides, her head high and jaw squared like she was daring him. The tough side of her warring against the gentle. Then she reached out and they met, both taking a few steps before going into each other's arms.

"What are we going to do? It makes me want to scream and rant and rave like a madwoman. I waited all my life, Mitch. All ... my ... life for someone to love. And so now why does it hurt so damn bad I can't draw breath? I swear to you I won't let you ride away from me if I have to hogtie you to that cot over there."

He held her tightly, chin resting on top of her head. "I know, I know. There's a pain, a pain so raw and mean, when I even think of being separated from you. There must be something we can do. Something. Only I just can't come up with it. They'll string me up or shoot me if they catch me. And as long as we run somewhere, sooner or later there'll be someone who'll do that. And God only knows what might happen to you."

He sighed. "God, I used to wish he'd come along. The man with the bullet in his gun meant for me. End it all. Stop what was tearing through me like some kind of mad storm. Now, all I can think of, all I want is to go somewhere safe and be with you. In peace. Oh, Charlie, in peace."

She lifted her tear-stained face and their lips met, their tears mingled.

"Make love to me," she said into his mouth. "Now, and make it last forever."

He slipped his hands under her shirt and caressed the flush of her bare skin, then tenderly lowered her to the floor where he undressed her. Leaning over he saw twin reflections in her black eyes, himself and all he would ever be. Then he slipped out of his clothes and lay beside her, holding her close for a long time before parting her legs and slipping inside.

She cried out once, an ecstatic, sad, happy sound, and then rode with him in silence until they came to a land so far away no one but God and his angels could possibly find them. There they remained for a very long time. Until the fire burned down and the johnnycakes turned dark and crusty, and cold slipped in around the door like a silent thief.

He brought her back as he had taken her, with gentle kisses and the touch of his bare skin on hers; his hair spread upon her breasts, his silken warm lips at the pulse in her throat.

And he didn't know what to do, but he did know that he could never leave this woman and he could not take her with him either. Now he stood on the edge but he wasn't alone, and he no longer wanted to plunge over, not as long as she held so tightly to his hand.

"Charlie," he said finally, the sound of his voice startling them both back to reality.

She jerked as if slapped. "I was just dreaming," she said.

"I know, me too. And I've had an idea."

No reply came, and he lifted to his elbows to study her shadowed face. "You're cold, let me put some wood on the fire." He rose and added a couple of logs behind the cooking food. His bare thighs glistened in the dancing flames and when he turned she saw a glimmer of hope in the firelit sheen of his features.

"What is it? Tell me."

"We'll go to Virginia City. I'll give myself up to the marshal."

She sat up, grabbed her shirt, and angrily tried to turn it right side out, not looking at him. "No. No, I won't let you do that!"

"No, listen to me. It was a long time ago, right after the war, maybe I can get amnesty. They did that then. We were outlaws, I reckon, and me the leader. But we never killed. We robbed and shot up some towns. Hell, most of us had no home left to go to. The war ravaged the South. What were we supposed to do? Men like McGrew. Look at him. A successful rancher and a pretty rich wife. He rode with us too."

Charlie stood there holding her shirt and staring at him. "So that's what he has against you."

"Not just that. The day the posse rode in to round us up, we were having a free-for-all. McGrew and some of his cronies wanted to rob the bank in town. I wanted to stop, go to Canada with my wife, put an end to it all." He shrugged, and tried on a weak grin. "We got away, they didn't. He spent time in prison, others died. He'd like to get back at me for that."

Thoughtfully she slipped on the garment. "And what about this amnesty thing? How does it work? Do you think you could qualify?"

"I'll wire my sister Dessa and her husband, Ben. They can help. Amnesty is sort of like a pardon for all your sins, if you promise to go and sin no more. It's because it's easier and cheaper than spending the manpower to chase an outlaw down. Jesse James and Frank, plenty of others were offered pardons, if they'd just quit what they were doing and ride in."

She studied him a moment. She tried not to think of Crane lying in a pool of his own blood, a bullet in him fired from her Winchester. This wasn't about her but about Mitch, who had a bounty on his head. Crane's death might be explained away somehow. "Did any of the outlaws take them up on it?"

He shrugged. "I don't know. I think most of them would rather not. Jesse, he didn't, but I reckon plenty did."

"But you're not up to no good and haven't been, so why would they do that?"

"As far as that lying sheriff tells it, I murdered those two worthless hands of the colonel's. I don't know that I can prove different. I've not committed a foul deed in years, not really. I reckon I could threaten to go back to my outlaw ways if they didn't grant me amnesty."

The attempt at humor fell short and he shrugged.

"Charlie, I don't know if they would offer me amnesty, but it's worth a try." Excitement colored his tone and he stood on one leg and then the other to put on his pants, talking all the while but not really looking straight at her. "But Dessa and Ben, they have a lot of influence. They own half of northern Montana, the railroads, hotels. Everyone respects them. With their help, and the fact that I give myself up and tell them everything ... about Yank and all that ... well, just maybe it would work."

"And if it didn't?"

He slipped into his shirt and grinned broadly at her. "Well, then I guess you'd just have to bust me out and we'd go on the lam. We could take up robbing trains and banks, or maybe—" he broke off, losing enthusiasm for his weak attempt to lighten the mood.

Hope surged through her and she answered his grin with one of her own. Maybe, just maybe there was a chance for him. And if there was, she would take her own chances where the killing of her cousin was concerned. Surely, when she told her story about how he had hit her and threatened her, the law would show mercy. What was most important was to free Mitch Fallon once and for all from the cloud of his past. Underneath his brash toughness he was a good and gentle man, and deserved happiness.

They talked and planned into the night, and the next morning, as if the fates had decided to give them at least one chance, a warm wind swept in off the mountains. The snow began to melt. By noon the high drifts were quickly turning to water that rushed down the steep inclines in numerous noisy cascades. The first thing the next morning, they would leave. It would be a long hard trek on foot without Mitch's big black horse. No telling where the beast had gotten to.

Chapter Twenty-one

It was pure entertainment, the way the colonel flapped his arms and ranted. Ritter figured if the man didn't stumble head first into a snowdrift soon, he'd have some kind of fit. Yet all he really cared about was seeing that Miss Charlie came out of this with no trouble. With Crane flapping his mouth all the way back to Miles City about her having shot him, that was going to be tough.

Ritter saw McGrew and a couple of his men saddling up and the sheriff, who up to now had been receiving the brunt of the colonel's wrath, including the threat that the man would never be elected in any county in Montana if he didn't catch this outlaw killer, followed suit. The way the warm wind was kicking up off the mountains, this snow would soon be mush and they'd be shedding gear right and left.

McGrew rode his piebald mare right up to the colonel and looked down on him. "Shut up, you old fool. Why don't you git in your fancy little buggy, sir, and ride on back to town. We'll take care of this little problem for you."

The colonel yelled right back. "This little problem is not mine, it is all the good people's of this territory who don't need a bloodthirsty killer riding free."

McGrew glared down at the man, enjoying his advantage. "Far as I see it, you are the bloodthirsty one, trying to steal all our ranches. Someone ought to hunt you down, same as we're doing to this Fallon, and back-shoot you. That would do the people of this territory a real favor."

The colonel struggled to his feet, fuming until each word sprayed foam. "You mouthy Irish trash, marrying money to get what you want. I ought to run you through."

McGrew tossed back his head and laughed heartily. "Run me through? You old fake. If you ever carried a saber you wouldn't know what to do with one. The closest you've ever come to being in the army is when you run the other way when the conscripters come to town."

Sheriff Newton shoved between the colonel and the mounted man. "McGrew, you don't want to start something here you can't finish. Just look around and use the good sense you were born with."

McGrew glanced to his right where the colonel's big bodyguard stood holding a rifle that could easily blow his head off, and it was pointed right at him.

Colonel Dunkirk began to laugh, an evil sound that chilled Ritter's very soul. McGrew's reply didn't ease his fears any either.

"You bastard. Someone will catch you without your hired guns someday and blow you to kingdom come. Solve everyone's problems."

Angrily McGrew reined his mount aside and joined his cohorts, fuming at them because they didn't back him up. Ritter's attention was caught by the sheriff, who was making an effort to organize the straggly posse.

"Now listen up, men. We're no more than a day's ride from Red Rock Bluffs. If that killer is still holed up there, and he very well may be seein' as how his stallion is here with us, we stop him any way we have to. The bounty don't say he has to be alive, and he's a dangerous man. Biggest chunk goes to the man who guns him down, pure and simple. Now, let's ride."

Miss Charlie was going to get hurt before this was over, Ritter just knew it. He fell in beside Yancey and Wolf, who was leading the big black stallion Jeb, saddled and ready.

The mud was almost worse than snowdrifts. Mitch and Charlie made pretty good time on the rocky trail, but once they reached flat land, their boots sank ankle and calf deep in mire. Each foot sucked up out of the mud carried clumps of the stuff, until the added weight became a burden that slowed their progress. She had insisted on bringing Mitch's rifle, but they carried only the barest of necessities in the way of food, water, and bedrolls. Tucked in her pocket was the deed to the Double H Ranch. The beloved music box was left behind. If they survived, they would come back in the spring and rescue it. Mitch wore his Colt .44, but even with it on he didn't vaguely resemble the gunslinger she'd first met at spring roundup. He might as well have been someone else, he had changed so much since that day. But then, she supposed she had too.

Water stood like a lake in the meadow grasses and flowed in furious rivers in every ditch and gully. The sun climbed higher and higher in the sky and they continued to make little progress. As the temperature climbed their spirits faltered. Sweat made their skin itch and prickle under the woolen underwear and heavy winter clothing both wore.

Finally the exertion took its toll on his wounded body and he staggered and went to his knees. She knelt beside him and locked an arm around his waist, afraid he would fall facedown in the snow-crusted water.

"Let's rest awhile," she said. "There's some high

ground up under that patch of trees yonder. Can you make it?"

He nodded, stumbled to his feet awkwardly, and together they climbed the rise into the small grove of scraggly pine. With a weary groan, he backed up against one of the scaly barked junipers and slid to the ground on his butt.

"Wet but fine," he said and grinned at her.

The bravery of the gesture made her want to cry. Instead she bit her lip, touched his brow, and found it clammy.

"I'm all right," he said and captured her hand. "Whoo, didn't know I was so wiped out."

"It'd be easier to walk if we kept to the high ground," she offered.

He buried his lips in her palm, and she closed her eyes. Oh, God, let this work. Let him be okay. Let nothing happen to him. It was a silent prayer she dared not say aloud, for it would show him how worried she was.

"Not a good idea," he finally said. "There are stretches where there are no trees, no cover at all. If they're out there looking for us we have to stay off high ground, and if that means wading mud and water and snow, then we'll do it. Hell, we don't want to get shot before we can give up, do we?"

"At this rate we're liable to be old and gray before we make it. I think we should circle back to the ranch and get horses. We can wait till dark and sneak in in case they're watching. Ritter and Yancey will help us if we can find them, I know they will."

He held up a hand, signaled for quiet. He shifted around to the other side of the small tree, moved to his knees, and peered out. She stood behind him.

"What?" she whispered.

"There," he said and pointed. "Riders, coming

through the gap in those trees at the break of the hill. See?"

She could barely make them out, but he was right. At least a dozen men rode toward them, their horses struggling through the mud and slush.

"Posse," she said close to his ear.

"Vigilantes," he said.

Between them they had only the ammunition in the Winchester and his Colt .44. Neither carried any spare shells.

She lifted the rifle; he laid a hand across it and pushed the barrel down to point at the ground.

"No more," he said. "No more killing."

"I won't let them take you, even if you will," she said through gritted teeth.

He didn't reply, but continued to watch the riders. If they kept to their present course they would pass within a few hundred yards of where the two of them hid. Maybe they wouldn't see them. It was a slim hope for the small clump of trees offered little cover.

"I have an idea," she said softly.

"What?"

"I'll walk out there, give myself up. While they're distracted you drop down the other side of the ridge and make a break for it. They won't shoot me. I'll tell them you got away, went west into the Bighorns. I haven't seen you in days. Not since before the big storm. You got out ahead of it. For all I know you froze to death out there somewhere." She spoke low and fast, all the while preparing to rise and reveal herself.

He didn't say anything for a few seconds as the riders drew closer. Then, "Won't work."

"Yes, yes it will," she practically hissed.

"Even if it did, what happens after that?"

She looked at him closely. She couldn't think, her mind was blank. After that? After that he would be alone out here in his weakened condition and she would be alone wherever those men took her; home or jail.

"Whatever we do, we do together, you said so."

Immediately she knew he was right. They had both been too long alone. Whatever their destiny, they would face it together.

At the head of the posse, the leader called a halt. The weary horses hung their heads, some kind of conversation was conducted, and then the riders headed up the rise toward the scant patch of trees where Mitch and Charlie waited. There was no place to go, nowhere to hide, and so she took his hand and helped him to his feet. Then, holding on to each other they stumbled out to meet the approaching posse.

He said to her, almost in jest, "You'd think in country this big they could have ridden another draw, or we could have walked down a mile in the other direction. Then we would have missed each other altogether."

"That's what you'd think, wouldn't you?" she agreed. She wondered if he could feel her trembling.

As Mitch and Charlie approached them, Yancey, Ritter, and Wolf acted in unison. No secret signal had been exchanged, but it might have been, for they swung their mounts into a barrier between the surrendering couple and the rest of the riders. McGrew, Sheriff Newton, and the colonel's bodyguard all had their guns cocked and pointed. Scabbards and holsters murmured with the sound of guns being drawn.

Yancey's weapon spoke before anyone could fire, the bullet cut dirt and threw the horses into a crazy hoof-stomping dance.

He shouted at the posse, "They're surrendering, and if you're gonna kill Fallon, you'll have to explain away five bodies." He glanced for confirmation toward his two cohorts and they nodded, grimly keeping their guns aimed.

Sheriff Newton roared, "You sons a bitches. Throw in with that outlaw and I'll put you all on the same scaffold."

"Now, Sheriff," Yancey said, "we're not throwing in with anyone. We're just seeing that things are done fair and square."

"Ain't no fair and square with a killer like Yank. And she went with him, she's painted with the same brush." Newton looked to the colonel and McGrew who nodded in unison.

"You ain't shooting Miss Charlie," Ritter yelled and brought up his rifle.

"Easy, boy," Yancey said out of the corner of his mouth.

A man beside McGrew drew and fired, hitting no target. It was unclear what he had aimed at, but with the crack of the gunshot all hell broke loose.

Mitch threw Charlie to the ground and covered her with his body, at the same time drawing his Colt from the holster. Wolf dismounted and knelt on one knee in front of the fallen couple. He carried an old Sharps and it belched clouds of black smoke and boomed so loud the ground shook.

McGrew's attention never wavered from Fallon. He spurred his mount through the melee of men and screaming horses, intent on only one thing. Killing the man he'd known as Yank. The outlaw leader who had abandoned him and his friends so many years ago. The man who could reveal his own secret identity.

In a flash of memory Mitch recognized the man, and it was as if he had been propelled back to the day at Alder Gulch when his guerrilla band had been attacked and destroyed by Sheriff Moohn outside Virginia City.

The man had been one of the leaders of the revolt

within the ranks of Yank's gang; the uprising that had ultimately caused its defeat. Mitch could no longer remember what name he'd gone under, but it hadn't been McGrew. All this flashed through his mind in the instant that McGrew drew bead, and Mitch shouted at Wolf to look out. At the same time he aimed his own Colt and squeezed the trigger. The big .44 shell caught McGrew in the chest and blew him backward from his saddle, but not before he pulled off his own shot. The bullet slammed into Wolf's arm, spinning him around. The big man let out a grunt, righted himself, and shifted the heavy Sharps to his other hip.

By this time Mitch had struggled to his knees so that he and Wolf formed a solid shield for Charlie. He heard her scrambling around in the mud, muttering her own special curses. But he didn't realize that when he'd thrown her to the ground she'd lost the Winchester, not until he saw from the corner of his eye her making a lunge for the rifle.

He swung around, shouted, "No, Charlie," just as she landed and came up with the Winchester. There she crouched, out in the open with no cover, no protection at all.

Rage twisting his face, the colonel raised his rifle and shot her.

Mitch aimed, fired, and tried to throw himself between her and the deadly bullet, his fevered brain screaming, "Not again," over and over, into a world black and empty. She went down, flying up into the air and landing on her back almost like one of her graceful dances. His ears drummed and darkness closed in upon him, until there was only an endless tunnel and her sprawled in the mud at the end of it. And he couldn't get to her, his feet kept bogging down, and no matter how hard he tried, she was still far away and fading from view.

He heard a tremendous, ungodly roar that he

thought was the sound of his heart exploding, his blood erupting, and then he had her in his arms. He didn't realize that the shooting had stopped until much later. All he knew was that the woman he worshiped beyond life itself lay cold and gray and unmoving against his chest, and he had no life, no heart, no love left in him. She had taken it with her.

Mud plastered her dark hair to one pale cheek, and he brushed it away tenderly. She was soaked, her skin icy, and he wrapped his arms around her, held her close, rocked and cried. Someone brought a blanket and wrapped it around both of them.

Voices repeated his name, told him things he didn't want to hear, but he just kept shaking his head, saying, "No, no. Go away and leave us be."

He touched her inert lips with his own. When she didn't respond, he talked to her, told her he loved her, held her against his breaking heart.

Finally words got through to him, oozed into his hearing like tiny echoes from another place and time.

"Let us have her, Fallon. Come on, Fallon, let go."

Enraged, he screamed, "No, you son of a bitch. You've killed her."

But then she jerked in his arms, gasped, made small mewling noises, moaned.

He couldn't believe that it was anything more than his imagination. He breathed her name once, twice, then foolishly, "Is that you?"

Her eyelids fluttered, her lips moved into a wan smile. "My darling, who ... else ... would ... it ... be?"

Weak, but alive. She was alive. He sobbed and laughed and held her close.

"Let Ritter take her, Fallon. Let's get her to town to a doctor. He'll carry her."

"No," he said, glaring ferociously at them and trying to hang on to her.

"You can't even stand, dammit," someone said.

He peered through the haze that still surrounded him, that cut him and his love off from the rest of the world. Hovering there he made out the kid, Ritter.

"I'll carry her myself," he told the boy, but he couldn't get up off the ground with her. What was wrong with him? He wanted to shout to the heavens, "She's alive. Damn, she's alive," thought he did, but maybe not.

Ritter grinned, white teeth gleaming out of a muddy face. "You damn right she is, but if we don't stop all this jawing, she might not be. Now, give her up, man. You've done all you could. You shot the bastard that gunned her. That's your part, now let us do ours."

Ritter touched his shoulder, and Mitch let go the tension and hate and bitterness and fear that had held him together. He allowed Ritter to lift Charlie from his arms, then he remained there a moment, fists clenched, head drooping. He no longer held the Colt and had no idea what had happened to it. Trampled in the muck somewhere, he supposed.

Slowly he took in the battle scene. Several bodies lay about on the ground while the men still on their feet loaded the dead and injured belly down on their horses. No one seemed interested in the man they'd been riding out after with such hellacious intent. Their leaders were down, wounded, maybe dead. The bodies of McGrew and the colonel were among those being loaded up. The colonel's bodyguard was nowhere to be seen. Perhaps he'd simply ridden away when his boss fell. The sheriff could be one of the bodies so coated in mud as to be unidentifiable. Mitch didn't know or care.

In the midst of it all, in the smoke and the fury and noise, waited the great black stallion. Looking at him, beckoning.

"You son of a bitch, where'd you come from?" he

muttered and swayed to his feet. All he had to do was mount up and ride away. No one would pay him the least attention, nor would they challenge him. The shooting of Charlie Houston had sobered them. Numbly he watched Ritter hand Charlie up to Yancey. The ramrod settled her into his arms and immediately rode off. Ritter and Wolf mounted and followed. He thought about his earlier brief desire to just ride away. It would be the easiest way out for all of them, Charlie included. Someone had saddled the stallion and brought him along. For him, so he could ride away? Everything was a confused mess, and he tried not to think anymore or it might cause his head to burst with the effort. Instead he captured the reins, stepped into the stirrup, and swung onto Jeb's back. Then he touched his heels to the horse's flanks and rode off in the direction that Yancey had taken Charlie. He might not be thinking too well, but he was sure of one thing. He was through running.

Charlie had a bullet in the fleshy part of her backside, the doctor told Fallon when he carried the spent shell over to the jail in Miles City. It had lodged there after plowing through her upper thigh and nicking her hipbone. Doc handed the smashed lead through the bars with a grin and a spark in his brown eyes.

"It'll be more embarrassing than anything else for the little lady. It'll be a spell before she can set down with any ease, and she won't be walking for a while, but everything looks fine. I've put her up at the hotel as we run out of bed space."

Mitch took the misshapen piece of lead. "Thanks, Doc. You sure she's going to be okay?"

The doc grinned. "She's already madder than a cornered bobcat because someone told her you're over here in jail. She's threatened to burn down the town if someone doesn't do something to get you out. With her acting like that, I'd a been here sooner, but had some more patching up to do. Quite a fracas you started out there."

Mitch rolled the lead in his fingers. "I didn't exactly start it, but I think I can finish it. You tell Charlie I've already done just that. My sister and her husband are on their way and they're bringing a newspaper reporter with them. Dessa has telegraphed the governor and Marshal Bracken down in Virginia City. Bracken'll be riding up too. Folks jump when my sister hollers, I guess. You tell Charlie everything's going to be just fine. This whole mess will be straightened out real quick.

"Damn, I wish I could see her. Is she really okay? Doc, is there any way she could come see me? They won't let me out of this place."

The doc studied Mitch for a moment, then shook his head. "Not a chance, not for a few days. I don't aim to see that little gal moved, and if she don't quit acting up the way she is I aim to chloroform her or tie her to the bed. Maybe both.

"You just be patient, young man. This'll all work itself out. By the way, how's that shoulder of yours? It looked pretty good when I cleaned it up for you. Bothering you any?"

Mitch flexed the arm and grimaced. "Nah, it's fine. Almost good as new. Now, about Charlie—"

The doc held up his hand. "Don't know which one of you is worse, I'll swear I don't." The doc started out the door, then turned. "Oh, by the way, I've got another fella over there at the hotel who's recuperating too. Says he's kin to Miss Houston. Goes by the name of Crane Houston. They found him shot out at the Double H a few days ago. He's been kicking up a fuss to see his cousin. I guess I might let him visit with her a bit just to keep her company."

The doctor pulled the door shut behind him.

Mitch stared. What the hell was going on? Charlie

said she'd killed that no-good bastard when he tried to ... "Hey, Doc," he yelled. "Goddammit, Doc."

The door opened and a young man peered in. "Shut up the blamed caterwauling."

"Listen, you've got to take a message for me. Now," Mitch said.

The deputy raised his shoulders in a sigh. "What now, Fallon. I swear you're more trouble than a cell plumb full of Saturday night drunks."

"This is important."

"Of course it is."

"Go to the doc's place and tell him whatever he does not to let Crane Houston anywhere near Charlie. You tell him that, now, you hear?"

"You mean that fella we found shot out at the Double H?"

"That's who I mean. Now, go, dammit! It fact, you take a pair of handcuffs and you put them on that no-good son of a bitch. You arrest him. He tried to ... I mean, he wants to steal the Houston ranch."

"Aw, dang, I can't do that."

Fallon ground his teeth. "Where the hell's the sheriff?"

"We ain't got us no sheriff."

"What happened to Sheriff Newton?"

"You got me."

"And just who are you?"

"Name's Acorn and no cracks."

"Is he dead?"

"Who?"

Mitch gritted his teeth. "The sheriff."

Acorn studied Fallon a minute. "Now why the hell would you ask me that? Of course, he ain't dead. I don't reckon. He rode off, said they didn't pay him enough to fool with the likes of you and all your friends. Now this town don't have any law."

"I want to see Ritter and Yancey, now," he roared

at the deputy, who had continued to ramble on about the sorry fate of the town.

"Don't get your hide all stretched out of shape. I'll find them, anything to get you to shut up."

"And you'd better get over to the hotel and watch Crane Houston, if you don't want me to wring your scrawny neck right through these bars." Filled with frustration and helplessness, Mitch kicked the slop bucket clear across the cell, spilling its contents all over the dirty floor. He immediately regretted that.

"Now look what you've gone and done," Acorn yelped.

"Dear God, will you do what I told you to?"

"I'm going, I'm doing it," the deputy said, and backed out the door, face screwed up against the offensive odor coming from Mitch's cell.

Ritter sat beside Charlie, twisting his hat round and round in nervous fingers.

She peered closely at him. "You're sure it's over? I mean, the whole thing?"

"Colonel Dunkirk is dead, ma'am." He grinned at her expression, but went on without apology. "McGrew was wounded, and they've sent him to Denver to be with his wife. Where he shoulda been in the first place, if you want to know what I think. The bounty has been removed off Fallon's head for gunning Cross and Neddy, Sheriff Newt had a knot on his head the size of a goose egg and was so mad when he came to riding belly down on his horse that he resigned as soon as he got back to town and rode off God knows where. Course everyone knows it was really 'cause he no longer had the colonel to protect his job. The whole town is in an uproar, trying to come up with someone they can vote in as sheriff before the marshal arrives from Virginia City and lots of 'em are saying Wolf would be just fine if he'd—"

"Whoa, Ritter. Wait a minute. Why is Mitch still in jail?"

"Well, ma'am, he . . . I mean, the telegram from the marshal ordered us to . . . well, to hold him till he gets here. Something about his actions after the war. Why, did you know he was as famous as Quantrill? Led a band of marauders just the same as him, guerrillas, they say."

"And the marshal is going to send him to prison for something that happened ten years ago?"

Ritter shrugged. "I don't know. All we know, Yancey and me, is that we're under strict orders from a U.S. Marshal, and we can't go agin them, now can we?"

Charlie sighed. "I suppose not, but dammit, Ritter, he doesn't belong in jail. Hasn't he been through enough without this? I want to see him, make sure he's all right. I can't stand just laying here like this."

Doc came in then and chased Ritter off.

The doc pivoted, the brown bottle of laudanum in one hand and a glass of water in the other. "I got someone in the other room who wants to see you as soon as you're up to it. Says he's your cousin. A fella by the name of Crane Houston?"

"That's not possible, he . . ."

"Are you all right? You look pale as ashes. My word, child."

Charlie gasped, clung to the bedcovers as the room revolved crazily. She swayed, her mouth went dry, then filled with saliva that choked her.

Doc let the laudanum and water glass clatter to the bedside table and wet a cloth to press to her forehead. "You've had too much excitement, that's all," he soothed. "Now just relax. I'll give you this and you can sleep. There's nothing to worry about."

"No, no. You don't understand." Why wouldn't he listen? The man she thought she had killed lay in the next room, obviously quite alive, and this man refused to listen to what she had to say.

He poured a measure of liquid into the water and held it to her lips until she drank. She sipped and swallowed, frightened eyes wide and pleading, until the glass was empty.

"Now calm down, go to sleep."

"Don't let anyone in here, please," she said through numb lips. "Don't let him . . ." Gentle darkness crept over her like blankets of thick wool, and the fear oozed away.

Chapter Twenty-two

Radine glared down at Ritter and Yancey, slamming down their mugs of beer so that the foam sloshed all over the table.

"You men are always up to some orneriness that nearly gets women folk hurt. You never can just let things go along and work themselves out." She paused a minute, but not long enough for either of them to reply. "Course, all I really care about is that Charlie is going to be okay."

The three broke out in wide grins and the two men sipped their beers for a while in silence.

Instead of leaving and tending to her other customers, Radine leaned on the table and ogled Ritter. He gazed openly at her breasts pushed up by a corset so that the blush of her nipples peeked out at him. He was beginning to feel pretty randy, now that everything was done and settled, and he toyed with asking Radine to go to a crib with him. The idea crawled around in his groin and he shifted in the chair.

She winked at him, but what she said didn't match her actions. "Hear about Red Cloud and Sitting Bull?"

"No," Yancey said. "They finally get the savages?"

"That ain't all. After Crook attacked at Slim Buttes

and American Horse surrendered, Red Cloud's bunch was disarmed. Army took their horses and guns."

"Well, dang!" Yancey said. "Well, ain't it about time?"

Radine took a deep breath and went on. "Then Colonel Miles followed old Sitting Bull to Cedar Creek and him and all them Sioux just flat surrendered. Some say there were thousands of them."

"Soldiers?" Ritter asked.

"No, Indians."

"Aw, bull. The army defeated thousands of Sioux? I don't believe that."

"Well, it's true," Radine said, hand in the air for emphasis. "I heard it from some soldiers themselves."

She blushed and fiddled with a little bow ribbon between her breasts. Once again, Ritter's glance skittered into place there.

Radine ran her hand down his arm, and he gulped audibly. She whispered in his ear, "I got some things I could teach you."

He slammed the empty beer mug down and kicked back his chair.

Radine giggled, touched her red hair, and led Ritter toward the stairs.

Charlie hitched one eye open, felt the bed spin, and groaned. Her stomach roiled. Crane was in the next room. What would he do to her when he recovered enough to move around? She had to get away from this place before he did. He was supposed to be dead, killed by the bullet from her rifle. Well, at least she didn't have to worry about being arrested for his murder. Still, he must have told someone who had shot him. Why hadn't anyone said anything?

As her head cleared she remembered Crane's threat with more clarity, the ace up his sleeve he'd spoken about. Something he claimed would prove she was not

Matt Houston's daughter, and therefore not his legal heir. What could it be? She had to find out, and if she couldn't walk, then she would crawl. After everything that had happened, she would not lose the ranch too. She would be there when Mitch was set free, no matter how long it took. He would have a home to come back to.

Her heart ached with loneliness and despair. How would she stand it if they sent him away to prison?

A familiar voice interrupted her thoughts, and she clutched at the mattress when she rolled her head on the pillow and saw Crane Houston leaning heavily against the door frame and grinning with all the evil he had in him.

"Well, well, lookee who's here," he said and shuffled toward her.

Charlie stared at her cousin in the open doorway as if he were a coiled snake. The pain in her hip grew more intense. She suppressed an urge to leap from the bed, rake at his eyes, seeing as how she couldn't move. The animosity of his ugly grin told her he'd not come to inquire after her health.

She shifted, tried to lift the injured leg with both hands and work her way to the edge of the mattress. Face him on her feet. Sweat beaded her forehead, and she felt giddy, finally gave up on the impossible task and lay back against the pillows. Her gown was drenched, her hair hung in wet strands that clung to her face and neck, and she was totally exhausted by the effort. Not once during the ordeal did she move her gaze from the man in the doorway.

He looked about as drained as she felt but managed to take several shuffling steps toward her, one arm wrapped around his right side. Without the door facing to support him it appeared as if he might fall at any moment, but he made it to the foot of the bed and leaned there breathing heavily.

At last she could croak out some words. "What do you want?"

"You shot me," he gasped.

She sent a quick look toward the door. The hallway was empty, quiet. "I thought you were dead."

He nodded, fingered around in the pocket of a loose robe he wore over pajamas, came out with a folded square of newspaper. "See what you think of your folks now, cousin," he sneered and skimmed the paper in her direction. It floated onto the coverlet just within her reach.

For a long while she just stared at the offering. It would be best if she didn't read it, but there was no way she could manage that, she knew. And so she stretched her arm out, leaned forward until she could pinch the clippings between two of her fingers.

"Get out of here," she told him.

"No. I want to see your face when you find out all about your real daddy and his whore. Read it, go ahead. And then I'll leave." He stopped and took several breaths. She could tell he was in a great deal of pain, but felt no compassion for him.

Licking her dry lips she began to unfold the small square of yellowed newsprint.

After pacing what seemed like a hundred miles in the tiny cell, Mitch was relieved to be interrupted by the sound of the outside door opening and closing. He hoped to see someone with a message from Charlie, but it was the young deputy Acorn.

"Did you tell the doc—?" Mitch didn't finish the question before Acorn interrupted him.

"Someone's here to see you." The deputy's eyes bugged, as if he didn't quite believe his own announcement. "It's Mr. and Mrs. Ben Poole. They're right outside, and there's this reporter fella with them. He says he's going to write all about you. How you were a hero in the war and afterward your whole family thought you were dead, only you were really an outlaw trying to right the wrongs of the . . ."

A tall blond gentleman filled the doorway behind the deputy and interrupted the tirade with a hearty laugh. "Mitchell Fallon, I thought we'd never see your ornery hide again. Have to confess, though, I'd have figured you to be behind bars when I did. How in the world are you, anyway? I've got someone here who's just dying to see you."

Ben Poole turned without waiting for a reply, took the arm of Mitch's sister Dessa, and pulled her through the doorway.

Green eyes met matching green eyes and Mitch extended his arms through the bars in an attempt to hug his tall, beautiful sister. "Oh, God, it's good to see you. How are you? You look wonderful. How was your trip? Damn, it's good to see you."

Dessa laughed delightedly and reached through the bars too so that they were hugging even with the unyielding iron between them. "We've missed you so much. How could you go away for so long and only write twice? I was so sorry to hear about Celia and the baby. What a tragedy.

"But we're all here now and together again. You've gotten yourself in quite a fix, haven't you? When are you going to settle down like the rest of us?"

Mitch stared at Dessa. How lovely and elegant she looked, not at all like the young girl who had ridden off to make her fortune with an equally young Ben Poole.

He beamed at her, despite all his worries about Charlie. "I'm ready, truly ready. I swear if I get out of this mess I'm going to spend the rest of my life just behaving myself."

Ben laughed uproariously. "That'll make the law happy."

The shy, soft-spoken, and gentle young man Mitch remembered had certainly changed. Despite his self-assurance and sophisticated demeanor, though, Ben still eyed Dessa in that hauntingly adoring way Mitch remembered.

"Well," Mitch said, "what's this about some reporter?"

"That's James Magruder, the fella with the pencil glued to his hand." Ben indicated a studious man with thinning hair and a round, childish face that lit up when Mitch nodded in his direction.

Ben went on. "You two will have plenty of time to talk later. First, let's see what we can do about getting you out of here."

"They told me I had to stay until the marshal arrived from Virginia City," Mitch said.

"That's ridiculous." Dessa lifted her skirts and swept past Ben to hail an enraptured Acorn, who had squeezed his way back into the outer office but still gaped in awe at the impressive visitors. "Young man. Yes, you. Kindly bring the keys to my brother's cell. He has business to attend to and it can't be carried out in this filthy jail cell. And please get someone to clean this place up, it stinks."

Acorn grinned and nodded, then grinned some more.

Then Mitch thought again of Charlie's predicament, and his ensuing outburst drew everyone's attention. "My God, we have to do something about Charlie."

Deputy Acorn came through the door, amazingly offering a key to the cell. Mitch addressed him. "Did you talk to Doc?"

"About what?" the young man asked, wearing his usual befuddled expression.

"Dammit, I sent you to check on Charlie and that no-good ... you remember, I told you about Crane Houston. Unlock this damn door. Now!"

Ben grabbed the key, stuck it in the lock, and swung the door open all in one efficient motion. Mitch remembered that about him. He never wasted time on useless questions.

"Come on, come with me. Everyone," Mitch yelled as he ran from the sheriff's office out into the street. "That son of a bitch better not have harmed a hair of her head."

"Oh, I can see you've really changed, brother," Dessa called, but again hiked up the skirt of her expensive silk dress to hurry after him. Ben, Magruder, and Acorn brought up the rear.

Mitch busted through the door of the hotel without bothering with the usual amenities. An elderly woman seated in the lobby huddled into her chair and stared wide-eyed as he led his entourage up the stairs. At the top he paused only a second after spotting four doors along the hallway. The first one on the left stood open to reveal Crane and Charlie.

Startled, both turned an amazed gaze toward him. Charlie's lovely dark eyes were awash with tears.

"You son of a—" Mitch headed for Crane, intent on mayhem.

Ben and Dessa grabbed his arms, held him back.

For a fraction of a second everyone remained frozen in place, then Mitch shook loose and went to Charlie, touched her, half turned to make another grab at Crane. "What'd you do to her, you thieving piece of—"

Crane cowered backward, whimpered.

"No, Mitch, no," Charlie said. "Don't."

Latecomers Magruder and Acorn crowded into the room.

"Why not? Give me one good reason why I shouldn't wipe up the floor with this worthless piece of . . . what's that?" He pointed at the newspaper clipping.

She ignored the last question, tried to calm him. "Because I love you and he is worthless, but you aren't. Please, Mitch, don't. Let's just let it all be over, please."

Dessa clamped his arm tighter. "Listen to her and don't go off half-cocked. Remember where you've just been."

For Mitch, when Charlie professed her love in front of everyone, it was as if his wild intent to do Crane bodily harm slammed up against a rock wall. Loving her would prevent him continuing in the direction in which he'd been aimed all these years. He would have to turn and face up to reality, take a hand in his own destiny. Though his inclination had been to choke the life out of the little runt hanging over the foot of the bed, all he really wanted was to be with Charlie. Taking another look at the pitiful Crane Houston, he figured the man might die on his own without any help from anyone.

Mitch extended his hands, palms down. "Okay, I won't kill him. Not yet, anyway." He turned in disgust from the lowlife to concentrate on Charlie who looked pretty peaked. He wiped tears from her cheeks with his thumbs.

"God, how I've missed you," he said and kissed her gently, once, twice, then yet again but with much more intensity.

She sighed, reached for him, then let herself go limp in his arms. "Who are all these people staring at me? Can't we go away somewhere and be alone? Oh, Mitch, you should read this. It's ... it's just so ... sad." She broke into great racking sobs.

He held her until the sobbing faded. After she came to her senses, wiped her face, and apologized to her visitors, Ben took over.

"I'm Ben Poole, Mitch's brother-in-law. This is my lovely wife, Mitch's sister Dessa, and this young man scribbling frantically is the fellow who will help see that Mitch doesn't go to jail, James Magruder. And back there, peering in like a hooty owl, that's the only law this poor town has to offer at the moment. Afraid I didn't catch the young fellow's name."

"Acorn," Mitch muttered and patted Charlie to re-assure himself she was real and okay.

She caught his hand fiercely and nodded up at the blond giant, then her ebony eyes searched out Mitch's gaze once again. She held up the newspaper clipping without saying a word.

"Aw, don't cry. It's not good for you. You have to get well."

"I . . . am . . . well. I just . . . oh, dammit to hell, Fallon, read that."

Dessa gasped and Mitch couldn't suppress a slight chuckle. The old Charlie was surfacing, despite everything she'd been through lately.

He moved to the window to read. There was no sound in the room except for an occasional sniffle from Charlie. Both Dessa and Ben tried to comfort her while Acorn quietly escorted a protesting Crane Houston from the room.

El Grande, Texas, June 15. A most heinous crime was committed in this small quiet community Tuesday when the fifteen-year-old daughter of the prominent Hernando Florez family was kidnapped and violated by three notorious Texas bandits. According to Sheriff Clark the men abducted Miss Dolores Florez as she strolled about the grounds of her family's hacienda. They shot and wounded three servants in their escape with the young girl.

Miss Florez was found unconscious in a shack some fifteen miles from town the next morning. Doctor Northrup stated that with rest and care she will recover.

Mitch glanced at Charlie and she nodded miserably. Every time she closed her eyes she saw her poor mother, herself a mere child, fending off those horrible men.

Mitch went back to reading:

Sheriff Clark reports the men who committed the dastardly deed are still at large. A bounty of $500 has been placed on the head of each of the outlaws, dead or alive. Posters are on display prominently around town.

Mitch frowned. Clearly, this proved to Charlie what her cousin had claimed, that she was not the child of Matt Houston, but of some low-life bandit. She would be able to count back from the date of her own birth and figure it out.

He only wanted rid of the entire matter. While he might understand how this could make her feel, it made no difference to him at all where their lives were concerned.

To show her so, he wadded the newspaper clipping into a tiny ball and tossed it in a receptacle near her bed, then sat gingerly beside her. Holding her hand in his he studied her drawn features.

"What is it, Charlie? Are you feeling worse? None of this means anything to us, nothing at all."

She gulped air as if she were drowning. Emotions choked her. Since her father's death she had never really allowed herself to break down and mourn. Now that she had more to grieve than his death, it was as if she couldn't stop crying. Matthew Houston was not her father. He had lied to her all those years. How could she ever reconcile such betrayal? She was truly some bandit's bastard child.

She clung to Mitch's hand, gazing at the way their fingers gripped. She couldn't meet his gaze.

"Darlin', none of this matters. All I care about is

you and me, us, together always. This, it means nothing. Matthew Houston loved you and that's all you need to remember. You are his daughter, more truly than any of this. Otherwise, he'd have left you." He spoke softly but urgently. "You're tired now. We'll leave, let you get some rest. But couldn't you stop crying, or at least tell me why you're so upset."

"No, don't go. Stay a few minutes. We need to talk, and I'm fixing to shut up this bawling. It's pretty undignified." She wiped her face on a corner of the sheet and Ben passed her a large white handkerchief.

"We need to get to our hotel and freshen up," Dessa said quickly. "James, you come with us if you don't mind. There'll be plenty of time to get your story when the marshal arrives."

Dessa swept from the room, shooing everyone ahead of her, including Acorn who had returned to hover outside the door. He murmured a mild protest, but it did him no good. Dessa Poole was in charge.

Mitch grinned toward the closed door, then turned back to Charlie. "Now, what's going on here? This isn't like you at all. A woman who rides herd on a bunch of ornery cows after being caught in the middle of a stampede doesn't let much get her down."

Charlie didn't know where to begin. With trembling fingers she touched Mitch's face, grazed their tips over the scar that cut through his eyebrow to the white streak of hair. A forever reminder of his own tragic loss. "Oh, Mitch, I do love you so. But I'm afraid."

"Of me? You've nothing to be afraid of. I know I get pretty stormy—"

She touched his lips, shushing the words. "No, not that. That." With a slight movement of her head she indicated the receptacle in which he'd thrown the clipping.

"What does that—"

"I'm trying to get up the nerve to tell you, but I'm

afraid you'll hate me, or be so disgusted you'll just walk away."

"Aw, hell, Charlie. Nothing could make me leave you now. Nothing in the whole wide world. I'm finished with running away, especially from you." He leaned over and kissed first her forehead, then each eye before trailing his warm, moist lips down her jawline to her throat, then up along her chin to her mouth.

She tasted of his precious love, afraid that this would be the last time he offered it. The thought emptied a great hole within her and the pain seared far worse than the bullet that had torn through her flesh. "Oh, Mitch. Mitch, please love me."

He trailed his fingers over the flannel gown and cupped her breast so that his thumb brushed the nipple. "I do, darlin', but we can't right now. Not here. It'll wait till we marry."

She crooned down in her throat, and he silenced the sound once again with his lips.

He realized that his greatest fear had been that she would not marry him or that something would happen to her. Now here she was expressing a like fear over some damned old yellow newspaper clipping that dated back twenty-five years or more. No matter what it proved, it didn't matter to him, and he wished with all his heart that it didn't matter to her either. He loved her. Yet, he could tell that until she explained she would never be free of whatever awful burden she carried.

He pulled reluctantly away from the kiss, cupped her face with one hand. Although from what little she'd told him he could pretty well figure it out, he sensed she needed to talk about the past and lay it to rest.

"Okay, tell me, now, and then we'll forget all about it."

"Do you promise?"

"Oh, yes. I promise."

And so she told him everything. How her father had come for her when she was a child after her mother killed herself. How her grandparents had let her go because she reminded them of her mother's shame.

"I'm a bastard, Mitch. I thought Matt Houston was my father. All those years of calling him Daddy and loving him, and all the time some dirty murdering bandit sired me in a filthy shack. A man who doesn't even know I exist and wouldn't care if he did. And even my mother probably didn't even know which one of them fathered me."

Mitch rubbed at her temple with a thumb. "None of that was your fault or your mother's, or even your . . . I mean Houston's fault."

"But he lied to me. I wasn't his daughter and I loved him so much. He could have told me the truth."

"And what would he have said? He probably didn't know what to tell you when you were a child, then when you grew up he just loved you so much he didn't think it mattered. He was your father, Charlie, in every way. Don't you see that?"

"But Crane said he was taking money from my grandparents all along. That's how he bought the ranch. If he truly loved my mother and me he wouldn't have taken money to raise me," she said. Anger had replaced tears and he thought that a good sign.

"You only have Crane's word for that. All that clipping proves is that your poor mother endured a horrible experience. You may have been conceived before your parents married, I guess you could tell that from the dates. But on the other hand, you may have been born early, or your mother and father might have . . . well . . . had a little fun out back in the barn. Be realistic, none of the rest of the story is anything but that filthy man's lies, and I won't have him hurt you like this anymore. I'll kill him, Charlie. I swear I will."

Frantic, she grabbed at his arms. "No. No, don't do that. They'll put you back in prison. He has to stay alive. Oh, God, if I had killed him I'd be in jail right now. Oh, Mitch, hold me."

He gathered her close and she nestled into the curve of his embrace. "Don't talk nonsense. He attacked you and you defended yourself. No one would ever have put you in jail for that. We talked about this before."

"What will happen to him now? Can he claim the ranch as my father's ... Matt's only heir?"

Mitch's eyes shimmered with rage. "Let him try. It'll do no good at all. He has no real proof. When I get through talking to him I believe he'll be glad to get away from Montana Territory with his scalp and hide intact."

"Oh, Mitch. Don't do anything else to get in trouble."

"Don't you worry. Now, close your eyes and go to sleep. I'll just sit in yonder chair awhile and watch over you."

She smiled and it felt good. Never had she thought she would be happy to let a man watch over her ... never had she thought that man would be Mitchell Fallon. Things certainly had a strange way of working out.

Chapter Twenty-three

Doc allowed Mitch to move Charlie that evening. He took her gently in his arms and carried her down the hallway where Ben and Dessa Poole met him in the doorway of a large suite of rooms. Yancey and Ritter came along because neither was willing to completely release Miss Charlie to the care of this reformed gunslinger who had stepped in and taken over her life.

Dessa and Ben insisted that Charlie take the larger of the two suites they had rented. There was an adjoining but separate room for Mitch.

Yancey eyed Ritter and he returned the wry look. Wasn't this just too cozy? Miss Charlie and that outlaw separated only by a thin door. Ritter figured he shouldn't be too surprised, seeing as how they had been together alone in that line shack for so long. He thought seriously about riding out for Idaho Territory and finding him a job in some bar where he could drink away his woes and be spared watching Miss Charlie make a complete goggle-eyed fool out of herself.

Yancey muttered as they left the room, "Reckon she's too good for him, but what do we know?"

"I got me an idea," Ritter said. "Let's go over to the Powder Keg and have a few more beers." It was

going to take a heap more than a few beers to get
him over loving Miss Charlie.

"I got a better one," Yancey said. "Let's ride to
Virginia City and file claims on all that land Dunkirk
has that's just going to waste before someone else
beats us to it."

Ritter stopped in the middle of the hallway and
stared at Yancey. "You mean start our own spreads?"

"Or throw in with Miss Charlie and Fallon. Whatever works. Hell, maybe we can build our own dynasty
and do it fair and square without killing anyone."

Ritter grinned great big and followed Yancy from
the hotel, slapping the Stetson on his head as he
went outside.

After the door closed behind them, Mitch said,
"Somehow I don't like the idea of you two putting us
up. We can take care of ourselves."

"Oh, don't worry," Dessa said, green eyes sparkling
like she had some gigantic secret. "It's your money
that'll pay for this suite. We can't let the half owner
of the P & F Railroad and the Great Montana/Dakota
hotel chain sleep in just any old room."

Mitch plunked down beside Charlie on the large
overstuffed divan where he'd carefully placed her.
"What exactly are you talking about? You and Ben
own ..."

His sister began shaking her head and laughing.

"She insisted on investing your money in it too,"
Ben said. "I told her she should ask, but she just took
your half of the inheritance and smacked it right in
there with ours. God knows how she would have explained it to you had we gone bust." Ben joined his
wife in laughter.

"What are they talking about?" Charlie asked.

"I have no idea," Mitch said. "I had no money,
no inheritance."

Dessa leaned forward in her chair. "Oh, yes you

did. Daddy never gave up looking for you. He believed you were alive and he left half of everything to you in that event. I'm sorry I gambled with it. I do hope you'll forgive me. You're rich, Mitchell. Aren't you happy?"

He stared at Dessa, then at Ben, and finally down at Charlie, who looked as astounded as he felt. "But . . . but . . . I can't take—"

"Nonsense, of course you can. We'll never miss it, honestly. Besides, we've been very careful in our accounting, and your share of the profits is in your name in a trust. We couldn't touch it if we wanted to. The capital, now that's another matter, and one Ben handles.

"Of course, if you want to continue the investment and just draw on your profits, Ben has some wonderful ideas for expanding westward in the near future. In fact, we're on our way to California when we leave here."

"I'm not a businessman," Mitch protested. "I'm a . . ." He broke off. What was he? For years he'd been a wanted man, an outcast, an outlaw, a gunslinger. How did that fit into this new turn of events? And suppose the marshal from Virginia City decided to arrest him and put him in jail for the rest of his life. What then?

He turned once again to the woman he loved. "Charlie?"

She peered up at him. All she wanted this very moment was to be alone with the man she loved in their own home.

Mitch continued, pressing her hand in his. "We'd better wait until we hear what the marshal has to say before we make any plans."

Dessa squirmed, a little of the young sister Mitch remembered flashing across the sophisticated features. In a soft voice she said, "He's coming to offer you amnesty, just like you wanted. The governor authorized it, in fact insisted upon it."

Charlie gasped, dread evaporating like river mist on a summer morning. "Oh, it can't be true."

"Yes," Dessa cried. "It is true. There'll be some compensation to be paid. You did rob some people, Mitch, and even if you felt justified because of what happened in the war, you'll have to pay it back."

"How in the world did you manage that?" Mitch asked.

Dessa's green eyes, like a reflection of his own, flashed through lowered lashes. "I told the governor how embarrassing it would be to have the hero of James Magruder's novels languishing in jail. That bright young man has a publisher interested in what he'll write about you. You behave now and tell him some good stories, will you? Not anything that will embarrass the fine family name. I convinced both the governor and Marshal Bracken that it would be better this way, for everyone."

Ben slapped his leg and laughed. "A little gentle blackmail never hurts."

Mitch stared at the window. Outside, lamps flickered on all over town, little pinpoints of yellow light like beacons in the falling darkness.

He thought of the men he'd killed in the war, and how oftentimes what came afterward was a war of sorts too. That was certainly forgivable when it couldn't be helped, wasn't it? Was it possible, though, that the law would give him another chance?

The Colt he'd carried still lay buried in the mud somewhere out there in the foothills of the Bighorn Mountains, and it could stay there for all he cared.

"Mitch?" Charlie said. "Are you all right?"

He turned from the window. Her dark eyes reflected the points of light from outside and telegraphed to him so much love that he felt wrapped in it, warmed and protected forever. That other life belonged to someone else, someone he no longer even knew.

"I think we'll build a house out at the Double H, if it's all right with Charlie," Mitch said after a long silence. "I think we'd both be happy living out there."

Charlie stared at him, filled with a love so genuine and sensual she could scarcely speak. "And Yancey and Ritter can run it for us when we want to travel."

Mitch, Ben, and Dessa all laughed.

"Sounds like she's got the right idea. Believe me, it doesn't take long to get used to having money," Ben said.

Dessa smiled and touched her husband's cheek. "I can remember when Ben didn't have anything but a blanket and a beat-up old rifle. And look at him now."

Ben hugged his wife. "Yeah, just look."

"And when will you two get married?" Dessa asked from the comfort of her husband's arms.

The question brought another laugh from everyone.

"As soon as I can walk down the aisle," Charlie said.

Mitch took her hand and brought it to his lips. "Why wait till then? I can always carry you."

A little over a week later, on a beautiful and crisp Saturday afternoon in early November, Mitchell Fallon and Charlie Houston were married in the small church in Miles City.

A disgruntled Crane Houston sat behind the bars of the jail where acting Sheriff Wolf Springer had put him when Marshal Bracken announced the man was wanted all over the territories for fraud of various kinds. He might truly be Charlie's cousin, as he'd claimed, but he was definitely the black sheep of that family. Probably the reason Matthew Houston never mentioned his name to either his beloved daughter or his friend and ramrod Yancey Barton.

By this time Charlie truly believed that her father

had loved her. It was tough to forgive him for his deception, but she thought she understood. As Mitch kept telling her, forgiving was easy when you loved someone enough.

"At least I certainly hope so." He gazed at her with a familiar gleam in his shining green eyes and rested his hands at her waist.

She put her arms around his neck. Of course he was right.

Determined to walk down the aisle, she and Yancey practiced every day until she could manage the short stroll without stumbling.

On her wedding day Wolf lifted her from the carriage that brought her and Yancey to the church and carried her as far as the entrance. Then he stood in the center of the street, a sheriff's star gleaming on his chest, and watched Marshal Therm Bracken ride out of town to the strains of the wedding march. Then he slipped silently into the church.

Charlie ignored twinges of pain and tried not to limp as she and Yancey started down the aisle. Through glimmering tears she looked from Dessa Poole, her dark beauty stunning in peach organza, to her husband Ben in silver-striped trousers and morning coat, and then finally to Mitchell Fallon who wore black trousers, a boiled white shirt, and a waistcoat that he looked ready to tear off at any moment.

There hadn't been time to get fancy clothing for the wedding, but Charlie wore a stunning cream silk-and-lace dress that belonged to Dessa and had been altered for her smaller build. A cloud of organza cascaded around her shoulder-length dark hair.

Mitch caught his breath as Yancey brought his bride to him, then hid a smile behind his hand when he noticed the tips of her riding boots peeking from beneath the hem of the dress. Just like Charlie not to wear the white slippers. He'd never tame this one, he knew, but decided he didn't mind at all. She was his Charlie, wild and a little stubborn, but for a man like him that was perfect.

He accepted her hand, tucked it firmly into the crook of his elbow, and together they faced the preacher.

WE NEED YOUR HELP

To continue to bring you quality romance
that meets your personal expectations,
we at TOPAZ books want to hear from you.
Help us by filling out this questionnaire, and in exchange
we will give you a **free gift** as a token of our gratitude.

- Is this the first TOPAZ book you've purchased? (circle one)
      YES   NO
  The title and author of this book is: _____

- If this was not the first TOPAZ book you've purchased, how many have
  you bought in the past year?
      a: 0 - 5   b 6 - 10   c: more than 10   d: more than 20

- How many romances in total did you buy in the past year?
      a: 0 - 5   b: 6 - 10   c: more than 10   d: more than 20 ____

- How would you rate your overall satisfaction with this book?
      a: Excellent   b: Good   c: Fair   d: Poor

- What was the main reason you bought this book?
      a: It is a TOPAZ novel, and I know that TOPAZ stands
         for quality romance fiction
      b: I liked the cover
      c: The story-line intrigued me
      d: I love this author
      e: I really liked the setting
      f: I love the cover models
      g: Other: _____

- Where did you buy this TOPAZ novel?
      a: Bookstore   b: Airport   c: Warehouse Club
      d: Department Store   e: Supermarket   f: Drugstore
      g: Other: _____

- Did you pay the full cover price for this TOPAZ novel? (circle one)
      YES   NO
  If you did not, what price did you pay? _____

- Who are your favorite TOPAZ authors? (Please list)

- How did you first hear about TOPAZ books?
      a: I saw the books in a bookstore
      b: I saw the TOPAZ Man on TV or at a signing
      c: A friend told me about TOPAZ
      d: I saw an advertisement in_____magazine
      e: Other: _____

- What type of romance do you generally prefer?
      a: Historical   b: Contemporary
      c: Romantic Suspense   d: Paranormal (time travel,
         futuristic, vampires, ghosts, warlocks, etc.)
      d: Regency   e: Other: _____

- What historical settings do you prefer?
      a: England   b: Regency England   c: Scotland
      e: Ireland   f: America   g: Western Americana
      h: American Indian   i: Other: _____

- What type of story do you prefer?

  a: Very sexy   b: Sweet, less explicit
  c: Light and humorous   d: More emotionally intense
  e: Dealing with darker issues f: Other

- What kind of covers do you prefer?

  a: Illustrating both hero and heroine   b: Hero alone
  c: No people (art only)   d: Other_____

- What other genres do you like to read (circle all that apply)

  Mystery   Medical Thrillers   Science Fiction
  Suspense   Fantasy   Self-help
  Classics   General Fiction   Legal Thrillers
  Historical Fiction

- Who is your favorite author, and why?_____

  _____

- What magazines do you like to read? (circle all that apply)

  a: People   b: Time/Newsweek
  c: Entertainment Weekly   d: Romantic Times
  e: Star   f: National Enquirer
  g: Cosmopolitan   h: Woman's Day
  i: Ladies' Home Journal   j: Redbook
  k: Other:_____

- In which region of the United States do you reside?

  a: Northeast   b: Midatlantic   c: South
  d: Midwest   e: Mountain   f: Southwest
  g: Pacific Coast

- What is your age group/sex?   a: Female   b: Male

  a: under 18   b: 19-25   c: 26-30   d: 31-35   e: 36-40
  f: 41-45   g: 46-50   h: 51-55   i: 56-60   j: Over 60

- What is your marital status?

  a: Married   b: Single   c: No longer married

- What is your current level of education?

  a: High school   b: College Degree
  c: Graduate Degree   d: Other: _____

- Do you receive the TOPAZ *Romantic Liaisons* newsletter, a quarterly newsletter with the latest information on Topaz books and authors?

  YES   NO

  If not, would you like to?   YES   NO

  Fill in the address where you would like your free gift to be sent:

  Name:_____

  Address:_____

  City:_____Zip Code:_____

  You should receive your free gift in 6 to 8 weeks.
  Please send the completed survey to:

Penguin USA•Mass Market
Dept. TS
375 Hudson St.
New York, NY 10014